,93

# Getting Even

# Getting Even

## *Carolyn Haddad*

PIATKUS

First published in Great Britain in 1991 by
Judy Piatkus (Publishers) Ltd of
5 Windmill Street, London W1

*The moral rights of the author have been asserted*

British Library Cataloguing in Publication Data

Haddad, Carolyn
  Getting even.
  I. Title
  813.54 [F]

  ISBN 0-7499-0020-2


Phototypeset in 11/12pt Linotron Times by
Computerset, Heathrow
Printed and bound in Great Britain by
Mackays of Chatham PLC

To Abe, for twenty-five years

*I have found you an argument; I am not obliged to find you an understanding.*

Samuel Johnson

# Chapter 1

# Funeral with Greek Chorus

It was to be a private funeral, but only a gate separated Tommy Patterson's casket from the thousands of admirers who surged inward, pressing against the wrought iron to get a good view. Helicopters filled with newsmen circled above the grave site, creating a draught. One could almost imagine Tommy's soul ascending in the turbulence, if he had not fled already.

What brought the faithful out to view this all too final departure? Here they were, young and old, rich and poor, and even some of the vestiges of the fast-fading middle class. Tommy had touched them all with his books, cassettes, lectures, seminars and media appearances, which constantly echoed their own drifting angst and gave them palatable answers to the eternal questions confronting all humanity. The *New York Times*, reviewing his last book WHAT IS A COMMITMENT AND HOW TO MAKE ONE IN 10 EASY STEPS, called him the 'King of Psycho-Babble', though many challenged Tommy for that title. But the *Times* missed the essence of Tommy's appeal. In the metaphor of the California surf, Tommy Patterson caught the wave, he rode the crest; he knew where people wanted to go and he jumped on board to take them there. Many sneered, but everyone needs a bit of comfort now and then. For some it's pizza, for others a massage, for women an orgasm, for men sex without condoms. And for many comfort meant reading and relating to Tommy Patterson.

Now he was dead and they were bereft, despite the fact that in a full-page ad in the *Los Angeles Times* and other papers around the country, his publishers announced, to stifle the tide of woe, the upcoming, now to-be-posthumously published LOOK BACK FOR LOVE, Tommy's reminiscences of the love he had shared throughout his short but meaningful life. So there was hope. The voice that had calmed so many hearts would not be stilled forever.

The tendrils of grief slowly drifted inside the gates of the cemetery where an open pit stood ready to receive the mortal remains of

1

Tommy Patterson. According to his wishes, he was having only a graveside service. Even though he had been a man of faith, he had not been a man of religion. Further, following his instructions, his four wives came to bid him that final adieu which three of them thought had taken place years ago with their divorce decrees. They stood dressed in black, commemorating either their mood or their belief that there are some situations when even the wildest among them must conform. Their thoughts were as disparate as Tommy's life.

Naturally, Kitten Fairleigh, being the Hollywood star that she was, attracted the most attention among the four women to whom Tommy had made his commitment. She was a gold and honey blonde of exciting proportions whose last movie was a breakthrough for her in the acting division. She had always looked good on the screen – that was usually all directors wanted from her. Finally, she got her chance to emote, and the critics loved it for the very novelty. Kitten, though, was well aware that her career was teetering on a precipice. While everyone who read the tabloids knew her marriage to Tommy was rocky, no one must come away from the funeral thinking she didn't grieve. Tommy's fans were the same people who brought tickets to the movies. She didn't want to alienate anyone. Bad publicity, when she was just about to shoot through mere celebrity status to major-time actress, was the last thing she needed. Perhaps that's why she was a bit less polite than she should have been to Odelle Hampton, Tommy's first wife. What did Odelle's grief matter? She was simply a surburban housewife. It was her sorrow, Kitten knew, that must be made publicly manifest.

So, 'Get out of my way,' Kitten Fairleigh whispered fiercely, distinctly aware that she was being crowded out of the photographer's view-finder by Odelle's never-ending presence at her side. How could the photographer get a clear shot of her alone? Kitten wanted to know. And that's what they would want to show on the front pages of tomorrow's papers: her tears for her dead, murdered husband.

'Dear,' Odelle broke into Kitten's calculations, 'I was his first wife. Don't you think people want to see what I look like? After all, they already have a picture of you throwing yourself on his corpse during visitation at the funeral home.' Odelle Hampton neatly adjusted her white kid gloves.

'Would you two watch out what you say,' Grace Mandling whispered a warning to them. 'Who knows who has a hidden mike on him. Or her.' She, Tommy's second wife, did not want to be here. But the newspapers had printed Tommy's last wishes and, like Kitten, Grace Mandling had a public she could not afford to offend. People who read romance novels tend to look at life through pink chiffon. At this

2

point, she didn't want to discourage her readers by giving them a glimpse of real life with Tommy Patterson, especially with the cost of paperbacks rising steeply. All she wanted to do was get this over with and fast!

'What's happened? Is Tommy really dead?' Trudi Surefoot wondered.

'No, coke-head, they're just burying him alive because the world got sick of him,' Grace snapped.

'Well, that's an awful thing to do,' Trudi replied, definitely troubled.

Odelle turned around and gave Grace a reproachful look. Well could Odelle be generous and noble towards Trudi. She had flown in from Chicago. It was Grace who had made the onerous journey from Newark to Dallas-Fort Worth, taking a commuter flight to Taos, New Mexico to pick up Trudi, then hopping on to Albuquerque for the flight to the coast. 'It would be so much easier for you,' Odelle had said, almost pleaded. And Grace decided to play the good sport. But it hadn't been easy. It had been dreadful. At each airport there were delays, and then Trudi wasn't where she should have been in Taos. It was unfair, Grace thought, that she always got stuck with the most burdensome tasks. Next time it was Odelle's turn.

'Don't listen to Grace, Trudi. Tommy isn't alive; he's definitely dead,' Odelle assured her. 'I held a mirror up to his nose and mouth just in case. He was always such a faker.'

'A mirror?'

'It was a literary allusion, Trudi,' Grace said. 'When you learn to read, we'll point a few out to you.'

'Oh, thanks, Grace. It's my dyslexia, you know.'

The sound of sobbing called their attention back to the occasion at hand. Kitten Fairleigh was once again composing her own mournful dirge; and the cameras, allowed to record this moment not only for posterity but for Tommy Patterson's many fans, who would buy the cassette of his funeral when it hit the market, zoomed in on the stately blonde's moment of intensely private suffering. Odelle put a comforting arm around Kitten's shoulders. She could feel Kitten stiffening, so leaned closer to her, whispering a few words of solace into her ear. 'Do you think Tommy's fans believe that little titbit in the gossip column this morning – that Tommy was about to serve you with divorce papers?'

Kitten weakened at the knees, but Odelle held her firmly in a sisterly embrace. The minister was finishing his graveside homily about Tommy and the Golden Rule. 'Yeah,' Grace said quietly from the second row, 'fuck them before they fuck you.'

3

Odelle turned back to her for a moment. 'And he fucked just about everyone,' she said softly, not letting her lips form the words clearly for fear of lip-readers in the crowd beyond the gate.

'Tommy, we hardly knew ye,' the minister concluded.

'And he was the lucky one,' Grace noted under her breath.

Odelle beckoned Grace to her and Grace dragged along Trudi. The four of them, Kitten, Odelle, Grace and Trudi, stood at the brink of the narrow opening as Tommy Patterson's mortal remains were lowered into six feet of emptiness, similar to the contents of his philosophical musings. The coffin at one point looked as if it might tip and land on its side, but the skilled gravediggers righted it and set it on its prescribed course downward until it thwacked bottom.

The minister nodded at Kitten. Delicately, she lifted a handful of soil up to eye level, then let it sift down on to the coffin below. She sighed and draped her hand over her heart. Odelle, not wanting either to remove her white kid gloves or get them dirty, kicked a piece of dirt over the edge of the grave with her black, high-heeled shoe. Grace found a stone and gave it her pitcher's throw downward, denting, she believed, the brass nameplate. Trudi took a flower from her hair and tossed it into the grave with a sweet, vacant smile.

Slowly, the four women walked off together towards the gates, while others behind them took their turn at paying Tommy Patterson their last respects, finally able to do him dirt.

As the wives of Tommy Patterson reached the gate, the roar of the crowd overtook them. Voices called out to them: 'He meant the world to me.' 'I touched him once.' 'He cured my sexual dysfunction.' 'I never knew what love was until I took Step No. 5.'

Grace Mandling tried to remember what Step No. 5 in WHAT IS A COMMITMENT AND HOW TO MAKE ONE IN 10 EASY STEPS was. She thought it was 'Learn to Have a Vaginal Orgasm,' which would have been typical of Tommy's belief in the quicker the better, but she wasn't sure. And she couldn't really concentrate with this crowd surrounding her. Where were the police? There were supposed to be police here to protect them.

Ahead of her Grace could vaguely see the limousine with its open door. She felt her arm being pulled, but by whom she had no idea. Someone grabbed hold of her silk blouse and was tugging on her from behind. She turned and found it was Trudi. She grabbed Trudi's hand. Step by tiny step, they inched forward. Tommy's fans, having come all this way, were intent on at least being next to someone he had loved, Tommy's four commitments.

Suddenly, she was inside the limo. Trudi fell in behind her. The door was shut, it looked like on a few fingers. But were those tears of

4

pain or simply of loss outside the sound-proofed, four-wheeled sanctum?

The limousine started up and began slowly pulling out, away from the crowd, which soon faded into the background. All four women gave a sigh of relief. 'Excuse me,' Kitten said, 'but I believe I'm going backward.'

'Single again,' Odelle noted wistfully.

'No. I mean, I get sick when I ride backward. I remember the first time I went to Cannes . . .'

'Oh, Jesus!' Grace spat at her. Patience was not Grace Mandling's strong suit, and today especially she had no patience for Kitten Fairleigh, who was a stranger to all of them. She, Odelle and Trudi had become interlinked over their many years of being Tommy's ex-wives, but this was the first time any of them had met Kitten Fairleigh. How could they sympathize with a woman who had no apparent flaws – except that she got sick riding backward?

'Here, Kitten, you can have my seat,' Trudi offered, ever the good soul, even to strangers. Unfortunately, Trudi was sitting next to Kitten, facing the same direction.

'I'm going to vomit,' Kitten promised.

Grace Mandling took off her hat and handed it to her. 'Take this. It's from K-Mart. I bought it especially for this occasion. I don't think I'm going to wear it again.'

'I should hope not, Grace. It's not you at all,' Odelle commented.

'Here it comes,' Kitten said, leaning over the hat. Grace and Odelle moved their knees aside and pulled up their skirts just in case it splattered. But even Kitten, wonderful actress that she was, had no way of faking vomit. It just wasn't as easy as tears. 'Any moment now,' she warned them.

'Good,' Odelle said. 'Something to look forward to on the long drive home.'

'It's not your home,' Kitten pointed out. 'It's mine. Mine and Tommy's.'

'It was just a figure of speech, Kitten,' Grace pointed out. 'After all, we know that home is where the heart is – those of us who have a heart, that is.'

'What was it Tommy always said about that?' Kitten wondered tearfully, twisting the brim of Grace's hat out of shape.

'Follow your cunt,' Trudi recalled happily.

'Ah, Tommy,' Odelle said. 'A man of many words, all of them four-lettered.'

The limo swept them noiselessly north, off the Freeway and on to the curving road that separated the California hills from the Pacific

Ocean. Then the driver took a right from the public highway on to a private drive that led up to the top of a steep incline where sat a house, not large but many-splendoured in its architectural sweep. The driver would have pulled around to the front steps of what Tommy had called "Mi Hacienda", but unfortunately, several police cars were blocking his way.

'Oh my God!' Kitten said, tossing aside the black hat, fully recovered. 'Not another murder!'

But it was only the man in charge of investigating Tommy's untimely demise, Detective Sam Morris. He said he had a few more questions to ask, just a few. Kitten Fairleigh turned dramatically to her all-female audience. 'He thinks I killed Tommy!'

Grace looked past the flaring nostrils of the honey blonde temptress and assured California's finest, 'To know Tommy Patterson was to want him dead.'

# Chapter 2

# A Balm in Gilead

Tamar Litowsky, Tommy Patterson's lawyer, sat in her office with a cup of coffee and the morning newspapers. Again the headlines screeched of Tommy Patterson, this time his funeral, featuring photos of Kitten Fairleigh, overwhelmed by grief. Tamar's eyebrows rose in surprise, though as a law student she had been warned often enough to be surprised by nothing.

Still, Tommy's murder had been a shock to everyone, probably even to Kitten. Tamar couldn't believe that just two days before his murder, he was sitting right here in her office, drawing up a new will. Did he know? Did he even then have a presentiment? 'Why, Tommy?' she had asked him, as she carefully crafted the clauses he desired. 'Are you making amends?' she teased.

'Amends?' he laughed. 'I have nothing to apologize for. You know that, Tamar. I am what I am. That's always been my philosophy. Be ME. Isn't that what my books have urged people?'

'But this will – '

'Protection. Or maybe you could call it the final payoff,' Tommy mused. 'I've just had a run-in with one of my ex-es. It's made me realize how much damage these wives of mine could do me after I'm dead. If they wanted to. This last testament will shut them up. They'll be trapped forever in the web of the master weaver.' He smiled, well pleased with his verbal imagery. Tommy Patterson was his own best audience. There wasn't a mirror he didn't love.

'But you're giving away everything,' Tamar objected.

He laughed. 'What can I keep after I'm dead?'

Death. It had seemed so far away when they were talking, joking, constructing his web of defence. And yet two days later, death surprised Tommy on the cliff outside his home.

The assumption was that a burglar had murdered him. The glass front door of the house had been shattered. Glass fragments were

7

tracked inside the house. Tommy must have come home and surprised whoever was within. But there were still so many unanswered questions. For example, why was nothing taken? And if Tommy surprised a burglar, why wasn't he killed inside the house? The police said Tommy had backed from his patio up the dirt path to his death. His body was so mangled from the quick descent down the cliffside, there was no way of telling if he put up a struggle before he died – if he received blows other than from bouncing off the cliff's outcroppings of rocks and trees.

Tamar Litowsky sighed. The police had a problem. The whole world waited for them to answer the question: Who murdered Tommy Patterson? She too had a problem. How was she to deal with Tommy Patterson's four wives?

They weren't the only ones included in Tommy's will. Tommy Patterson had left a long list of bequests and many beneficiaries, but Tamar had no intention of using the state's money to fly them all to her office for the reading of the will. All she really wanted present were the four women who, Tommy claimed just a few days ago, had meant so much to him, one way or the other. That in itself would be enough of a side show. After all, what would the couple who lost a son to cancer, didn't have the money to pay the medical bills, but had claimed spiritual renewal after reading Tommy's book, have added to the occasion? Or the cocktail waitress Tommy met in Kansas City, the one who was studying to be a classical pianist? Or the director of a clinic set up on an Indian reservation to deliver fast and safe medical care? Tommy's publicist would receive a list of all these bequests this morning by messenger. He could make of them what he would. The bulk of the estate was going elsewhere.

Tamar had sent limos around to collect the four wives of Tommy Patterson. She had seen them together at the funeral, giving a semblance of getting along. But what choice did they have with the press using its telescopic lenses? For all Tamar knew, they were bitter enemies. So she sent four separate cars to pick them up and deliver them here safe and unruffled.

The reading of the will was set for ten o'clock. At eleven she was meeting Detective Morris to discuss how Tommy's estate was divided. He would want to know when his latest will was drawn up. She was going to have to tell him that Tommy changed his will just two days before he plunged over that cliff. And then Detective Morris would ask who knew. Tamar had a feeling Morris was trying to pin the murder on Kitten Fairleigh. He would certainly make a name for himself, arresting the new darling of the silver screen. But reports in the papers continued to indicate that Tommy surprised a burglar. Did Detective Morris know something L.A.'s fearless reporters didn't?

Anyway, Tamar wondered, why would Kitten kill Tommy? True, she might not have known about the divorce papers before Tommy's murder, but she and Tommy had signed a prenuptial agreement. Their finances were always separate. Besides, Kitten had an air-tight alibi: she was in bed with another man. Too bad she hadn't made it a threesome. The more witnesses, the better.

Tamar Litowsky's intercom sounded softly with its almost Oriental tone. She pushed a button and was informed that the women were waiting for her in Conference Room 2. She picked up Tommy Patterson's last will and testament and went to greet them.

The four wives of Tommy Patterson sat quietly in the plush conference room. All four were slightly hung over. Only three of them knew it. For Trudi Surefoot the condition had become natural over the long years of her chemical dependence. When the police finally left them alone, after two hours of intensive questioning, last night had become a time for drink and shared confessions.

They rapidly reached a consensus. Like a weed, Tommy Patterson had taken over the perfumed garden of their life. Someone had finally applied enough pesticide to shrivel him. It would take time for the garden to grow back to its natural lushness, but it could be achieved. That was the promise Odelle held out to them, she being the longest out of her first husband's clutches. 'Though one never forgets the pain,' she added.

'Or the toll on the emotions,' Grace remarked. 'And the worst part is that he always got away with everything.'

'Until the night he was murdered,' Kitten noted dramatically.

'Maybe Tommy committed suicide,' Trudi suggested.

'Tommy!' they all shouted at her at once.

Now there was a closeness between the four of them, a realization that they shared the experience of being screwed by Tommy Patterson. Were they simply unfortunate or merely dumb? They sat in the conference room, each considering the biggest mistake of her life.

'It was just like Tommy to pick a woman lawyer,' Odelle broke the silence, addressing no one in particular. 'He trusted women. He thought we were easy marks.'

'We were,' Grace reminded her.

'There were some good times with Tommy,' Trudi vaguely recalled.

'He did a lot for me emotionally,' Kitten agreed. 'It was the way he treated me. I guess I had to lose my self-respect to gain it. In that way, he freed me from my insecurities. Infused by this freedom, I realized

9

it was my insecurities that led me to attach myself to him in the first place.'

'Look at this room,' Trudi said wistfully. 'I wish my apartment looked like this.' And indeed, what was labelled Conference Room 2 was more like an old-fashioned parlour, with comfortable armchairs and sofas all upholstered in various floral patterns. Even the curtains were dotted with flowers. The tables were delicate, rosewood and maple. The desk behind which they presumed the lawyer would sit could have passed for a French antique, which it very well might have been. None of them was a collector.

When the door opened and Tamar Litowsky stepped inside, the women were not surprised to find she was as much of a type as they were. She was in her forties, but looked fit and strong. She was determined, a success. And wasn't this one of the troubles of their age? Women had to succeed. It was impossible any more, almost criminal, to let life simply happen. Life was to be moulded and shaped so that it could fit into a busy appointment book. Beauty, position, power, youth – with the help of modern science and a good education, all were attainable. Only love escaped that net of control. Love alone was the elusive nectar that one flitted desperately about searching for. And why? Love, when found, left one weak, distracted. Love didn't lend itself to the image of success because love meant surrendering power into another person's hands, trusting that person withyour heart. Trust could be foolish, could even be fatal. It led only to betrayal.

Tamar Litowsky looked as if she trusted no one. She sat down behind the fake – or real – French desk and smiled at them. 'I'm not going to read you all of Tommy Patterson's Last Will and Testament,' she assured them. 'Though certainly copies of it will be made available to you, should you so wish. Needless to say, we all knew Tommy was a generous person. Aside from his family, he has made a list of over fifty bequests to people he met along the way, whose lives touched his, touched his heart. The bequests are small. I think he just wanted these people to remember that he cared.

'Now, as to the four of you . . .' She watched while they squirmed. No, "squirm" was pejorative. The wives of Tommy Patterson slightly adjusted themselves in their chairs. 'Tommy left a message for each of you in his will, and it was his express wish that you four be in the same room while his comments were read. Thank you very much for complying.'

Tamar meticulously turned the pages of the will to the appropriate section. She began to read. 'To Odelle Lacy Patterson Hampton, in recognition of the comfort we gave each other in our early years, I leave the sum of $10,000 for her personal use. In addition, in acknowledgement of her caring concern for battered women and children, I hereby assign the copyright of my forthcoming book LOOK BACK FOR LOVE to Sisters of the Storm, Inc., the shelter of which Odelle is executive director. I know that Odelle will make good use of the funds she now will have available for this most important work.'

Odelle was stunned. She couldn't believe her good fortune. After so many years of struggling to provide even the basics for her family shelter, having to beg for food and blankets and soap even, now she could give these women and children what they really needed, first-rate accommodation and first-rate counselling. Tommy's books sold and sold and sold. None of them was out of print. LOOK BACK FOR LOVE, wouldn't this be his last book? Wouldn't this be the book everyone had to buy? 'When is it being published?' she asked.

'In approximately four months,' Tamar answered. 'Since his death, his publishers are trying to speed up the publishing process to – '

'Cash in,' Grace finished for her.

'However, I must warn you, Ms Hampton, that Tommy's decision to assign the copyright to your shelter was made only recently, so the paperwork will take time.'

'Not too much time,' Odelle warned her. 'My needs are immediate. My women – '

'I'll work as fast as I can in getting the money for you,' Tamar assured her with a professional smile. 'We all recognize the problems that exist in this field.' Tamar turned her attention to Grace. She looked down and continued reading from the will. 'To Grace Louise Mandling Patterson, in appreciation of the years we had together, full of artistic endeavours, I leave the sum of $10,000 for her personal use. In addition, I appoint Grace Louise Mandling Patterson as my literary executor and instruct her to use my unpublished writings as she sees fit. As my literary executor, Grace Louise Mandling Patterson is to receive fifty percent of all monies accrued from her endeavours on behalf of my work. Having followed Grace's career with interest, I know that my writings are in good hands.'

Grace Mandling tried not to let her dismay show. What in God's name was she going to do with Tommy's writings? The man never stopped. He left his dribble everywhere, including matchbook covers and tablecloths. This was totally unfair of him, but oh so like the man she once knew so intimately. To perpetuate Tommy's work – and hadn't the world heard enough from him already? – she would have to let her own slide. What a dumb thing for Tommy to decide. And so typical of him to think she would be so self-sacrificing. Of course, if she got fifty percent, his work could make her rich. But she was rich enough already. How much money did she need? Damn Tommy Patterson!

Seeing that Grace was unlikely to express thanks or regrets, Tamar Litowsky moved on to Trudi Surefoot. 'To Trudi Heidi Halley Patterson, also known as Trudi Surefoot, I leave, in appreciation of many mystical memories, my house in California, "Mi Hacienda", and all its contents. Also, because I am aware of Trudi Surefoot's delicacy, sensitivity, sense of decency, and most of all her all-encompassing, compassionate heart, I appoint her executive director, with the assistance of Tamar Litowsky, of the Tommy Patterson Fund for the Betterment of Humanity. As executed by Tamar Litowsky, under my direct supervision, this fund will allow those among us who are momentarily down and out to gain strength, knowing that this is a place where they can apply for small bequests to tide them through the darkest of times. It is said only too often that money cannot buy happiness, and perhaps that is true. But money can keep the wolf from the door, the shadow from darkening the heart. Trudi understands wolves and shadows. The largeness of her heart will allow all who enter into her presence to be nourished. Trudi, you always wanted to make the world a better place to live in, and now's your chance. You and I both believed that moving the masses wasn't as important as saving the individual. Now you will have the chance to carry out this philosophy. My love and encouragement will always be with you.'

'Of course, you understand, Ms Surefoot,' Tamar said, 'that the foundation will be under our joint control. Tommy expressed the fear that you might be too easily swayed and taken advantage of. I'm sure that, by working together, you and I can make the difference Tommy wanted.'

'Oh, yeah, sure,' Trudi said agreeably. 'I can't believe this. Tommy gave me that nice house on the hill?'

'Where exactly is the money coming from for the Foundation?' Odelle asked. 'Not that it's any of my business of course, but – '

'I'm sure Tommy wouldn't object to your knowing,' Tamar said agreeably. 'After the bequests are paid and various family members of Tommy's receive what he left them, all the monies from Tommy's already published books, except LOOK BACK FOR LOVE, and the fifty percent of his unpublished work that Ms Mandling will be handling, will go into the Foundation. With careful investment and disbursement, it should go on in perpetuity.'

'So the world is not yet rid of Tommy Patterson,' Grace said almost under her breath.

Tamar turned her attention to Kitten Fairleigh. Now it was the turn of the lawyer to shift uncomfortably in her seat. 'To Gretchen Marie

12

Corelli Patterson, also known as Kitten Fairleigh, I leave exactly what she gave me – nothing.'

Tamar closed the will and sat back, waiting for the fireworks. But Kitten was an actress and developing into a good one. She sat there, showing no emotion at all, perhaps waiting for a director to cue her as to what was expected.

The other three women were all shocked. At least in death Tommy had given to them, even if in life he had drained them dry. But for Kitten – nothing? 'Never mind,' Odelle said to her, reaching over to pat her hand. 'You don't need anything from Tommy Patterson. You have it all already.'

'You're lucky to be totally rid of him,' Grace leaned forward to say. She was still pondering how she could get out of being his literary executor.

Finally, Kitten reacted. She stood, her breasts heaving slightly under the cotton knit, pale blue dress. 'It was cruel of you to have me here,' she said to Tamar.

'It was Tommy's last wish.'

'Tommy's dead. I'm alive. I can still feel. Not that he ever gave any thought to anyone's feelings but his own. After all, in his own way he managed to destroy us all, didn't he?' she said, calling upon information gathered last night. 'He turned Odelle into a martyr, Grace into a writer of trash, Trudi into a junkie and me into a whore. And now we have to pretend we're grateful for knowing him! Oh yes, I'll act the part of a woman who cared because Tommy has too many fans out there who have commercial clout at the box office. I'll act shocked and hurt that he chose to spurn me in his will. I'll make a play for their sympathy like you wouldn't believe. But you want to know something? I'm glad Tommy's dead. I only wish I *had* killed him.' She turned smartly, making Odelle envy the firmness of her rear, and left the room.

Grace also rose. 'And that, if anything, should serve as Tommy Patterson's benediction. I'll be in touch,' she told the lawyer.

As Grace was leaving, Trudi leaned forward to say to the lawyer, 'Kitten was so sad, maybe I should give her the house. After all, she is living in it.'

'Don't be too hasty,' Tamar said. 'Tommy bought that before he married Kitten Fairleigh. Besides, you'll need some place to stay when you're out here. We're going to have to work closely on his Foundation.'

'I don't know,' Trudi said softly. 'This whole thing comes as such a surprise. Why would he put me in charge of a foundation? When we were living together, he only allowed me spending money. I had to ask him for everything. I'm sad. I think I might cry. Because I'm lost. I'm always lost. Sometimes I don't understand this world.'

Odelle sighed. Over all the years she had known Trudi, she had come to realize how true this was. But she had her own problems now. She stood and walked over to the desk where Tamar still sat. 'I want to stress how urgent my need for money is. I would appreciate anything you could do to expedite matters.'

'Naturally, I understand that need,' Tamar said. 'I also do charity work.'

'This isn't charity work,' Odelle replied. 'I've dedicated my life to helping these women and children.'

'I'm bound by the will, by the laws of California, and there are still Tommy's relatives to hear from. What if one of them challenges the will?'

'Aren't there clauses covering that?'

'Yes, there are. But the law grinds slowly.'

Odelle saw that she wasn't going to get any further along than vague promises. 'Why don't I have my lawyer call you?' she suggested with a touch of menace.

'I'm sure all lawyers understand – '

But Odelle waved away the ending of Tamar's sentence. She had several lawyers, from some of Chicago's prestigious firms, sitting on her board of directors. One of them had to be able to move mountains. She would not let Sisters of the Storm string along under-budgeted now that she was sitting on a perpetual gold mine. She was a woman of action, not reaction, as Tamar Litowsky would soon learn to her dismay.

Odelle turned from the lawyer and saw Trudi staring vaguely into space. Again, she became the keeper of the lost sheep of Tommy Patterson. 'Come on, Trudi. Let me take you back to the hotel.' Hand in hand, Odelle and Trudi left the conference room. And with their departure, the wives of Tommy Patterson scattered, leaving behind them a few tears, a few laughs, momentary expectations, and a murder.

# Chapter 3

# A Younger Man's Love

When Grace Mandling flew into Newark Airport from the coast, she looked a far cry from the portrait on the back cover of her latest book HELL HATH NO FURY. Her hair was not windswept. Her eyes were only lightly made up. Further, they lacked the dewy look the photographer had captured after he had turned on the fan and some dust or something had struck her contacts. Today she was wearing a sensible tweed suit with a turtleneck silk blouse. Her last book jacket picture had shown her in a plunging, frilly affair, but the unretouched proofs revealed a neck that had begun to crease. Since seeing those proofs she had been careful not to expose her neck. Now she knew why designer scarves were such a hot item.

Grace Mandling was only thirty-eight. She didn't think it right that she should begin to age. She supposed her problem, as usual, was refusing to accept reality graciously.

Galen Richards was at the gate to meet her. She had told him not to bother. By now she had been around enough airports to be able to make ground travel arrangements anywhere. But there Galen was, waiting for her, and she was thankful. Sometimes she was just so tired of being independent and successful. Her fantasy was to be thought of as a weak, delicate, fragile, waif-like woman who needed someone constantly to lean on. She had been involved with many men since Tommy dumped her all those years ago and whenever she became intimate enough to confess this dream, this terrible need of hers to be watched over and cherished, she was laughed at. 'You, weak and dependent!' was always the comeback. The implication was, "A ballcrusher like you?"

Galen didn't laugh at her needs. Why should he? He probably didn't even understand them. He was only a baby. Twenty-seven years old and with his whole life ahead of him. What was she doing with this innocent?

15

'Hi,' he said when she had finally passed through the crush of embracing relatives. She fell gently against his chest. His arm awkwardly encircled her across her garment bag and overnight bag which he soon took from her hands as they made their way out toward the parking lots. 'Rough?' he asked her.

'Rough enough.'

They didn't say much as they walked, just exchanged a few bits of information, like what was in the mail, on the answering machine. Grace occasionally caught Galen's admiring glances and wondered why she couldn't just accept his love, his adoration. Had she been around the block too many times or was she simply unwilling to admit that fantasies can come true? Fantasies. Galen Richards looked as if he had jumped off one of the covers of her books. He was the artist's conception of how every hero appeared in the eyes of the women who loved him.

Galen was young – there was that word again – and sort of sandy-haired, neither blond nor brown. He could never be a model because there was something wrong with his mouth. It showed perpetual, sarcastic amusement. This mouth of his was what had drawn her to him in the first place. Grace had assumed Galen had the same outlook on life as she, but had been mistaken. His expression was deceptive. He took life at face value. He might know what the word "sarcasm" meant, but he would never employ it. He could be a schmuck on occasion, but never a sarcastic one.

He had worried brown eyes. They always seemed to sense some calamity about to happen. None had so far, but his eyes were wary.

She loved his body, and that wasn't only because he knew how to use it in bed. He looked nice standing upright also. He was still lean. Most men her age, a near-doddering thirty-eight, had begun to fill out along the torso; and while she didn't find it unattractive – it was sort of sweet really – she liked the hardness of Galen's body, the fact that when she touched him, she could feel his ribs. It annoyed her that he didn't work out to maintain this perfection. Perfection was just a part of him.

Out in the car park, she discovered that Galen had brought his battered station wagon. He knew perfectly well that he could borrow her Sable at any time, but he chose to drive around in this wreck with its paint fumes. Now she would have to sit with her nose to the window. She didn't even think Galen smelled paint fumes anymore. They were too much a part of his life. That was another thing about Galen Richards. He was still struggling against his fate while she had accepted hers. He didn't want to be a commercial artist. She had acquiesced to the fact that commercial was all she would ever be.

16

She had met Galen in Nyack, New York, along the waterfront one delicious summer's day, when sailboats were skating along the Hudson and tourists had flocked into the still small town to have a look at the artistic wares. As she recalled, the first thing she noticed about Galen was his mouth, not his paintings. His paintings were abstract, blobs within cubes or cubes within blobs. He explained the concept to her after their first meeting, about form and free form, constrictions and expansions. They still looked like blobs and cubes to her. She remembered overhearing a woman about her age asking Galen if he had anything a bit bigger and in browns and golds. She caught Galen's eye and smiled in sympathetic amusement. Even then she should have known Galen was an idiot, or, as he called himself, an idealist, artistically speaking. He could have handed the woman his card and said he took commissions, but he didn't. He just answered politely, 'No, I'm sorry, I don't have anything in browns and golds today.'

After the woman left, Grace approached him and said, 'Was that wise? After all, she might pay well for what she wants.'

'She wanted something to match her carpet,' Galen replied. 'And you?'

She confessed to her ignorance about art. And artists. Yes, even then she was coming on to him. He caught on to that fast. He wondered if she wanted to hang around for a few hours so that he could explain art to her over dinner. She laughed. The entire encounter sounded like one from her books, and maybe she would use it as such. For more verisimilitude she accepted his invitation, though she was sure she would have been able to invent the scene before it happened. He would take her to some chowder house overlooking the Hudson, and probably the Tapan Zee Bridge, since that was hard to escape in Nyack. They would order a chilled bottle of white wine. He would discuss the longings of his soul. She would let him rest his head on her bosom, maybe. If he spoke prettily enough. She was a sucker for sweet talk.

She returned in a few hours. He was already packing up that nasty station wagon of his. 'I have my own car,' she confessed.

'I'll drive you back to it.'

That was the first time she entered that rolling abomination and discovered that paint fumes gave her headaches.

The chowder house of her fantasies, turned out to be a Burger King along the highway, well away from the river. 'I like it because there's a custard stand next door,' he confessed.

Custard? Hamburgers? Oh, he was so young! Galen hungered for grease, while Grace longed for a glass of clear, cold white wine, hot soup, warm bread, white table cloths. She didn't think of herself as being sophisticated, just civilized.

17

'I'm a commercial artist,' Galen confessed over his Whopper. 'I work in the city five days a week. Then on Saturdays and Sundays during the summer, I exhibit around the state.'

'Sell much?' she wondered.

He shrugged. 'I paint all winter. I've got to clear out my workroom for next winter's efforts. This last winter I was trying to deal with the issues of freedom and constraint. My job change erupted in my art. I moved from a cosmetics firm to an ad agency.'

She asked if he lived in the city. He didn't. 'I should have thought that was the place for a young artist to be,' she suggested.

'I can't speak their language,' he confessed. 'I've always had trouble fitting in. I'm sort of on the cusp between art and life. Besides, I like the fresh air, the easier life.'

'You live in Nyack then?'

'New City.'

She was surprised. 'So do I!'

'Yeah?' He smiled. 'Then you have the same trouble I do. People ask where you live. You say New City. They say, oh, New York City. And you say, no, New City. And they – '

She would have edited his conversation for him, but she was too busy studying his sarcastic mouth and his worried brown eyes.

That night she went to bed with him. He was a child, and she felt he needed her experience. But she had misjudged him. Not only was his technique reliable, but he possessed a creative flair. His artistic temperament, thank God, he kept out of the bedroom. She didn't like bedroom scenes. She had been through too many of them.

That first summer with Galen was one of the most enjoyable of her life. When he finally wanted to know what she did – being typically male, he was mainly concerned with himself – she told him she was a typist, which, in any case, was exactly what so many of her critics called her. Galen's curiosity was satisfied.

That was the summer she had a book come out in August. She was furious. True, it was debuting in early August, but the beach season was almost over. What would her sales figures look like? What was the title of that one? Yes, it was THE BLOSSOMING OF BEAUTY BANCROFT, all about a young woman who comes into her own one summer along the Maine coast. God, the scene with Beauty and Lance becalmed one night just off Mount Desert, letting the ocean rock them into a mutual orgasm, was one of her most moving. Trash? She thought not!

Galen discovered her true occupation one Sunday when he spotted an art lover carrying Grace's book under one hand and a straw basket under the other. He recognized Grace's photo on the back cover instantly. She was pleased because sometime she couldn't recognize herself. He confronted her that evening. He was angry. 'All the time I was going on about art, and there you were, the true artist, and you never gave me a hint!' he accused.

She loved him for that. True artist indeed. 'What difference does it make?' she asked him, smiling, almost laughing at his anger.

'What difference? I thought we knew each other.'

And then she did laugh, while he dramatically stormed from her house, back to his crowded townhouse along the commercial strip.

After Galen left, she missed him. But she didn't go after him. August was fading rapidly toward September. Summer romances were like summer flowers. Now it was back to the cold reality of working for a living and waiting for love.

The whole affair with Galen had been dumb, she finally concluded, as the days passed by without him: young artist, older woman, consummation of several fantasies. Reality always struck with the falling of the leaves.

But he came back to her one Sunday when she was outside mowing her lawn. She had a maid clean the inside of her house, except for her workroom, because she hated doing things like vacuuming and cleaning bathrooms. But she loved being outside on her plot of land with its grass and trees and vegetable garden. He came round the back and surprised her. She turned off the mower and watched him approach. 'I've read several of your books,' he said when he reached her. 'It's funny, I even know the guy who did your last cover.'

'Really?'

'The books aren't like you at all. I can see why you didn't want to tell me about them. They're like me and advertising. You're so much finer and more delicate than what you write. Sensitive, maybe even fragile.' He shrugged.

Sensitive? Fragile? The magic words, so far removed from manipulative, cold, bitchy, independent. 'Would you like to come in for some lemonade?' she wondered.

Yes, even then she was planning on serving it in bed. Galen offered no objections. My God, how they tore into each other, clothes scattered from the back door on up the stairs. He was already hard when they reached her unmade bed, and she was so desperate for him, so really desperate, that she didn't bother waiting for him before she came, shouting with fulfilled desire.

After Labour Day, he moved in with her. It was dumb and she knew it. She could already write of the inevitable break-up, the pain, the agony, the weeping, the anger when she would find out he left her for a younger woman, someone his own age.

19

But that was over two years ago now, and Galen was still in her bed. He was in her house too, though not painting there. As a Christmas present that first year she had a studio built in the back yard for him with skylights and everything. She just could not stand the smell of paint.

But other than that, they got along well. They were friends, lovers, companions. Lately, though, Galen was beginning to press her for more than his loving relationship. He wanted to get married. How sweet of him and how totally unrealistic. How could she possibly publicly marry a man eleven years her junior? It would make her look like a fool. She didn't care what all the magazines were saying, she had her public to think about. They would see Galen as her stud. Of course, she loved him, she assured him over and over again. But marriage?

He wanted children. She pointed out to him that one day he would leave her, find someone his own age or probably younger. Then what would happen with the children? He would never leave her, he promised. But she had been married before. She knew how much a man's promise was worth.

'What is it?' he asked finally. 'Don't you want children?'

She was thirty-eight and, yes, she did want a child. She was beginning to want one desperately, so much so that she would spend spare time in the children's section of department stores, watching mothers with their offspring buying clothes. That sight, if any, should have turned her off motherhood. But it hadn't. Then she thought of that other time so very long ago, when – but she had promised herself that she would never think of that again.

# Chapter 4

# Ultimatum

He laughed at her. 'Stop sticking your nose out of the window! The smell's not that bad.'

'Not for you maybe,' Grace replied.

Galen pulled smoothly on to the Garden State Parkway and headed north. 'Look, I've done something. I don't know if you're going to like it. I've designed a condolence card and printed up about a hundred.'

'Are there a hundred people who are sorry Tommy Patterson's dead?'

'Come on, Grace. Hold the bile. I didn't even know you were married to him.'

'I told you I had been married before.'

'But you never told me to whom. I don't understand you. Why are you always so secretive? If I were you, I would have bragged about being married to Tommy Patterson. I read some of his stuff in college – '

'Sophomore year, I presume.'

'And a lot of it made sense. He made me feel better about myself.'

'He could do that – from a distance.' She sighed, then said, 'Look, Galen, I've heard enough about Tommy for a while, with his funeral and all. Let's talk about something else, okay?'

She didn't mean to encourage him to talk about his troubles with his boss at the ad agency, but he did anyway. It was something about defining a car bumper. She listened with half an ear, held her nose to the window, and they got home sooner than she would have thought.

The first thing Grace did when she got home was check her mail. Perhaps it was a throwback to her earlier days when the mail was so overwhelmingly important. Then she was a budding author who sent out manuscripts with such fervent hope, only to receive rejections in return. She still found the mail fascinating, even though nothing important was mailed nowadays. It wasn't only the lousy service. Younger people had taken over the publishing business, every business, including her doctor and dentist. They couldn't remember a time when long-distance calls meant trouble, either illness or death in the family. Now it was reach out and touch everyone you could get your hands on – except, it seemed, when offering your condolences. Galen was right. There was a stack of mail, which, when opened, revealed a delicate overflowing of sympathy for her recent loss. Hallmark was missing something here. It should definitely have developed a sympathy card for the loss of an ex-husband. But how could such a card be generic? You could hate the bastard. Or you could still love him, which would be even worse.

She didn't know how she felt about Tommy. When he was alive, she found him an annoyance, not that there was much contact. Occasionally they found themselves at the same booksellers' convention. Tommy would be his pleasant, concerned self. Of course, there was that one time when they slugged it out in public. But lately she found out about Tommy only through the media. He was never far from the front page, especially after his marriage to Kitten Fairleigh.

When she heard about his death, she was shocked. He was only a few years older than she, and the first reports didn't make it clear he had been murdered. Yet when it turned out to be murder, she wasn't shocked. She was even grimly amused. Tommy got his. At last. She tried not to be bitter but he had stolen something precious from her, and it wasn't her maidenhood. He had destroyed her ability to believe in love.

Grace had had no intention of going to Tommy's funeral, but that lawyer Tamar Litowsky called to let her know his last wish: each of his four wives was to attend his funeral. It would also be advisable, she said, to show up for the reading of Tommy's will.

Was she sorry she had gone? The funeral had had its amusing moments. But she still felt so much anger towards Tommy, and couldn't let it go. Which meant, she supposed, that he was still controlling her life.

'A penny for them?'

Galen was downstairs now, after stowing her bags up in the bedroom. He put his arms on her shoulders. She shrugged them off, the ghost of Tommy still lingering. 'That's such a cliché, Galen. Can't you think of anything better to say?'

Puzzled and hurt, he backed off. He went into the living room and sat down, staring vacantly at the grass outside the picture window. She sighed. She was such a bitch. Sometimes she spent months acting as if she had PMT. Why should she take everything out on Galen?

She walked into the living room and sank down next to him. 'I'm sorry,' she said prettily.

'Yeah.'

'Honestly, I am.'

'You always are.'

Oh oh, he was annoyed. She loved it when he got annoyed with her. Usually, he was so even-tempered when it came to their relationship that it drove her crazy. She laughed. He turned and gave her a warning glance. Then he got up and started to walk away. 'Come on back here,' she urged. 'Please, Galen. I promise I'll be good.'

He stood at the picture window like a stubborn little boy. She got up and went to him, put her arms around him and held him tight. He had to reciprocate. 'You know I'm a bitch,' Grace told him.

'That you are,' he agreed. Then he whispered in her ear, 'Do you want to go upstairs?'

She didn't really want to, but she could feel he did. 'Let me shower first?'

The shower was her sanctuary. She liked the water hot and comforting. As she had when she was a child, she still used Yardley's English Lavender. It always made her feel so grown up.

Galen was waiting for her when she came out, all fresh and powdered. He lay naked with the sun streaming down on him. He was so beautiful to her that sometimes she wished she were an artist so she could capture him. What was his essence? Youth?

He cupped her breasts in his hands as she joined him on the bed. They used not to dangle so. Did he mind? He never seemed to. He pulled her down on top of him, then tumbled her so she could feel the weight of him on her body. 'Galen, I love you. I'm so glad you're here.' And she meant it.

Afterwards, she lay smiling into his chest. He could feel her smile. 'What is it?' he wondered.

'Do you mind that I moan so much when you touch me?'

'No, it turns me on.'

'I love your fingers. I love your teeth. When you put your mouth on my breasts, I think I'm dying.'

'I think I'm dying too.'

She giggled. 'You're so eloquent.'

'Thanks.'

'Physically.'

'Oh.' He propped himself up and away from her. 'Another insult,' Galen noted.

23

'No, it wasn't – '

'Listen, Grace, I know you've been through a lot lately. And maybe I shouldn't dump this on you now. But I've been thinking about it the whole time you were gone.'

He was leaving her. That's what he was thinking about. She just knew it.

'Now that your first husband is dead, you can't possibly have any ties to him. I mean, it's like the past is dead with him. So now maybe you can focus on our future. Together.'

Trapped, she sat up on her elbows. 'There's the phone. I'd better – '

'The answering machine is on. I want a commitment, Grace. I want you to say you love me publicly.'

She smiled. 'Publicly?'

'You know what I mean. By marrying me. Then people will know I'm the one you love.'

'People already know that, Galen.'

'Oh yeah? Then how come I'm always reading about Grace Mandling, unmarried queen of romance?'

'The Elizabeth I of lovesick souls,' she mused.

'Look, Grace, here's another cliché you won't like – either shit or get off the pot.'

'Fish or cut bait, for Chrissakes!'

He fell back on to his pillow. 'Okay, I give up. I've got to move on, Grace. I know what I want. If you don't – '

She sighed, annoyed. Galen was such a thoughtless bastard. Did she really need this now? Okay, he had been pressing her for months, but why give her an ultimatum now? She wanted to tell him, you're young, I'm old, but he had heard it all before. He came home with statistics that proved women live an average of ten to fifteen years longer than their mates. By marrying him, she wouldn't have to be alone. They could have children, grandchildren. They could have life.

'I got you something,' Galen said.

'What?'

'A present.' He turned over to his bedside table and leaned down to reach for her gift. While he did so, she admired his ass. He came up with a book, wrapped in Galen's own inimitable style.

'What's this?' she wondered, feeling the heft of it, which was not much. Galen wasn't a great reader.

'Open it,' he demanded.

She tore through the paper. She hated to do it, as Galen always made his own. She thought it should be framed instead of ripped.

24

Underneath the paper was a copy of WHAT IS A COMMITMENT AND HOW TO MAKE ONE IN 10 EASY STEPS. She laughed. Would she never escape Tommy Patterson, world class bastard?

# Chapter 5

# Communications

When they finally got out of bed, Galen trailed down to the kitchen to stir up some spaghetti sauce from a recipe that had been in his family for at least ten years, he assured her.

While Galen was cooking and watching television, Grace decided to catch up on her answering machine. One tape had run out of space, so Galen had put in a second one. Now she rewound the first to have a listen. The calls were mostly from her publisher Adams & Westlake, wondering if and when she was going to finish her book tour for HELL HATH NO FURY, which was interrupted in Atlanta by the news of Tommy's death. Then there were two interesting calls interspersed with business. One was from her mother, the other from her sister. Both offered condolences on poor Tommy's death. They knew how he had abused her but considered that all in the past as Tommy became a world-class celebrity. Grace just bet they flaunted their acquaintance with her throughout their social circles. She noted with pleasure, however, that she hadn't heard from her brother. Either he was too busy in the lab, or his silence, as usual, expressed disapproval. Her brother was never taken in by Tommy. She guessed if you dealt with rats all day the way her brother did, you learned to recognize one when you saw one.

The second tape contained more desperate calls from her publisher, begging her to get in touch. And then came several interesting calls that surprised her. One was from a woman who introduced herself as Carman McCall, and then said, 'You don't know me, but I'm Tommy's agent. I understand you've been appointed Tommy's literary executor. I think we should get together and have lunch.' She left her number, warning that she would call again. After that came a call from Grace's own agent, followed by one from Tommy's publisher, then one from hers again. Obviously, the contents of Tommy's will were out in the open. She was glad Galen had refused to let her answer the phone. Better to confront her beloved than the world of publishing. God, what a mess. She had enough work of her own. She didn't want to have to start worrying abut Tommy's crap too. 'Hey, Grace, get your butt out here!' Galen called.

Some sauce. It must have been simmering all of ten minutes. She hurried to the kitchen, glad of the diversion from business problems. Galen pointed his wooden spoon at the television. '*Entertainment Tonight*,' he reported.

Kitten Fairleigh was sitting very cosily next to the hostess of the show, blonde near blonde. Her eyes were moist, and she was dabbing them ever so slightly with a hankie. God, Grace hadn't seen a hankie in years. Kitten leaned forward to say earnestly to the hostess, but actually into the camera, 'Tommy and I loved each other deeply, but he was hurt. He hurt just like a little boy.' Dab, dab. 'He was just – ' a shake of the blonde mane ' – innocent of the Hollywood scene, and didn't really understand the close working relationship we actors develop during the filming of a movie. We become a family, you see. Tommy didn't understand about David.' A picture of David Turner was flashed on the screen. What a hunk, Grace thought. Go for it, Kitten! 'Tommy was,' Kitten continued mournfully, 'jealous. Oh, I know it's a horrible word to use about anyone, especially someone as sensitive as Tommy. But he was a man.' She nodded. 'Yes, he was definitely a man.' Smirk, smirk. 'I'm sorry he died when he did, before he had a chance to understand the depths of my feelings for him,' Kitten concluded. And Grace could only bet what those feelings were.

'So you weren't surprised when he left you nothing in his will?' the hostess asked.

Kitten looked up and sighed tremulously. 'He left me a lifetime of memories.'

'Do you have any idea at all who killed him?'

'Oh, Janquelle,' Kitten said, reaching out to touch the hostess, 'I don't believe anyone could or would have wanted to kill Tommy Patterson. I know what the police are saying, but I – I simply have to believe it was an accident. He was a good man, a man who cared. And that's all we can ask from each other, isn't it, that we care?'

The camera cut to a picture of Tommy Patterson, smiling and caring, then faded to a toothpaste commercial.

'That woman has a body I could go for,' Galen admitted.

'Oh, really?' Grace replied. 'I was too busy admiring her acting to notice.'

Galen turned to her, dripping sauce on the floor tiles. 'Okay, tell me the real story. What's Kitten Fairleigh like and who murdered your ex-husband?'

Grace smiled. 'Kitten is – ' The phone rang. 'Oh, shit! Galen, please get that for me. I can't speak to anyone right now. It's all about this literary executor thing, and I haven't even sorted it out in my own mind. Please?'

Galen picked up the phone. 'Galen Richards speaking.'

'Grace Mandling, please.'

'I'm sorry, Ms Mandling isn't here at the present time. May I please take a message?'

'This is Odelle Hampton. Could you please – '

'Oh! Hang on a second.' Galen put his hand over the mouthpiece and said, 'It's Odelle.'

'Odelle?' Grace frowned as she took the phone from Galen. 'Odelle, hi. Were you listening to *Entertainment Tonight*?'

'Heavens no! Why?'

'Kitten Fairleigh just made her exculpatory appearance.'

'She did? No, I didn't see it, but I'm sure it was – um – emotive. Listen, darling, I know I have no right to ask you this, but I was thinking on the plane ride home that – well, are you putting out a book of Tommy's right away?'

'Oh God, Odelle, I don't even want to think about Tommy and his inanities. Not now anyway. I have enough on my mind.'

'Because if you were, it would cut into the sales of LOOK BACK FOR LOVE, which would mean that my shelter would get less money than it might otherwise receive.'

'You have nothing to worry about. His publishers won't want to crowd the field either. They'll probably simply reissue all his old books in new paperback editions at higher prices. But his latest, his last, should be a hot seller.'

Odelle sighed. 'Thank God for that. It's just so hard to help people nowadays. No one seems to care any more. But I was thinking after this book, maybe a year or so after, you could publish something like TOMMY PATTERSON LOOKS AT LIFE ON OUR PLANET or THE WIT AND WISDOM OF TOMMY PATTERSON, something like that. You know, just jottings. Then I could apply for a grant from his Fund for the Betterment of Humanity. It would keep Sisters of the Storm in money. That's all I'm worried about, keeping the shelter going. Look, I've got something else to tell you also.'

'Yes?'

'Trudi's signed over "Mi Hacienda" to Kitten Fairleigh.'

'The idiot!'

'What's more, Trudi's here with me in Chicago. She flew in the flight after mine. She says she wants to cleanse herself.'

'Of what?'

'I don't know. I put her in a hotel for the night. I have my own problems to sort through right now.'

'Keep in touch, Odelle. Let me know what I can do to help. Call me before the first of the year about the shelter. I'm sure I can give something.' She put down the phone, then rushed to the answering machine to turn it on again. But should she? Maybe her mother and sister – well, she'd call them later. Meanwhile, she could finally smell the sauce, and she was hungry. She went back into the kitchen to set the table. Galen was boiling the spaghetti, testing it every few seconds to make sure it didn't overcook. She always hated it when he served the pasta almost crunchy. She liked it slack. But he was in charge tonight.

'Beer or wine?' she asked, as she went to the refrigerator to get the cheese.

Galen gave it a thought. 'Beer.' He placed her spaghetti delicately on a plate and dolloped too little sauce on it for her liking.

'God, Galen,' she complained.

'Do you want to smother the taste?'

'Yes!' She took the plate from him and dumped another ladle of sauce on the spaghetti. She hated purists.

They sat down together, while ET droned on in the background. 'So,' Galen said, 'what did Odelle have to say?'

'Trudi's with her, Trudi Surefoot, Tommy's third wife. Trudi says she wants to cleanse herself. What do you think that means, Galen? Do you think she killed Tommy, and she's ready to confess?'

# Chapter 6

# Give Me Shelter

Odelle Hampton was the founding member of Women Tommy
Patterson Dumped On. So, naturally, Odelle was not surprised that
Trudi Surefoot had found her way to Odelle's doorstep when she
needed help. She was used to taking charge in a crisis. She learned
how to early, when Tommy walked out on her.

But that was long ago. Now she had other worries, like Trudi, like
the shelter. Trudi she had already managed to do something about.
The shelter was a more enduring concern.

Who would object to Tommy's will? When Odelle could answer
that question, she would know how soon she would get the money left
to Sisters of the Storm. Would Kitten Fairleigh? No. Certainly not
now that Trudi, spaced-out, bleeding heart that she was, had signed
over "Mi Hacienda" to the silver screen's latest Valkyrie. Besides,
Kitten had more going for her than Tommy's money. How much did
movie stars make anyway? Lots, Odelle figured.

Would Tommy's family make trouble? What about her own sweet
daughter Julia? Ms Litowsky said Tommy had left bequests to family
members. Was Julia included? Somehow Odelle doubted it. Over the
years Tommy had forgotten he even had a daughter, especially since
Julia was older than his fourth wife, the delightful Kitten. Tommy
didn't want anything or anyone around him that would make him
seem as if he were ageing. Children definitely demonstrated the years
were piling up.

But Julia probably wouldn't make a fuss. After all, when Odelle
called her to tell her her father had died, Julia simply said, 'I heard it
on the news. So what?' Years ago, after Julia discovered that Sy
Hampton was not her real father and *the* Tommy Patterson was, she
introduced herself to Tommy for the first time at one of his lectures.
He pretended not to know who she was or what she was talking
about. How bitter Julia had been. Now she was merely indifferent.

Odelle only wished her husband Sy were here to help her through this. He would know what to do, whom to contact, what to say. But he was off somewhere in Saudi Arabia or Dubai or was it the United Arab Emirates? She could never get those countries straight. She had contacted him through his office, and he had sent a telegram via the shelter, which passed his message on to her in Los Angeles. If she needed him, he'd come home. But she knew she couldn't ask him to do that. He had his work, and couldn't just be lifted off the desert floor, or wherever he was searching for oil and minerals, simply to fly home and hold her hand while she contemplated the death of Tommy Patterson.

So who could she lean on? Their son Luke was a senior in high school. He had enough worries of his own, writing his college application essays. Besides, what did he know about the law or what Tommy's family would do?

Who was left of Tommy's family anyway? His mother was in a nursing home. The last time Odelle saw Tommy, he bragged about how Medicare was paying for some of it, even though he could perfectly well afford to keep his own mother in splendour. His father was dead. His brother, with whom she still exchanged Christmas cards, had a car dealership. Tommy's sister might be a problem because Odelle understood her husband had left her recently. In such an eventuality, there definitely could be money problems.

"Money problems" about summed up Odelle's work at the shelter. Why hadn't she stuck to volunteer work? That's how this all started out. She supposed she first volunteered for work at Sisters of the Storm, the shelter for battered women and children, because it was so distant from life as she knew it. Her marriage definitely, and thank God, lacked that sort of drama. Was it because she and Sy were such well-balanced people? More likely their marriage held together so well because Sy spent half his time away from home, operating his own petrochemical consulting firm.

At the outset Odelle felt her stable, happy marriage qualified her to act as care-giver to those less fortunate in their choice of husbands. How little she knew! How innocent she was. She did not yet have any idea of the degradation to which women and children were being subjected in this supposedly enlightened culture.

At first she couldn't believe what she heard. She couldn't conceive of being slapped for smiling at what your husband considered an inappropriate moment, or kicked for not having gravy for the mashed potatoes, beaten just because your husband needed something to punch. And what about the children, the poor, little, helpless, innocent children, looking up at her with grieving eyes, wondering what they did to deserve such pain?

When she started working at Sisters of the Storm, it was for half a day a week. Arriving home, she could barely let Sy near her, she was so full of hatred for all men. Men were big, strong. All the power was in their hands. They could wipe the floor with you, and often did with the women in the shelter. There were social workers in the shelter who would try conciliation and therapy. Odelle's solution, as the months rolled on and she became more and more involved, would have been to put men up against a wall and shoot them. She didn't go for this mumbo-jumbo familial history crap. Anyone, even a man, must know it was wrong to knock around a women and a child.

Sy was so disturbed by her burgeoning hostility, he suggested she drop the shelter and do volunteer work at a blood bank. That was before AIDS. But she continued at the shelter, increasing her hours. In the meantime, she went back to school to get her graduate degree in public administration. She already had her undergraduate degree in child psychology. She had finished it course by course while Luke was a baby. These degrees qualified her to turn from a volunteer to a paid worker. So from a half-day-a-week volunteer, she went to full-time employee at the shelter.

When the director left for browner pastures in New Jersey, she recommended Odelle for her job. Odelle had her doubts. Being director of the shelter meant for the most part that she would be removed from the day-to-day work with her women. It also meant she would be spending all her time scrounging around for funds. Sisters of the Storm, Inc. was private. It got grants from the city and had access to city social services, but basically it was funded by the director going on bended knees to various charitable organizations, businesses and churches in the Chicago area. She discussed it with her husband, naturally. Sy told her if she felt that strongly about what was happening to women and children, she should do it. By then she had learned to hate men selectively, so Sy wasn't on the defensive all the time.

So Odelle took up the gauntlet. For two years now, she had held the shelter together. But charities are like fads. One year it could be battered women and abused children, but the next year it would be hospices or cancer research. She was banging heads with equally worthy causes for the shrinking charity dollar. That's why she had approached Tommy.

Odelle supposed she should have told that detective Sam Morris about her visit to L.A. a few days before Tommy died. But why? She wasn't there when Tommy was murdered, so what difference did her visit make? Besides, if she explained to Detective Morris what she had been doing in Los Angeles, he could have accused her of blackmail. Might that negate the will? Or would she have had to murder Tommy to lose her inheritance?

Odelle sighed. She wished Julia were here to answer all these nagging legal questions, not that she could tell her daughter the full story. How could Julia understand her passion? Instead of doing something worthwhile with her life, like working for Legal Aid, Julia had joined some large commercial firm and was making over $100,000 a year now, specializing in foreclosures or something equally dismal.

Where did she go wrong with that girl? Both she and Tommy had such ideals when they were young. The young had nothing any more, only the vision of being rich. Well, perhaps Luke would want to do something more noble, though he kept talking about majoring in marketing. Hopeless.

The doorbell rang. Odelle wasn't surprised. Glencoe was a wealthy suburb of Chicago where everyone possessed everything advertising could recommend. But ever since word got out among her neighbours of her work at the shelter, she received these late night visitors: women who spent their days golfing or having their hair done, then their nights living in terror of their well-heeled, well-dressed husbands making an appearance. Nothing could shock Odelle. That was the problem with knowing too much.

She went to the door and looked cautiously out. A terrified woman could have an irate husband following her. That's what had happened one time. The husband kicked his foot right through the front door, and Sy was not a little bit put out. But tonight it wasn't one of her neighbours visiting her, it was Trudi Surefoot.

Odelle opened the door wide. 'Trudi, I thought you were all tucked in for the night.'

Trudi stepped inside, looking lost, as usual. 'That hotel you sent me to? They were selling drugs in the lobby, Odelle.'

'Don't be ridiculous! Not in that hotel. That's one of the best in the area.'

'Do you think I don't know a pusher when I see one!'

Odelle gave that some thought. Trudi had a point. Was no place safe any more?

When she thought about it, she realized no place was. If it wasn't drugs, it was alcohol or guns or religion or channels. That's why Tommy had been so successful. No one wanted to deal with life as it was. There always had to be some enhancer. People wanted to believe that only magic could make life better, that nothing they did by themselves could make a difference. Was it global despair or simple laziness?

33

'Can I stay here tonight?' Trudi meekly asked.

Odelle looked sternly at her. 'Do you have any drugs on you?'

'No, nothing. Honestly, Odelle. That's why I'm here. I want to quit. I owe that much to Tommy, don't I?'

'You don't owe anything to Tommy. You owe it to yourself to straighten out your life.'

'It's the fund Tommy put me in charge of. If I'm drugged all the time, how can I help other people?'

'A point well worth remembering,' Odelle said, leading Trudi into the living room.

Trudi sat on a sofa and looked around at the tastefully decorated living room, a far cry from her apartment in Taos, with its wild, eccentric pottery and Indian rugs and blankets. 'I've never been here before.'

Odelle was surprised because she felt as if she had known Trudi forever. But it was true. Odelle had been to Taos, and she and Trudi kept in touch over the years, but Trudi practically never left the Southwest. 'Have you eaten?' she wondered.

'Oh, no,' Trudi said. 'I was afraid of going out anyplace. I might not have known how to get back.'

The story of Trudi's life, Odelle thought. She went into the kitchen and made them some sandwiches. When she came out, Trudi was still sitting in the rather fixed position of a little girl at her first tea party. Odelle set the tray down and made sure Trudi was eating before she began. 'I've made arrangements for you to be admitted to the River Range Clinic. It's up north, almost on the Wisconsin border. I think you're going to like it.' Odelle didn't bother going into the details of the bargaining she went through to get Trudi jumped to the top of the list. Her friend Madelaine Stevenson had people begging to get into the clinic. She had met Madelaine while they were both searching under the rugs of government agencies for funds. To get Trudi admitted, Odelle made a vague promise: when Trudi recovered from her addiction, Odelle was sure she would remember the River Range Clinic fondly. She would have hundreds of thousands of dollars to distribute. Madelaine hadn't believed a word of it. 'If you knew someone that rich, you'd get the money for yourself.' Then Odelle mentioned those magic words "Tommy Patterson", and Madelaine relented.

'I don't know if I'm really ready to do this,' Trudi said, picking the bread from the sandwich and rolling it into little balls.

Odelle frowned. That was something little children did. Exactly how far gone was Trudi's mind? 'You'll love this clinic, Trudi. It has a very high success rate. You won't even miss drugs. Aside from

34

therapy, it puts a huge emphasis on physical activity. The body can heal itself.'

'But what about the mind?' Trudi wondered.

Yes, as far as the mind went, it was entirely possible nothing would be able to save Trudi Surefoot. She had once confessed to Odelle that she started taking drugs when she was ten. Perhaps it would be best if no one did a brain scan on her for a while at least. 'Come,' Odelle said kindly, after it looked as if Trudi was done eating, 'let's go make up a bed for you.'

Trudi trailed along like a shy little girl. Half an hour later, she was asleep. Odelle was left alone in her room with the bedlight on, trying to read. But her mind wouldn't let her. So many years had passed and it all came to this. Death, despair, loss. Where was their happy innocence?

# Chapter 7

# In The Beginning

Odelle Lacy and her mother slugged it out, verbally, the spring of her senior year in high school. Blessed with acceptances from both Mount Holyoke, her mother's alma mater, and Cornell, Odelle swung wildly between the two. Her mother wanted her to go to Mount Holyoke because of the "intellectual stimulation" she would find among the women there. But Odelle wasn't looking for the scholarly, almost monastic, life she expected to find among the Seven Sisters. She wanted to be where the boys were, as Connie Francis so aptly put it in one of Odelle's favourite movies, especially as seen in the drive-ins. So Odelle Lacy chose Cornell.

Who cannot recall the excitement of being dropped off on campus that first time, suddenly discovering that there are no more parents hovering over one's bedside to make sure the daily routine is followed, good manners prevail and common sense reigns? Aside from house mothers and strict dorm curfews, still holding sway in 1960 when Odelle entered Cornell, suddenly freedom was there for the taking. Up to now, life followed certain rules, especially if one's family were Republicans from Connecticut. Growing up, Odelle knew very well what was expected of her and which boundaries she could not cross. Suddenly to wake up in her own dorm room and find that no one was guarding the door – well, it was emancipating and at the same time scary.

Like many women of her age, Odelle Lacy went to college because it was the thing to do. She had no game plan, no driving ambition. This didn't mean she didn't know what she wanted to do with her life. Odelle wanted to get married, have children, live in a house just like her mother's in Connecticut, except she could do without the consistently beige decor. In other words, Odelle had come to Cornell, as that tasteless, tacky, sexist joke had it, looking for her MRS.

While she was waiting for Mr Right to come along, for that Prince Charming on a white charger, Odelle was faced with the chore of checking the time table to plan her semester's coursework. It was confusing, and her advisor was no help at all. Perhaps if she had some idea of what she might like to major in, he could have pointed her in the right direction. But she didn't know yet what really interested her. Fortunately for Odelle, at the dawn of the Sixties universities had prescribed coursework, so she had little freedom of choice her first two years in any case. She was sure she would find something that grabbed her. She did. His name was Tom Patterson.

Odelle met Tom Patterson the second semester of her freshman year at Cornell. She had already pledged Kappa Kappa Kappa, and most of her weekends involved working and partying at the house, being a little sister to a Chi Phi, being all around Miss Jane College. Even then Odelle felt there might have been a fatal flaw in her character, because when her roommate, who really would have fit in much better at Mount Holyoke than at Cornell, called Odelle's sorority Crappa Crappa Crappa or the Tri-Craps, Odelle laughed.

It was her roommate Bobbi Baker who introduced her in a roundabout way to Tom Patterson. Bobbi was dating Tom's roommate, and one weekend she begged Odelle to go double with them. Tom had just broken up with his girlfriend and they needed a fourth for a play they had tickets to. Odelle was upset because it meant giving up a Pikes-Go-Hawaiian party, but she and Bobbi had weathered a lot together and she owed her roommate that much.

When Odelle first saw Tom Patterson, she knew it was going to be a long evening. He was not the sort of man to catch one's eye. He was neither tall nor short, handsome nor ugly. He seemed to lack any distinction at all, except for possessing a very warm smile.

Tom definitely wasn't Prince Charming. Odelle knew that from the beginning when it was time to go and he didn't even bother to assist her on with her winter coat. While Bobbi and her boyfriend trooped ahead of them, Odelle was left to walk behind with Tom, trying to make conversation. It would have been helpful if he had answered in words of more than one syllable. For example, after she had ascertained he was from Oneonta, New York, she asked, 'What's in Oneonta?' 'Cows,' he replied.

It was a long, brutal walk to the theatre, Odelle all the time staring daggers into Bobbi's back, not that her roommate seemed either to notice or care. Bobbi at least was having a good time.

The play they saw was Eugene Inonescu's *The Bald Soprano*. Odelle was sure she could have enjoyed it had it been in English rather than the original French. The only benefit she got from attending was that her French teaching assistant saw her there and gave her a short wave. Maybe this would help boost her C-average.

They went out for hamburgers afterwards. Fortunately, they sat in a booth so that Bobbi's bubbly personality took the dead weight of conversation off Odelle's shoulders. And then it was back to the dorm in order to make the twelve o'clock Friday night curfew.

It was ten before twelve when they arrived before the wooden door of the long-standing, antiquated hall. They stood in the middle of what was affectionately known as the kissing pit, where with careless abandon dates would get in their last minute licks, kisses, feelies, whatever, before the house mother would flash the light, letting the girls know they had sixty seconds in which to reach sanctuary. Bobbi and her boyfriend weren't going to waste a minute of their time together in the darker outer fringes. This left Odelle standing awkwardly with Tom, wondering how she could thank him for this interesting evening while at the same time indicating she hoped never to see him again.

She held out her hand and said, 'It was nice meeting you.'

'Uh, yeah,' Tom said. He took her hand in his. Then he looked slowly to the left and right of him. 'We're out of place,' he told her.

He certainly was, she had to agree.

And then he did the most disagreeable thing in the world. He gently pulled her to him and kissed her full on the mouth, only his mouth was open and she could feel his tongue against her teeth!

She broke away, shocked and stunned. French kissing on a first date! 'That was uncalled for,' she said sternly, hearing her mother's voice in her own.

'I just wanted to let you know how much I enjoyed being with you,' he told her with a disingenuous smile.

That makes one of us, she wanted to tell him. But good manners prevailed, as always, and she merely gave him a curt nod, turned on her heel and strode into the dorm before the lights flicked madly.

'He likes you, you know,' Bobbi said the following week.

Odelle couldn't have cared less. 'Not my type,' she assured her roommate, while at the same time wondering why the hell she had taken History of Central Europe. These people couldn't even agree on a name for their countries, much less a border.

'He's a bright guy,' Bobbi continued, not at all concerned about her classwork. She was taking both psychology and sociology. 'He got all A's last semester. He's not in liberal arts. He's in the ag school, taking health sciences or something like that. Though he actually wants to be a writer. Not your type, of course. He's not a conformist.'

'And I am!' Odelle turned on her roommate. Bobbi just stared back at her with open eyes. She knew how to be cruel.

Conformist. To be labelled one was worse than being a commie pinko, at least to Odelle. She had read THE MAN IN THE GRAY

38

FLANNEL SUIT in high school, so she knew how destructive denying one's individuality could be. And yet she never really was an individual. She had always been one of a group – her crowd in Connecticut, her sorority, her rightful place in society. Was there any other way to travel through life?

About a month after her first meeting with Tom Patterson, three weeks after her rejection of his offers to take her out, he called once more. She was ready with a line of excuses until the semester ran out, but he said almost immediately, 'I didn't call you for a date. I just wanted to know if you'd help me with my sociology project?'

'Hmm.'

'It means getting together for ten minutes. I'll ask you a series of questions. You answer them, and that's it. Please, Odelle? I need the demographics.'

She believed him. All her friends in sociology had the same problem, papers due demanding original research. She had already answered the most off-the-wall questions for many of them. She supposed she could do the same for Tom Patterson. 'Ten minutes is all I have to give,' she warned him. They agreed to meet at the Student Union for a Coke and the questions.

When Odelle arrived at the Union, she saw him in line and caught his eye. He waved. She found a table and sat down. He came her way, carrying a tray with two Cokes and a large order of fries. He placed the tray between them. It was a boundary line. Then he took his notebook out of a grey backpack and placed it on the table, flipping it open to a clean sheet. He looked up at her, peering over his glasses. 'Are you a virgin?'

'What!' she objected.

'I'm doing a study of orgasmic responses among freshman women. Now, are you a virgin?'

'Yes, I am a virgin; and if I weren't a virgin, I wouldn't tell you!' It was only when she looked around and noted people were staring at her that Odelle realized she hadn't kept her voice as low as she should have.

Tom leaned toward her and soothed, 'Please. This is for science.'

'I'll bet!' she snapped.

'Look, I lost my virginity when I was fourteen. It was in the back of a school bus late at night. We were returning from a class trip to Albany. We used the side-to-side position. I barely got in before I went off.'

'Aii, God! You're telling me all this over limp fries!'

'You're sensitive. I can see that. Would you rather write your answers?'

39

'I would rather not be here,' Odelle said.

She stood up to go. Tommy grabbed his notebook and backpack to follow. 'It's no shame if you're not a virgin,' he told her, as they strode across the campus green.

'I am a virgin,' she assured him.

'Answer No. 1.' Somehow he got his pen out and wrote this down. 'How often do you fantasize about sex?'

'I don't fantasize about sex,' she lied.

'You're assexual then.'

'What?'

'You have no sexual feelings.'

She stopped. 'Of course I have sexual feelings,' she informed him. 'But well-mannered people don't talk about them.'

'How much of your day is consumed in sexual fantasies? Estimate percentage, please.'

She stormed away from him. He called after her, 'Do you masturbate? If so, how often and is it to orgasm?'

The man was a maniac.

At her next Tri-Kaps meeting, Odelle was surprised to find their sorority president standing seriously before them with mimeographed sheets in her hand. 'Girls,' Brently Moffat said, 'I have a difficult task to set before you tonight. As you all know, we women of Kappa Kappa Kappa have a certain reputation to uphold on campus. We've always been one of the top sororities at Cornell and we aim to keep it that way. Unfortunately, there are those outside the system who have been spreading all sorts of rumours about us. That we're cold, feckless, thoroughly Episcopalian. That our dates go away from us with a condition which I understand is called blue balls. Please, no tittering. This is serious.

'Girls, throughout campus tonight, in various dorms and sister houses, these sheets are being passed out, dealing with a certain delicate matter. To wit, sexual response. It took me many hard hours of thought before I agreed to pass out these questionnaires – and much consultation went into this with Mrs Swickey. But these questionnaires are anonymous. You don't have to fill them out if you don't want to. If you do fill them out, be honest. We don't want to be known as sluts. But we also don't want to be known as ice maidens.'

Odelle couldn't understand what Brently was talking about until she received her copy of the survey. On top it said, "Please return to Tom Patterson, Box 320, Campus Mail."

Tom independently published the results of his survey under the provocative title of "Where the Whores Are". It was grabbed up by almost the entire student body for $5 a shot. Not only did it have

40

titillating quotes from various coeds, it also contained charts indicating the fastest place to get laid. The information was colour-coded, red for hot, yellow for medium, blue for cold. The Tri-Kaps just made it into the red.

Tom Patterson was placed on probation by the administration. But the severity of his punishment left little impression on him. He had come to Cornell as a scholarship student. After the sale of "Where the Whores Are", he had enough money to put himself through college. He also got an A in sociology.

*Chapter 8*

# Why Do Fools Fall in Love?

Was it fate? Kismet? Simple bad luck? Those were questions Odelle asked of herself later – much later. At the time, she merely panicked as she walked into her first chemistry lab, saw the long black tables and the bottles of reagents. How was she to survive this course? And why did she need science anyway? Couldn't nature go on without her?

The summer had been too long, too glorious. She spent it life-guarding at Richaven's public pool with Tony Manuella. It was an act of rebellion, her association with the delicious Tony. 'He's Italian, dear, and Catholic,' her mother pointed out gently one night at the club. 'There are so many – '

Yes, there were so many of her own kind, as Odelle well knew. But none of them was as exciting as Tony Manuella, with all his curly, black hair and his white, white smile. The forbidden fruit of their relationship had consisted of fumbling in the back seat of his parents' car, having her bare breasts caressed in the warm, moist summer night.

But all that fled with September. Here she was, back at Cornell, forced to take all the distribution requirements she had put off from her freshman year, courses like economics, logic, and – chemistry! (She would have taken physics, but she dropped out of that even in high school.)

She was living in the Kappa Kappa Kappa house now, with its extensive access to former tests. And she was also the beneficiary of much excellent advice on how to pass the course. 'Get a lab partner who's premed.' Then she wouldn't have to do anything. He'd do it all because he wouldn't want her to mess up his results.

It seemed as if every other girl in chemistry had received the same advice, because by the time Odelle showed up for the lab section, all the premeds were taken. She was stuck with a frightening choice: an English major, a business administration type, and – Tom Patterson.

God! What was he doing in her lab section? And he treated her as if she were an old friend!

Everyone on campus knew Tom Patterson now. He was notorious. For the sake of her reputation and that of the Tri-Kaps, she planned to stay well away from him.

This she managed to do, until her first hourly. She got an F. Her lab grade wasn't much better, hovering in the D-range. Both she and her English major partner had to do everything under the hood, whether it was called for or not. Their lab instructor just didn't trust them.

'I can help you,' Tommy told her, after glimpsing her grade.

'No thank you,' she replied coolly. She saw the grade of his hourly sticking out of his chemistry book, along with the slide rule. It was an A. 'Uh, Tom.' He turned. She smiled that sweet, helpless, innocent smile of supplication that women learn practically from birth. 'Do you think you really could help me?'

He wasn't as bad as everyone said he was. That's what she constantly had to reassure her sorority sisters. Not that Tom ever got inside the house, not after "Where the Whores Are". She didn't date Tom exclusively that semester, but she saw enough of him to appreciate his finer feelings, the shades of grey in which everyone lived, even Tom Patterson.

Oh sure, he was in his own way a hayseed, lacking her Connecticut sophistication. He was brash, over-confident, the kind of kid who knew he was smart but didn't as yet know where his intelligence would take him. He had no idea of what he wanted, except he wanted the world. But underneath this brash overcoating, Odelle found the little boy in Tom. Here was a guy who insecurely ordered his first bottle of wine, then had to have Odelle hint to him how to taste it and give his approval. Tom was different. As with Tony Manuella, Odelle valued this difference above all things, even common sense.

Still, Odelle wasn't a rebel. She wasn't cut out to oppose society. The pressure from her sorority sisters got to her so much that she once confessed to Tom, in the dead of winter, 'I don't know why I see you.'

'You see me because you like me.'

'But is it worth liking you?'

'You know what you feel. That's what's important. That's what you should hang on to. You've got to be your own person, Odelle.' Long before the phrase became popular, Tom was a believer in getting in touch with your féelings.

It was tough being her own person, especially during the Mom's Day Weekend of her sophomore year. Her parents drove up to Ithaca from Richaven; and although the sorority had many festive events planned for the families, there were those odd moments when

43

daughters would be alone with Mom and maybe Dad. It was definitely an odd moment when Odelle introduced her parents to Tom.

Odelle previously made the mistake of telling her mother about Tom Patterson and her brief association with him the summer before, all about his pamphlet "Where the Whores Are". And here she was, introducing Tom as her boyfriend. Unfortunately, her mother, being a staunch Republican committee woman, had a memory like an elephant. She smiled politely, shook hands, and said, 'I hope you've given up writing, Tom.'

But he hadn't! If only her mother knew, though thank God she didn't. Tom had written an actual book, and it was going to be published by Black Mountain Press. He was thrilled. 'If you only knew what this means to me,' he confessed to Odelle. 'These guys at Black Mountain, they publish everything that's esoteric.'

'Esoteric?' Odelle could not hide the worry in her voice. 'Tom, you haven't written anything – '

'You have to read it,' he insisted.

And that's how she first got her hands on the manuscript TO LOVE A DUCK.

Odelle knew a lot about English literature. She had taken several courses in it. She understood that writing came from one's experiences. So she looked for Tom and Oneonta in TO LOVE A DUCK. She found neither. And then she thought, well, maybe this was Tom's version of 1984. Maybe the duck symbolized something, and she was just too dumb to get the imagery. For example, she had to ask Tom, as she reread the first few pages, 'Do ducks have nipples?'

He threw up his hands, figuratively. 'Don't you get it? It's not about ducks; it's about – fucks,' he finished in a whisper.

Fucks! As in male/female reproduction organs, getting together to screw? She re-examined what she read. Was this how sex really was? So physical, so – wet, so – lacking in depth? But Tom should know, shouldn't he? He had done IT. She meanwhile had merely dreamed of what s-e-x would be like. Innocent that she was, Odelle still labelled the stirrings between her legs as romantic longings. She saw sex as an act of warmth, tenderness, affection, love. Sex was good feelings, although she knew it involved some physical aspects. Hadn't she felt Tony Manuella hard against her thigh when he was nibbling on her bare breasts? Didn't Tom often talk to her about his needs when they were alone together, making out, with only the trees and grass for company?

But the act, the act of sex – what did it consist of? How she pored over her D.H. Lawrence and Ernest Hemingway in an effort to find out. And all of a sudden, here was TO LOVE A DUCK giving her the act

44

of sex in explicit if gooey detail. She handed the manuscript back to Tom, and said to him with all the sincerity of a convert, 'I think you're going to be as famous as Jonathan Swift.' His baffled look told her he had no idea who Jonathan Swift was. And if he had, he wouldn't have approved of her critique. Tom Patterson took himself very seriously. Reviewing his own book, he said to her more than once, 'I'm freeing an entire generation, opening them up to their own sexual needs and desires.' Was this the beginning of his megalomania?

But the reaches of Tom's mind exceeded Odelle's grasp. She didn't concentrate on his broader urges to impact on American society. She focused in on the sex, on her own "sexual needs and desires". For example, the more she dated Tom, the more she wanted him to touch her. And yet, she knew, as did every other good girl at Cornell, that sex was wrong. Virginity was still a prize to be captured on one's wedding night by that knight in shining armour. No blood-stained sheets had to be exhibited after he had pierced his woman with his lance, but still, everyone knew what was right, what was proper.

Sex was very big in the early Sixties, mainly because no one was having any. Oh, there were rumours here and there of a couple actually doing IT, but Odelle always discounted these. There was a way to behave. There were rules and standards. Everyone adhered to them. They would be excised from society if they didn't.

Sex. It hung over her and Tom's head like the sword of Damocles, or, had she but known, like an engorged penis. She wanted Tom. Not that she would admit it when he asked her, 'Don't you want me?' But God, did she ever. She loved the way he touched her neck, the way he whispered into it and nuzzled there. She ached for Tom's touch, for his hand on her breast, his fingers gently pinching her nipples. He called it collecting material for his next book. She called it heaven.

She yearned for the moment when he would undo her bra and put his hands on her bare skin. But then she got scared when he wanted to go further still. Sometimes his hand would rest on her thigh, and she would feel those shooting pains go up to her groin. And then there was the first time he put her hand on his thing. 'Touch me,' he begged her. 'Touch me. Please.'

In a way, she was disgusted. In her romantic visions, she didn't actually consider the physical organs themselves. And she didn't know how men could live with themselves, using the same organ for peeing and for sex. She was afraid. She didn't want to touch someone else's pee, not even Tom's. But he took her hand in his and rubbed it all over him down there. Then she heard him groan and moan and jerk around a bit, after which he would relax on her shoulder, getting her blouse or skin, whatever lay between them, all sweaty.

45

He led her slowly along the path to tingling despair. He would work her up into a frenzy, slowly tempting her through her sweaters and blouses, then opening them up, undoing her bra, placing his teeth on her bare nipples, causing such an awful need inside of her. Unzipping his pants, he would remove his penis from his underwear. He would place her hand on it and show her how to do it to him, how to rub it so that he would come. And then there was that time when he forced her to kneel before him, take his penis in her mouth and suck him off – after which he told her how much he loved her.

She suffered. When she left one of her dates with him to make it back to the sorority house before curfew, her hips would feel heavy and she would have a band of painful engorgement across her abdomen. She told Tom how she felt, and he replied that there was a prescription for her ills. He placed his hand on her thigh, and she wanted to object. But he was the doctor. He had the cure. His hand slid up past her garters to her panties, and she said, as she knew she must, 'No, Tom, no, no, no.' But he pushed the heel of his palm down on her pubic hair and her legs heard this open sesame. His fingers went inside her panties and lingered in her hair, twisting and turning, until they descended to her vulva and dug sweetly into her. She was scared, she was excited, she had been overstimulated for months. She had an orgasm. From that moment on, she couldn't get enough of IT.

Naturally, she never let on to her sorority sisters what was happening, but she was afraid she rather neglected the cultural events of the Cornell campus. Thus does sex detract from civilization. 'What are we going to do about this?' she asked Tom, filled with the sweet guilt of illicit activity.

'Enjoy it,' he responded.

If only she had left it at that.

By the end of their sophomore year, both Odelle and Tom were under the mistaken impression that they couldn't live without each other. They had sex at least five times a week, and they called it love. In that they weren't unique. Everyone in the early Sixties called sex love. It took a later generation to face reality and get down to the nitty gritty of free sex and endemic cynicism. But in the early Sixties, romance held sway. Sex was love, love was sanctified by marriage. Tom and Odelle gloried in a Labour Day weekend wedding in Richaven. The Pattersons and the Hamptons uneasily mixed and vowed that their son and daughter would live happily ever after. Champagne sometimes has that effect.

Fortunately for the newlyweds, neither family saw the need for immediate independence for son and daughter. Both Odelle and Tom received not only their tuition but a weekly allowance that

46

allowed them to live comfortably. Odelle, on the eve of her wedding, watched her mother squirm as she was about to speak. Odelle assumed the talk would be on the physical aspects of the marriage bed. But what her mother really wanted to say was, 'I hope you'll finish college. It's very important to me.' Odelle, spared the embarrassment of acknowledging that she knew just what to expect that first night of wedded bliss, fervently promised her mother that she would indeed finish college. How was she to know that several months into her junior year she would discover herself pregnant?

Odelle was overjoyed. She was living the American Dream. She was in love, she was married, she was pregnant. Now she could become the woman she was always meant to be.

Tom was pregnant himself, giving birth to the first burst of psycho-sociological articles that would lead to his omnipresence on the American culture scene. His editor/publisher at Black Mountain Press was practically begging him for a second manuscript. TO LOVE A DUCK had been picked up by an obscure but still financially rewarding mass paperback house, one that published mainly soft porn. Its success would keep Black Mountain Press in business for at least another year. But Tom was torn. Being husband and expectant father and majoring in sociology left him little time to come up with another book-length masturbatory fantasy. Instead, he turned to everyday matters of psycho-socio import, such as, why do men prefer blondes, what does your choice of colours say about you, do opposites *really* attract, what do you see when you actually look across a crowded room? Unfortunately, the magazines which would later come on the scene to report specifically on these important questions did not as yet exist. So Tom changed his name to Tommi and wrote for the women's magazines and the younger market like *Seventeen*. His editors thought he was a woman, he had such great insight into the female psyche. Odelle felt she had given him that insight, and was proud.

Julia Lacy Patterson was born the first week in August, 1963. When Odelle's waters broke, she was sitting at the typewriter, typing from Tom's handwritten manuscript one of his efforts for *My True Story*. 'Sleaze pays,' he told her. Those were words he would come to live by. She tried to ignore her contractions because she knew Tom wanted to get this manuscript out today, and he didn't like to type his work himself. He claimed a loss of freshness. She herself wasn't the best typist in the world, mainly because she got lost in his stories, especially ones like this, a wife torn between her husband and her husband's younger brother. God, there was such trouble in the world. Odelle was glad she had Tom around to protect her from it.

She finished typing the manuscript, then left it on the kitchen counter with a note to Tom, letting him know he could find her in

47

hospital, giving birth to their child. She was from Connecticut, after all, and understatement was a way of life.

Natural childbirth was not as yet in vogue. Her mother even suggested, when the time came, Odelle be put totally out. 'Believe me, it's better not to know what's happening,' she stated emphatically. But Odelle, with her doctor's prodding, decided on a caudal.

Labour went fast. Odelle was taken to the delivery room before Tom showed up. It didn't matter. In those bygone days, when women were women and men were men, fathers were considered superfluous to the birthing process. What surprised Odelle was the pain. It was horrible. She had never felt anything so wrenching, and she swore over and over to anyone who would listen that she would never again have a child. The nurses smiled sweetly down at her, as if they had heard all this before.

The caudal brought some relief. The doctor told her to push, but she didn't know what she was doing. Thank God. Then people were yelling at her that they could see the head. 'Not long now,' the doctor assured her. She was lying on her back looking up at the operating room lights, wondering what she had ever done to deserve this.

'Here are the shoulders. We're ready for delivery!' the doctor exclaimed, maybe feeling it was more his baby than hers.

And then Odelle felt a sense of release. Sweating and cold at the same time, she heard this little burp of a cry, followed by these mewing sounds that a sick cat might make. And that was her daughter.

The doctor held the baby up for Odelle to see before the nurse took it from his hands so that he could deliver the afterbirth. Odelle was not allowed to touch the child. The child no longer belonged to her. For the next five days her baby belonged to the hospital and its routine. 'Is she all right?' Odelle asked.

'A beautiful baby girl. Ten fingers, ten toes.'

'You've got a winner here,' one of the nurses said. 'Six pounds, thirteen ounces; nineteen and three-quarters inches. Good size, beautiful colour.'

The baby was wrapped and carried away from her. Then Odelle was slid off the operating table. The cart with her body on it was wheeled out of the operating room. Tom was in the hallway, waiting for her. He grabbed her hand. 'I saw her!' he said excitedly. 'She's beautiful.'

'You got my note,' Odelle assumed. 'The manuscript – '

'I sent it already. Oh, Odelle, I can't tell you how happy you've made me.'

She didn't think about what he said at the time. But it occurred to her later, maybe the next day, maybe the next week or month, that he had stopped by the post office to send off his manuscript before he came to the hospital to see her. She tried to figure it out. Why was he so happy? Because she had finished typing his story before she went in to deliver their child?

# Chapter 9

# Breaking Up's Not Hard To Do

'Would you keep that kid quiet!'

Tommy Patterson was working. So the world should stop moving. All Julia was doing was dragging her bumble bee around the kitchen table, which Tommy had appropriated as his work space. All she was doing was being a normal two year old. But that was too much of a strain for Tommy Patterson (who would later win a humanitarian award for his pioneering look into the minds of the very young. Now what was his thesis? "Seeing God through the Eyes of Your Child". The award had come from the Catholic Archdiocese of St Louis, during one of their fund-raising campaigns. Tommy Patterson, as honoree, was a big draw. Of course, all that was years after he had dumped Odelle and abandoned his daughter.)

Now Odelle, ever mindful of Tommy's special needs, scooped up Julia and took her into the bedroom. 'Come on, honey, we can play with your bee in here. Zzzz, zzzz, zzzz.'

'Shut up, will you!'

Odelle closed the bedroom door on her daughter and came steaming out to the kitchen. 'Why don't you work at the office? This is our home too!'

'I hate the office, that's why. I hate the piddling little assignments I've been given. I don't really care if people prefer stick deodorant or cream. I don't care if they prefer their cookies firm or soggy. I just don't give a shit about this job. But I had to take it, didn't I? Because of you. Because of you and that brat in there.'

Odelle stood there, red in the face, blood pressure rising. But what could she say? What was she supposed to say? Wasn't that a man's duty, to support his wife and child? What did Tommy want from her? The job choice was his decision. She hadn't asked him to come to New York to work for a research firm that investigated such weighty matters as personal preference in deodorant or dough. As far as she was concerned, he could have continued with his writing. They would have made do somehow. She could have gone to work while he stayed home, wrote and watched the baby. But he was the one who insisted that child care was woman's work, that he needed to get out in a man's world and make a buck. So she stayed home and did woman's work. She took care of Julia. She cooked and cleaned. She went to the park and compared notes with the other mothers, coming home with Julia in her push chair, wondering if her daughter was up to snuff. Their division of labour was clear and conventional. Now Tommy had decided he didn't like it. What was she to do? They were living in Brooklyn, for God's sake.

Lately all Tommy did was scream at her and the baby. What did he want from her? Instead of screaming, why didn't he talk to her, tell her what was wrong, what was bothering him? All she wanted was to share. They were man and wife. Burdens were easier borne by two. But when she talked to Tommy about it, he would always say to her, 'You wouldn't understand.'

'Understand what?'

'The real world. You live in a cocoon. What do you know of the pressures I'm under? How do you think I feel, selling out like this?'

'Maybe you should get another job.'

'I don't want another job,' he insisted. 'I don't want a job at all. I want to live!'

'Well, what does that mean?' she faltered.

'As I told you,' he replied coldly. 'You wouldn't understand.'

Odelle, during her first ten months in Brooklyn with Tommy and Julia, often debated fleeing home to her mother. Lately she had definitely considered it. For the first three months after they moved in, everything was fine. Tommy was still excited about his work. 'You get to meet real people,' he told her. She was busy putting shelf paper in the cupboards while keeping an eye on Julia who was becoming recklessly active. But after the excitement of the move and the new job, life settled into a dangerous routine. 'I think I'm dead,' Tommy once said to her in the middle of the night.

What was she to do?

Summer came. Brooklyn was stifling. 'I think I'm going to go home for a week, get some fresh air,' Odelle informed Tommy. 'You don't mind do you?'

Tommy smiled meanly and shrugged. 'Why should I mind? You're free. I'm the one who's stuck with a two-week vacation for the next ten years.'

'I could wait. Do you want me to wait here with you? We can plan something together.'

51

'No, dear. Run off to Mommy and Daddy in Richaven. I'm sure I'll find ways of fending for myself.'

Now what was that supposed to mean? Was it some sort of threat? Odelle was exhausted. Tommy exhausted her. All she wanted was some respite from the constant toll he took on her emotions.

And yet was it safe to go up to Connecticut? She couldn't let on to her parents that anything was wrong with her marriage. Even though Tommy hadn't been a choice they were crazy about, they would just tell her that, "It's up to you to make things right." Hadn't she been trying to do that for so many months now? If only she could understand where she had gone wrong.

Go or don't go? She debated. In the end, after one last impossible scene, Tommy not understanding why Julia had to sniffle all night with a summer cold, Odelle decided she had to get out.

The week in Connecticut was heaven. Freed from Brooklyn's hot cement, Julia blossomed in the magical green of Richaven, working alongside Grandpa in the garden, going to roadside stands with Grandma and Mommy. As for Odelle, the absence of tension made her realize how much pressure she had actually been living under. Loyally, she didn't tell anyone about it. When her parents inquired politely about her husband, Odelle merely said that he was working hard. They all left it at that.

The week ended all too soon. Odelle hated to leave. But what excuse could she find to stay? Could she tell her parents that she didn't want to return to her husband? 'Come back again soon,' her mother urged. 'Julia is such a doll.'

So she and Julia got on a train, arrived at Grand Central, then took the subway to their stop in Brooklyn. It wasn't the easiest thing to do. Odelle had a baby to carry as well as their suitcase. But she hadn't really wanted to call Tommy and ask him to come and meet them at Grand Central. She didn't want to put him out when he always seemed to be in a bad mood no matter what she requested, even to switching off the light so she could get some sleep.

Odelle knew the apartment was empty when she turned the key in the lock and opened the door. She called anyway. 'Tommy?' No answer, and in a way she was relieved she wouldn't have to deal immediately with her husband's sour humours. She could still carry within her the well-being from Connecticut.

The first thing she did was get Julia settled. Then she decided to tackle the suitcase. She hated unpacking suitcases. It always meant the trip was over and she was back to reality. But at least this time she didn't have to worry about dirty clothes. Her mother had put them through the washing machine before Odelle boarded the train. All

Odelle had to do was hang them in the wardrobe or shove them into drawers. It was then that she noticed she had more wardrobe and drawer space than she expected.

All of Tommy's things were gone.

Like an idiot, she raced through the apartment, looking for signs. At first she stupidly thought maybe there had been a break-in; in which case why was none of her stuff missing? And then she realised: Tommy's left me. After which she wondered: What did he take with him?

The household money was gone from the kitchen drawer. Odelle grabbed Julia and rushed down to the bank, only to discover that their joint account, where she had foolishly deposited the little cheque her parents sent every now and then, had been emptied.

All Odelle had to her name was her child and the fifty dollars her father had slipped her at the train station. What in God's name was she going to do?

She called Tommy's work number. A woman answered. Odelle asked to speak to Tom Patterson. 'Just a minute, please,' the woman said. And then Odelle was frightened. What was she going to say? How was she going to get back the money he stole from her?

'This is Steve Rosen,' a deep male voice said. 'Who's this, please?'

Steve Rosen! That was Tommy's boss. 'This is Odelle Patterson, Tom Patterson's wife.'

'Could you let me speak to your husband, Mrs Patterson?'

What was he, crazy? 'I – I was calling the office to speak to him there.'

'You mean he's not at home! He's not sick or something?'

'I – I just got home from Connecticut.' What should she say? How much should she admit? 'Could I ask when you last saw him?'

'We saw him yesterday,' Steve Rosen said, enunciating every word in a clear, cold voice. 'He left at noon, claiming a severe headache. He took with him various figures he was working on for a demographic study of ours. We need those figures for a presentation to clients. You'd better tell your husband to get that material back in here now. Today!'

'Mr Rosen, don't shout at me! I just came home from Connecticut to find all of Tommy's things missing and our joint account cleaned out!' She slammed the phone down.

A minute later it rang. She picked it up, hoping it was Tommy, coming up with some explanation. It should have been no surprise that it was Steve Rosen once again. 'He's cleared out?'

'Yes!' She slammed down the phone.

This time when it rang again, she knew it was Tom's boss. 'Please,' he said quickly, 'don't hang up. Could you please look around and see

53

if you can find a dark brown folder? It looks like fake leather. It is fake leather.'

'Your dark brown folder is the last thing on my mind.'

'I know, I understand, but we need – '

She slammed down the phone. Then she realized he would only call again, so she took the phone off the hook.

Julia came over to her and put her head in Odelle's lap. 'Milk,' the child said. Even then she had healthy eating habits.

With her fifty dollars, Odelle dragged Julia along to the corner grocer's and got some milk, bread and bologna. Then she slowly walked back to the apartment. Like an accident victim, she was in shock. She just didn't know it. No sooner had she arrived back at her apartment and set out a glass for Julia's milk than the doorbell rang. Tommy. Coming to say it was all a joke!

She threw the door open. A strange man stood there. 'Steve Rosen,' he said, hand semi-outstretched.

She sighed. 'What the hell do you want?' she asked, already defeated.

'Please, can I have a look for that folder?'

She shrugged and ushered him in. 'Why not? What does it matter?'

Steve Rosen's search was fruitless. He could barely contain his rage as he realized the brown folder was missing for good, along with Tommy Patterson. 'Your husband's a real schmuck,' he told her on departing.

'On that we can agree,' she assured him. As he was going down the hallway, she called, 'Does he at least have any pay coming?'

Rosen turned. 'Are you kidding? If we find him, we're going to sue him!'

Odelle spent the night alone in her marital bed with the light on. What was she going to do? What does a woman alone with a child do? How does a woman whose husband deserts her cope? (Had she but known she was ahead of her time in asking these questions, she might have been somewhat comforted. As it was, she was simply worried sick.)

The natural solution would be to run home to mama. But there was something within Odelle that would not let her do that. Was it pride or stupidity? She didn't know. But, she figured, she had got herself into this mess, and she would get herself out. Unfortunately, not on fifty dollars.

The next morning she put in a call to her brother Mason. He lived in Massachusetts and sold yachts for a living. He was surprised to hear from her. They usually got together only at Christmas. Mason had been another one of those who didn't really understand Tom or her

54

attraction to him. But she wasn't about to lay the whole mess before him yet. Mason would just go squealing to her parents. She didn't need parental outrage on top of her own. 'Hi, Sweetcakes,' he said to her when he realized who it was.

She hated his nickname for her, but beggars, et cetera. 'Mason, I have a big favour to ask you. Remember that time I broke my piggy bank so you could have enough money to buy that new model you wanted?'

'The piggy bank fell, and I got to the money before you did,' he corrected her.

'Mason, I'm desperate. I need money. I need anything you can spare.'

There was silence at the other end of this tenuous telephone wire. 'What happened?'

'I can't tell you. I'll pay you back. You know that.'

'How desperately do you need it?'

'All I have to my name is $47 and change.'

'I'll send you something,' he promised. 'You want to tell me about it?'

'I can't now, Mason. I haven't digested it myself.'

Three days later, she received a check from him for $1,000. By that time, her plan of action was already in gear. True, she hadn't graduated from college, but she knew how to type. That was a skill she planned to use now in becoming gainfully employed.

It took her two weeks to find a job. She could have taken one faster, the first week even, because her typing speed was good and she had a certain polish, left over from her days in Connecticut. That was before Tom got hold of her, making her feel like a worthless rag. But she wasn't looking for just any job. She wanted one with benefits that would safeguard both her and her daughter in case of dire emergency, as if she wasn't living through one right now.

She got a job at Aramco, as a receptionist. It didn't pay much, but the benefits were what she was looking for. She would have to travel into midtown Manhattan every day and back home every evening. Through the women at the park, she found out the names of several older women in the neighbourhood who took care of children from time to time. Odelle picked the one she had seen outside actually playing with her charge. The woman was doubtful about going full-time with this child care business. But perhaps she sympathized with the desperate nature of Odelle's predicament, because she finally agreed to work for her. Odelle sighed in relief. One of the main, bothersome questions every prospective employer asked her was did she have children and, if she did, what did she plan to do if the child fell ill? Now at least she had an answer.

55

Her last chore, before starting work, was to move from her two-bedroomed apartment to a smaller, dingier, cheaper apartment in the same general area of Brooklyn. She lost a month's rent and her deposit, but that one-time expense would more than be made up for by the saving on the new apartment. 'Yuck!' Julia said when she first saw it, and yuck it was, but also cheap. Odelle needed cheap because most of her salary would be going toward Julia's day care. For the first time in her life, Odelle would have to count every penny to survive.

# Chapter 10

# News from Far Distant Places

Odelle told her parents about Tommy's desertion two weeks after she started working at Aramco. Until then, she wrote letters home, detailing Julia's young life and the weather. She hadn't even given them her new address, hoping against hope that the Post Office would forward her mail. But at the end of two weeks, she knew that, while life wouldn't be pleasant, she could survive. So she wrote a long, gruesome account of what had happened to her since she last saw them.

The weekend after the parents got her letter, they came into the city. For the first time since Tommy had gone AWOL, Odelle allowed herself to cry. Her mother ranted – not about Tommy, surprisingly, but about how awful the new apartment was, unfit for a granddaughter of hers. Furthermore, how could Odelle leave her child and go off to work? And, finally, why did she marry that bum anyway? Her father just stood in a corner, looking dour. Then Odelle's mother had the nerve to order her back home and to bring Julia with her.

'I can't go backward,' Odelle protested.

'What do you call this?'

'Mom, I'm not a little girl any more. I have adult responsibilities, including a child. And they're my responsibilities, not yours.'

Her answer was final, but it took her parents longer than that weekend to accept it. Even though she wouldn't change her mind, she welcomed their concern. It was nice to know that somebody in the world still cared about her. Life alone, even with a child as sweet as Julia, could be very empty.

During Odelle's first six months of working, she was tired all the time. It seemed as if all she ever did was get up, drop Julia off at the babysitter's, get the subway into New York, type, smile, answer the phone, eat lunch, type, smile, answer the phone, get crushed on the subway going home, pick up Julia, do the laundry, the dishes, the

57

cooking and cleaning, go to bed and fall from one type of exhaustion to another, because even sleep didn't seem to refresh her.

In all those six months, no one heard from Tommy, except maybe his family. They were evasive so they must have known something. She left a message with them that she wanted a divorce and she wanted it now. But she never received a reply.

After six months, her body began to get into the swing of things. She started to enjoy her job at Aramco. There wasn't much of an intellectual challenge, but she liked the social life, exchanging gossip about bosses, having lunch with friends, shopping together, being a part of the city. It was the only social life she had. She didn't date. Not only did no one ask her, but she was sort of in limbo, neither married nor divorced. The neutral term "separated" seemed not really to define what had happened to her. So the only thing she could really say when anyone asked, which was rare, was that she had been deserted. And "deserted" brought so many curious questions that she'd rather just avoid the subject of her marital status entirely.

Most of the women in the Aramco office were single. Either they were old single or they were young single. The old had a devotion to duty; the young were dedicated to exploratory manoeuvres among eligible male candidates. Aramco was better than most companies in that respect. Oil was an arena where men were men and women were babes.

After six months at Aramco, Odelle received a transfer to another department and a promotion. She was no longer a receptionist; she was not officially a secretary. She no longer greeted people in the main office and brought them coffee, while asking if they were comfortable. Now she worked in sales for a very nice boss who travelled most weeks, thus leaving her in charge of his office. She was free and yet she wasn't free. She had a lot of paperwork which she had to take care of. At any minute her boss might call and demand details of one deal or another, so the information had to always be at her fingertips. But at least she had more control over her work day.

In late December of 1969 her boss told her, confidentially, that he was leaving Aramco. He had received a job offer from a Houston firm and was taking it. Needless to say, she was upset. Odelle had spent three years working for this man. He at least provided some stability in her life. Was everyone planning to walk out on her?

When he left, just after taking his Christmas bonus, she was stuck training the new boy who came in to take his place, and Odelle did mean "new boy". He was younger than she was and dumber than she was. It was time for her to look around for another job.

But she hated to leave Aramco, where she had put in so much time to gain certain benefits. Over lunch, discussing her problems with one of the old singles, she was told there was an opening for an assistant in research and development. The position required some college. Odelle had some college. She would have had even more if she hadn't met Tommy.

Not bothering to go through personnel, Odelle approached the head of R & D herself. She knew him from office parties and chatter in the hall. He was one of Aramco's cowboys, and she though it might be quite interesting to work with him. Right away he took her into his office, started the globe on his desk spinning, and asked her to find certain countries. She stopped the globe several times and only missed Burma.

Then the head of R & D got up and threw open what turned out to be a map drawer. She was tested on longitude and latitude, degrees this and that. He nodded thoughtfully as she stumbled through the degrees bit. 'I think you can handle it,' he told her.

She had the job and, more important, the raise that went with it. After the first few weeks in her new position, she realized she would be earning that raise. She was busy all the time, trying to find maps that someone had stowed in the wrong drawer, or if they were in the right drawer, in the wrong file. She took calls from overseas, asking for specifics on locations. Soon she was learning how to determine which geological formations gave evidence of oil or other minerals. Odelle became confident and quite pleased with herself.

Into this office one fine day came Sy Hampton. He was just home from six months in Saudi Arabia. Sy barged into the office in khakis and field boots, wearing a *kafiyah* wrapped around his neck. He looked as if he was trying out for a bit part in *King Solomon's Mines*. 'Haven't met you,' he said, as he went into her boss's office without being announced. She soon learned that geologists and petro-chemical engineers were beyond the bounds of normal convention. They were to be treated as precious substances in their own right, until they made enough wrong guesses. Sy Hampton hadn't guessed wrong yet.

'What's your name?' he asked, when he came out of her boss's office.

'Odelle.'

'Odelle,' he repeated with a smile. 'I'm Sy Hampton.' Then he reached over the desk to shake her hand. His was browned by the sun; hers was coated with dust from the maps. But Sy Hampton seemed to like dust. He held her hand long enough to prove it.

Sy was in the office often the first few weeks he was back in the States. But with him it was business first. It took him a month to ask her out, even though she had been primping in readiness every time she caught sight of him. 'Where can I pick you up?' he asked, after she readily agreed to a Friday night date.

'I live in Brooklyn.'

It was as if she said she lived in Outer Mongolia, which he probably would have been delighted to go to. Even though he was quite the world traveller, Brooklyn gave him pause. 'Perhaps I should just meet you here in the city,' she suggested, afraid he would suddenly discover something better to do Friday night.

'Nonsense,' he told her. He took down her address and had her draw a map from the subway to her apartment. 'Eight o'clock,' he warned.

Now all she had to do was find a babysitter.

At seven fifty-nine that Friday night Odelle was ready. She was dressed sedately but alluringly. A teenager from downstairs had arrived and checked out her refrigerator, worried about starvation for the few hours Odelle might be missing. Julia was in her pyjamas with her favourite blanket wrapped protectively around her. At eight precisely the doorbell rang.

Odelle opened the door and with a big smile said, 'Hi!'

Sy nodded and stepped inside. With one sweeping glance, he took in the situation. 'Not only do you live in Brooklyn, you have a child,' he accused.

Well, okay, so it would be only one date. What the hell? She was planning to have fun.

They stayed in Brooklyn to eat. Sy chose an Italian restaurant where they could see the Brooklyn Bridge. The setting was very romantic. Of course, the evening lost a little of its glow when Sy, over the mussels sautéed in garlic and wine sauce, explained exactly how the bridge was built and how many lives were lost. At least he didn't talk sports, she thought, even though she had been boning up on them all week, just in case.

She spoke too soon. Sports came with dessert. And she was ready. But not for camel racing and falconry. Somehow these hadn't made it into the sports pages of the *Post*.

She found out a lot about Sy Hampton that night. She didn't think he was self-centred exactly, but he liked to talk and she didn't mind listening. By the end of the evening, she knew where he went to school, how he came to Aramco, the countries he worked in and, most important, the fact that he wasn't married. Of course that might not do her much good. First, she lived in Brooklyn. Second, she wasn't divorced.

After dinner, he suggested they walk across the Brooklyn Bridge and back. She was in high heels; her hair was swept up; she wore only a light coat. It was late February and it was cold. But so desperate was she to stop the evening from ending that she readily agreed.

'Stimulating, isn't it?' he pronounced. They were halfway across and had stopped to stare at the water and the lights reflected upon it.

She couldn't cogently reply to him. Her teeth were chattering. He turned to her and said, 'You aren't cold, are you?'

No, she wasn't cold. She was numb!

'A brisk walk will do you good,' he insisted. He hit his stride while she hobbled along behind him in her heels.

The walk did do her good. It cured the evening of its aura of romance. She was only too glad to get back to the apartment. So much for the glories of dating. But she had to say that Sy was a real gentleman. He paid for the babysitter, over her protests.

After the babysitter departed for a fuller refrigerator downstairs, Sy came in and joined her. She hoped he didn't expect anything vital in exchange for dinner. 'Coffee?' she suggested.

He shook his head. 'Nah. It keeps me awake. Anyway, I can't get used to American coffee. In Saudi Arabia they have this rich, thick brew that's – oh, well. When in Rome.'

'You like to travel, don't you?'

'Yes,' he agreed half-heartedly. 'I don't know. I'm getting old though. I'd like to settle down. Travel, yes, but I'd like something to come home to. Do you realize I don't even have my own apartment? I stay in one of Aramco's when I'm in New York. I can pack all my worldly possessions inside one tan leather suitcase.'

'Travelling light through life,' she joked.

'Not in your case,' he noted.

'No,' she agreed.

'Divorced?'

'Deserted. If I ever find the bastard, and it's been four long years now, I'll be divorced.'

'You mean – '

'He just picked up and left one day, cleaning out the bank account as he went. No one's heard from him since, except maybe his family, and they're not talking.' God, she had to watch herself. She was going to sound like one of those cold, bitter women men hate so. Of course, that's exactly what she was when she thought of Tommy. 'And you?' she wondered. 'No women in your life?'

'Well,' he said, leaning back, 'I find most societies very accommodating when it comes to women.'

'Not this one,' she snapped before she had time to think.

He laughed. Then he stood up and took his leave.

She closed the door with few regrets. It had been a pleasant evening, a treat, really. But she knew it wasn't going anywhere.

61

Her opinion was confirmed when she arrived at the office on Monday to discover that Sy was on the move again, this time to South America. He came by to tell her he had had fun on Friday. And then as an afterthought, he said, 'Hey, would you mind if I write to you while I'm away? Just to keep in touch with America.'

She shrugged. Why should she mind if Sy saw her as the Statue of Liberty?

She told her mother later that she and Sy fell in love through their letters. He wrote as he talked , long and glowingly. She wrote back shorter, chattier letters about work, her life, about Julia. She was pleased to note that in all his replies, he mentioned her child, asking how Julia was getting on, if she really liked finger-painting as much as Odelle said – stupid little homey things.

Odelle didn't want to build this letter writing into too much. Sy said he wanted to keep in touch with America. She assumed he meant what couldn't be found in the papers – the protest marches against the war in Vietnam, the continuing struggle for civil rights, the trouble with Richard Nixon. She unfortunately had no time to be too involved in any of this turmoil. She had a daughter to raise. And to do that she had to work.

Sy Hampton returned to New York just before Christmas, 1970. He burst into the office, wearing an Inca blanket around his shoulders, beads around his neck, and a shrunken head hanging from his belt. 'Anyone I know?' she asked.

But he was called into a conference immediately. When he came out, before he was ushered to lunch, he said, 'Christmas?'

'Connecticut.'

'New Year?'

'I'm free.'

'Not any more.'

This time she couldn't get a babysitter. But she had an idea. When she went home for Christmas, she said, 'Mother, how would you like to spend more time with your grandchild?' Yes, she dumped Julia on her parents.

The New Year, 1971, started off with a bang, if she could use such an atrocious pun. It was like something from *The Barratts of Wimpole Street*. She and Sy had been writing to each other for so long, and now the supreme consummation.

Odelle concluded immediately that Sy was a lot more experienced than she. She could tell because, even during the act itself, he gave her an anthropological account of various tribal women he knew, along with their sexual customs. It was sort of off-putting until he mentioned one that entailed using a leaf and a caterpillar. All of a she could see where his meandering was taking them – to the top of the Andes. Orgasms. She loved them. They were so healthy, and the perfect way to start a new year.

On New Year's Day they went out to Connecticut, not only to pick up Julia but also to meet her parents. The day went smoothly, mainly because there were so many football games on, no one talked. Her mother laid out her traditional cold ham and roast beef; the men made sandwiches, drank beer, grabbed handfuls of peanuts, and thoroughly enjoyed themselves. Meanwhile, Odelle was left in the kitchen, expecting to have to fend off her mother's questions.

Even if her mother had asked any, there would have been no answers. Two weeks later, when her mother eventually did call to ask about Sy, he was in South East Asia, into harm's way, still looking for oil.

Sy didn't ask her to marry him until March of that year. 'I want someone to come home to,' he explained.

So this was what romance boiled down to? 'Are you going to give up your tribal encounters?' she wondered.

'Dear Odelle, I don't know how to explain this to an American, much less to someone from Richaven, Connecticut, but to give up such encounters would be an insult to the people I live among. Would you prefer that I insult these people?'

'Yes.'

The problem with Sy's proposal was that she was already married. 'We'll hire a private detective,' he told her. 'Maybe, better, a lawyer first. Even without his approval you ought to be able to divorce Patterson for desertion. How many years does it take?'

'I don't know, Sy. I keep thinking some day he's going to turn up and I can nail him then.'

'Some day?' Sy queried. 'We have to take some action now because I'm not waiting forever.'

But more pressing needs hovered. Sy had to fly to Oklahoma, where she assured him there were no tribal customs more outlandish than those in Brooklyn. She, meanwhile, had chipped her tooth and needed to make an emergency appointment with her dentist. She hated going to the dentist. Not only was she afraid of the pain, she couldn't bear the expense.

She'd forgotten besides the long wait one must endure in the outer office. She saw patients go in looking fine and come out with big bulges where their lips used to be. She had learned when Julia was born that she was basically a coward when it came to physical pain. So Odelle grabbed a magazine to keep her mind off her impending time in the chair. But like so many dentist's waiting rooms, this one had only an esoteric selection no one could concentrate on: *Organic Farming, Parent's Health Letter, Mr Toothbrush, Society Today*. She picked up *Society Today*. Nothing interested her. It was full of articles that belonged in a textbook: "Changes in our Dietary Habits with the Coming of the Blender", "Do Women Secretaries Prefer Male Bosses and Why", "Demographics – Bending the Truth".

"Demographics – Bending the Truth", by Thomas Patterson. Jesus!

Her name was called. She waved the assistant off. 'Come now, Mrs Patterson. It's only a chipped tooth; this won't hurt a bit,' the assistant insisted. 'You can bring the magazine with you.'

What was worse? The pain of the dentist or seeing Tommy's name again? Or Tom. Or Thomas. Whatever he was calling himself.

"List of contributors". With the cotton in her mouth and the novocaine not working, Odelle flipped to the back of the magazine. "Thomas Patterson, Ph.D. candidate in Sociology, University of Michigan."

Eureka!

# *Chapter 11*

# Business Blues

The first thing Grace Mandling did every morning was turn on her answering machine. Unlike many writers, she could not work all day. She had only a few good hours in which to concentrate wholly on the book in progress. They occurred after Galen left for work up until the start of *The Young and the Restless*, at twelve-thirty, during which she ate lunch. After lunch she turned her mind off, occupying her time with chores, like picking up the cleaning and doing the shopping, not to mention considering what kind of fertilizer she needed for her grass, which looked a little less green of late.

This morning Grace turned on her answering machine and threw on her track suit. She was ready for the day ahead. Unfortunately, the peace in which she and her computer coexisted was shattered by the grinding noises from a lorry outside. At first she though it was a new dustcart being broken in. But then it grunted to a halt, she could swear, outside her house. Damn!

She went from the back of the house to the front. Yes, indeed, an Airline Express truck was parked almost on her lawn, and several men were unloading boxes on to trolleys, making ready to assault her house.

Jesus! They were running the trolleys over her already suffering grass!

She threw open the front door. 'Hey! What're you doing!'

The men looked up, startled. 'You Mandling?'

'Grass doesn't grow on trees, you know! Get yourselves off it!'

They rolled the trolleys back, but the indentations in her precious blades remained. Now her lawn would look like some teenager and his car had assaulted it over the weekend.

The men came up the path, bumping up the three stairs that led to her front door. 'What is this?' she asked, as they approached.

'Boxes,' one answered.

Great, she'd have to deal with a comedian. 'I didn't order boxes.'

'I didn't say you did. They were sent from L.A. We got about ten more in the truck. Where do you want them?'

'I don't want them at all.'

He leant on his trolley. 'You refusing delivery?' he menaced.

No wonder the heroes of romances are never truck drivers or delivery men. Grace looked down at the top box. As she suspected, even dreaded, these were the remains of Tommy Patterson, his notes, his notebooks, his scraps of paper, his detritus. Why had his lawyer been so prompt in delivering these to her?

Or was it Tamar Litowsky? Maybe it was Kitten Farleigh, cleaning out "Mi Hacienda", which was now her hacienda.

'Lady,' the delivery man said, not hiding his impatience.

'Oh, all right! Hang on a second while I go and open the garage.' She was damned if she would have Tommy's stuff inside her house, polluting her own work space.

Grace ran into the kitchen and pushed the magic button. The garage door slid upward, and she told the men to set the boxes down near the back wall, stacking them up so they would be out of the way. Five rows the men made of the boxes; five rows, four boxes high. Tommy obviously suffered from writer's diarrhoea, unless that crafty Kitten had sent all of Tommy's worldly goods eastward.

The men left. Grace turned firmly away. She could not think of Tommy now. She had her own work to attend to. She returned to the computer and sat calmly before it, waiting for the magic of her mind's imagination. 'Sir, I may only be your maid, but who's to say I am not the better person?' Perky, yes, but too perky? Shouldn't the maid be a bit more humble to begin with, so that when it's discovered she's actually the illegitimate daughter of the Fifth Duchess of Wexworth, it would be a celebration of the unexpected? Or should the story focus on the lord of the manor, prematurely raised to such a high estate by the sudden death of his father, via cobra bite in far-off India? Yes, the lord, in the great tradition of *Pygmalion*, sees to it that his humble, illegitimate maid becomes the belle of the London season?

Groaning, Grace cleared the screen. She was sick of the Edwardian era. Her book before last also took place in that era, before the world's loss of innocence on the battlefields of World War I. That novel was about an American girl, Lydia Gainsworth, who entered London society, giving everyone the impression that she was rich. Actually, she had nothing to her name but a one-way ticket to London and a truckful of elegant dresses she designed herself. Three men fell head over heels in love with her. Which man would she choose? Then calamity struck. A real American heiress spotted

Lydia at an elegant reception and unmasked her by asking loudly, 'And what is my dressmaker doing here?' Would Lydia ever find happiness now? Two of the men who claimed to love her faded quickly from her side, but Cecil, Earl of Montcrief, remained steadfast. It was he who showed her the meaning of true love. They had a quiet little wedding in Westminster Abbey with only the King and a few other close friends in attendance. That book, what had it been called . . .? Ah, yes, LOVE IS A WALTZ. That book had done so well. The tears shed when Cecil discovered what a fool he had been momentarily to distance himself from the woman he loved simply because she was a pauper induced a downpour from Grace's own eyes. Love is so simple on paper.

Hmm. Maybe instead of *Pygmalion* – after all, hadn't GBS said it all! – she should continue the story of Lydia and Cecil? Cecil, poor sod, would have to die in the trenches of World War I. Lydia would fight valiantly on as a nurse in France. Or should she have a child? Yes, why not? Cecil and Lydia would have a child, Edward. Yes, Edward William George Henry, Duke of Davenport until he obtained the title Earl of Montcrief. He could be born in 1910, have vague memories of his father the Earl before Cecil's gallant death. Lydia would be not only mother and nurse but also a designer, burying her grief in a dizzying array of lovers during the Jazz Age, coming to her senses only when Edward William George Henry, aka Teddy, discovers her in bed with – whom? Ah yes, Jake Domino, black sax player from East Chicago.

Grace's mind worked overtime. Her fingers flew over the keys. She had to get this down, get it all down, before it fled from her. It was too good to lose!

The outline of the plot for her new book to be called – RAGTIME? No, someone had used that title. LYDIA TAKES A LOVER? No. Everyone would guess that anyway. LOVE TRIUMPHS? Too obvious. LOVE NEVER DESPAIRS! She liked that. Yes, she really liked that. But then, who was the anthropomorphic love? Hell, she'd worry about that tomorrow. GONE WITH THE WAR?

Stuff and bother. This was getting her nowhere. She had her ten-page plot outline. This should be enough to get her the advance she needed. Unfortunately, once she got the advance, she would be forced to write the book. She'd never given back an advance yet. Though there was that one occasion when they had tried to take it away from her. Fools!

Now whom should she call, her agent or her editor? Why not call her editor and give the man a tantalizing hint of what was in store for him? He would be so excited! Then she would call her agent.

She dialled via her computer. That was the handy thing about a computer. Once she was sitting in front of it, she didn't have to move. 'Hi, Mary,' Grace said, when the phone was answered. 'This is Grace Mandling. Is Craig there?'

'He's in a meeting, but just a minute. Hold on, and I'll see if I can roust him.'

Grace held. This was a far cry from earlier days when she was just starting. Then everyone was always in meetings, and no one could be bothered to return her calls.

'Gracie!' Craig Epstein's voice came on line. 'I'm a bit rushed.'

'That's okay, Craig. I just wanted to let you know I'm writing a sequel to LOVE IS NOT ONLY FOR THE VERY RICH.'

'What? Oh, you mean LOVE IS A WALTZ.'

'I still prefer my title, Craig.'

'Yes, but it was so similar to – '

'I'm not going to argue that with you again, Craig. I just wanted to let you know that your dreams are about to come true. I'll have my agent contact you, and you can – '

'Hang on a second Grace. What are we doing about the Tommy Patterson papers?'

'What?'

'Tommy Patterson, remember? You're his literary executioner.'

'If only, Craig.' She just loved him for these little mistakes he made. With most editors nowadays getting their MBAs instead of a degree in English literature, one couldn't expect perfect word usage. 'It's executor. And don't remind me. I've just been inundated with twenty cartons of his crap.'

'Listen, Grace, we are hot for his work. Whatever you can throw together, we'll pay the world for it. Or ask for the moon, you've got it. Matter of fact, that's just where I was, discussing the possibilities.'

Grace was a bit nonplussed. She had called Craig to discuss her work, not Tommy's. 'I – I'm not even planning on opening the cartons for a while, Craig. I'm just getting ready to start on my new Lydia Gainsworth book.'

'Lydia can wait, dear. There are thousands of people out there who could write a book about someone like Lydia. There's only one Tommy Patterson.'

Grace slammed down the phone. Thousands of people could write the way she did? Thousands of people could bring tears to the eye and a glow to the heart? Thousands could renew the tremors of romance in a love-starved universe? She thought not!

It was obviously time for a new publisher. Plus, she would have to go out and order up a plaque to sit on her old editor's desk – Craig Epstein: Illiterate Asshole!

Her phone rang. She was in a rage. She couldn't possibly answer it. She would listen via her answering machine. It was, as she suspected, Craig. 'Gracie dear, what's the matter? Did I say something wrong? Call me. We love you here. You know that.'

Grace waited until Craig hung up. Then she picked up the phone and dialled her agent, Edna Waitz. 'She's taking a London call right now. Can she call you back or could her assistant help you?'

'I will hold!' Grace insisted. And hold she did. For ten minutes. Talking to London for ten minutes? What was the world coming to? Think of the cost!

'Yes,' Edna came on the line.

'Edna, it's Grace.'

'Oh! You should have said who it was. The receptionist had no idea.'

'I'm sure you offer the same consideration to everyone who calls your office, Edna.'

'Hmm.'

'I want to change publishers.'

'Oh?'

'I've just been insulted – mortally wounded by Craig Epstein. I refuse to have him touch another book of mine.'

'What happened?'

'It's just so painful, I don't know how to tell you.'

'Do you want me to call him and get his side of the story?'

'He doesn't have a side, Edna! He's an asshole.'

Edna sighed. 'Well, he's a man, dear. What do you expect?'

'I hinted to him that he would shortly be offered the sequel to LOVE IS A WALTZ.'

'You're doing a sequel? Great!'

'Despite my great news, all he wanted to know was what was happening with Tommy's work. He came right out and said there were thousands of people who could write the way I do, but only one Tommy Patterson.'

Edna was silent, no doubt weightily deliberating this gratuitous insult. 'Craig can be tactless at times. There are certainly not thousands of people who can write the way you do, and he knows it. You're a brand name, Grace. When people see your work, they pick it up. They don't bother with reviews or any of that garbage. They know exactly what they're going to get, and that's what they look forward to. So you write that sequel to LOVE IS A WALTZ. We won't have any trouble placing it.

'Now, on the other matter, why won't you even talk about Tommy Patterson's work?'

69

'If you had been married to him, you wouldn't need to ask that question.'

'But I wasn't married to him, and you're sitting on a gold mine.'

'How do you know?'

'I know Patterson's sales figures.'

'You talked to Craig, didn't you? While I was hanging on hold, which will add zillions to my phone bill, you took a call from Craig, and he told you Tommy's work was delivered to me, didn't he?'

'I didn't know you were holding, Grace. I did take a call from Craig, only because he is, or was, your editor; and I always have your best interests at heart. That's why I'm telling you, you can make a fortune from what Tommy Patterson left behind. You get fifty percent of everything. So what's the problem?'

'The problem is that Tommy Patterson is a cancer, and once you let him invade your system, you never get rid of him. The problem is that I'm me and it took a long time to become me. And I won't be a part of him.'

'The name of the game, Grace, is money.'

'There are some things I won't do even for money, believe it or not. Letting more of Tommy's works loose on an unsuspecting world would be worse than being responsible for the Bhopal disaster.'

'A slight exaggeration?'

'I will be working on my sequel, Edna, should anyone want me.'

Grace hung up the phone. What a sad state of affairs her life had come to. Tommy Patterson was back.

She thought she had shaken free of him years ago. To do so, she had to destroy what was finest within her: her belief in the nobility of humanity, her belief in evolutionary progression, her faith in the old cliché, "The cream always rises", her sense that justice prevails, her faith in love triumphant. But she had no regrets. She was alive, perhaps a little bit warped, but she had made it. Now Tommy, in death, wanted to make her dependent again. That was the secret menace of his will. He left her to perpetuate his poison. Could she let others fall, as she had fallen, under the spell of Tommy Patterson, Pied Piper to the innocent and unsuspecting?

*Chapter 12*

# University of Michigan, 1969

As Odelle Hampton was a woman of the Fifties, Grace Mandling was a child of the Sixties.

Grace was a small town girl. That was tough to take at the time, in the fall of 1969, because everyone, certainly the people who lived there, thought of Grand Rapids, Michigan, as a city. But Grace found out what "city" meant when she arrived at the University of Michigan.

At her high school in Grand Rapids she was considered far out, part of the literary crowd, mainly because she read more than was assigned to her in the classroom. She was also a contributor to the *Oxtail*, Regent High School's literary magazine. She wrote what she realized later were trite little poems on such subjects as death and longing. Her mother thought she needed a psychiatrist. What she really needed was someone to tell her to stop writing poetry.

Even before she arrived at the University of Michigan, she knew she wanted to be a writer. Consequently, she joined the staff of the *Michigan Daily*. In the newspaper's offices she discovered how very provincial she was. So many of the *Daily* staff were from big cities: New York, Detroit, Chicago. And they were ethnic, rough, quick-witted, insensitive, demanding and aggressive. She wilted. She didn't survive on the paper for more than six months. But that six months was a useful experience. She discovered within herself absolutely no interest in politics or movements of any sort. Hers was a mind turned inward on a nation's soul. Far from the surface politics of the times, she was to devote herself to society's psychological underpinnings.

Grace Mandling was a good student. She couldn't just cut classes the way so many of her friends did. She attended each and every lecture and discussion, taking copious notes. She was serious. She was diligent. And with her, as yet, undefined personality, she was lost. The University of Michigan was a very big school, where, the

71

administration bragged, you could either sink or swim; and if you sank, nobody gave a damn.

Her first semester at Michigan, Grace lived at Alice Lloyd Hall, a healthy choice on her part, as she had an energetic walk back and forth to campus several times a day. She took the standard course-work, trying to get rid of as many requirements as possible so she could devote herself to – what? She wanted to learn the process of creation, but aside from theology – she didn't believe in God – and astronomy – she couldn't even spot the Big Dipper – she could find no classes that concentrated exclusively on that most mystical of subjects.

By her second semester Grace still hadn't found her path to creation, so she took an English survey course instead. Even though she had hated her rhetoric course, taught by a jerk from Wesleyan who wore a suit and tie and thought he was hot shit, she felt that English literature was where she belonged. Also, the English depart-ment had a strong creative writing program, fortified by the Hop-wood Awards, given each year to the best student writers the University could vomit up.

Aside from her survey course, Grace took a course in history to give her more background. She had finished her French, which completed her language requirement. She hoped never to see the Frieze building again as long as she lived! There was still science to get out of the way, so she took her second botany course, a big mistake. It was Applied Botany. As it turned out, she would get a C in the course because mealy bugs had eaten the plants in her hanging basket, and the instructors told her it was her fault! To round out her semester, she wanted a real gut course, so she could concentrate on the more important things in life. She took Sociology 1.

The professor for Sociology 1 was a kindly gentleman who stood before them at the first lecture, listing the books they must buy and letting them know, despite what they had heard, that Sociology 1 was a C course. She was concerned; but on her way out of the hall, she overheard several fraternity boys telling each other not to worry. They had all this guy's tests in the exam file. He gave the same tests year after year. So she guessed she would have to make it her business to date someone in a fraternity, though frat rats were definitely a mindless lot.

Grace was almost late for her sociology discussion session. She bounded in as the bell sounded and took the first seat available, which was right in front. That's how she found herself staring into the eyes of the mesmerizing Tommy Patterson.

72

His eyes were brown. But did that really describe them? They had the power to warm or to freeze. Tommy himself wasn't that impressive. He looked like a slob, with rumpled chinos and a wrinkled sports shirt. But that was the way all the sociology teaching assistants dressed. They were making a statement. What the statement was they'd have to find out by survey.

Tommy also wore a fine, thick moustache and a scraggly beard. Truly, she thought, as she stared up at him in glazed admiration, here must be an intellectual. He confirmed her hypothesis with the first words out of his most beautiful of mouths. He said, 'This class is about confinement.'

Grace was thrilled. Confinement. She knew the feeling! Hadn't she felt confined by the expectations of others (her parents and teachers) all her life? And now here she was at the University of Michigan, confined by her own lack of direction. Her epiphany came the moment she realized that here stood the man who had the answers.

Even then the Pied Piper was playing.

Tommy Patterson's discussion sessions had nothing to do with the professor's lectures. Tommy's sessions were always about "us", you and me against the system, the system being the crazy regulations the university threw up as a smoke screen for its vacuity, like attending class, getting good grades, conforming.

Tommy was against conforming. 'I conformed once,' he told them. 'I tried to fit into the system, and the system nearly destroyed me. I have to breathe. I have to let my mind take me where it wants to go. Sociology is about society. But whose society? We in this class can be our own separate society. We can be a tribe with our own customs and decrees. We will not let anyone destroy our individuality. We will not conform!'

They all loved him. This adoration was enhanced when, before every hourly, he would arrive in class with a list of questions they "might" be asked. He was their friend. There was no phony Mr Patterson and Miss Mandling. It was Tommy and Grace, Tommy and Jim, Tommy and everybody. Perhaps Grace was so attracted to him because he was one of the few human contacts the students had with the faculty, most of whom were too elevated to open their doors to mere students.

Grace left Sociology 1 with a B. That was just before the flames from the Vietnam War rose to such intensity that its draft began to lick at the heels of the university's best and brightest, thus leading to a remarkable grade inflation where everyone, even the dummies, got A's and B's. Then a B meant something, as C was the average. She was happy. She would cherish the memories of Sociology 1 with Tommy Patterson.

Grace didn't see Tommy again until autumn 1970, when she started her sophomore year at the University of Michigan. That semester she was inching along the steps toward creation by taking her first poetry writing course, and she felt very good about herself. The professor had to read your poetry before you were admitted. The students in his class were all alike, anxious and dedicated to their craft, or was it art?

One Tuesday afternoon when it was dank and wet out and the professor was depressed, he suggested that they adjourn for five minutes, leave Angel Hall to hold class at the Union. What could be sweeter? And this would give the students a real feeling of camaraderie with their professor. Everyone, mindless of the killing traffic, dashed across the street, lined up for a quick Coke from the cafeteria and headed to one of the big round oak tables with names of former students and their glories etched into them.

It was during the warmth of that class that Grace spotted Tommy, surrounded by his own coterie. She waved to him and he waved back.

No matter where they were held, class broke on the hour. Time is the master of us all. Tommy's class also started to drift away from him. With a tenuous sort of courage, Grace didn't stay to hang on to the last words from the master poet. She moved instead towards Tommy's table. 'Hi,' she said, when the last student had finished what she was saying to Tommy, leaving his intense brown eyes to focus on Grace alone.

'Hi,' he replied. 'Another sociology class?'

'No. Poetry writing,' she answered with a bright smile.

His eyebrows rose, revealing not only interest, but more of those deep brown irises. 'Oh! I'd like to read some of your work some time.'

'Would you?' Her heart gushed, like mercury rising from a broken thermometer.

He asked her out. It was so casually put, she didn't even see it in her mind as a date. They were, after all, just friends. Or perhaps – what was the word she had just learned – Tommy could be considered her mentor. In any case, there was a new French film at the Garden. Tommy was sure she would enjoy it. Then they could go back to his place and read her poetry.

It was only later, as she walked from the Union back to her dorm, a mile and a half away, that she wondered. Could Tommy Patterson like her? Not like her as a student, but as a human being, a woman? What a silly thought. She was only a sophomore, Tommy a sophisticated graduate student. But still, stranger things had happened, hadn't they? Her mind was already spinning its own romantic web for her to be caught in.

The French movie – pardon, film – was very French. There were shadows, bare bosoms and angst. Men rode while women moaned. Grace sat next to Tommy, dying of embarrassment. How could she face him when the film was over? But when the lights went up, all Tommy said as he led her out was, 'Not as good as his last one.'

Grace tried to shake herself free of her mood of stimulation created by the sexual frankness of the French film. Why couldn't she be more adult, more sophisticated? It was just a movie. It didn't mean anything. Why was she so turned on by seeing two people making love? Or in that one case, three?

His place, as he called it, was a room in one of the big boarding houses on Washtenaw, right next to a fraternity. 'I like to watch them frolic,' he said with a superior air when she noted the frat house's proximity. He offered her a soda and then asked, 'Now, did you bring your poems?'

Before leaving her dorm, she had carefully folded newly typed copies of her poems and placed them in her bag. Now she drew them out and handed them over. Tommy turned on his lamp and sat in his arm chair, while she nervously placed herself on the edge of his very ragged sofa. 'Such beauty,' she heard him mutter. 'I never knew there was such beauty.' When he looked up, she thought she saw tears in his eyes.

After he regained his composure, and that took a long time, he said to her, 'You realize of course that, even when you were in my discussion section, I always knew there was something special about you? There was something so delicate, so sensitive, even about the way you sat, the way you leaned forward to catch everything, as if my words were dew falling on the golden leaf of your skin.' He sort of sighed and smiled. 'You know, those women on the screen tonight possessed not half your – freshness.'

She blushed. 'They really aren't very good. The poems, I mean. I know I can do better. I'm working at it.'

'Working hard,' he agreed. He stood up and brought the poems back to her. She folded them carefully and replaced them in her bag while he stood before her. When she looked up, she found herself at eye level with his crotch. It was bulging. Had she not been an innocent virgin, she would have known he had a hard-on. 'May I sit down next to you?' he asked.

She smiled. 'Of course.'

Tommy sat down next to her with his hands dangling on his thighs. 'I knew it,' he said, after what she found to be an uncomfortably long silence.

'What?' she wondered.

'I can feel your aura.'

'My aura?'

'I am within its shadows. May I come closer and be enlightened?'

'I don't feel my aura,' she confessed.

'Let me show you where it is.' Carefully, he lifted her right hand and placed it on her heart, his on top of it. 'This is the centre of your being,' he said. He let his forehead drop on to his hand which was now encircling her breast.

'I feel uncomfortable,' she confessed.

'Don't be selfish, Grace. And that name is perfect for you. You've got to spread your aura, offer its protection for those who would dwell within.'

Well, actually, it was her legs he wanted her to spread, but they didn't get quite that far their first night together. He worked into her aura slowly, carefully, precisely, so it was as if she were inviting him in, though in actuality even after she lost her virginity, she was still an innocent.

# Chapter 13
# Wedding Bells

Love. Real love. It was as rare as a perfect day in June.

Grace Mandling found love with Tommy Patterson. She had expected only to show him her poems and drink at the fount of his wisdom, but he endowed their relationship with a special quality. Love. Blind love. Love is one of the seven deadly sins of stupidity all women succumb to along the wretched climb to the pinnacle of true happiness, which can usually be found in an apartment devoid of husband and children.

But what did Grace know of all this? She was *in love*. She floated through the day, her gaze clouded by thoughts of sex and tenderness. Her poems took on a new warmth, a new realism. They were, as one of her classmates had the nerve to tell her, "icky". But after all, she thought, wasn't that true of love and sex itself?

Grace didn't write home and tell her parents she had fallen in love. They held a very middle class view of love – that it came along only once in a lifetime. Had she told them she was in love, they would have rushed over from Grand Rapids to meet her fella. She loved her parents but were they enlightened enough to understand Tommy Patterson?

She supposed love made her unbearable. She noticed over the first few months of her relationship with Tommy that her friends began to avoid her at mealtimes, or, should she sit with them and start talking, they would change the conversation or not allow her to speak at all. Love is all encompassing, but its circle is small. She smiled secretly to herself. If these mere girls only knew what it felt like to be a woman!

Love is an act of completion, a vessel of perfection. And yet it is also a commitment to madness. Because nothing, not even love, is perfect. But Grace still believed her case was different. How wildly disabused of that notion she became when Grace met an old classmate in the bathroom of the UGLI, Michigan's undergraduate

77

library. 'Saw you with Dr Tommy,' the girl said casually, as she combed her tousled blonde hair. 'What line did he use on you, the aura or the vibes?'

'What?'

'You know? To get you to go to bed with him?'

'What makes you think I'm going to bed with him?' She was, of course, but that this girl should make such an assumption was insulting!

'Hey, what else would he want with us?'

Now there was a girl with very little self-respect, Grace concluded. Tommy had his choice of all these adult women. He didn't have to run after students. Besides, she did have an aura. She could even feel it herself sometimes. Her pen emanated aura whenever she sat down to write her poems.

Yet – and here was the first crack in the vessel – how far could she really trust Tommy? Of course this cheap bottle-blonde was lying – except what if she were telling the truth about him? Was Grace not the only woman Tommy was sleeping with?

Nonsense! She couldn't believe it. After all, Tommy was in love with her. He told her so many, many times.

Doubt is a weed just as pernicious as honeysuckle. Once it appears, how can one stop it from strangling the blossoms of love? Grace was suddenly in a state of doubt. But how to broach the subject to a man she knew to be as noble as any of the knights of the Round Table, which she was studying in her Making of Myths course.

Taking the bull by the horns, or whatever, Grace confronted Tommy one evening after an especially trying session on tangled white sheets. Or should it be pale and tangled white sheets, or just pale and tangled white? No, that wouldn't make any sense. It had to have "sheets" in it because people in poems were always loving each other on white sheets. She didn't know why. Didn't they have money for patterns or colours? Or was white the symbol of the purity of their love? Or love's sterility?

Weeks ago when she was devoured by the sheer romance of their love, before she met the blonde in the bathroom, nothing could have shaken Grace's faith in their commitment to each other. And yet, even then – when she considered it, as she had been for the last seven days – in the first flush of the sun's light on the steamy, bodily commitment to love's ideal, Grace realized something was missing from her relationship with Tommy. She believed it was called an orgasm. Hers.

She had already once said to Tommy, 'I don't feel what I'm supposed to.' And she knew what she was supposed to feel because she had read a dog-eared copy of FOREVER AMBER as a child.

78

'It'll come in time,' he assured her lovingly. 'You have to get used to sex first, my sweet little virgin.'

Virgin no longer, she thought, though Grace didn't particularly mind sacrificing the precious commodity of her maidenhood. After all, if she was going to be a writer, she would have to experience passion. And she was making every effort. However, frustration was the overwhelming outcome of her layabeds with Tommy.

Now, how could that be?

Before they consummated their love, he had spent a long time massaging her neck, her breasts, kneading her belly, caressing between her legs. She could feel herself flowering with expectation. And she thought of that first time – if there hadn't been so much pain, would she not have come, to use the vernacular?

Yet, after that first time, while love remained constant, a paean to John Donne's imagery, the primordial mating changed. Tommy was busily working on his dissertation, already having one article accepted for publication. Love filled only a tiny time slot in the day. So she got a cursory nibble at her nipple and sometimes four, five, or at the most six pumps from Tommy. She felt nothing. But she would have found the fault within herself, not the stars, certainly not Tommy, if this snake in the grass, his former classmate, had not indicated that Grace was not alone in sharing the fecundity of Tommy's love.

Now she wondered. She wove and rewove the suspicions in her mind, much as Penelope at the loom. Maybe that's why Tommy didn't have the energy for her? He was saving the hot thrust of his iron for a maiden other than herself!

And so on that fatal evening – *J'accuse*!

Tommy denied it. She was the only woman in his life. He swore it. To prove it, he would do what he had been dying to do since the moment he first laid eyes on her. He would marry her.

Married?

All she had asked for was his undying love and an orgasm thrown in here and there, not for him to pledge his troth. Grace didn't want to get married. She was too young and wanted to finish her studies. Furthermore, what would her parents say!

Tommy smiled when he saw the confused horror on her face. He had called her bluff and now she had to bid or fold.

Marriage.

Would marrying Tommy make everything right?

After she left him the night of their confrontation, she went back to the dorm. She took a pad of paper, drew a horizontal line across the top and a vertical down the middle of the page. On the very top of the

79

page she put "Marriage". The two columns were labelled "For" and "Against".

For: Tommy had taken her virginity. He loved her. She loved him. He was a graduate student. He would be a success. If she married him, she would see more of him, bedwise. Maybe then she would have an orgasm.

Against: Did she really want to get married. It was scary. Her parents would have a shit-fit. She really wanted to finish college.

On the other hand, For: What if she didn't marry Tommy? She wasn't a virgin any longer. What was she to do, spend her life going from man to man, sharing one bed after another?

Against: Her parents were Republican.

For: She could elope and tell them afterwards. Once they got to know Tommy, they would love him. Didn't everybody? Besides, how romantic this would be to tell her children and grandchildren!

Grace Mandling and Tommy Patterson got married at the Washtenaw County courthouse in downtown Ann Arbor on spring break. They then took a quick ride over to Grand Rapids to break the news to her parents. By that time, Grace had convinced herself that her parents would be ecstatic. After all, she was marrying a graduate student who had a brilliant future once he got his Ph.D. in sociology.

Her parents' reception of the newly married couple, glowing with wedded bliss, was a little less than Grace had hoped for. Her mother, terribly Presbyterian, tried to keep up a good front. Her father, a distributor for Goodyear, said, and here she would have to quote, 'What sort of shit subject is sociology?'

Grace left her parents' house in tears. But deep in her heart, she had no regrets. All artists have to suffer. What she was going through now would some day be grist for her writer's mill. Meanwhile, she had the love of a good man and the expectation of an exciting future.

## Chapter 14

# Have I Got News For You!

Late March of 1971 was picture-perfect in Ann Arbor, the exact time of year when the university's botanical gardens turn less into a place for roving Botany 1 students, more into a place for lovers' trysts. The air was sweet across the city of Ann Arbor, and happy days were a hamburger at the Brown Jug, followed by a double scoop of ice cream at Miller's. Despite their vehement displeasure with her marriage, Grace's parents had not cut off her allowance. With Tommy's small stipend the newly-married were just making it, especially since Grace continued to eat in the dorm. But she spent as much time as she could over at Tommy's, playing at being married. That's where she was when the phone call came.

The phone rang and naturally she picked it up. Why not? She was Tommy's wife. A woman on the other end asked to speak to Tom Patterson. 'I'm sorry. He's not here right now. May I take a message?'

'May I ask to whom I'm speaking?'

'This is Tommy's wife.'

'Tommy's wife?' the voice said. 'How very – very interesting.' And then the woman hung up.

Grace thought nothing of it. She didn't even bother to tell Tommy about the call.

Two weeks went by. During those two weeks, Grace noted with distraction that she had missed her period. It was probably from the stress of being married. Her physical timing was off. And then one day when she was over at Tommy's, trying to straighten all the periodicals flooding from his desk, the downstairs door bell rang. 'Tom Patterson,' Grace heard the landlady's voice say, 'he lives right at the top to your left.'

Grace hurried now. They were going to have visitors! She didn't want Tommy to be disappointed in her ability to entertain.

81

When the knock came, Grace was ready. But not for three people who didn't even look like students. 'Hello,' she said in her simple, open Midwestern way.

'You must be Tom's wife,' the woman said. But still Grace didn't connect this visitor to the voice on the phone, until the woman said, 'We talked before.'

Grace nodded agreeably.

'I'm Odelle Patterson, this is Sy Hampton, and this is Wayne Harris. Wayne's an attorney.'

'Oh,' Grace said. Attorney? Did this mean trouble?

'May we come in?' Odelle asked.

'Oh, certainly. Please do.' Grace indicated they should sit wherever they found space. 'May I get you something to drink?'

'Nothing, thank you,' Sy Hampton answered.

Grace sort of crouched down on the floor and smiled at Odelle. 'You must be a relative of Tommy's with the same last name and all.'

Odelle smiled, cold and sweet. 'I'm his wife.'

# Chapter 15

# Vengeance is Mine, Sayeth Odelle

'I want to ruin him,' Odelle stated simply to Sy Hampton. This was right after she got off the phone from speaking to Grace, after she found out her husband Tom had, among his many other sins, committed bigamy.

Sy was in Louisiana, and either the connection was bad or he was in a bar. 'Look, let me take care of this.'

'Castration is too good,' Odelle continued, almost to herself. 'Ever since he left, I have been living at poverty level, working, taking care of Julia, fending for myself in a very cold, cruel world, while he's been sitting pretty, at a university, getting his Ph.D. And on top of that, he has a wife? He hasn't even divorced me yet!'

'The thing about the law is the less emotionally involved you are, the better off you'll feel later,' Sy tried to convince her.

'I will never feel good again, Sy! To think of how he's using her and how he used me.'

'But you have him by the short hairs now, don't you?'

'I'd rather not even think about Tom Patterson's short hairs.'

In the end, Odelle let Sy persuade her that he would take care of everything. She would just be along for the ride, an observer, keeping her mouth shut, he emphasized. Odelle was offended and relieved. She was offended because there was so much she wanted to say. She was relieved because it was so good to have someone take the burden off of her shoulders. She was a woman, and she really needed a man to lean on. Finally, she had one. Sy was there for her.

Now here she was in Ann Arbor and what did she feel? Mainly pity for this young, sweet, stunned girl before her. Grace was her name. Grace Patterson. 'Not really Patterson,' Odelle pointed out as kindly as possible.

'Grace Mandling then,' Grace said. 'But I don't believe you.'

Grace was thin and intense. Odelle always noticed thin and intense girls. It was a look that at one time she tried to cultivate. But she had

83

never quite managed it. Odelle supposed it was because she was basically a round person, round face, round breasts, welcoming hips. And Grace had her hair the way the girls wore it now, long and jumbled.

Grace kept looking worriedly at the three of them. She was more than confused. She was stunned, a poor shivering rabbit caught in the flashlight of revelations. 'What exactly do you mean, you were married to him?' she tried to eke out more of the story from Odelle.

Odelle neatly folded her gloves on her lap and straightened her fingers. 'He married me when we were both students at Cornell. He seduced me, married me, and got me pregnant. You mean he's never mentioned Julia, our daughter?'

Grace's mouth dropped open, and she looked as if she might be going into shock. 'I can't believe you,' she said. Naturally. If she did believe Odelle, what would be the consequences?

'Julia was born in 1963. Would you like to see her picture?' Odelle opened her bag. 'Of course, Tom hasn't seen his daughter since 1965, which is when he took off, cleaning out our joint bank account first. I haven't heard from him since then. I wouldn't have known where he was except that he published this very interesting article in *Sociology Today* about demographics.'

'He's getting his Ph.D.,' Grace said numbly.

'Isn't that fascinating.'

Grace stood up. 'I have to call someone.'

'Not so fast,' Wayne Harris said. Then he turned to Sy and Odelle and added, 'We don't want her alerting him. Who knows where he might take off to.'

'I'm not going to try to get in touch with Tommy,' Grace said. 'I have to call my father. He'll know what to do.'

Odelle was touched. The poor girl was so young and so dumb, much as she had been when she was enamoured of Tom Patterson. 'I'll go with her,' she volunteered.

'Let's just wait here until Patterson returns,' Sy said.

'But, Sy, who's she going to fall back on? We can't leave her to face this alone. I remember all too well how that felt when it happened to me.' Odelle stood, took the girl by the hand and led her down the stairs to the pay phone. To be on the safe side, Odelle asked the girl for the number she wanted, called information to make sure the area code was Grand Rapids, then had the operator call collect. She listened, sick to her stomach, while Grace poured out her story to her father. She knew it had to be the girl's father because she could hear the growling in the background and then the barking.

After Grace put down the phone, she lifted her head. There were tears in her eyes. 'Daddy's coming over,' she said.

84

Odelle brushed the hair off the girl's face. 'You're not really married to him, you know. You're the lucky one.'

'I'm such a fool.'

Odelle shrugged. 'We're women.'

They returned upstairs to continue their vigil. Grace couldn't really tell them when Tommy would return. He had office hours, and he always got "so involved with his students". As she should well know!

Three hours later the door opened, and they heard footsteps on the stairs. 'That's him,' Grace whispered, now joining the conspiracy.

Odelle stood. She wanted to kill.

An unsuspecting Tommy Patterson opened the door to his room and walked in with a smile on his face.

The smile quickly turned to recognition, then alarm. He made an about face and tried to flee. Sy tackled him, turned him over and pinned his arms. Odelle couldn't help it. She very delicately stepped with her heels on to Tommy's body and mashed his balls.

He was trying to grasp what he considered his manhood while Sy sat on him. Wayne Harris served him with divorce papers and explained his legal situation. Odelle begged for another chance to do her grape-mashing step across his penile extremity. At that point, the downstairs door burst off its hinges to admit Dale Mandling, Grace's father.

Grace knew her father was a big man, but she didn't realize exactly how strong he was until he grabbed Tommy by the hair, causing Sy Hampton to tumble off. Then he pushed Tommy up against the wall and socked him over and over again, despite Tommy's every effort to fall down.

Poor Dale Mandling. When the police came, his knuckles were raw. They were just about to arrest him for assault and battery when Sy Hampton stepped in to save the day. 'This man just held him,' Sy said. 'I'm the one who actually hit him.' At which point, Odelle felt she had to say something, so she confessed.

Then Grace knew she had to do something to save her Daddy. 'I really did it,' she added tearfully.

The only one who hadn't confessed was Wayne Harris. It was to him that the police turned for the true story. 'I didn't see a thing,' the lawyer claimed.

Tommy Patterson didn't see a thing for a while either. When he arrived at the hospital, they naturally tried to reduce the swelling around his eyes, but with little success. Neither the doctors nor the police would understand why Tommy refused to press charges. All he could get out of his mouth, with its broken teeth, was, 'Family matter.'

So Odelle flew back to New York, finally assured of her divorce. And Sy flew back to Louisiana, promising her that as soon as the papers came through, they would be married. Odelle was happy. And yet she wasn't. She worried about that young child, Grace Mandling. A few years ago she herself had been Tommy's victim. She knew how it felt to have her life thrown off course by Tom Patterson. She knew what it was to hate and to suffer. It seemed to Odelle that Tom had done little enough of either.

The article ripped out of *Society Today* that led to Tom Patterson – "Demographics – Bending the Truth" – continued to haunt Odelle, hinting there was a step she had not taken. Tommy would recover from the beating he had received. Weren't there other ways of getting even with him? She reread the article, and it made her wonder.

The next day at Aramco, she xeroxed "Demographics – Bending the Truth". Then she called Tommy's old firm, the one he left in the lurch at the same time he was shitting on her. Steve Rosen was now a vice-president. 'You won't remember me,' she began. But it turned out he remembered her very well. Tommy's theft had caused him to lose an account. Tommy absconded with all the research, and they could neither recollate the information nor duplicate the results in time to please the client.

'May I buy you lunch?' Odelle suggested.

'Why?' Steve asked surlily.

But he finally consented. Odelle picked Heavenly Burgers. It was cheap enough for her budget, yet manly enough for Steve Rosen. He met her there at twelve-thirty on Thursday of that week. They ordered their burgers well done, which meant they would be lucky if the outside was seared. 'I'm a busy man,' he told her, 'so why the sudden call?'

'Mr Rosen, I am not my soon-to-be ex-husband, so why be hostile towards me?'

'I'd rather forget that episode with Tom Patterson.'

'I've found him.'

'Really? Well, take my suggestion and lose him again.'

Odelle then explained the circumstances in which she had found Tom Patterson and further elaborated on his bigamous relationship.

'Nothing would surprise me about Patterson,' Steve said with a shake of his head.

'There's something that interests me about that article, though,' Odelle said. She pulled the xeroxed copy out of her purse. 'It might interest you too.'

She handed it over and watched while Steve Rosen scanned the pages. He quickly lost his appetite for lunch. Well, who wouldn't?

Raw meat is only occasionally appetizing. 'This – this is the work he stole from us,' Steve gulped.

'As I suspected. You went to college, didn't you, Mr Rosen?'

'Yes. Columbia.'

'Do you know, Mr Rosen, that work has to be original for you to be granted a Ph.D.? You can't steal someone else's research. Did Tom do all this on his own?'

The smile that slowly crept across Steve Rosen's face was very gratifying indeed.

# Chapter 16

# Wedding Bells Redux

Grace Mandling was pregnant. When her period didn't come and didn't come, she went to the health service and got tested. 'You're pregnant,' the woman doctor told her. 'How do you feel about that?'

When Grace filled in the health service form, she had marked single as her marital state. They didn't have a box for "Married, but not really". So she guessed the doctor was asking her if she were going to jump off a bridge or something.

Grace told her mother first. 'We'll fly to London to get an abortion,' her mother immediately decided. 'I've always wanted to see London.'

'Mother, I want the baby.'

'How can you want the baby? Look who the father is. I'm assuming. Besides, having a child means the end of life as you know it. There is a time to have children, when you're married and ready to settle down. You haven't done anything yet except get involved with this, this – oh, honey, how could you?'

Her mother told her father. During the whole time the issue was discussed, Grace never spoke directly to her father about it. Confronting the sexual side of life was something he just didn't handle well. If he could, he probably would still be giving her dolls for Christmas. So it was always between Grace and her mother, with 'Your father says', or 'Tell Daddy – '

The problem was keeping track of Tommy Patterson, because Grace's father insisted, if she was going to have the baby, it would not be illegitimate. But the divorce papers hadn't as yet come through dissolving Tommy's marriage to Odelle.

Dale Mandling found this out from Wayne Harris, whom he also retained to handle Grace's problems with Tommy Patterson. At first Harris thought it might be a conflict of interest. But then Dale Mandling let Harris know what he had in mind.

Both her parents insisted that Grace should return to school for her junior year. The baby wasn't due until December. She might as well get in as much school work as she could. They went with her in August to the campus and scrounged around until they came up with a small apartment in a rundown house near East Quad. She would be on the first floor and near enough to both school and a few grocery stores for her to be able to manage, no matter how large she became. Furthermore, if anything happened, she had the university hospital less than a mile away. 'And don't you worry,' her father told her before they departed for Grand Rapids, 'you'll be married when you have that baby.'

Grace wasn't quite so sure. She heard rumours about Tommy being suddenly cut from the Ph.D. program at the university. So she called Wayne Harris, figuring he must be keeping on top of things. But Mr Harris was under the impression that Tommy was continuing with his thesis and thus had a valid reason to hang around Ann Arbor.

The lawyer called Grace back that very same evening. 'It seems Patterson was called before the chairman of the sociology department and dismissed from the program. The original research he was supposed to have done for his thesis on demographics was actually stolen from a company he worked for in New York. He took their raw research at the same time he cleaned out Odelle's bank account. But don't worry, Grace; I'm keeping him here in Ann Arbor until he can marry you.'

'How can you do that?' Grace wondered.

'By threatening to get a warrant issued for his arrest as a bigamist. And by the time I'm through with him, Patterson knows he'd be spending time in jail.'

'He always spoke about the confinements of society,' Grace said almost wistfully.

'If he tries to decamp, he'll find out just how confining society can be.'

And so late in November, when the rest of America was buying turkey and cranberry sauce in preparation for Thanksgiving, Grace Mandling once again married Thomas Patterson, this time with her parents and Wayne Harris in attendance. Grace was in her eighth month of pregnancy and worried about getting her paper on Alexander Pope in on time. The judge said to them, as he looked over the supposedly happy couple-to-be, 'Not a moment too soon.'

This shotgun wedding lasted as long as it took for the wedding party to leave the judge's chambers and walk down the hall to another office of the Washtenaw County Courthouse. There Grace Mandling Patterson and Thomas Patterson filed papers for divorce. 'Don't bother trying to get child support,' Tommy snapped, when his signature was on the dotted line.

'We don't even want you to see the baby,' Dale Mandling informed his soon-to-be ex-son-in-law.

He need not have worried. Tommy didn't stay around Ann Arbor a minute longer than it took to get from the courthouse to the city limits. His Volkswagen was packed. Last seen he was headed for Detroit and the bridge over into Windsor, Ontario. Tommy Patterson was headed north into Canada where the law couldn't touch him.

Grace returned home with her parents for the Thanksgiving feast, which turned out to be less festive than usual. A sort of gray pall hung over the gathering. By now everyone in the family, including her brother and sister, knew the story of Grace's disastrous lack of judgement. Even if they hadn't they could certainly read it in the bulging of her belly. How did a smart woman become so dumb?

Grace headed back to the university, determined to finish her coursework and take her finals. She was cheered by news of a philosophy graduate student who had given birth, then returned to teaching class a week later. Maybe she could be like that, finish her degree and go on with her life, wherever it would lead her. As to that, she had no idea.

On her way out of the apartment to take her last final semester, and that in critical reasoning, her worst class for obvious reasons, Grace's waters broke. They sort of gushed down her legs and on to the carpet. She sat down for a moment, shaken. She was going to have her baby. But she was also going to have her final. She put in a call to her doctor and asked if it would be all right if she just took that last final. He was doubtful, but she was desperate. Critical reasoning was a course she didn't want to think about ever again. She was on her third out of four essay questions when the contractions became unbearably close together. When one stopped, she stood up and walked to the front, her face sweaty, her body shaking. She said to her professor, 'I hope you can grade me on these answers alone. I've got to – ' Her face contracted along with her belly. Her professor called a graduate student out of the hall to supervise the rest of the final while he rushed her to the hospital. Gee, he was a sweet man. He even gave her a B – for baby.

Grace's labour at the hospital was short, so short that her doctor barely made it to the hospital in time. He came into the labour room to check and see if she was dilating. He stared, said something about seeing the head already, and she was whisked into delivery. She thought this was what always happened because the pain was so great she really couldn't do more than moan. 'This will be a natural,' the

90

doctor said. The nurses clucked sympathetically. Grace remembered having one pat her forehead with a cool towel. And then she felt this extreme urge to push. The doctor placed his hand on her abdomen, and the baby plopped out of her. She didn't see it, but she could feel it.

She couldn't hear it.

She could hear voices, some calm, some rising; she could hear the door to the delivery room slam open; but she couldn't hear the baby crying. All babies were supposed to cry when they were born.

'My baby?' she wondered.

But no one had time for her. They were working furiously in a corner of the delivery room, while she was lying there, looking up at the lights and the metal and wondering what was happening.

Finally, the doctor came back to her. He was not the smiling, jovial man she had seen over the last six months. He was sad and solemn. 'My baby?' she asked.

'I'm sorry. There was nothing we could do.'

'Do about what?'

It turned out that her baby was born with only half a heart. They had to do an autopsy to find out what the problem was. Afterwards, after she had had the baby baptized Charity Mandling and buried in Grand Rapids, Grace came back to her doctor and asked him how this terrible thing could have happened to her, to her child. She took such good care of herself. She followed all his instructions.

The doctor said, 'There are so many things that could go wrong, and nobody knows why. Just for my own peace of mind, let me check something out again. I asked you when you first came to me if you ever took drugs.'

'And I told you no, I never have.'

'It doesn't matter to me, Grace. I just want to know.'

'Drugs have never appealed to me. I fantasize a lot instead.'

'And the father of your baby?'

Tommy and drugs? 'But would it have mattered?' Grace wondered. 'After all, I was the one who carried the child.'

'Drugs can alter a genetic pattern and lead to defects. Whether it led to this one, I don't know.'

Tommy smoked pot. She knew that for a fact because she could smell it on him. But what else he did, she had no idea. They never discussed it. And since she would never see him again, it didn't matter. Her little girl was dead.

She wrote a poem about the death, an elegy. That was her offering. Years later, when she accidentally came upon the poem in her papers, she cried. The tears were both for her baby and herself, for

91

the young, innocent, tender, sweet, unsuspecting girl she used to be. If life could be replayed, meeting Tommy Patterson was the moment she would have chosen to delete.

# Chapter 17

# Dependents

Trudi Surefoot did not understand why River Range Clinic was making her wear a uniform instead of her own clothes. She had packed her special, hand-decorated jeans. But no, she was ordered to wear the jeans the clinic provided – probably, she suspected, because they were being put on her bill at three times the cost of regular jeans. And why the sweatshirt, pink for women, blue for men, yellow for those who couldn't decide? Emblazoned on its front was "I Took the Cure" to be followed on the back by "At River Range Clinic". Did the clinic want its patients to be spotted the moment they escaped over the high wall and into the nearby town? What had Odelle Hampton got her into?

In group yesterday Trudi was condemned for not trying to fit in. How in god's name was she supposed to fit in with five cocaine sniffers, two heroin addicts and one drunk on speed? What did she have in common with them? Did they have any concept of the use of the sacred mushroom?

And all this individual psychotherapy she was undergoing because no one took seriously the fact that she had actually been reincarnated three times. Dr Sabon, after faking concern and compassion, showed his true colours. He actually scoffed at the possibility of reincarnation. If only Tommy were alive. He would put Dr Know-It-All Sabon in his place!

But Tommy was dead.

Trudi started to sniffle.

One of her group members was passing by. He stopped, stood over her, and looked down. 'Yeah, it's awful when the nose starts to go, isn't it? That's what scared me. That's why I'm here. I paid good money when I was a teenager to have my nose fixed, and now I'm losing it.' He waited for her to say something. When she didn't but turned from him instead, using direct body language to send a message even he could understand, he walked on. Druggies. She was stuck with a bunch of druggies.

Why had she allowed Odelle to plant her in this unfertilized soil? That was the question she had to focus on. Sometimes it was so, so hard to focus. What exactly did she recall? Tommy died and just everyone, like Odelle, Grace and Kitty – or, no, wait, Kitten – was so upset about it. Then the police reported something about Tommy not having time to reconcile his spirit with its upcoming journey. Oh yeah, someone had pushed him off a cliff. But couldn't Tommy fly? She remembered a time together when he told her he was flying. He wasn't levitating like some of those jerks claim to do or walking on hot coals, like who needs it. Everyone knows hot coals are for barbecues. Tommy flew. She flew too. Her mind just –

Her mind. That's why she had come willingly to this clinic, this place of unending regulations. Her mind no longer functioned the way it should, the way it had when she was in kindergarten and learning to fingerpaint. She loved fingerpainting. It was so squishy and messy, and it made you feel so good. She told that to her psychotherapist Dr Know-It-All, and he replied that fingerpainting was anal. What was the point in talking to a man who couldn't accept the simple joys of life?

Trudi supposed she had always liked art. Her first life, the first one she could recall under the influence of the sacred mushroom, was as Rising Surefoot. She couldn't remember when that life occurred. Ten thousand years ago, two thousand years ago, what did it matter? It was in the past. Rising Surefoot was a sand artist in what Americans now call Arizona, what her people called Land of the Sun, Sand, Cacti, Moon, Sweeping Waters Once a Year. She didn't actually understand why, as Rising Surefoot, she was a sand artist, until Tommy told her, after he induced this mystical experience within her, that she was a priestess and that her sand paintings foretold what would happen to the tribe. Obviously, they didn't like what she had to say because she was hacked to death at a very young age. But her spirit lived on. It became a part of the ceremony of the soul. In other words, the men of her tribe ate her in their effort to capture her very essence.

Her next life, at least the next she could remember, was as Jennifer McBride. She was a member of a wagon train headed west. The wagon train was overtaken by hostile Indians (what we now call Native Americans, what we then called savages). Of course, they weren't savages. Jennifer learned to appreciate that after she was taken captive and brought into their midst. She was called Yellow Hair. This part of her reincarnation always bothered her because, as she recalled, Jennifer had brown hair. But Tommy always told her not to dwell on the minutiae, just to inhale the broad sweep of things. Anyway, as Yellow Hair, she was taken to the bed of Talking Brave, the chief's son. Everything would have been all right if she hadn't taken up sand painting again, this time with even more disastrous results. She painted a picture of a white god ascendant. Politically, it was an unwise move. Talking Brave set out at the head of a scouting party the day after her drawing caused so much unease among the tepees. The scouting party never returned. Poor Yellow Hair was left out alone on the desert to die of dehydration, while her people folded their skin tents and migrated towards where they thought safety lay.

And now what was to happen with this life? Would something disastrous come her way again?

This time she had been born Trudi Heidi Halley from East Diablo in West Texas. She supposed she had a normal upbringing for someone born in 1953. She could remember her whole early life centred around the television set, first the children's shows, then *I Love Lucy*, then – oh so many memories. Like the time she came home from school to find her mama sitting in front of the television, crying, when John F. Kennedy was murdered. 'Why did it have to happen in Texas?' her mama kept bemoaning.

'We had the Alamo and now this,' her father agreed.

Despite national turmoil, Trudi recalled a happy childhood as Trudi Heidi Halley. She didn't know what marijuana was until junior high when her father's cousin came back from Vietnam. She didn't know a lot of things until Cousin Earl came home. Then she found out about things like sex, V.D., and drugs more complex than marijuana. The drugs helped her through the pain of her sinful experiences with Cousin Earl, because the drugs helped her see that there was life beyond pain.

Trudi suffered from a bad reputation in high school. The guys said she was easy. But she wasn't really. The closeness of sex just made her feel good. You had to do things that made you feel good, otherwise you'd feel bad. After Cousin Earl, she felt bad about herself a lot; that's why she needed to feel good. Anyway, she took a lot of art courses, so nobody really cared. Art courses sort of labelled you as different.

Trudi supposed the worst moment in high school was discovering she was pregnant. She missed three periods in a row and felt slightly nauseous, but she hadn't really connected either with getting pregnant. After all, the nurse had told the girls in one of their special once-a-year health classes that periods could be irregular. As for the nausea, there was always a lot of 'flu going around. But then when she

95

missed her fourth period, she had a suspicion that it might just be because she was with child.

She panicked and immediately thought of suicide. Her family were Pentecostal Christians, and things like teenage daughters getting pregnant just didn't happen if you were born again. But then she realized it wouldn't just be suicide if she took her own life, it would be murder as she would also be killing her child.

She turned to her mother, who unfortunately told her father. From then on her father never called her Trudi again. Whenever he wanted to refer to her, he always called her 'the tramp' or 'the slut'.

Trudi had the child. She was six months pregnant when June rolled around, so she finished the academic year, despite some anxious hints from the principal that she might want to drop out of high school. This her mother refused to allow. So Trudi wore the scarlet A of her maternity clothes, and suffered the indignity of whispers behind hands whenever she walked down the hall. She couldn't even name a father, as her own father insisted she do. She didn't know who the father was.

And she never would either. After the baby was born, a beautiful, perfect, little boy, Trudi gave him up for adoption. In September, she went back to school for her senior year. She remembered it as the most horrible year in her life. The boys, seeing she was no longer pregnant, wanted more of her. She couldn't convince them she had changed, that she had no desire to get pregnant a second time. And her father hated to see her around the house. He made her eat in her room, so he wouldn't have to sit across the dinner table from her. She didn't think anyone was more happy to graduate and leave East Diablo than she was.

After she left high school, and her mama was so proud of her because her mama never got her high school degree, Trudi headed off to this commercial art school in Abilene. She didn't know if it was any good and neither did her teachers, but the school promised to help her get a government loan to pay for her education. It was there that she learned how to throw. After that, she and the potter's wheel became inseparable. Her fingers in that wet clay made her feel better than sex or drugs or just about anything. And she was glad, later on, when she learned she had lived so many different lives, that she had taken to pottery this time, because in West Texas it would have been just as easy to take up sand painting.

And now here she was at River Range Clinic. Even though there as no one eating her or deserting her to die on the cruel sands, she felt something somewhere had gone wrong with her life. Somewhere between Cousin Earl and Tommy's bodily departure from this earth, she had lost her way. She was looking for that way now, but without drugs it was so hard to illuminate the path. Drugs were like magic. They lit up alleyways you couldn't see if you didn't use them. Unfortunately, drugs dimmed everything else.

But why did she want to get clean now? she wondered, as she sat on the grass at River Range Clinic. Where was she in her own time-space continuum that she had decided upon this drastic step?

Ah! Tommy. He had left her in charge of the Tommy Patterson Fund for the Betterment of Humanity. That was it. How could she, a drug addict, as that dunce of a group leader called her, lead toward the betterment of humanity if some days she could barely get out of bed, due to a drug-induced haze lasting from night into morning?

Damn it, she was going to change! She was going to be the person she was meant to be, clear-headed, forceful, yet compassionate. Hadn't she proved that with Kitten Fairleigh? She gave Kitten "Mi Hacienda" because she knew that Tommy deep down wanted Kitten to have it, even if he hated her when he wrote his will.

Will. That was the word she had to remember. She had the will to recover from all her addictions. And she would. She was determined.

'Hey!'

Trudi looked up. There was some guy standing above her. He had on jeans and a grey sweatshirt that said on the front "Ask Me", on the back, "I'm Here to Help". All the staff wore these. Was she supposed to be at some activity? She hoped it wasn't fingerpainting she forgot about. She loved fingerpainting. 'I can see you're suffering,' the guy knelt down to say.

Trudi wondered if he was seeing into her inner soul or did she just look bad that day in full sunlight? She waited. She always waited where men were concerned. She was a passive person, basically. She guessed that's why she had been hacked to death and eaten, deserted and molested by Cousin Earl at too young an age.

'Look,' the staff member continued, 'I'm not supposed to do this, but when I see someone like you suffering, my heart goes out.'

'Where?'

'What?'

'Where does your heart go to when it goes out?'

He smiled a little uneasily. 'Just an expression.'

'That's funny,' she said to him, 'because it's not really just an expression. During our religious ceremonies with the sacred mushroom, I have seen hearts leave bodies.'

'Uh, yeah,' he said agreeably. 'Well, look, I don't have any sacred mushrooms, but I think I can get you some uppers or some downers, whatever you prefer.'

'Gee, that's nice of you.'

'Yeah? Well, it'll cost you. Like, I'm putting my job on the line for your benefit. But I hear you're rich.'

'My spirit has been well-endowed.'

'Your body too.'

'But as far as money goes, I'm afraid I'm Miss Empty-Pockets.'

He stood up and backed off with a shrug. She was glad, because she was filled with will and determination.

Her will and determination lasted about fifteen more minutes, then she considered the possibilities. Was going cold turkey right for someone with her delicate system? After all, she had been consuming the sacred mushroom in one form or another for over ten thousand years. Perhaps she should just ease off gently.

But she didn't have any money. That lawyer in California was taking care of everything. However, maybe Odelle . . .


It was past seven when Odelle opened the door of her Glencoe house and heard the phone ringing. Her machine was on, and she didn't want to answer it. She had just left the shelter, after making sure the food stretched to serve all the women and children and that the security guards had arrived for the night. Now she wanted some time to herself. Still, maybe she'd better see who it was. She couldn't leave her workers stranded.

Odelle turned up the volume on the machine and heard a crab-like whisper: 'Odelle, it's Trudi.' Odelle whipped the receiver off its resting place. 'Trudi?'

'Gee, your machine answers back.'

'Trudi, it's me, Odelle. I just got home. What's happening? What happened to your voice?'

'I can't talk loud because I'm not supposed to be communicating with anyone from the outside yet. I had to break into an office to call you.'

'What's the matter?'

'I need money.'

'For the canteen?'

'No. I found this guy who's willing to sell me some pills, and I don't have a cent on me.'

'Gee, Trudi, that's awful,' Odelle faked it. 'Listen, dear, I don't want to alert the staff to what you're doing, so why don't I just send the money to the staff member for you? That way they'll never suspect. What's his name?'

'I don't know. He didn't say.'

'What did he look like?'

'Do you think he'll get it if you just put his description on the envelope?' Trudi sounded doubtful.

'Of course he will. When you write to the President, you put White House on the envelope, don't you?'

'Gee, Odelle, I never really thought of that. Well, he's kind of medium height with dirty blond hair. He has blue eyes, and, oh, golly, yes, a dimple on his chin just like Kirk Douglas, or is it Michael? I can never get those two straight.'

'Okay, Trudi. You just hang in there, and I'll make sure this guy gets exactly what's coming to him.'

'Thanks, Odelle. Everyone counts so much on you.'

As soon as Trudi hung up, Odelle put in an emergency call to her friend Madelaine Stevenson. She gave Madelaine a large piece of her mind and a description of the errant staff member. When she put down the phone, she discovered two messages waiting for her. Maybe Sy had called from Brazil. But no, the first one was from Grace, asking her to call. What now! Why had she been Tommy's first wife? It seemed as if all she had done since marrying and divorcing him was serve as a nursemaid to others whose lives he ruined. Thank God she could count on not hearing from Kitten Fairleigh. Now there was a woman who would never need help.

The second message was from – Kitten Fairleigh. 'Odelle? I just thought you might like to keep up to date. My sources tell me that Detective Morris knows you came out to visit Tommy two days before he changed his will.'

## Chapter 18

# Domesticity – Sort Of

Galen Richards called the bus ride back and forth to New York City his rides of passage. In the morning he stepped lively on to the bus, gave the regular driver his ticket, nodded to those that he knew already in their places, and made his way to a window seat midway towards the back. Most people liked to sit on the aisle, but not Galen, even though he sometimes suffered for it by being crushed. He was one of the few people left in this world who did not have a claustrophobic personality. He liked to look out of the wide, dirty window and watch the passing scene, note the seasons of the year, observe the changes, wondering if they were for better or worse. Sometimes he even thought about work, especially if something exciting, even stimulating, was about to happen, like maybe a presentation or the creation of a new storyboard. Life held promise in the morning.

His passage home was always one of despair. Nothing ever seemed to go as well as he expected, even when it went very well indeed. The day's disappointments weighed him down. But as he stepped off the bus in New City, his mood swung once again. His spirits picked up. Soon he would be home in his house with his love, and she would be warm and comforting. Or, depending on her humour, cold and hostile. Or bleak and despairing. Or simply castrating and bitchy. It was hard to tell with Grace. But none of that mattered. She was there, and he would soon be there with her. Never before had he had such a satisfying relationship. He had never known what it meant to feel really good about being with someone twenty-four hours a day. Though twenty-four hours a day never happened. Even on weekends they both worked somewhat, he more than she with his painting, which she encouraged. She needed her solitude, and he needed time to contemplate his ideal.

Now he had brought a cloud to the perfection he had been enjoying for the last two years. But it was time to take a stand.

He often told Grace that he never thought of their age difference, and that was true in one respect. Between the two of them it didn't make any difference. Man was fated to die ten to twenty years before the woman he loved, if he had to die at all, which at twenty-seven was difficult to believe. But there was also a time element for women which determined when they could have children and when they could not. Galen was an only child. His parents were high school teachers in Knoxville, Tennessee. His mother married late. She had been considered a spinster before his father came along, the new coach in town, and swept her off her feet, after his divorce became final. All of Galen's aunts and uncles asked him if he thought it a shame that his parents were so old, but it never bothered him. They were his parents; and as long as he didn't get on their nerves or get into trouble with the neighbours, they let him do pretty much what he wanted to, except his father never let him go out for football. He said there were too many injuries.

Galen's regret was being an only child but his mother was forty when she had him and she was too afraid to try to have another. Grace was now thirty-eight.

He knew Grace loved him. They could be married and she could get pregnant right away. Then they could have another one eighteen months after the first. He knew a lot of people who spaced their children eighteen months apart. It seemed ideal to him. Grace, if she didn't want to be bothered with the day-to-day mothering, could hire a nanny. She had the money. But he wanted those children. He had reached the stage in his life where he sought the solidity that a wife and family would give him. He wasn't terribly driven. Galen understood that. He knew that for him having a middling career and painting on the side would be enough. If he had that family to love.

Grace was afraid. 'There's a lot you don't know about me,' she would sometimes say in the depths of the night. What deathly secret could it be? True, one had to pry Grace's life from her or discover it on the front pages of the paper, like with Tommy Patterson, her former husband, whom she had told Galen nothing about. But Galen couldn't believe there was anything deep and dark about Grace.

He could arrange for her to get pregnant. After he told her that he didn't particularly mind using condoms, she left birth control up to him. He could just forget one night when he knew she was fertile, and he always knew because she was the type of woman who went into heat. But then what if she did get pregnant that way and decided to have an abortion? That would end it for him, shatter the entire romance. And he didn't want to lose her comfort.

He sighed. It was a problem. It was something they would have to work on.

101

As he pulled his car into the driveway, he noted Grace's was missing. Damn. Did this mean he'd have to make dinner? He hoped not. He wasn't in the mood to cook tonight. She'd have to settle for frozen food.

He unlocked the door to the kitchen and discovered a note from Grace on the table. "Toothache. At dentist. Will bring something back from Cantata's."

Italian. Did he really feel like Italian tonight? Well, Galen supposed it was better than cooking himself. He walked through the kitchen, into the hall and on to the living room, flickinnng on the lights as he did so. There was a huge bouquet of flowers on the coffee table in the living room. What a still life they would make. And their perfume delighted him. He walked over to the table and looked down at them, his eye spotting the card. "Grace, my love. Please say you forgive me. You're the only romance I'll ever cherish. Craig."

Craig? Who the hell was Craig? The only Craig he had heard Grace mention was Craig Epstein, her editor. What was he doing sending her flowers? Still, if Grace had anything to hide, she would have put the flowers in her workroom. Wouldn't she? Unless she were planning to torture Galen with them. Damn it! Maybe he should call the dentist to find out. But no. That would make him look stupid. Grace would call him her puppy again, and he would get annoyed. He marched into the downstairs study and left his portfolio case alongside his chair. Then he went upstairs to the bedroom to change into something even more casual than what he was wearing.

Back downstairs he went into the hallway to check the answering machine. Maybe she had called and left another message for him, or maybe Craig Whoever had called and Galen could find out more: 'Grace, this is Edna. What's it to be with Tommy's papers? I have so many offers here you wouldn't believe it. I called Craig. He honestly loves the idea of a sequel to LOVE IS A WALTZ. What about going into a contract for several books? I know you don't like to do that, but Craig is ripe for the picking. How long would it take to slap together something by Tommy? Something like NOTES FROM A WANDERING MIND. That way you don't even have to open all the boxes. Call me. We've got to move on this while interest is still high.'

'Grace, dear, it's Craig. Why have you left me pining away for your answer to a very simple question: How much do you want? Did you like the flowers? They cost a fortune. Let's bridge our differences and get on with our task of enlightening the American public. Call. Or must I come there on my knees over broken glass? Oops. Sorry for the suggestion.'

'Is this Grace Mandling's residence? It's so hard to tell from your cryptic message, especially since a man left it. I know I reached the number I dialled and that you'll get back to me as soon as possible if I leave my message at the sound of the beep, but who are you? I'm Holly Berrenson, a feature writer for *People* magazine. I'm sure you've had many offers before, but we'd like you to tell your story the way you want it to be told. I suppose you realize that the next issue of the *National Inquirer* has an article on you and Tommy called "The King and Queen of Love". It has some really revealing stuff in there, like tales of bigamy and quickie marriages and divorces. I understand there was even a child, stillborn. Wouldn't it be better for you to tell us your side of the story, instead of letting it linger in the mud of a million minds? Here's my number. Call me.'

Galen rewound the tape and listened to the messages again. Again, the last one blew him away. Grace pregnant? Bigamy? What was all this shit? Why did she never tell him anything?

He retreated to the solitude of his study. He sat in the dark, realizing only too well that he was a mere plaything to Grace Mandling. There was neither love nor trust between them.


Grace returned home with one side of her pleasantly formed face puffed up with novocaine. She was definitely considering changing dentists. This one kept finding decay where she knew none could possibly exist. Did he delight in giving her pain?

She got manicotti from Cantata's. She figured in an hour or so when she denumbed, this would be soft enough for her and Galen to eat.

She pulled in well away from Galen's station wagon. She was always afraid in the early morning hours he would dent her car when he backed out. He was always in a rush to get to his parking spot in the shopping mall and then dash to the bus. For Christmas this year, or maybe for his birthday, she was going to get him a jeep, four-wheel drive. Sometimes she worried about him, coming home late at night from the city, especially when it snowed. The jeep should be secure. She didn't want anything to happen to him, not that she was ever going to admit to him how much she needed him. There was no good in making him feel too secure.

'Galen!' she called, as she entered the kitchen. Her note was still on the table. But he must have seen it. Yes. The light was on in the hall, and in the living room. All the men she had ever known hated the dark. She liked the dark. She could walk around the house in total darkness and not bump into anything. But Galen turned on lights wherever he went and never turned them off when he left a room. She should really make him pay the electric bills.

'Galen!' she called from the living room. Craig's flowers blossomed out toward her. She went over and took a sniff. She loved flowers. They made her feel so – so feminine. It was a dirty trick of Craig's to send them.

Hmm. Maybe Galen was upstairs. She went up to their bedroom and found that he had indeed been there. The light was on and his city clothes were scattered at the edge of the bed. But the bathroom door was open. She turned off the light and went to the window. There were no lights on in his shed, so he wasn't there.

Oh well. Maybe he went out for a walk or something. Sometimes it was harder to judge Galen's moods than it was her own, and she was moody enough. She hopped downstairs and put the manicotti in the refrigerator. Then she went to check her answering machine. Oh damn. The light was blinking furiously. No one called her before Tommy died. And now this. It was so totally unfair. She reversed the tape and listened to the messages. Then Grace knew where Galen was.

'Hi,' she said, as she stood in the doorway of his little study.

He was sitting in the dark. She could see his slight figure outlined on the couch. Carefully, she stepped around his portfolio and sat down next to him. She was very close. Their hips and torsos touched. But he didn't say anything. He didn't even move.

'You listened to the messages,' she told him. 'I'm sorry. I suppose you want to know how much of what that jerky *People* writer said was true. I'm afraid it's all true. When Tommy married me, he was already married to Odelle. By the time I found out, I was pregnant. So when Tommy's divorce became final, my father arranged a quick marriage and divorce in the same courthouse, the same hour. The baby was born with only half a heart. Symbolic, huh? You see, Galen, I had every intention of keeping that child and raising it, loving it, being a mother, even though by then I hated its father. I went through the pain of childbirth and got death in return. I was young then. Stronger. Dumber.'

She thought that about covered the *People* call. She took Galen's hand and gave it a squeeze. He didn't respond. She sighed. He was such a little boy. But then all men were. Whose fallacy was it that men were put on earth to take care of women? They couldn't even take care of themselves. 'What do you want me to say?' she asked Galen with some asperity.

'I want you to explain to me why the hell you never told me about any of this,' he shot back.

'Because it was none of your business. It has nothing to do with us. This is past history. You should remember I have a lot more past history than you do.'

104

'Oh, cut it out, Grace. You use our age difference as an excuse for everything. None of my business,' he repeated disgustedly. 'I've been living with you for over two years. I'm in love with you. I want to marry you. I want to get you pregnant. And all of what happened before is none of my business?'

'That's right. It has no bearing on us.'

'Hasn't it?'

Grace sank back and let go of his hand. He turned to her and placed his hand roughly on her cheek. 'Ahh!' she screamed and slapped his hand away.

'What!'

'My tooth!'

'Oh, Jesus, Grace, I'm sorry.' He put his head against her breasts and she held him tight and rocked him. What did she need a baby for? She had Galen.

'You're afraid to have a child,' he told her. 'I understand that now. But things have changed. Medically. They have so many tests that can be done to see if the baby is okay. And if it's not? Well, hell, it can be aborted. We can try again. I know it sounds cold and cruel, but it's done all the time. See, there won't be a problem. We'll have a healthy child. We'll be a family.'

'You're asking too much,' she warned him.

'Why? What am I asking for?'

'An act of faith. I don't have any. I'm not young. You are. The future came and went for me a long time ago.'

'You're thirty-eight, for Chrissake's, Grace! Stop talking as if you're at death's door! I'm sick of it! You want to drive me away? You want to spoil paradise? Fine. You've done it!'

He stood up and rushed out of the room. Grace heard his footsteps on the stairs as he headed toward their bedroom. To pack? Ah, impetuous youth. She had been impetuous once. Experience taught her where it got her.

She walked slowly from Galen's study, past the living room, into the hall. 'Galen, do you want to have the manicotti first, or should I pack you some to go?'

The phone rang. Grace checked the hall clock. Six-thirty. It had to be someone trying to sell her something. They always called at the dinner hour. That's because no one was home at any other time any more. She found these calls both annoying and insulting. She especially hated it when these sales people called her Grace, as if she had known them for years. She grabbed the phone, at last having someone to really unload on. 'Yes,' she practically shouted into the phone.

'I'd recognize your voice anywhere, Grace. This is Odelle.'

105

'Odelle,' Grace said. 'Listen, this isn't a good time. Galen's about to walk out on me. It seems the *National Inquirer* is doing an in-depth story of that time at the University of Michigan, which both of us remember all too well.'

'Why should that bother Galen?'

'A: he didn't know about it. B: he wants a child.'

'You should have a child, Grace. I've always said it would make your romances more realistic.'

'Then they wouldn't sell.'

'Trudi called me earlier.'

'Another case of Odelle Hampton taking the troubles of the world on her shoulders. You must believe there's a heaven, Odelle.'

'Only because I hope there's also a hell. For Tommy.'

'Why? He'd only write a book about it that would become a best seller. So what's with Trudi? I thought she was safely locked up at some clinic.'

'She is, but she almost found a way to get drugs. Fortunately, I've blocked that path. And also, Grace, I was wondering what you've decided to do about – '

'Tommy's papers? Everyone's been wondering about that, Odelle. To be honest with you, and this is sheer sincerity here, I don't know. The thought of touching anything of his revolts me. And yet, as they say, money is green. However, ethically, can I really force myself to deceive the public any longer?'

'They won't care, dear. Look, you know what I'm concerned about. I just think with that money, we can do so much good. It's time something good came from Tommy Patterson.'

'I don't know,' Grace said tiredly.

'You owe me,' Odelle reminded her.

Grace smiled. 'I know.'

'And, Grace, one other thing. Get pregnant.'

Grace was still smiling when Galen came into the kitchen, haphazardly packed. He looked so much like a little boy about to run away from home, it broke her heart. Was he old enough to have children? What if in a few years they separated and there was some gigantic custody battle? She got custody and he kidnapped their child during his visitation? She never saw the child again, or only on milk cartons?

God, why was everything in her life a plot?

'What about a prenuptial agreement?' she suggested, as Galen stood stupidly before her.

'What about one?'

'Not only covering financial matters but also child custody.'

'Child custody?'

106

'In case of divorce. If I have a child, I don't want to lose it.'

'Well, I don't want to lose the child, either. But, first of all, I wouldn't get a divorce.'

'Famous last words.'

'Second, we're both adults. If that eventuality ever came up, we would handle it in a civilized fashion.'

She laughed at him. 'You're such an innocent, Galen. You say you're in love with me; you believe that love conquers all. You don't even know the meaning of love. Love is passion, anger, even hatred. But most of all, love is getting even.'

## Chapter 19

# Christmas in Chicago, 1972

'But I don't believe in Santa Claus any more,' Julia Hampton whined. She was going through her ballet stage and insisted on wearing her hair long and scraggy so that twice a week it could be put up in a dancer's bun, which lasted for all of the one hour each class took. Now she wore her light brown hair down, pinned back behind her ears by two butterfly barrettes. She was still thin, but Odelle didn't as yet have the heart to tell her daughter that her legs were not those of a dancer. Julia was mostly torso, like her mother.

'I haven't believed in Santa for the last two years,' Julia confessed. 'So why should I pretend any more?'

'For your brother's sake, if nothing else,' Odelle said, as she wheeled Luke's pushchair through the crowded aisles of Marshall Field's downtown Chicago store. What madness had possessed her to bring the children down here on the Saturday before Christmas? This must be one of the sacrifices mothers make. If only Sy were home. But no. He was in Borneo or some other place she had only vaguely heard of before.

'If there really were a Santa Claus, then why do all these strange presents I get always come from the same countries Daddy works in?' Julia asked.

Just then Odelle felt the pushchair tipping forward. 'Sit down, Luke!' Jesus Christ, she was going to have a nervous breakdown right in the middle of Marshall Field's. Lord help her. All she felt like giving her kids for Christmas now was a bat across the teeth. Control, Odelle! she warned herself. 'Let's find Santa,' she suggested cheerfully.

'I won't sit on his lap,' Julia warned.

'Fine. Just walk Luke up to Santa and let the elves take a picture of the two of you.'

'Mommy, there aren't any such things as elves!'

The line to Santa was long and winding with brattier kids than hers standing in it. Odelle felt grateful. She'd thought perhaps God had handed her the worst of the lot. Maybe she should have gone home to Connecticut for this Christmas, but it was such a hassle to travel with two children. Plus, Sy claimed he was going to try to get home for the holidays.

Sometimes she resented Sy a great deal, though she knew she was being unfair. After all, he travelled before they were married. Why should he stop now? On the other hand, he and his friend didn't have to set up as consultants on their own. They could have kept working for Aramco. But Sy wanted to be his own boss, taking on himself both the risks and the profits. So two months ago they had moved from New York to Glencoe, Illinois, just outside Chicago. Why Chicago she had no idea. She supposed she should be grateful it wasn't Houston with its hot, muggy weather. Of course, the Midwest with its snow and wind wasn't much to write home about either.

Odelle supposed she had made a good choice marrying Sy. He certainly was loyal – in his own way. It was he who suggested that he adopt Julia, and she was glad of it. It would be easier for her to have the same last name as the rest of the family. Furthermore, it would give Odelle less reason to contemplate her disastrous first marriage to Tom Patterson, a man Julia had never really known. It was nice to hear her now refer to Sy as 'Daddy' instead of 'Uncle Sy', as she had before they were married and for a while afterwards also. And Julia hadn't even been particularly jealous when Luke came along almost ten months after the wedding. She proved herself to be a great little helper.

Still, despite the pleasing domesticity in her life, the fact that now that she was married, she no longer had to work, Odelle felt a certain dissatisfaction. She was lonely. She felt cut off. She was away from her family. Her friends were either in Brooklyn or New York. Here she was a stranger. She didn't even have the social life she would have had if Sy worked normal hours. There were no business acquaintances to entertain. And when Sy did have visitors to Chicago to discuss business, he took them out on the town. 'They're not the sort of people you'd really enjoy meeting,' he assured her. So she was basically left alone to make her own life, and she wasn't really doing too good a job of it.

She jointed the PTA at Julia's elementary school. But she really didn't volunteer to do much. With the move and Luke being only fifteen months old, she didn't have much energy left for volunteering. She spent her day rising early enough to get Julia off to school, then feeding Luke and clearing away the breakfast. Then she would take him out for a stroll or they would do their grocery shopping. There wasn't a playground where mothers gathered. And while the neighbours were friendly enough, she didn't really know any of them that well. So, it was a hectic, busy life but not really a satisfying one. Yet. But she had known worse times in her life; she could hang on.

They were nearing the head of the line. Odelle removed Luke from the stroller. He stood wobbling on his feet. Odelle took a comb out of her pocket and pushed it through his thin, reddish locks. Julia was primping all by herself. 'Okay, you're on,' Odelle said. 'Remember to smile.'

Odelle grinned as Santa took Luke on to his lap and asked him what he wanted for Christmas. Luke stuffed his fist in his mouth and looked as if he were about to cry. Meanwhile, Julia pronounced in a loud voice, 'I don't believe in Santa Claus. You're just a fake.'

Santa looked as if he could kill – tears began streaming down Luke's face, while Julia stood there with a smug expression on her face. The elf took their picture and caught this moment for posterity. Odelle paid for a print, then captured her children at the other end of the line, where the elf handed each a candy cane. 'There now,' Odelle said grimly, 'wasn't that fun?'

'Can we go look at the toys now?' Julia asked. 'Or maybe let's go way up to the top and see the tree. Or – '

Odelle plopped Luke back down into his chair. 'We've got to get Daddy a Christmas gift.'

'Why? You said he probably wouldn't be coming home for Christmas.'

'Well what if he does? It wouldn't be nice not to have a present for him.'

Julia smirked. 'Why don't we just let Santa bring him one.'

Odelle was pleased to find that the men's department wasn't as crowded as the rest of the store and there definitely weren't as many children around. Of course, hers made up for that. While she was checking one of the dress shirts, Luke somehow managed to reach out and grab a mannequin, which was now tipping desperately from side to side.

'Mommy!'

Odelle glanced up in horror as the figure in double-breasted pinstripe looked as if it were about to tumble on to her son. She reached out to forestall the calamity and found she was not the only one to have noticed the impending carriage crusher. Another woman had grabbed for the dummy also. Together they soon stood it upright once again, while Luke pounded on his stroller's tray, delighted by all the activity.

110

'Thank you so much, I – ' Odelle began. But then she stopped because there was something very striking about the woman before her, and it wasn't just the fact that she was well dressed, with a straight skirt, frilly blouse and heels. It was her hair, the same sort of hair that –

'Mrs Patterson?' the woman wondered.

'You're – '

'Grace. Grace Mandling.'

'Oh my God. I can't believe it! I saw your face, but then I thought it couldn't be because what would you be doing in Chicago?'

'I work here. I'm a buyer. Women's sportswear.'

They stood staring at each other until Grace continued by saying, 'Are these your children? Well, that's a silly question. Of course they are. But why are you in Chicago?'

'I – I live here now.'

'Really?'

'I remarried and had Luke,' she explained, indicating the trouble-maker in the pushchair. 'We moved out to Chicago in September. Look, can I buy you coffee or anything? At least for saving my son from getting the braining he deserved.'

Grace looked at her watch. 'Sure. That would be fine.'

Coffee turned out to be an early lunch. The line to the restaurant was long but moving briskly. Odelle just had enough time to find the ladies' room for Julia, while Grace chanced it by rocking Luke back and forth in the stroller. When Odelle returned, she found her son hadn't even noticed she was missing. They were soon being led to a table next to four old ladies, who gave the children very doubtful looks. 'Julia, we have to behave in here,' Odelle warned.

Grace smiled. 'Everything's so mad at Christmas time. It's not going to matter.'

It did seem to matter to the four old ladies. They wanted a nice, dignified, chatty lunch. Odelle's children sort of put a damper on that, especially a drooling Luke. But Odelle and Grace chose to ignore Julia and Luke, especially since they were being as quiet as children can be when out in public. Instead the two former wives of Tommy Patterson concentrated on what had happened to them since their first meeting in Tommy's boarding house.

'I knew you were pregnant,' Odelle said, when Grace finished her recital. 'Wayne Harris told me. But after the final divorce papers came through, I sort of lost touch with the situation. Sy and I were just so happy to be married. I'm really sorry you lost the child.'

Grace shrugged. 'My parents say it's for the best. It was awful though. Really awful. Anyway, it gave me a chance to finish my education. And here I am.'

111

'Do you like working for Marshall Field's?'

Grace grimaced. 'What else could I do with a degree in English?'

'What did you want to do?' Odelle wondered.

'Write,' Grace confessed shyly. 'Not that I was any good at it. I entered all the literary contests that last year at Michigan. All the winners were in my writing class. But I wasn't among them. So.' She shrugged again. 'I guess I just wasn't good enough.'

'You never know. You have to keep plugging away at that sort of thing.'

'No time now. I've got to earn a living.'

Odelle sighed knowingly. 'I'm glad I'm out of that rat race.'

Grace laughed. 'You don't sound very liberated.'

'I was liberated after Tom dumped me. Believe me, it's not all it's cracked up to be. Call me old-fashioned or just unambitious, but I enjoy staying home, taking care of the kids. Besides, with Sy gone most of the time, who else would do it?'

'You're lucky. To have a life you find satisfying. Sometimes I feel I'm just drifting through mine,' Grace mused.

'You haven't found anyone yet.'

Grace laughed. 'Women aren't supposed to need to find anyone any more, Odelle. But to answer your question, no, I haven't met Mr Right. I'd like to fall in love. It's just – ever since Tommy, I've had this fear that I'm not bright enough to make the right choices. But it would be nice to love someone, especially at this time of year when it can get so lonely.'

'But you're going home to Grand Rapids for Christmas, aren't you?'

'No. The store needs me, or so they have informed me. I'd be spending most of Christmas day travelling if I tried to make it to Grand Rapids and back before the after-Christmas sale. So I'll be having frozen turkey dinner.'

'Nonsense.'

'Not nonsense at all. My roommate for the last year has met her Prince Charming, and she's taking him home for the holidays.'

'You'll come and have Christmas dinner with me.'

Grace looked shocked. 'I couldn't.'

'Why not? Sy's in God knows what jungle. Even if he made it home, he'd be delighted to have you. And if he doesn't come home, I'm going to be alone too. If you discount these two delightful children,' she added, giving her offspring a baleful look. 'I'll make turkey, stuffing, cranberry sauce, the works. What about it?'

'Well – '

'Please. It'll make my holiday much merrier. Come Christmas Eve. There's a spare bedroom and everything.'

Grace brightened. 'You know, Odelle, I think I'm going to take you up on your offer.'

'Great! We can discuss old times.'

'Foolish mistakes.'

'Innocence.'

'Love,' Grace concluded.

Like the man who came to dinner, Grace Mandling came and she didn't leave. Not that she broke a leg or anything, but the two women discovered they enjoyed each other's company. Sy didn't make it home that Christmas or for New Year. He did come home for Valentine's Day, and his family had his carefully wrapped presents saved for him. By that time, Grace had moved permanently into the spare room. Odelle convinced her to do so by asking why she should bother to look for a roommate to replace the one getting married when it was just as easy for both to move out. With the train it was a fast commute into the city. Grace didn't have to pay rent, just for her food.

If Sy ever had a mind to object, he changed his mind when he noticed how contented Odelle was. Plus, they now had a built in babysitter for times when he was home. It was strange, he supposed, two former wives of the same man under one roof, but he had seen stranger customs in countries where he worked. And was he really around long enough to complain?

Odelle found herself re-energized by knowing Grace would be there in the evening in case there was anything she wanted to do. She got involved in several district classes, one called "How to Parent" and another "Make You Own Tiles". Those two evenings out a week were heaven. She made friends in the community, and she began to feel at home.

But all good things must come to an end, and this particularly heavenly arrangement came crashing to a halt the week after Nixon resigned from the Presidency in August 1974. Amazingly, Sly was home at the time. That was good because otherwise Odelle might have humiliated herself by begging Grace to stay; though she doubted whether anything would have stopped Aunt Grace, as Julia called her, from leaving.

Grace came home with a copy of *Rags* in her hand. Odelle had seen her walking around with this particular magazine printed on fuzzy newsprint before, but had never paid much attention. Odelle assumed it had something to do with Grace's work as a buyer for Marshall Field's. But Odelle was mistaken. *Rags* was actually devoted to experimental fiction and political manifestos.

Odelle remembered the moment of Grace's announced departure perfectly. Sy and she were home enjoying the cocktail hour, that

113

fabulous hour between five and six she had learned about at her mother's knee. The cocktail hour followed the children's hour, and it was so desperately needed by the time the children's hour was over. Sy made a perfect martini, one of the many reasons she loved him. They were sitting calmly in the living room. As they sipped their drinks and nibbled on cheese and crackers with a side of raw vegetables, Grace stormed into the house and tossed *Rags* down on the Jarlsberg cheese.

'Something wrong?' Sy surmised.

'Read it!' she sort of growled. Her expression didn't even brighten when Luke came out of the family room with the request that Aunt Grace come and inspect his Lego rocket ship. 'Not now, darling,' she said, and slammed herself into the arm chair opposite Sy and Odelle.

Odelle picked up the magazine and thumbed through it. What exactly was she supposed to read? She thought maybe she'd better study the table of contents. There it was! "The Age of Women", by Grace Mandling. 'Why, Grace, that's wonderful! You got a story published!' she exclaimed, as she handed the magazine to Sy.

'I never knew you wrote, Grace,' Sy said.

'Oh, Sy, how many times have I told you that's what Grace really wants to do,' Odelle chided.

'So if your story was published, what are you so upset about?' Sy wondered.

'You haven't read the entire table of contents,' Grace remarked.

Sy went down the list while Odelle peeked over his shoulder. "Why I Went to Canada", by Tommy Patterson. 'Oh my,' Odelle said.

'Jesus,' Sy agreed.

'I'm not going to read it,' Odelle promised, mainly herself.

'I already did. On the train ride home,' Grace said. 'He went to Canada, if you can believe this, not to escape possible bigamy charges or child support payments. He went to Canada because of his fear of what was happening to this great nation of ours. He went to Canada because he refused to be netted by an unlawful draft. As if he was ever in danger of being drafted. At his age, in his condition! He went to Canada to show solidarity with his brothers. He claims he was a member of the underground railway which led soldiers about to be shipped out to Vietnam from the ports of California to the streets of Vancouver. And now, with the impending downfall of Richard Nixon, Tommy Patterson feels the time has come. His country needs him. He is returning to our shores. I hate him! There is murder in my heart.'

They were all silent for a while, catching just a hint – thank God – of Julia practising her flute. 'Well, maybe he'll be arrested,' Sy suggested hopefully.

114

'It's funny, you know, you and him being published in the same magazine, the same issue,' Odelle noted.

'If you'll read the biographies in the back of *Rags*,' Grace suggested, 'you'll discover that Tommy is having his Canadian diaries published by the John Brown Society. It's to be called MY YEARS IN THE WILDERNESS: A SPIRITUAL SEARCH FOR THE MEANING OF LIFE.'

'Darling, you'd better pour me another martini,' Odelle requested of her husband.

'The editors say that Tommy Patterson is at the forefront of American thought.'

'Of course, Americans don't think much,' Sy pointed out. 'We're not really a philosophically attuned society.'

'Meanwhile, I'm a buyer at Marshall Field's,' Grace said bitterly. 'But no more. I quit. I handed in my two weeks' notice.'

'Grace!' Odelle was shocked. 'What are you going to do?'

'I'm going up to the University of Iowa. They have a writers' program there, and I'm going to be admitted to it.'

'Grace, that's a very well-known program,' Sy said. 'Don't you have to apply and submit samples of work and things like that?'

'I'm sure you do. But I'll go up there and work for a semester before I'm admitted, if I have to. That way at least I'll establish residence. But I'm not going to waste any more of my life while people like Tommy are acclaimed American cultural heroes. His voice has to be drowned out. And I'll do it with my own, if I have to.'

So Odelle didn't plead. She understood it was time for Grace to move on. And as much as it killed her and would play havoc with the very comfortable life Grace had helped establish for her, Odelle wished Grace all the luck in the world. Then she gave her one last piece of advice. 'Don't try to compete with Tommy, Grace. You'll never win. In this world, evil triumphs.'

## Chapter 20

# Rip Me Apart, Why Don't Ya!

Grace Mandling sat in class, listened carefully and tried to under-stand. She knew she was not one of these people yet; she had a lot of catching up to do. Her work was so primitive compared to the labyrinths of the soul traced by her fellow students in narrative writing at the University of Iowa Writers Workshop. Everyone had a statement to make. She, as yet, only existed. That was her problem. Existence was minimal. She needed to flower forth with a philosophy of her own being.

Her philosophy for the last six months had been one of survival. The Administration, the big A of college life, as in Asshole, informed her there was no way she could get into the Writers Workshop program on less than a month's notice – unless it was overwhelmingly obvious that she was fearsomely talented and gifted. An upturned nose by one of the registrars seemed to indicate Grace did not fall into that category.

Why had she been so impetuous? She could have stayed at Odelle's and applied from there. But it was too late. She had quit her job at Marshall Field's and moved to Iowa City before she found out she would have to wait at least a semester.

She found an apartment in one of the newer buildings of Iowa City, and bought a car. Both financial obligations cut deeply into her financial reserves. So she took up waitressing. She understood that all real writers had at one time been waitresses or waiters, that she was really serving herself more than the public, piling up the real life experiences she would soon be able to use in her fiction. Though at the end of the day she could never figure out exactly what knowledge she was accumulating, except that standing on one's feet for long periods of time made them hurt, people were rude, and students didn't leave big tips. But it didn't matter. This was her time in a garret, so to speak, and she was ready to suffer.

Actually, she never found out what real suffering was until she walked into her narrative writing course. Here she was, twenty-five years old, and she felt like little girl lost. Her problem was she had no cause, no raison d'être that could stir the soul.

There were twelve people in her class. A Vietnam vet had trouble bringing his work in on time because he had this slight problem with heroin. And when he did read for the class, it was so elemental, like See Spot Run. Their professor and mentor Leslie Brownlow called it Hemingwayesque. If Grace were to label the writing, she would call it mentally disturbed. She sat well away from Mr Vietnam.

On the other hand, there was a draft resistor who had spent a year in prison rather than fight in Vietnam. He came with stories of prison violence, rapes, knifings, love affairs. Talk about life experiences!

In these intimidating classes, Grace usually sat next to Michelle. She was a political lesbian. In actuality, she was a heterosexual, but she felt strongly that men were users and oppressors to be scorned and avoided. However, she didn't really like women all that much because, 'their minds aren't quick enough'. Her head was in the right place, she assured Grace. It was just that her heart and body kept wandering.

Grace preferred Michelle and her political rantings to Sarah, who was the star of the class, the one Leslie Brownlow foretold would go far. To Grace, Sarah's narratives were like her days – long, drawn-out, and boring. One of her short stories focused exclusively on an old woman arranging gladioli in a vase. 'It's all about life, isn't it?' Leslie said. 'About that space between life and death that we call time.'

Another story of Sarah's centred on a husband of ten years who was taking a carpentry class after work. The legs of the table he was making were uneven, so he kept sawing away at each of them, trying to make the table stand without rocking. 'Yes,' Leslie intoned, 'despite his yearning, he finds within himself the inability to conform, to accept the inevitable, and you've captured it perfectly, Sarah.'

Were they sleeping together? Grace wondered, until one of Sarah's stories was accepted by the *New Yorker*. They didn't even ask her to edit it! It made Grace's poor effort in *Rags* seem pretty pitiful.

Grace's first story to be presented to the class was about hypocrisy. She thought it had a lot going for it that would appeal to several members of the class. It was about a man and a woman. They lived together without benefit of clergy because they were making a statement. They were both artists. The man had a fetish for dead animals. He captured animals, killed them, painted their dead portraits, then left the models to rot around the house they shared. He had become quite the *in* artist within a certain crowd. The woman

117

focused on enamel work and was much less successful financially. But her art meant as much to her as the man's did to him. The man pretended to encourage her, but his every act was meant to undercut her. He left the household chores to her. He did things troubling to her psyche, like gutting a goat in the bathtub. He insisted she set aside the project she was working on and make jewellery to sell at a Christmas craft show. In the end, she lost confidence in herself as an artist and got pregnant. He had her where he wanted her.

'Lief gazed fondly down upon his woman,' Grace read her last paragraph. 'And Erica looked up into his eyes and knew she had been betrayed. She had betrayed herself.'

Grace put down the neatly typed pages of her story and looked up at the silent faces surrounding her in the seminar's circle. She was nervous. She would admit to that. When she began reading, her voice trembled. But as the strength of her story rose within her, she became steady and sure. She finished her reading with the power of her conviction. She knew she had written a first-rate story.

'I had trouble with your use of language,' Margaret bounced in after that first, dramatic, empty pause. Grace wasn't worried. Margaret had trouble with everyone's language. 'It's too – pedestrian. People *use* language like that. You can hear it every day on the street. Why would one want to read it?'

'Well – '

'Perhaps you should invest in a good thesaurus.'

'But words are – '

'Where were your images?' Sarah wondered.

'They were there,' William said. 'You just didn't see them because they were so obvious. Dead animals. God!'

'Why was she living with this guy anyway?' Michelle wondered. 'I mean, it was obvious he wanted to see her dead. It was too obvious that he wanted to kill her spirit. That was the symbolism behind the dead animals, right?'

'Why get pregnant when her child might have to go off and fight in a war?' Vietnam vet asked.

'I don't understand why she worked in enamel,' Cell Block No. 1 confessed. 'What was the meaning behind that?'

'There was no meaning. It just – ' Grace started to explain.

'Grace,' Leslie Brownlow cut in, and everyone in the class leaned forward to catch his pronouncement. 'I think what we're saying is, this has been done before. Love, as a subject for literature, is passé.'

'Love is passé?' she questioned.

'Oh, not for commercial artists, of course. But we're serious in here. We're trying to advance writing to a new plateau. We want to be

118

able to capture each second of every day. We want to show the significance of ordinary actions. Your effort was melodramatic at best. Let's not rebreak old ground. Okay?'

After the reading of her story and the critique thereof, Grace found herself shunned. Her classmates avoided her like the plague, to use a cliché no one else would bother with. She was cut off from intimate conversation about word usage and writer's block, grants and new literary magazines. They made it obvious that they didn't think she had it as a writer.

At the end of the term, Leslie Brownlow approached her. This was after she had read a second story, a whimsical piece about a woman and her seeing eye cat, and again garnered the same censorious reaction. Leslie suggested she might be happier in another field.

'But I know I'm meant to be a writer,' she insisted.

He looked at her askance, not wanting to say it but suggesting few shared her supreme faith. 'Maybe you should try journalism,' he meant to comfort. 'All I want you to understand is that students here are seriously dedicated to their art. Many will go on to get Ph.D.'s in creative writing, so that they may go out to other schools and spread our gospel of good writing. I'm afraid, Grace, that I cannot in all honesty encourage you to do likewise.'

She might have taken Leslie Brownlow's words to heart if she hadn't the same day entered the one bookstore at the University of Iowa that carried every little literary magazine in existence, plus all the mainstream periodicals. There she found on the front page of the *New York Review of Books* a rave for Tommy Patterson's MY YEARS IN THE WILDERNESS: A SPIRITUAL SEARCH FOR THE MEANING OF LIFE. Tommy was called "a major voice of the emerging generation." And she was called a dud!

She *had* to stay on at Iowa. Now, if ever, she must show everybody how wrong they were. She was talented. She knew it. And somehow Grace Mandling was determined to prove it!

## Chapter 21

# Faces in the Mirror

They left the Eden of Iowa together, outcasts from a sodden plain. Eve was white; Adam was black. It was to be the story of their lives together.

Grace Mandling met Darrell Templeton in a seminar called "Controlling Your Epic". She hadn't written an epic as yet; but she knew, when she did, it would need to be controlled. Meanwhile, a second short story of hers had been published, this one in the *North/South Review*. She sent the tear sheets to Leslie Brownlow in hopes of obtaining admission of hasty judgment on his part. She received by return campus mail a note that said, "I see you're still trying." God! The impertinent prig!

But Leslie Brownlow affected her less now that she had a more important emotional commitment in her life, more important even than her writing: Darrell Templeton. Meeting Darrell in her class on "Controlling Your Epic" simply confirmed her belief in the goodness of Cupid, who waits for us in the most unexpected of places.

She wasn't even looking for a lover when she entered the classroom, whose second-storey window opened out on to the branches of a gothic oak. Darrell was the one who started what would turn out to be their intense, conversational duet of the spirit. He asked what she was working on. It was a matter-of-fact question because everyone was working on something. That's why they were at the Writers Workshop. Though there was a class devoted to writer's block and how to get over it.

In answer to Darrell's interrogatory, Grace had to say something, even though at the time she was merely thinking, trying to gather the threads of a story together. But thinking seemed so – so passive. So she said she was working on women and their concept of freedom. That was safe enough. All the women at Iowa were trying to deal with the revolution in choices that suddenly confronted them. The new world came perhaps a bit before they were ready for it.

'And you?' she replied politely.

'The struggle for black liberation.'

Safe. They were both playing it very safe. Matter of fact, the entire length of their affair, she never admitted to him that the theme that most attracted her was love, and he never admitted to her that his theme was black alienation. Had they been truthful with one another in the beginning, they probably never would have found the common ground to get together. However, since they both claimed to be dealing with liberation, there was a lot to discuss. They started having coffee together after class. They went to the movies and the theatre. They joined other friends at poetry readings, offering their own scintillating comments on images and the colour of words, more for each other than for anyone else. Finally, they went to bed.

What was it that attracted her to Darrell? Grace pondered late at night, once again lying on tangled white sheets with some man, though this time one wholly unlike Tommy Patterson, thank God! Was it Darrell's blackness? In truth, he was light enough to have passed as a fraternity man with a tan. Was it the cultural gap between them? Actually, Darrell's mother was a school teacher, his father an auto worker in Detroit. (What was it? she later had to wonder in her agony of self-reproach when she tried to pin it down. Her continued lack of judgment when it came to men?)

Or was it her simple love of love? She was in love: with Darrell, with herself, with her daring. They were the odd couple, a revolutionary couple, even in a university town. They would walk down the street together and draw stares. It excited her. It meant she was finally accomplishing something. She was receiving notice as a liberated artist. She was different. She was to be applauded for her differences.

They suffered indignities together. They shared the silence of the insult. They both believed that pain made an artist grow. Maybe that was another reason why they chose each other.

Pain! Grace knew she received a sharp bout of it the day Darrell came to her apartment to announce he had received a Reiseman Fellowship to complete his novel. 'I didn't even know you had applied,' she said, shocked.

'I didn't want to tell you. I didn't want you to feel the hurt of rejection if it didn't come through. I wanted to spare you my humiliation.'

'But I told you I was applying,' Grace pointed out. 'You saw me. You helped me fill out the last part of the form. You even mailed it for me.'

They stood staring at each other. The first betrayal of intimacy cratered between them.

121

'Have you heard yet?' Darrell asked.

'No. Not yet.'

'Everybody's heard,' Darrell stated.

In her heart she thought black, black thoughts. Blacker than Darrell would ever be. In her heart she thought he had received the Reisemen because he was black. Minorities were in, while she was a woman and what did women have to say anyway? She would never admit in her heart or any place else that she wasn't good enough to win the Reiseman. She could not face an assessment that her work was light and trite and unfit for consideration as true literature. Grace knew in her soul – and she did have a soul – that she had something to say. She just didn't know what it was yet.

'Look,' Darrell said, 'I'm leaving the Workshop at the end of this semester.'

'Why?' Why would anyone leave this warm, cosy, killing environment?

'Because they have nothing more to teach me. I have to find my own voice.'

She was upset. Wasn't that just what she was standing there thinking herself? And yet she never came right out and said it. Others said it for her. Others formulated the words for her thoughts. Didn't she also, like Darrell, have a voice to find? There was still somewhere repressed within her the person she was going to become.

'Can you come with me?' Darrell wondered. 'I know it's a lot to ask, but I want you by my side. I don't think I could write without you there.'

And how could she refuse? Could Grace be responsible for the failure of another artist? She thought not. 'I don't know if I want to get married,' she said weakly, ready to be convinced.

Darrell looked stunned. 'I – well – marriage is in the future, isn't it? When we both get where we want to go.'

Even then, if she were to be truthful with herself – and what woman ever is when it comes to love? – she knew in her heart Darrell had no intention of marrying her. Ever. Still, wasn't marriage passé? It was an old-fashioned convention, suitable for some people, sure, but she and Darrell were too revolutionary, too creative, to follow standard conventions. She would go with him. Whither he wentest, her star was tied to his.

Darrell went to Chicago. They found an apartment near the University of Chicago where the quilted pattern of their skin colours would be of less interest to those around them. In two months her savings ran out. The Reiseman provided just enough money for one person not to starve. It did nothing for two people. 'I can't stop now,'

Darrell told her. So she approached Marshall Field's. She didn't get her old job back. She had been gone too long. Plus, she still wanted the flexibility to work when she wanted to, in order to continue contributing to America's belles lettres. So she got a job as a sales lady.

Her new job worked out well. She rose at six each morning, wrote until 8.30. Then she dressed and took the bus to Marshall Field's, where she worked all day, sometimes into the night. Upon coming home, she would make dinner for Darrell and herself, do the dishes, the laundry, watch a little television, then fall into a deep, dreamless sleep, the sleep of exhaustion. It was exhilarating what the freedom of women's liberation could do for one.

But her sacrifice was not in vain. She was rewarded by seeing Darrell blossom as a literary force. Pieces of his upcoming novel were being published in magazines and journals. Excitement was being generated. Darrell Templeton was going to make it as a literary super star, and she would be at his side!

She begged him all the time to let her read what he was writing, but he refused. He said he didn't want any comment on it until he was through and it was in galleys. She thought that strange. Here they were so intimate, and yet he refused to share his work with her. So she gleaned what she could from the published excerpts and encouraged him to forge on. Meanwhile, she was lucky enough to get a piece of fluff published in *Ladies Home Journal*, "Sales Ladies: Are They Human?" It was really quite amusing, and another article was requested of her. Perhaps fiction wasn't her thing. Maybe all this time she should have been concentrating on real life.

But what did she know of real life? She and Darrell were living a fairy-tale romance. The only time she saw glimmers of reality, aside from her job, was when she and Darrell visited Odelle Hampton, still ensconced in Glencoe, still spending half her life alone while Sy was out God knows where, searching for oil. Odelle and Sy Hampton were two of the few people Grace knew who were benefitting from the oil crisis. While others were waiting in line, fucking, shoving, assaulting and murdering each other to gain a full tank of gas, Odelle was considering building an addition on to her house.

It was a good time for Odelle. Julia was fourteen and in her first year of high school, while Luke had already started first grade. 'I cherish the freedom,' Odelle told Grace once when they were alone in the kitchen. Sy was home for that particular visit. He and Darrell were in the living room, watching the Cubs lose another game.

'Soon you'll have to think about getting a job,' Grace said thoughtlessly.

123

'Why?'

'Well – ' Grace was surprised that Odelle even had to ask. 'The children are in school. Surely you must get bored without anything to do.'

Odelle laughed. 'I have something to do. I spend about half an hour tidying the house. I go out to get groceries. I read. I work in the garden. I take my art classes. I've started taking an aerobics dancing class. Lots of fun.'

'But you don't *do* anything,' Grace protested.

'I've just told you what I do, Grace.'

'But, I mean, where's your career?'

'I have a career. I'm a wife and mother.'

Grace groaned and shook her head. 'I mean a real career, Odelle.'

'Like working as a sales lady to support the man I'm living with?' Odelle wondered.

'That's only to get money,' Grace objected, 'before both our careers take off. The galleys to Darrell's book should be in for proofing any week now.'

'And then?'

'And then he'll write another book. And I'll get more published.'

'Loved your article on sales ladies, by the way; though I still don't believe they're human.' Odelle turned to her more seriously and said, 'Look, Grace, be careful with this affair of yours, will you? I don't want to see you get hurt again.'

'You don't understand my relationship with Darrell.'

'I understand more than you think. You're giving everything to this person. Not everyone is the foolish romantic you are. What if Darrell some day decides to walk out on you?'

'Darrell's not the walking type.'

'And pigs can fly. There's a natural order of things, Grace. Men work, women take care of the children.'

'Oh, God, Odelle, where have you been for the last ten years?'

'Part of it working for a living to support myself and my child after my husband deserted me. You think you're living in a brave new world, Grace, but it's still the same old world. Just watch yourself because men do one thing very well – they give other people the shaft.'

'Sy included?' Grace countered.

Odelle smiled grimly. 'Some men are different. Besides, I don't ask Sy what he does when he's not with me. He provides me with love and security; I provide him with a home and children. I call us evenly matched. What do you get out of your relationship with Darrell?'

After that, Grace was careful to stay out of the kitchen with Odelle. What Odelle didn't seem to understand was that when one loved someone, one made sacrifices. Grace was sacrificing for Darrell now. And she knew, when the time came, he would sacrifice for her.

The day Darrell got a thick packet from his publishers, he was back up in Iowa, giving several seminars on how he got published. It was a two-day trip, and the galleys came on the first day he was gone. Grace knew she shouldn't have done it, but she was so excited for him, she ripped open the packet, getting the confetti stuffing all over their kitchen floor. She gazed lovingly at the neat, manilla pages. RAGE IN WHITE AND BLACK screamed the title page. "A Book of the Revolution by Ahmed Jemal Mohammed."

Who the hell was Ahmed Jemal Mohammed!

The dedication page read: "To my brothers and sisters who share in our continuing struggle for a homeland."

Grace trembled briefly in disappointment that the book wasn't dedicated to her, or at least to Darrell's parents. She had never met Darrell's parents, only spoken to them over the phone. They seemed like very decent people. But who were his brothers and sisters? He was an only child.

She opened the book to Chapter 1. "I was born and raised a Christian, but now I'm free."

A nice, strong beginning, but where would it lead?

Grace sat in the kitchen, oblivious to time and sank herself into Darrell's book. When the phone rang, letting her know she was late for work, she replied that she was sick. She didn't care if she didn't sound sick, she *was* sick. In that she wasn't lying.

Darrell's story was simple enough. The main character, Dick Stomp, was a poor black boy from the ghetto who went on a scholarship to the University of Michigan. There he met a rich white girl from Benton Harbor. He thought it was love, but on her part it was all forbidden lust. He was her stud. She was the all-American rich bitch, using him for kicks. She led him into every sort of degradation, from sex to drugs to working as a waiter at her father's annual Christmas party. Dick had once been full of hope that he could make America his own. That's when he was pure, in the ghetto, surrounded by his own people. Interacting with white America taught him otherwise. White America corrupted the black man's soul, castrated him, returned him to slavery. The only freedom was to be found among one's own people. The only revenge was to reproduce own's own kind. With realization and self-knowledge, Dick Stomp's character was rebaptized into the new religion of revolution with the name Ibrahim Ali Kemal. His story was told in flashbacks from prison where he was incarcerated for having killed his white, exploitative girlfriend when she dared to drive her Porsche into the heart of

Detroit, looking for drugs; more importantly, looking for more black meat she could corrupt. His white girlfriend's name was Grace Goldstein.

Grace's eyes were red the next morning, whether from tears or from staying up all night reading this result of a Reiseman Fellowship she didn't know. She had never appeared in a book before, certainly not as a character someone else had distorted and reshaped. And yet, here she was, a cold-hearted castrator. Darrell didn't even bother to change her description. To save him from a suit, she guessed, he changed her last name to Goldstein. Or was that simply to accommodate black anti-Semitism? She would have to ask Darrell for his motivation.

She stayed away from work a second day, knowing in all likelihood she would be fired. But she had to wait for Darrell to make his reappearance. He did so at four in the afternoon. 'Hey, baby,' he said to her, 'what's happenin'?'

So typically clichéd. Why hadn't she seen that about him before? With a deeper grimness than she had ever felt previously, she said, 'I read your book.'

'You what?'

'I read your book. The galleys came while you were out, and I was so excited, I opened the package and read it.'

Darrell looked stunned and, she was pleased to see, guilty. He was flustered. She had put him on the defensive. He glanced around the room, looking for either rescue or a way out. Then he said, 'Isn't opening someone else's mail illegal?'

What a street fighter he was! 'So have me arrested. You fucking bastard!'

'Oh. So you're in one of those moods.'

'You dishonest shit!'

He was nervous. He was sweating. 'Grace,' he began, then faltered. 'Grace, let me explain where I'm coming from.'

'You're coming from the middle class, Darrell. You're not streetwise, hip dude. You're like me. We're both from Michigan. We loved each other. Didn't we?'

'If you knew what it meant to be black – '

'Do you know what it means to be a woman? A woman who's supported you, and this is how you treat me? You hold me up to contempt, Darrell. What have I ever done to deserve this contempt, except love you?'

'It's not you. The book's not about you.'

'Then explain why the woman has my name and my features?'

'You know how it is when you write. You take from life experiences.'

126

'But you don't twist and destroy.'

He shook his head and placed his hands over his temples. 'I knew this would happen. I knew this would be your reaction when you read the book. That's why I didn't want you to see it before it was actually published. Don't you realize what you're doing to me now? You're destroying the joy that should be within me to see my work finally in print.'

The groan that came from within Grace was that of a downed elephant. Darrell was so startled that he backed up against the door to their apartment, readying his escape route. 'You've got to change this, Darrell,' she said in a voice so low, even she thought she was possessed. 'You've got to change this woman's name, change her description, change this message. It's all a fake.'

'Fake?'

'Fake. You have something to say as a black man in America, but you've taken the cheap way out. You're exploiting both black rage and white guilt. You come across as both a racist and an anti-Semite. Is that what you stand for?'

He came away from the door. 'I stand for the truth, the truth about white America.'

'What truth? What opportunities has white America denied you that you should write such shit? Are you writing the truth or what you think will sell and make you a hero in certain white and black circles? Are you writing about real people, black and white, or simply some political manifesto to get you in the news and on to the best seller list?'

He took a step towards her. 'Who are you to question my knowledge of black America? What do you really know about being black? I've lived with my blackness all of my life.'

She stood up and came to him, grabbed his shoulders, turned him, and pushed him in front of the mirror. 'Take a look at yourself, Ahmed Jemal Mohammed. If I got a tan I'd be darker than you. As far as soul, I already have more soul than you could ever fathom, because I would never destroy something I loved. But it was all fake, wasn't it? As phoney as your book. Maybe love was never what our relationship was all about. Maybe it was about using instead. You used me to support you. And then when you didn't need that support any more, you killed me off, first in your heart, because you couldn't have written about me that way if I wasn't dead to you already, then in the pages of your book.'

She turned from him, exhausted and unbearably sad. She went to the wardrobe and got out her suitcase. Darrell watched her, puzzled and angry. 'You're jealous, aren't you? That's what this is all about.

127

You're jealous of my ability to create something masterful. It kills you to see me successful.'

'I prayed for your success, Darrell. I just didn't think it would come over my dead body.'

'The stinking carcass of a white America,' Darrell said, repeating lovingly one of his own lines.

'An America that gave you a Reiseman.'

He sighed as she packed. 'Hell, the Reiseman people will love it. White Jewish liberals love to be flagellated, didn't you know that? They'll take me to their bosom.'

'As I did, only to be stung to death.' She laughed grimly. 'You've really opened my eyes to what it's all about, Darrell. Rage! Maybe now I too can aim again for the Reiseman.'

'And if you don't give it to me to mail, it might even get to the committee.'

Somehow she wasn't even surprised that he hadn't mailed her application.

It took her less than an hour to pack. She left everything she had brought to their relationship: the television, the clock radio, kitchen appliances and dishes, sheets, towels. Everything, especially her heart. With one suitcase she moved out and away. She passed the grocery where she did her shopping, the record store where she bought Darrell gifts of jazz, the laundry where she exchanged cooking tips with the neighbourhood women, the restaurant where she and Darrell went for ham hocks and turnip greens, which neither of them liked. And all along her walk away, she saw faces she knew, who knew her, and suddenly she saw them as hostile. Even without being told, she knew and they knew that she and they were once again foreign, apart from one another. They were strangers together in the same land. And then she took the train to Glencoe.

# Chapter 22

# Creating Love

Odelle stuck her head round the bedroom door and asked, 'What does Camille want for supper?'

Grace turned around and buried her head in the pillow. 'I'm not eating.'

'Come on, Grace,' Odelle coaxed.

'No.'

Odelle sighed and left. 'This is ridiculous, you know,' she called, as she walked down the hallway.

Ridiculous? What did Odelle know about ridiculous? She was safe and secure. She was married to Sy. She had two children. She had a house. She had everything she wanted in life. All Grace had to her credit was a bigamist relationship, a dead baby, a rotten ex-lover, and her name plastered all over a book that was bound to be read by someone. Sure, Odelle could well afford to eat dinner. But for Grace the pain was just too great.

There was a timid knock on the open bedroom door. Grace didn't bother turning around. 'Aunt Grace?' came Julia's less than authoritative voice.

'What is it, honey?' Grace asked. She couldn't possibly be rude to anyone who called her "aunt".

'Mommy says you're not coming down to eat again. You've been here a week now, and you've hardly eaten anything. Do you have the 'flu? 'cause Mommy says you're not really sick.'

Grace turned and faced the young teenager. While the girl definitely had breasts, her hips were still slender, still bespeaking innocence and hope. Grace almost cried when she thought of what Julia would have to endure in her life. Why? Why were men invented? What crazed moment of sadistic despair caused God to develop the seed of what would be hell on earth?

'So are you sick?' Julia asked, daring to come closer.

'The love bug's got me,' Grace confessed.

'Oh yeah.' Julia sat down on the edge of the bed. 'I know what you mean. Like, there's this guy I really like, he's football and all, and he thinks I'm just a sappy little sophomore. He's in my French 2 class because he failed last year. I don't know. Do you have any tips, maybe, like how I should attract him?'

Grace looked into Julia's earnest face. Why do we always fall for the bozos? Here was Julia attracted to someone who probably had muscles everywhere but in the brain. He was probably good looking and spoke in monosyllables. And yet, couldn't Grace remember being in love with someone like that in high school also? Sure. Then you would dress in the morning especially for him, try to spot him in the halls, in the lunchroom, hoping for just one glance in your direction. No wonder men acted like gods. Women were such easy prey. 'Dear,' Grace said carefully to Julia, 'I know you're not religious, but have you ever considered becoming a nun?'

'A nun?' Julia shrieked.

'To spare yourself the pain that life will inflict upon you.'

'I'm not in pain.'

'Not yet, Julia! Not yet!'

Julia backed out of the room and ran down the hallway yelling, 'Mommy!' From somewhere in the kitchen, Grace could hear Odelle laughing. Well could Odelle laugh. No one had ridiculed her in a book.

Heavy footsteps were coming up the stairs. Holy shit! It had to be Sy. It was. There was his shadow looming in the hallway. 'Grace, get out of that bed now!'

'No!'

'I mean it. Get out or I'll drag you out. Telling my kid to become a nun. What are you, crazy? Jesus, I've never seen a woman who screws herself up more than you do. If you had spent time in the Burmese jungle, you would have known . . .'

'Oh, fuck the Burmese jungle, Sy! No one gives a shit about the Burmese jungle.'

Damn. She had antagonized him. Odelle warned her early on that Sy like to talk (and talk and talk) about his foreign adventures. Everyone had to listen politely. And Grace had. But right now she was in too much pain to be polite. Sy should understand that.

'Out of bed, now!'

He didn't understand. So what should she expect? He was a man. 'I'm not getting out of bed, Sy, so forget it.'

'I'm counting to three. If you're not out of bed, there will be drastic consequences.'

What would he do? Kick her out of the house, her one sanctuary all these many years? 'One.' He wouldn't be so cruel. 'Two.' Odelle wouldn't let him. 'Three.' He came at her, tore off the covers, revealing her jeans-clad body, and lifted her out of bed, throwing her over his shoulder.

She shrieked. 'What are you doing? Put me down! Odelle!'

Odelle came from the kitchen as Sy was carrying Grace down the stairs. 'Sy?' she wondered.

'Open the front door,' he ordered.

God, he was going to throw her out! Grace was worried now. But no. He hopped down the front steps with her and started walking down the street of their neighbourhood. It was freezing out. She had no shoes on and just a sweatshirt to protect her. Sy at least had her draped around his neck to keep him warm. 'What are you doing?' she hollered.

'Fresh air taken in at a brisk pace will cure anybody of almost anything.'

They passed several neighbours walking their dogs. Sy very politely said good evening to them. Grace's feet turned numb and her nose started to run. 'Help,' she said to one of them.

By the time they reached the corner and turned around, Sy pausing to adjust her weight, a police car with blue flashing lights screeched to a halt in front of them. Two very young policemen rushed out with their night sticks at the ready. 'Is there a problem here?' one asked.

Sy stopped. Finally Grace ceased jiggling up and down. 'No problem,' Sy assured the cops.

'Uh. Do you think you could put her down then?' the other policeman said.

Sy let Grace slide to the pavement. 'Oh!' she shrieked. The pavement felt like ice. She hopped from one foot to the other.

'Miss, are you okay?' the first cop asked her.

'C-c-c-old,' she chattered.

'What's this all about?' the cop asked, frustrated.

'I'm in the midst of curing her of a bad case of depression,' Sy told them.

'By slinging her around like a sack of potatoes?'

'She's far heavier than that. And the choice of how she was to leave her bedroom was her own.'

'Can I please go home now?' Grace begged.

'Where does she live?' the policeman asked.

'With me,' Sy confessed.

'Oh,' he began to understand. 'You two are married?'

'No. We have a ménage à trois at No. 15.'

131

'Jesus!' the cop said.

'How's that for your community relations?' Sy replied with a smile.

'Ma'am, do you want to go home with this guy?' the second cop asked.

'Yes, yes,' Grace hurried them along. She started to hobble along on her bare feet, but she didn't get far before she stepped on something that would have sent her tumbling if Sy hadn't grabbed her and picked her up once more.

Once more in his arms, Grace was carried back to Odelle's house while the patrol car carefully trailed them. Up on the porch, Sy knocked the front door open. The police weren't far behind when he entered the house. Odelle had to come out of the kitchen and explain that Grace was a friend of hers who was suffering from depression over a broken love affair. They were trying everything to get her out of it.

'She's lovesick,' Julia added.

Luke followed the policemen out of the door to sit in their car for a few minutes and have everything explained to him. Then the quiet street in Glencoe returned to a neighbourly silence, broken only by the loud laughter coming from No. 15.

Grace's recovery dribbled forward for three months. During this time, Sy took off on two trips, one to Central America, the other to Bahrain. Meanwhile, Odelle began to do voluntary work at the Planned Parenthood Clinic, perhaps spurred on by Julia's continued interest in boys, despite Grace's sad experience. Grace herself found a job as an assistant manager in a local clothing store called Glad Rags. She did not take pen to paper except to handle the accounts. Her writing days were over. What had her "talent" ever brought her, except ridicule and remorse?

At the end of this three-month respite, Grace, who had the nasty habit of reading the paper every morning, found that the book review in the *Tribune* had been clipped before she could get to it. 'What's this?' she asked Odelle, who was always up before she was, getting the kids off to school.

'Oh that. I knew you wouldn't mind. There was a book of Tibetan recipes which I though might interest my gourmet club members.'

Odelle was lying. While she did belong to a gourmet cooking club, it was Sy who did the cooking. But Grace acted as if nothing was amiss. She went off to work as usual, making only one extra stop, the pharmacy, to pick up another copy of the *Tribune*.

RAGE IN BLACK AND WHITE by Ahmed Jemal Mohammed had come up for review. "A man who hears the singing of the ghetto's soul." "Mr Mohammed truly understands the underbelly of America's beast, racism." "The reader feels the wounds of humiliation inflicted by Grace Goldstein, as if he himself were wounded." "A blazing new black talent." "A must-read for anyone interested in understanding Chicago today." This sort of puzzled Grace as the story took place in Detroit. But no one said reviewers had to be accurate. Or even intelligent.

Grace got home at ten o'clock that night. Odelle was watching the evening news, almost snoozing. It was Tuesday, and she was waiting for a call from Sy. He was not a conscientious observer of their Tuesday connection, so Odelle could be waiting all night. 'Hi,' she said, when Grace had hung up her coat and come into the living room.

'I got a copy of that Tibetan review,' Grace said grimly.
'Oh.'
'You needn't try to protect me, Odelle. I'm not that fragile.'

That was put to the test next Monday night, when Grace sat down to watch *About Chicago*, an arts talk show. She liked to keep *au courant*. Sometimes she and Odelle would take the train downtown to a play or the opera or the ballet, while Julia babysat. During a discussion between Manny Green, the host of *About Chicago*, and a new playwright about why his work had closed after twenty performances – audiences weren't ready for him – Grace decided to get herself a salad and a soda. So it was Julia who called from the living room and said, 'Look, everyone, it's Darrell!'

Grace put the food on the counter. She knew she wouldn't be able to eat. She raced to the television, sat down on the couch just as Odelle came in from the laundry room. 'Ahmed – may I call you Ahmed?' Manny Green asked.

Darrell nodded condescendingly.
'I thought his name was Darrell?' Julia said, puzzled.
'Shh!' Odelle hushed her.

'About this book, which is creating quite a stir, certainly among my friends, what are you trying to say? In your own words, if you would, Ahmed. Because to me there are some very troubling aspects to RAGE IN BLACK AND WHITE. Now, not that I'm sensitive about my own ethnic status – hey, I'm Jewish, people know it – but what is the significance of naming this gal who dumps on you all the time Grace Goldstein? You see, what I don't understand about black people is that we have been walking hand and hand, brother and sister together. And now all of a sudden, in books like yours, the Jew is the enemy. Is this reality or is it part of your effort, black people's effort, to identify more closely with white Christian America?'
'Well – '
'Hold it, will ya, Ahmed? I see we have to go for a break.'

133

Grace and Odelle giggled. 'Gee,' Julia said, 'that guy didn't even give Darrell a chance to speak.'

Darrell rectified that in the next segment, where he explained his conviction that he had spent his life being shafted by the white establishment, by white women in particular. "Grace" was just a combination of all he found wrong in America. She was a user who didn't know it. Exploitation in love and business was the name of her game. Darrell had no idea when he named this character that Goldstein was a Jewish name. But if the shoe fit . . . No, he didn't feel at home in Chicago, even though he had lived here for several years after attending the University of Iowa. He didn't feel at home anywhere in America.

'And thank you very much, Ahmed,' Manny concluded, 'for bringing your rage into our living rooms.'

'I thought he felt at home here,' Julia said, hurt.

'I thought he felt at home in my bed too,' Grace muttered.

'What did we do to him?' Julia wondered.

'Nothing, dear,' Odelle said. 'It's just a way to sell books.'

'If he doesn't feel at home here,' Luke broke in to say, peanut butter jar in hand, 'why doesn't he go where he does feel at home?' He shrugged his shoulders while Odelle opened the jar for him.

'And now we have a real treat coming up for you,' Manny Green promised his audience. 'Hang on for this one. Have you ever met a woman who's led three lives?'

Fade into commercial. 'I think I've lived more than that already,' Grace said thoughtfully.

'Oh, I love these women,' Odelle squirmed in anticipation. 'They're all crazy, you know, and they come out and speak in different voices. Like ventriloquists. Wouldn't it be great to be a different person so you could act any way you wanted?'

'You already do act any way you want, Odelle,' Grace pointed out.

Odelle was about to protest when Manny Green's smile blazed on to the screen and stopped her. 'We have with us tonight, fellow hog city lovers, two people who come to us from Taos, New Mexico.'

The camera panned from Manny to include the guests. Odelle practically had a heart attack. 'Julia!' she screamed. 'Get out of the room!'

'Why?'

'Out now!'

'Do as your mother says,' Grace concurred. 'This isn't for you.'

There, on the couch with some very young woman, sat Tommy Patterson, older, longer hair, moustache and beard, but still recognizable as the man both women despised.

Julia retreated but only to the hallway, where she stood and watched.

'Shall we turn it off?' Grace wondered.

'And miss this sterling performance by the second schmuck of the evening?'

'Tommy Patterson,' Manny Green was saying, 'and his lovely young bride Trudi Surefoot.'

Trudi's head looked as if it wasn't screwed on tight. It sort of wobbled in one direction and then another, while Manny held up the book WOMAN OF THE THREE LIVES. 'Tommy, tell us how you discovered your wife was more woman than ever she knew herself to be.'

'Well first, Manny,' Tommy started, then paused to smile deeply at Manny and then straight into the camera, grabbing them all with those eyes of his, 'I assume your audience knows that spirituality, the inner being, the soul of man, has always been of interest to me, as you may judge from my previous book MY YEARS IN THE WILDERNESS: A SPIRITUAL SEARCH FOR THE MEANING OF LIFE, which is now available in paperback for those who want to understand the full meaning to young American men of the impact of Vietnam on our society at large, and the failing of the very American values that led to such misjudgment on the part of our self-annointed leaders.'

He took a deep breath. 'But you're asking about Trudi.' With that Tommy turned and put his hand gently on hers which was resting on her lap. She looked at the hand as if it were some sort of animal. 'When I returned from my exile in Canada, I sought out pockets of spirituality within the United States, areas which were not corrupted by hate, bitterness of factional fighting, as I think we've just heard illustrated by Ahmed Jemal – uh – you know. I found in Taos, New Mexico, the inner power I needed to free myself from any residual rage left from the war against young America, perpetuated by our self-anointed leaders in Washington – '

'Hold it a sec, Tommy. Isn't Taos, New Mexico, considered some sort of drug capital of the Southwest?'

'What do we intake into our system that is not drug-related?' Tommy wondered spiritually. 'Look at the pesticides on our food.'

'But do those pesticides alter our minds?' Manny wondered gamely. 'I believe in your book you state it was a vegetable that led your delightful wife to the discovery that she was more than one person.'

'Mushrooms,' Trudi leaned forward to say, almost tipping off her chair.

'When I met Trudi,' Tommy retook the conversation, 'our auras fused.'

135

'We met each other at a recreation of an old Indian ceremony, and we loved each other less than an hour later,' Trudi agreed.

Manny looked slightly uncomfortable. 'Why don't you tell us about your former lives, Trudi?'

'I'm an Indian really. I kept bringing bad luck on my tribe. I was killed and eaten once. I don't know how I tasted. I hope they didn't burn me. If one is going to eat meat, and I personally am a vegetarian, one shouldn't burn it and do away with all the natural flavouring and nutrients. Even humans have to taste good.'

'Hold that thought, Trudi. We have to cut away for just a second to our friends in the commercial world,' Manny warned her.

It did not surprise either Grace or Odelle that when Manny came back, he was talking with a woman who had sworn, if God spared her husband's life, she would tap dance her way across America.

Odelle got up and turned off the television. 'He's married again,' she said.

'I wonder if they have children,' Grace remarked.

'I hope not. At the clinic there are people who have taken drugs and had babies. It's not pretty.'

But Trudi Surefoot and Tommy Patterson did have a child, a daughter named Free. Grace read all about it, as the weeks and months passed. WOMAN OF THE THREE LIVES rose to the top of the Non-Fiction best seller list, while Tommy dragged Trudi Surefoot from one talk show to another, like a sideshow at the circus.

Meanwhile, RAGE IN BLACK AND WHITE was having its problems. Darrell took his book on tour also; and each time he spoke or was interviewed, he seemed to become more violent, more racial. RAGE did not make it to the top ten, nor even the top twenty, but it sold respectably and steadily. So now Darrell was finally living his big lie. Sometimes Grace felt the urge to call his parents and find out what they thought of their son. But it was none of her business any more. She was no longer a part of his life. No one had identified her as Grace. She could rest easy.

Or could she?

Something ate at her every time she picked up the book review section of the paper and checked the best seller list. Something gnawed at her every time she saw or heard of Tommy Patterson or Ahmed Jemal Mohammed. Was it simple envy?

Grace Mandling wanted to write all her life. As a little girl she made up stories for her paper dolls. In high school she was on the literary magazine. At the University she majored in English. Then Tommy came and sucked the spirit from her for years.

But she recovered. She bounced back. She went to Iowa. Okay, so no one there thought she had talent, but she was doing what she wanted to do, write. And then she met Darrell. She worked while he wrote. He had his book published, and all she had was her name on a despicable character. Again she was the loser.

Why?

At night she tried to answer that question. While Tommy and Darrell were living the lives of writers in America, she was stuck at Glad Rags as assistant manager. Had life done it to her or had she done it to her life?

She was dumb, let's face it. She wouldn't know a good man if he came along and pinched her bottom. And there was very little of even that available, working in a woman's clothing shop. She was getting old and she was going nowhere.

Grace smiled as she turned into her pillow. She remembered when she was young, in high school, oh, the lovers she invented for herself. They were strong and manly, but weak and gentle. One won the Nobel Prize, the other was voted Most Valuable Player. But the thing that her fantasy lovers all had in common was a deep and abiding commitment to romance. They loved her deeply, without question.

Where was there a man like that in real life?

Well, shit! Grace sat up in her bed, the blankets dropping away. If there weren't a real man like that in her life, she couldn't be the only one to suffer such a lack. All women want perfection. All women want romance. They want to be swept off their feet, even to have an orgasm. If they couldn't get that in the bars, the clubs, the museums, let them at least get it on paper.

Fantasies of love. Now there was an area Grace understood. Time to make her fantasies come alive!

137

# Chapter 23
# Bereft

'But, Tommy, what did I do wrong?' Trudi Surefoot asked, heartsick.

'Look around you,' Tommy Patterson ordered. 'Look at yourself in the mirror.' He took her by the shoulders and pushed her up against the mirror so that all she could see was her nose.

Tommy pulled back in disgust. How had he married this woman? How had he slept with her? She was totally dishevelled. When was the last time she had at least run a comb through her hair? Her eyes were vacant. Gone was the spirituality he first found within her the night of their initial intercourse. Gone was the piercing oneness of their aura. Gone. Their time together had come and gone.

He saw it out in the heartland, when he travelled with this space woman, promoting WOMAN OF THE THREE LIVES. Times they were a-changing, and he'd better change with them. He always had. That was the secret of life: Take a stand. When that stand is no longer profitable socially or economically, change your stand to what everyone else was thinking.

Everyone else was coming off the high of the late Sixties, early Seventies. Everyone else was hitting the ground running. Meanwhile, he was stuck with this druggie drudge and her brat.

I can change,' Trudi told him. 'What is it you want from me? You know how much I love you.'

'Love is just a word, Trudi,' he warned her. 'Look.' He took her more gently by the shoulders now. 'You and me, we've had some good times together. And isn't that what life's all about? Hell, you should know. You've lived through three lifetimes.'

'But they were short lifetimes,' Trudi protested. 'I wanted something more permanent this time. What is it, Tommy? Didn't I do what you wanted? I did everything you told me to do on all those shows. We were so good together. People liked us.'

'Trudi, I loved you. You know that. And I'll always love the ideal of my love for you. But now, can't you see that your ions are negatively charged?'

Trudi looked puzzled. She was trying very hard to concentrate, but she had taken so many pills lately and maybe too much liquor. What was Tommy saying to her? 'What ions are you talking about?'

'The ions of your aura.'

'My aura is the light around my body.'

Tommy stepped back with contempt. 'Jesus Christ, don't you know anything! Your aura is made up of ions, both positively and negatively charged. When we first came together, your ions were positive. Now the world's turning, babe, and we're just repelling each other.'

'But you're not repelling me,' she pleaded. 'What am I going to do without you? I love you, Tommy. You're my whole life. Before you came to me, I was just drifting.'

'Girl, each of us has to write our own script. Mine says exit stage left.'

Trudi wandered around in circles while Tommy packed his bags. She just couldn't focus her mind. All she wanted to do was understand what was happening. They'd had a few hits together last night, then there were the pills and booze and she thought he had made love to her. Now this morning he was leaving. Leaving her all alone with . . . 'What about Free?' Trudi asked him.

'What about her?'

'She's your daughter. You can't just walk away from her.'

Tommy looked at Trudi with infinite patience, compassion, no desire. 'You're honestly telling me you think Free is my daughter.'

'Of course she's your daughter, Tommy. ,We were sleeping together when I got pregnant. Don't you remember?'

He placed his hand on her cheek. 'Trudi, Trudi, Trudi, you dear, sweet, innocent child. Honey, can you name someone in Taos you haven't slept with?' He paused while the horrible unfairness of his accusation sank into her. 'I accepted responsibility for Free while we were living together because I'm that kind of man. I don't desert those I love. But now, hey, he travels fastest who travels alone, babe.'

Trudi's hands ripped through the tangled knots of her hair. 'But what am I to do? All these months travelling with you, I gave up my wheel, my time at the kiln, my share of the co-operative. Now what am I to do? I don't have any money, and there's Free to take care of. I don't have a cent for any of this.' Also, she thought selfishly, she had no money for drugs or booze or anything.

139

Tommy reached into his pocket and took out his wallet. Frowning, he looked through it. 'I can spare you a twenty,' he said, pulling one out and offering it to her.

'A twenty? But what about all that money from the book? You said it was such a hot seller. You said the contract with the paperback company was so good. Why can't I have some of that? It was my lives you wrote about.'

'Hey!' Tommy shouted. He was grim, almost threatening. 'You didn't even know you had those lives before I took you back into them. The money I got from the book was money *I* earned. I wrote the damn book, not you. And you lived high enough off the hog when we were going to all those hotels and things on the publicity tour.'

'Yeah, but – '

'Look, take the twenty and shut up, okay? I'm sick of your whining.'

Whining. She was whining again, and she knew how Tommy hated it when she complained about anything. She had to stop. She had to make everything happy and pleasant for him. 'Look, Tommy, why don't you stay for just a few more days, and I'll show you how great our lives together can be again? Don't you remember all the fun times we had? We laughed so much together. Don't you remember?'

He shook his head. 'The laughing's over.' He picked up his bags and walked out of their three-room, fake-adobe-walled apartment. Trudi grabbed Free, who was totally naked, and followed Tommy down the stairs. He placed his bags in the back of their Honda Civic, but he didn't get into the car. Instead he walked down to the street to Jake's Barber Shop. She trailed after him. Free was struggling in her arms, trying to get loose. It seemed everyone wanted to escape her clutches. But Trudi held tight. She stood outside the barber's shop, sometimes putting her head to the window and peering in. What was Tommy having done to him?

He came out more than forty-five minutes later. She was startled. She thought maybe she was suffering from a delusion. He wasn't even Tommy any more. Gone was his long hair. His moustache and beard were missing. He looked like – she could barely cope with it – some clean-shaven businessman.

'Tommy,' she called to him. But he didn't pay any attention to her. He walked back down the street, got into their Honda Civic and started it. She stood behind it. Let him kill her. She didn't care. She couldn't lose his love. But he didn't back up. He just drove forward. And in a few minutes all that was left of Tommy Patterson in her life was his aura so negatively charged against her.

That night Trudi took no pills, no liquor, no pot, no peyote. That night Trudi keened for her missing man. She was alone in this world, alone with Free. And there wasn't a friend she could turn to.

Where had they all gone? Before Tommy came, she had a million friends. She came here after a year at art school, when her money ran out, because she heard Taos was the place to go. Taos had everything. Beauty, art, drugs, and especially tourists. Taos was a place where she could set herself up as a potter and make money.

So she came and she thrived. There was even sort of a rapprochement with her family. A friend took pictures of her, selling her work on the square. And then her mother was so excited when Trudi became a television star. Oh, how envious the mothers in East Diablo's beauty shop were. Gone were the days when nobody mentioned Trudi because of – well, that one mistake, her out-of-sync pregnancy.

Everyone was now proud of Trudi, except for her father, of course. She would never be anything to him except a burden the Lord had placed on his shoulders. When Trudi actually came home that once for a family wedding, her brother Buster told her their father thought her claim of three lives was an affront to God. And they were all God-fearing folk in East Diablo.

Trudi feared God also. And now she knew why. God had deserted her. Those were hard times back then, when she was in high school and everyone rejected her. But they were nothing compared to this, this total loss of love.

Where is your rainbow, Lord? she wanted to ask. But she knew she was outside His loving embrace. Oh, how crooked were her ways.

Now that her husband was gone, Trudi asked herself one question. Was Tommy a mistake? None of her friends from Red Bull, her art co-operative, had come out and warned her about him. But that was their way. Everyone existed in his or her own space, that space wouldn't be violated. Her space was with Tommy. And at first everyone liked him. 'He talks a good game,' was the way one of the senior members of the Red Bull had put it. But then later some accused Tommy of being a user, of trying to gain from their talent. She supposed it was that article in *Art Focus* magazine, where he discussed the Red Bullshit Co-op and tried to make a distinction between artists and craftsmen. Truth was always important to Tommy.

But this truth drove her friends away from her. Then came that maddening book, detailing the many ventures of her spirit in other times. After the book was published, one of the women artists said to her, right to her face, like Trudi would never have the nerve to do,

141

'He's using you, Trudi. You don't have three lives. You've only got one. Watch out before he takes even that one away from you.' All the time no one but her really understood Tommy. She defended him against all comers. And now she was alone in the ring.

Free was crying. 'Food, Mommy,' she was saying. Trudi looked out of the window and saw that it was day. 'Food, Mommy!' Free insisted. But Trudi wasn't hungry. She slid down on to the straw pallet she and Tommy had so happily shared together and went to sleep.

Life became a daze. Somewhere in time she had visions of men in uniforms coming to her apartment to talk to her about something. What was it? A child? Was there a child to be born in Taos, New Mexico, that would set them all free? Free. Sometimes Trudi could fee Free patting her face or see her daughter, staring into her eyes. What was Free doing with herself lately?

'Ms Surefoot. Ms Surefoot!' Someone was calling her, shaking her rudely. Trudi didn't know what right a stranger had to be in her apartment. She opened her eyes and saw a black woman standing above her, poking at her. 'Ms Surefoot?' the woman said.

'Halley, I mean Patterson,' Trudi corrected her. How could she have forgotten? Halley was her maiden name, the one she gave up when she and Tommy were married. Married. She perked up. Tommy hadn't asked for a divorce. So he probably still loved her! He would come back to her. She sat up and smiled.

'I'm sorry,' the black woman said. 'Your neighbours across the way said your name was Trudi Surefoot.'

'That's – oh, well, actually Surefoot came from when I was Rising Surefoot in my first life.'

The black woman took in a deep breath and let it out slowly. 'I'm Ms Dolan, from the state Human Welfare Bureau?'

'Oh, good. I believe in human welfare,' Trudi said agreeably.

'You have a daughter.'

'Yes. Free.'

'Excuse me?'

'Free. That's her name.'

Ms Dolan looked down at the form she was carrying. 'Right, Free. Well, your neighbours seem to feel that Free is lacking proper supervision.'

'Oh, no,' Trudi objected. 'That's not true at all.'

'They say they have been feeding her all her meals, bathing her, letting her sleep at their place. They say you're usually passed out and incoherent.'

'Oh. I haven't had any drugs lately.'

'I'm not accusing you of being on drugs, Mrs – er – '

'What I meant is, I've been totally straight, and that's why I'm not thinking right. I'm usually high.' She smiled disarmingly up at the social worker. The social worker did not smile back.

'Ms Surefoot, you must realize we can't let your child just wander at will. She can't be more than three.'

'She isn't. And she's not wandering at will if everyone knows she's over at the neighbours.'

'Are you married?'

'Oh, yes. To Tommy Patterson. The writer. Surely you've heard of him.'

'No, I'm sorry, I haven't.'

'I'm the woman in WOMAN OF THE THREE LIVES.'

'Ms Surefoot, can we get back to your family situation? Where is your husband, exactly?'

'He split. Said our ions were negatively charged.'

'Then there's only you to take care of – uh – Free?'

'Well, gee, Free really pretty much takes care of herself.'

Which is how Trudi found herself in front of a judge in family court, being threatened with having Free taken from her too. She tried to explain to the judge how she had already lost one baby to adoption. She just couldn't lose Free. She couldn't! Ms Dolan said something about drug addicts and foster care, none of which Trudi could understand. Her court-appointed lawyer wasn't much help because he was busy working on someone else's case, some guy who had slit open his wife and boiled up her intestines for their cat. Gee, she was only sorry her case wasn't more interesting. The only helpful suggestion her lawyer made was for her to tell the court she had family to take Free in while she straightened herself out.

'And where is your family?' the judge wanted to know.

'East Diablo, in West Texas.'

That seemed to satisfy everyone because, if she took Free back to West Texas, it would be out of New Mexico's jurisdiction. It would no longer come under the court's purview.

Ms Dolan arranged busfare for Trudi and Free all the way back to East Diablo. It was a long dusty trip, and Free was none too happy about being cooped up in a bus. After a while, none of the passengers was too happy about being cooped up with Free. But Trudi made it back to East Diablo with only a few unkind remarks being exchanged.

East Diablo's bus stop was right in front of the gas station, so the first person who caught sight of Trudi was her Cousin Earl, he who had deflowered her all those years ago. 'Well, will ya looka here!' he said. 'Trudi Halley, what brings you back home?'

'None of your damn business, Earl,' she told him.

'Seen you on all them shows. You are the toast of this town, gal.'

He tried to come over and be cousinly, but his grime and body odour did Trudi in. She rushed up the street toward the yellow bungalow she had once called home.

No fatted calves were slaughtered in her honour, but Trudi honestly believed her mother was glad to see her. 'You're a celebrity now, girl,' her mother told her. 'Look. I've made a scrapbook all about you.' Her father said nothing, just gave her that stare of his. After that first meeting, he walked out of the room whenever Trudi came into it. He wouldn't even acknowledge his own granddaughter. It was as if everything Trudi touched was shit.

Finally, Trudi could take it no longer. She called her father into the living room in a peremptory voice he had never heard her use before. 'This here ain't a bastard!' she told her father, who simply gave her that stare back. 'This here's your grandchild. She's legitimate from my marriage to Tommy Patterson. Her name's Free.'

'A Christian name, is it?' her father asked.

'All of us are children of God,' Trudi replied.

'You think God believes in having three lives!' her father came back at her.

'Now, Jimmy,' her mother warned. 'Look how pretty this little one is.' Her mother had warmed to Free right from the start.

But Trudi was ready to slug it out. 'I can't help it if I've lived before,' she told him.

'Everyone's so proud of you. No one knew what you had in you,' her mother assured her.

'The devil. That's what she's got in her,' Jimmy Halley told his wife. Then he went outside and walked down the street for a beer at Marley's.

Anger was mixed with fear as Trudi was left alone with her mother. She knew why she was here, and she also knew she couldn't stay. East Diablo, with its small minds, especially her father's, couldn't hold her any more. But what to do about Free? 'I'm in deep shit, Mom,' she confessed to every daughter's patron saint. Her mother listened as Trudi poured out her sad and woeful story of love lost, desertion and drugs. 'Oh lord, oh lord, oh lord,' was all her mother could say.

'I was thinking, when I was on that long bus ride home, of maybe asking you to look after my daughter, just till I sort myself out. But now it's obvious I can't leave Free here,' Trudi said. 'I can't have Dad destroying her spirit. She has a beautiful spirit, Mom. Just look at her, and you can see she has a beautiful spirit.'

Myra Halley looked at her granddaughter more critically than Trudi expected. The little girl needed a bath and some clean clothes.

144

She smiled and took the child into her hands. 'Hey, sweetie, how'd you like to come out back with your old grandma and get yourself a bath?'

Free looked doubtfully at her mother, stuck her thumb in her mouth, but let herself be lifted up by her grandma.

Free stayed naked for an hour and a half while Grandma washed her clothes and let them dry in West Texas's desert sun. Then she was dressed crisp and clean like a proper young miss. All this time Jimmy Halley was down with the boys at Marley's, drinking his beer.

Soon Trudi and her mother were out on the back porch swing. Myra Halley was holding Free on her lap and rocking the child back and forth. 'I've missed you,' she admitted softly to Trudi. They sat there, silently swinging. 'It's awful to lose a daughter.'

'I'm going to lose mine, aren't I?' Trudi said fearfully.

Myra sat up, determined. 'No, you damn well are not!'

'I can't leave her here, Momma.'

'Buster.'

'Yeah, what about him?' Trudi dispiritedly recalled one of her older brothers.

'He's over at Cartersville, selling insurance. He's been married to Libby Seldes for two years now. Can't have kids.'

'Why not?'

'She used one of them metal things? Ripped her insides out.'

'Oh Jesus. Poor Libby.'

'They're waiting to adopt.'

Trudi shook her head. 'Momma, I don't want my child to be adopted. I want to be able to come back and take her when I get myself straightened out.'

'Until then,' Myra suggested, 'maybe they'll take Free in.'

Trudi gave it some silent thought. Buster? Yeah, he had been okay as a brother, but he sure wasn't anything like Free's real daddy, Tommy Patterson. What was it Tommy always said about nature versus nurture? Oh, why ever didn't she listen more carefully when he spoke, instead of just enjoying his presence? There was so much he had to teach her, but she was such a lousy student.

'Let's do it,' her mother said. 'Let's drive over to Cartersville right now and see what Buster and Libby say. See if we can set your mind at peace.'

'Dinner?'

'Your dad will be too potted to eat when he gets home anyway. And the boys, hell, they can fix their own meal for once. Or go down to MacDonald's.'

So the two women piled Free and her little bundle of clothes into the Halleys' old Buick and set off down the road to Cartersville.

145

There Buster and Libby lived in one of those new town houses that were amazing everybody with all their conveniences.

Buster was shocked to see his sister, Libby more so. But when she saw the child and heard what she was being asked to do, her heart melted. 'Oh, my baby,' she said, and already Trudi was worried. 'My little – what's her name?'

'Free,' Trudi stated emphatically.

'Free? Hey Trude, can I call her Carrie? I've always wanted a little girl called Carrie.'

'Well – '

'Free, Carrie, what's in a name?' Buster asked, as well he might since his real name was James Mason Halley, Jr.

'Yeah, well, I guess you can call her Carrie,' Trudi conceded, 'as long as she knows her real name is Free.'

'Oh lord, oh lord,' Libby said, and crushed the child to her bosom. 'Thank you, God. Praise your name.'

Trudi felt such an emptiness within her. 'I'll send you what money I can for her keep,' she promised.

'No need,' Libby told her. 'We've been saving up for two years for our little bundle of joy, and now we got her.'

'But it's not permanent,' Trudi tried to make sure Libby understood. 'The child's mine.'

'Of course she's yours,' Buster said. 'I just hope you haven't fucked her up with all those drugs I bet you've been takin'.'

'Hush, Buster,' Libby said. 'Don't dare talk like that in front of the child. Now, listen, Trudi, I have to ask, hon, how many lives has this little one had?'

'Oh Jesus!' Buster said.

'You stop that now, Buster,' Libby threatened.

'Only one,' Trudi admitted. 'Only one sad little life.'

Which about summed up her own at the moment.

Trudi stayed at her parents' that night, but she couldn't sleep. Her father's negative vibes, even in his drunken stupor, told her there was no place for her at this inn. She had to get out. She had to go away. She had to go back. Her home was in Taos. Her life here was over. But before she left, she went over to Cartersville to see how Free was doing.

Libby had taken Free shopping and brought her all the things everyone wants to buy for little girls: frilly dresses, patent leather shoes, barrettes and bonnets. Poor Free. All she had ever worn was a tie-dyed t-shirt and panties when she was with Trudi, except in the winter when she wore her bunny suit. And now she was to be dressed up to the nines. How would her little girl stand it?

146

Trudi watched in silence as her daughter delved into the boxes of delight and lovingly fingered the fabric of her new silky dresses. 'Remember me, Free,' she begged. But already her little girl's attention was focused on the flashy, store-bought objects before her.

# Chapter 24

# An Endless Torment

River Range Clinic was looking mighty bleak. Trudi Surefoot spent two days in an ever-increasing frenzy, seeking the man who had promised her the pills she needed to keep her life in a certain chemical balance. After two days, she concluded in despair that he was missing. Trudi hadn't the heart to break into another office and call Odelle once again to let her know they had been ripped off. The attendant obviously received the money from Odelle and then fled with it. Damn. Who the hell could you trust nowadays if not your drug dealer?

This whole clinic thing wasn't working out. Trudi wasn't meant to be confined. Yet that's what had happened to her ever since Odelle got her into this mess. Yes, it was Odelle's fault, all her fault. Why had Trudi flown to her in the first place? Okay, okay, Odelle had helped her out of messes before, but that didn't mean Trudi could rely on her now. Odelle was part of the process of taking away from Trudi her most vital part: the individuality which came only through drugs. But how could Odelle understand? She was so damned – what had Tommy called her once – square? And a two-dimensional square at that!

Trudi hated Odelle most at six a.m. in the morning, when wake-up call came. Trudi had exactly fifteen minutes to get dressed and get over to the gym or practice field for calisthenics. 'Waking up the body,' Morris, their drill instructor, called it. Morris – did he know the patients called him Moron? Sound body, sound mind? But her mind wasn't sound. It lacked its normal pharmacological mix, something it had craved for over twenty years now.

After their disastrous morning stretch session, with its horrid midlevel aerobic component to get that dreaded oxygen flowing to the brain, they trooped, sweaty and stinking, over to the main hall for breakfast. They passed through a cafeteria line – like big deal, there

148

were only corn flakes or shredded wheat, milk, coffee, tea and juice, and Trudi understood that the doctor in charge was trying to eliminate coffee and tea due to the caffeine – and then they took assigned seats. Assigned seats! Were they in kindergarten? She sat between Big Ed, an alcoholic who went through this Praise the Lord routine before he could eat his three boxes of raisin bran, and Little Nellie, a diet pill addict who was so afraid of gaining weight now that she was off her twelve-year pill habit that she only drank a glass of juice for breakfast. Between Big Ed, singing the Lord's praises, and Nellie's calorie counts, Trudi had no appetite at all.

At least after breakfast she could get back to her own room for "chore time". This gave her a chance to shower quickly, clean her teeth, make her bed and straighten up her spartan room before she set off to do her clinic chores. None of the clinic chores was fun, except groundkeeping. All chores put her in contact with other clinic inmates. Trudi hated them. That was another thing that had happened to her since she stopped eating the mystical mushroom, among other mind expanding edibles and swallowables. She discovered that she really didn't like people. Every single one of the patients and prison guards at the clinic possessed some fault that drove her crazy, like grinding teeth, running noses, crying too much, self-pitying whines, things she just wouldn't have noticed had she been stoned or levitated in other ways. Where was the goodness she once found so overwhelming in humanity? Had she just been looking through pupil-widened eyes?

After chores there was group therapy. She hated group. Everyone just sat there and dumped on each other. At the end of each hour, Dr Sabon kept telling them how much progress they were making. They weren't making progress at all – unless you considered keeping off drugs and booze for one more hour progress.

After group they suffered through more physical activity. 'Work off the pain of dependence,' that sadistic Madelaine Stevenson, Odelle's friend, urged. Not really urged – ordered would be more like it. They could go to the gym for volley ball or the playing field for soccer or baseball. Trudi tried all three. Her problem was she just wasn't aggressive enough for those competitive bastards, patients and coaches. Everyone ended up yelling at her. Obviously, she and balls just did not go together.

So she took to foregoing the pleasures of bashing someone's knee cap on the playing fields of River Range. Instead there was another program she was more attuned to. It was called Take a Hike with Mr Don, Don Harrington, or as his faithful following called him, Mr Nature. Now here was a man she could relate to. He would walk them up and down River Range property. They would stop every now and then to examine wild flowers, animal tracks, and watch for birds. It was her type of activity, peaceful, calm and non-competitive. Trudi felt almost at one with herself again, maybe because so few chose these nature walks. Sometimes she and Don were the only ones, especially when it rained.

After sports, lunch, another healthy meal with fruit for dessert because Madelaine believed sugar was dangerous for the addictive personality. Lunch was followed by meditation in one's room. In other words, rest hour, where you could listen to music and write letters, begging to be let out of this insane asylum. She wrote constantly to Odelle and sometimes even to Grace, though Grace was way over in New Jersey and probably wouldn't be able to do anything anyway.

Meditation was followed by occupational therapy. Madelaine arranged such coursework as investments and banking, which Trudi considered terribly unwise, sort of undoing all the good that meditation had accomplished. Or there was painting; basketweaving; reading and discussing great books – which couldn't be that great, as WOMAN OF THE THREE LIVES wasn't included. They were also offered the chance to play Madelaine's own game of Jeopardy, which was all about drugs; plus they could take medically-oriented courses to discover what drugs and alcohol had already done to your body and your brain. Trudi tried that one day but had been informed that half her brain might be missing, so she thought why chance it by using the rest of her brain to store irrelevant information? She wanted to conserve her strength so returned to pottery.

Madelaine's River Range clinic was ill-equipped for an expert potter like Trudi. The teacher, who doubled as the cook, was especially poor. But soon Trudi had the potter's shed well in hand and was directing the other inmates' efforts. Madelaine applauded her initiative and told her she had the makings of a great teacher. But it was all bullshit. Trudi had always been dependent, taking orders instead of giving them.

Dr Sabon was well aware of that fact. Her private sessions with him occurred during the afternoons, some time between occupational therapy and Tai Quon Do. They discussed Trudi's own particular problems. These were never very happy sessions. Dr Sabon, when she first came to the clinic, worked with Trudi on making up a list of all she lost by taking drugs. That's when she was in the burst of her first enthusiasm, before she realized that she was stuck here and they were expecting her to reform before they would let her out. What had Trudi lost? Years of her life when she didn't know what was happen-

150

ing. Her boyfriends, who came and went before she had the vaguest idea of who they really were. Her first child whom she put up for adoption. Her husband Tommy because she wasn't able to please him, because she never really understood what he wanted. Her child Free.

Her child Free, who was now her brother's child.

God! No wonder she always left these sessions with Dr Sabon crying. She wanted to dwell on the happier elements of her life, like her reincarnation, but he waved away her attempts. 'Let's concede,' he once said, 'that this is your third life. What are you doing with it?'

How could Dr Sabon be so tactless as to ask such a question!

Maybe that's why Tommy had put her in charge of his Fund for the Betterment of Humanity. Maybe he wanted her finally to develop her total potential as a human being.

Tommy was so hard to figure out. She tried sometimes when it was lights out at ten and she was still lying there on her bed, twisting, desperate for peace. Even though she knew Tommy was dead – unless he had just been faking lying there in the coffin and had really risen again – she continued to try to understand him. Understanding Tommy meant unlocking herself.

People loved Tommy Patterson. When he appeared on television or had that radio advice show for a while, critics called him charismatic. He could look into a person's soul and create a state of fusion. He was a giver of love and comfort. He knew the words to say to make people feel good about themselves. 'We're all on a spiritual journey,' he used to tell his audiences, when he held those sessions around the country during the eighties. 'Where you are is where you ought to be.'

Not for Tommy chastisement or rules. Morality is what *is*, that's what he preached. Values were relative. If it felt good, it was good. If it seemed right, it was right. Tommy wasn't the sort of person to impart negative feelings to his flock with terms like "ought to". No one ought to or had to do anything he or she didn't like. Responsibility lay in the eye of the beholder.

Tommy provided people who believed in themselves with a comfortable way to live. Only those who lived in doubt, who questioned rather than accepted, failed to see the greatness in this man. Trudi had no close knowledge of him after they stopped living together, but they definitely kept in touch, through their lawyers. Still she believed. Tommy didn't lead. Tommy didn't follow. Tommy was there as a chronicler of relevance. Like, after WOMAN OF THE THREE LIVES, his next best seller was WHY, LORD, ARE THERE OTHER PEOPLE IN THE CHECK OUT LINE? She knew what he was saying, even though she hardly ever went to a grocery store. He was saying ME. Get out of my way because ME is here. And people responded. Yes! It's all right to be ME!

With his next book THE DEVIL TAKE THE HINDMOST, reviewers said Tommy rewrote Darwin for the Yuppies. But was that fair? Wasn't that what the devil did anyway?

And his best book, the one Trudi loved most, was WHAT IS A COMMITMENT AND HOW TO MAKE ONE IN 10 EASY STEPS. Because there he was talking about love. ME was searching for WE. Everyone was searching for love. Tommy by then had found love with another woman, Kitten Fairleigh. Even Trudi had to admit that they made a splendid Eighties couple in their *People* magazine cover story.

Love was so tricky. Trudi was in love with Tommy from the day she met him until the day he died, and maybe even beyond that. But now Dr Sabon was telling her it might just be the narcotics, that maybe she didn't have a clear picture of what love was, after all. Certainly, the Tommy-is-love equation didn't sit well with either Odelle or Grace, and they had known him just as well as she had. Grace said to her once, 'To know Tommy Patterson is to understand perfect rage.'

Poor Grace. She was filled with fury. A few downers would probably have helped her out. Who out there, besides Trudi, knew that there was such anger in a woman who sold love for a living?

152

# Chapter 25

# May I Help You?

"Winning." "Every woman's fantasy." "Engaging." "We have here the next Rona Jaffe."

Grace Mandling sat back and read her reviews with the greatest of satisfaction. She didn't believe them, but she read them with relish anyway. What pleased her most was not that her first novel had received such encouraging reviews, but that she was working steadily, producing book after book. She had acquired an agent, and now enjoyed visions of supporting herself via her writing.

Grace never dreamed when she sat down in Odelle's house to write MAY I HELP YOU? that it would actually sell. The plot was rather trite, taken as it was from her own limited experience. Ashley, her heroine, from good blue-collar stock, was hired at Norman's, Chicago's premier department store, as a sales lady in women's lingerie. She met Mr Norman's son while he was embarrassing himself by trying to find the right gift for his sophisticated and expensive mistress, foreign and ten years his senior. Ralph Norman discovered, after about four hundred pages, that it wasn't his French mistress that he loved at all, it was little Miss Ashley. To close the book, they had the society wedding of the year. Old Mr Norman smiled happily on as Ashley's father, the plumber, explained how to replace the copper pipes in the downtown store without losing selling space. In other words, prince meets commoner, marries same, lives happily ever after, for all we know because Grace refused to carry the plot past the wedding ceremony.

In her second book, Grace varied an old theme. Her working title was DEBUTANTES DO IT! Sally Graystone, an Upper East side New York brat, is fleeing Tony Armstrong, her intended from the Hamptons, because of some silly disagreement over how one should serve pouilly fuissé. She rents a yacht for the weekend from this low life who takes her out on Long Island Sound. A storm comes up. They

153

are blown way off course and feared lost by all who know and love them. Tony is inconsolable. He refuses to drink another drop of the grape before Sally is found. 'What? You would give up Château Laffite Rothschild 1889 for a mere woman!' his father wonders.

Meanwhile, Sally faces the elements with the low life she rented the yacht from. She knows him only as Jack. During their days of danger together, he teaches her the meaning of life. It's not how you serve the wine, it's how you drink it that counts. Sally is finally saved after making a secret vow to the stars above to change her lifestyle. She rejects Tony in favour of Jack, but by then Jack has disappeared. That's because Grace was only up to page 200 when Sally was saved from the storm. It takes Sally another 200 pages to find Jack, who's actually a multimillionaire living in seclusion off the Maine coast. They're reunited and cast away in each other's arms with the simple but certain last sentence, 'Pour the wine, Jack.'

Her editor told Grace, 'I cried.' Grace decided at that point to change publishers. She didn't think she could really trust anyone who took this crap seriously.

LOVE YACHT, as the book was finally entitled, made the *New York Times* best seller list and stayed there for forty-two weeks. It also changed Grace Mandling's life. She was finally, irrevocably, rich.

But was she happy?

Damn right she was! She was rich and happy! Darrell Templeton, aka Ahmed Jemal Mohammed, faded from the literary scene after his first book RAGE IN BLACK AND WHITE ran its course. True, Tommy Patterson was still around, pushing his latest WHY, LORD, ARE THERE OTHER PEOPLE IN THE CHECK OUT LINE? But as popular as Tommy's self-centred advice was, it couldn't top LOVE YACHT.

Grace embarked on a new life. She left Chicago, Odelle, Sy and their kids behind her, and she moved to New York state, close enough to the city to feel its pulse, not close enough to be mugged. She started making public appearances. For this she needed a wardrobe consultant. Even though she was a former buyer for Marshall Field's, her taste seesawed between jeans for off-duty hours and tailored suits and skirts for work. But now her work was different. What did the well-dressed romantic floozy wear? In public she took to dressing in silk for day, lace for the evening.

She was not only a writer, she was also an actress. She lived her character, having a series of outrageous affairs with men who were dashing and daring and a little bit neurotic. Raw material, she told herself the morning after. Grace could take what these men gave her and spin it into marzipan for others. She would never again fall in love herself. She had tried that twice now, and each time she had picked a loser.

Oh, there were down moments in her life. LOVE YACHT was reviewed for the *New York Times* – only after it appeared on the best seller list – by none other than Leslie Brownlow, he of the Iowa Writers Workshop, who had encouraged her not to bother putting pen to paper. He called her work "verbal corpulence" leading to "illiteracy among the masses". All of a sudden, Leslie was worried about the masses? "Furthermore," Leslie continued, "there's not a single mention of furniture. Life without furniture is just an empty room." Was he being profound or did he have a furniture fetish?

Grace wasn't too upset. She understood she would never be a literary darling. But there were plenty of "serious" writers around, concentrating their novels on days in the life of. These were the ME writers, who couldn't see beyond their own constricted, constipated lives, their needs, their marriages, affairs, divorces, babies. The only questions they asked themselves were how much alimony to pay, whom to have an affair with, what to say to their therapists, and what the furniture in their living room said about their lives. Needless to say, most of these writers worked in short story form, not having enough to say to fill more than twenty pages at a time. At least she gave her readers their money's worth. Adventure, romance, a travelogue of some sort or other, the thrill that reading used to be before writing became a banal activity among banal people.

Another awkward moment in her career came when she appeared at the National Booksellers' Convention to autograph copies of her latest and glossiest THROBBING LOVE, her first with her new editor, Craig Epstein of Adams & Westlake, who insisted she show the flag at any convention that came along. She didn't know why. In its first week THROBBING LOVE shot to the top of the best seller list, whipped on by the frenzy of her many fans. But Grace could see Craig's point. These were booksellers, and nothing was too good, she felt, for those were who sweet enough to carry her books in their stores. So she gladly put purple pen to title page, smiled, and said a few meaningful, heartfelt words to each of the hundred or so who lined up for an autograph – until she spotted Tommy Patterson across the way, doing very much the same thing for his latest book THE DEVIL TAKE THE HINDMOST.

Her heart skipped a few beats, very much the feeling one of her heroines might have experienced, except that her heart was suffused with hate, not love. She shouldn't be resentful, she tried to calm herself. She was above it all.

But she wasn't. Her pain at his betrayal and the death of her baby was still there. She felt like yelling 'Stop, thief!' because this was the man who had stolen her innocence, leaving her with only nightmares of love and a stillborn child to keep her company in the dead, very dead of night.

He caught her eye as she was staring at him. And he smiled. He smirked. She could have killed him.

After she finished her autographing session, she descended from her little booth and sought out Craig Epstein. 'How dare you book me at a convention where you knew Tommy Patterson would be present?' she accused in a voice low enough only for the two of them to hear.

Craig was stunned. He was going to ask what Tommy Patterson was to her, but she rushed away without giving him the chance. Therefore, he also lacked the opportunity to tell her she was booked to speak at the same symposium as Tommy Patterson that very afternoon.

Grace consumed only cottage cheese for lunch. A good thing too. Even that curdled in her stomach as she was ushered in to the symposium on love and what it means today, only to be placed next to her ex-husband, who was busy burying his moustache in a cup of java, as the chairman called it.

'Grace,' Tommy acknowledged.

'Asshole,' she replied.

He smiled wearily. 'And your success excited me so.'

'Really? Well, you know what they say, "You can't keep a good woman down." Though I'm sure you've tried with enough of them. Like, what happened to your space doll? Following your career, as I have been forced to, via the media – you must have the best publicist in the business – I haven't seen you photographed with her lately. Dumped her too, have you?'

'I never dumped you, Grace. I fled from your fury.'

'Or was it the child support payments you thought you would have to make?'

'Our child – '

'Our child!' she shouted, and then realized she was bringing unwanted attention on herself. 'We have no child,' she said. 'She died at birth.' And realized with sudden horror that it had been almost ten years since she had suffered that loss, and that she suffered it still.

She looked towards the chairman and then almost back at Tommy. 'No one knows we were ever married. I want to keep it that way.'

'Fine with me. Though in my secret moments I can still hear you moaning when I put my tongue – '

She swung back her arm and slapped him. The picture made the front page of the *Miami Herald* and from there was syndicated all over the country. Some enterprising reporter found out the connection between Grace Mandling and Tommy Patterson. Soon she saw pictures of herself at her local grocery store check-out counter, splashed all over the *Inquirer* and the *Star*. The only good thing she could say about the incident was that it did nothing to lessen interest in her books or decrease the demand for public appearances, where she was constantly asked what Tommy Patterson was really like. Oh, how she wished she could tell them. But she demurred politely, each time repeating, 'Let me just say that he was not the role model for any of the heroes of my books.'

So, professionally, she thrived and Tommy thrived along with her, though she still felt the world wasn't big enough for the both of them. But how could she shrink it and squeeze him out?

Getting even with Tommy Patterson. What heaven that would be!

# Chapter 26
# Family Vacation

'This is embarrassing,' Julia insisted.

But Odelle was not to be put off. Okay, so they had been travelling in the car for eight days now, touring across America, listening to Julia complain about how she hated to be seen with them. It didn't matter.

'My friends' parents sent them to Europe as a high school graduation present,' Julia once again stressed. 'All I get is a tour through the great southwest?'

'You'll be lucky if you don't get a shot in the teeth,' Sy muttered.

'Look at that interesting rock formation,' Odelle pointed out.

'Which one?' Luke obliged by feigning interest.

'Oh. We passed it already,' Odelle noted sadly.

'I mean, why couldn't I have just worked as a cashier all summer to save money for college?' Julia insisted on continuing her whining, eight-day monologue. 'Why did you have to drag me off into this desert? None of my friends was forced to go on a family vacation.'

'None of my friends was either,' Sy agreed with her.

'Look, everybody!' Odelle boomed out. 'This is the last time we're all going to be together as a family. You're going off to college,' she reminded her daughter. 'You're almost never around for two weeks at a stretch,' she accused Sy.

'Thank God,' he muttered.

'I'm sorry I suggested this trip,' Odelle conceded. 'You're all being such pains in the butt, I'd rather have gone by myself!'

'I'm enjoying it Mom,' Luke pointed out.

'You would, you dork,' Julia told her ten-year-old brother.

'Everybody just shut up and look out of the window,' Odelle ordered.

'Can I keep my eyes on the road?' Sy asked.

Odelle didn't reply. She fumed. She hated them all. Try to do something nice for these ingrates and what did she get? A tension headache. Well, at least she'd have this trip to remember. She'd never forget what a miserable bunch this family of hers was, and she'd never travel with them again!

'Look, Mom, there's another cactus,' Luke enthused.

'Yeah. It's only the four thousandth we've seen in the last half hour,' Julia sneered.

'Why don't you read something, Julia?' Sy suggested.

'I'll continue with Aunt Grace's book,' she said.

'Aren't you a little bit young to be reading that – uh – romance?' Sy wondered.

'Everybody in school reads it,' Julia pointed out. 'We even passed the one that just came out in paperback around the classroom. With certain sections highlighted. Gee, you know, Aunt Grace never struck me as a sex fiend when she was living with us.'

'Don't mention sex in front of your brother,' Sy ordered.

'That's okay, Dad. I know about sex. Mom gave me a book explaining everything.'

'Everything!'

'That's in lieu of you explaining it to him,' Odelle said testily. 'Despite the many times I've asked you. I mean, how can you describe what it feels like to have a wet dream?'

'Odelle!'

'Yuch,' Julia agreed.

'Anyway, he'll know it when he has one,' Sy murmured viciously.

'Is it about time to stop for lunch?' Luke wondered.

'It's only ten-thirty, dear,' Odelle answered.

'Oh.'

Odelle wondered, as the day wore on, if she could stand another hour welded in the car to this wretch of a husband, a daughter who found adventure only in her local shopping mall, and a son who was fascinated by stopping to pee on the edge of the highway. It had all started out so well, their drive south from Chicago. They had stopped at Hannibal, Missouri, to see Mark Twain's old stamping grounds, then on to St Louis and the zoo and the arch. After that, it was down into Texas and Oklahoma so Sy could combine business with pleasure, the pleasure being his meetings with some oil men. Now they were trekking across the great southwest towards California. Julia was at least anxious to see California. Everything was happening there, she assured her parents. So maybe the trip would pick up as the days passed each other by.

'Here it comes,' Sy suddenly announced. 'So long, Texas. Hello, New Mexico.'

'Wow!' Luke exclaimed.

'Oh, shut up, will you!' Julia insisted. 'Do we have to eat Mexican again for lunch, Mom? Don't they have a MacDonald's here?'

'Sy, why don't you tell them one of your jungle stories, like when you ate that iguana.'

'Armadillo, dear.'

'Yuch,' Julia commented.

The situation vastly improved when Sy finally pulled into their first stop of the day, Taos, New Mexico, and everyone got out of the car to inspect the old Spanish town. 'Shop for trinkets,' Sy told his wife. 'I'm going to get an ice cold beer.'

But neither Julia nor Luke was interested in trinkets, so they just walked the streets of the old town – or, as some might call it, tourist trap – and gazed at the panhandlers and the left-over hippies. Odelle looked around her at the mountains and could see why no one who came to Taos would ever want to leave it. 'Isn't this beautiful, kids?' she said, but got no positive response.

They had a late lunch in a Mexican cantina. 'I'm beginning to like having tacos and refried beans every day,' Luke continued to be agreeable. Julia would have made some response, but Odelle grabbed her arm and gave her a warning grimace.

'Would you like a refill on the ice tea?' the waitress asked. She wasn't even Mexican but Anglo-Saxon, with long brown hair and sort of dopey eyes.

'Who does she remind you of?' Odelle leaned across to Sy.

'Julia?'

'No. The waitress?'

'The waitress?'

Sy was horrible about paying attention to who served them. Often, when they were out together, he would call the wrong waitress over. But this woman . . . Probably she was like someone Odelle knew in Chicago, but who?

Ever since Odelle had taken up painting as a hobby, she had learned to study faces. She examined them for shadows and contours, and she was sure she had seen this waitress's face before. 'Pardon me,' she said, when the woman came back with the tea, 'but have you ever lived in Chicago?'

'Oh, Mom,' Julia moaned.

'Chicago,' the waitress repeated rather dumbly. 'I was there once.'

'Yes? I thought I'd seen you before.'

The waitress smiled happily. 'Probably you saw me on television.'

'Oh? Were you an actress?'

'Oh no, no. I was the woman in the book, WOMAN OF THE THREE LIVES?'

160

'Not – !'

'Odelle!' Sy broke in. 'Thank you for the tea, Miss. We'll call you if we need you.'

The waitress looked puzzled. She put down the tea, only slightly slopping it over the lid of the pitcher.

'Odelle, you are not to say a word to that woman,' Sy stressed.

'Can you believe she's working here as a waitress?'

'Who is she?' Julia asked, suddenly interested in the world around her again.

'She must have made a fortune out of that book. So why is she working here? I still see the paperback on the shelves.'

'Eat your food, and then we're leaving town,' Sy ordered. 'I refuse to become involved with yet another wife of Tommy Patterson.'

'Who's he?' Julia wondered. Odelle prided herself on the fact that so far, despite several situations where it was needed as proof of age and birth, she had managed to keep Julia's birth certificate out of her daughter's hands. Therefore, Julia still had no idea that Tom Patterson was her real father. Some day though, some day soon, Odelle would have to face the music and tell her the grisly truth.

After their lunch at the Mexican cantina, Sy sped through New Mexico. He zipped through Arizona, across the Sierra Nevadas and into California, down to San Diego where he promised the kids no more Mexican food. Now they would have some really good seafood.

'Seafood?' Julia whined. 'Is that like – fish? I can't stand fish.'

161

# Chapter 27

# Grace 'Sherlock' Mandling

When the phone rang, Grace took her time picking it up. It was just after four in the afternoon, and she wasn't really in the mood to talk to anyone. She was lying in bed after her afternoon nap, thinking about what she would have to write tomorrow. Her working title for this one was NANNY'S BOY, and the plot was becoming slightly perverted. She was stuck with the sinking feeling that she would have to toss the fifty pages she had written already away. Perhaps the world wasn't ready for a story about a man who grows up to be Prime Minister of England and who confesses on his death bed that he always loved his Nanny best. She would have to call her editor and see what he thought. Craig Epstein always got so jumpy when they discussed sex, which he preferred to call "romance."

So Grace picked up the phone unenthusiastically. 'I have a person-to-person collect call for Ms Grace Mandling from Mrs Odelle Hampton. Will you accept the charges?'

'Who?' Grace asked, trying to focus her mind.

'Odelle Hampton.'

'Odelle? Why is she calling me collect?'

'Grace! Accept the charges!' Odelle shouted over the operator's growing objections.

'Of course I accept the charges,' Grace said in a tone ill-befitting her name.

'I will put you through now,' the operator informed her.

'Grace, I have to talk fast,' Odelle said. 'Sy's on the beach with Luke, but he's bound to be back any minute. So just listen. I met Trudi what's-her-name in Taos, New Mexico. She was waiting tables. Why was she waiting tables? What happened to the money she got from that book? What happened to her relationship with – '

'Who the hell is Trudi what's-her-name?'

'Tommy Patterson's third wife! She of the three lives. She's working in Cantina Sante Maria in Taos, New Mexico. Sy refused to

162

let me speak to her to ascertain a few facts. That's why I'm calling collect because if he knew I called you, he'd know why.'

'So maybe he could clue me in.'

'Have you no curiosity about exactly why our sister in suffering is working as a waitress instead of living in a *muy grande hacienda*? Shit! Sy's on his way in.' Odelle slammed the phone down before Grace could comment one way or another.

During the rest of the evening, Grace considered how much curiosity she did have. What business was it of hers what happened to this Trudi woman? As she remembered her from her television appearances, this Trudi was sort of spaced out anyway. And yet, she knew only too well what it was like to be lost in love and disillusionment with Tommy Patterson. It had all returned with telling force when she slapped Tommy and made front page news.

But what did she owe Trudi what's her name? Nothing.

Of course, she did have a score to settle with Tommy. Like a snowball on a wintry day, he was growing fairer and purer. He was crisscrossing the country, offering seminars such as "Watch Out, World, ME is Coming!" and "Make Way For ME", as he and his followers focused on aggressively attacking life to get the most out of it for ME. Testimonials even appeared in the *Rockland County Journal News* when Tommy was scheduled to appear at the community college auditorium: Jane Jackson, Securities Analyst for E.F. Hutton says, "I used to feel guilty if, when out with my friends, I took the last piece of pizza. But now I realize, hey, I'm entitled. If you want something, you have to grab for it. Come hear Tommy talk about ME. Because who he's really talking about is YOU!" The all-day course, held conveniently on Saturday, cost only $350. The workbook that accompanied the course, consisting of all sorts of self-help tests that would determine if you were killer enough for today's society, cost only $52 and included a motivational tape, recorded by Tommy himself.

Grace noted that except for the top of the ad, Tommy never used his last name. It was always Tommy, as if he were an intimate friend. Her gorge rose every time she saw that ad!

But what could she do about it? How could one blacken the name of someone whose espoused philosophy was that ME is the most important person in the word, that we owed nothing to anyone else.

At least he wasn't a hypocrite.

However, he was a shit! Could she prove it? Could she disembowel him before the world and let his guts hang out? Would anybody care?

Hate was destructive. She knew that. Still, that did not diminish her great capacity for it. She had been a victim twice, once with

163

Tommy and then with dear Ahmed. Maybe she had let herself in for it. She was so innocent and trusting in both cases, blinded by her belief in love. But was she always going to be the one who paid?

She called up Ray Steiner. He was a mystery writer she had met at a cocktail party in Connecticut about a year ago. They weren't really having an affair. They just slept with each other off and on. It was a fond relationship. Between fucking, they discussed the drawbacks of being considered category authors. Ray actually was having tremendous success with one of his characters, Adam Stead, a bisexual undercover investigator for an unnamed U.S. agency. He gave her an autographed copy of his latest, SNORKELLING TOWARDS DEATH, and it seemed authentic to Grace. Maybe he could offer some help now.

Ray lived in Boston, though he had a weekend cottage in New Hampshire. He said he had to live most of the time in Boston because he had to have access to its libraries. So she tried his Boston apartment first. 'This is not an answering machine. This is me. I'm not here. So don't bother me, his machine snapped at her.

'Ray, this is Grace Mandling,' Grace mewed into the phone. 'I need your help.'

Then she called his New Hampshire cottage, where she had recently spent a rather delectable weekend, all things considered, like on the down side he took her fishing. There he didn't even have an answering machine.

Ray didn't get back to her until after midnight, and then he sounded drunk. That's what Boston will do for you. 'How can I help my precious little Gracie?' he asked.

'Precious Gracie needs some big help from robust Ray,' she replied in kind. 'For example, do you know a detective agency that's good, discreet, and works out of Taos, New Mexico?'

He laughed drunkenly and said, 'Just a minute. Let me ask Adam.'

There was a pause while Grace considered what should be done. Obviously, Ray was delusionary. Adam was the character in his books, wasn't he? 'Okay,' Ray came back. 'Adam says try Continental Assurities. They're located in New York. They're mainly involved in industrial espionage, but they do handle the odd personal case now and then to break in their new hires. Get in touch with Jamie Ford. She's Adam's contact there. Hey, Grace, listen, I'll call you back tomorrow. I've got to heave.'

And on that romantic note, Ray hung up on her.

Continental Assurities. The firm's name was waiting for her on her telephone pad when she woke up. She knew there would be no such company and that Jamie Ford was another figment of Ray's imagination. But what the hell? She dialled information for New York City.

164

Continental Assurities was indeed listed. And Jamie Ford was a real and pleasant person.

She asked who had referred Grace to her; and when Grace said Adam Stead, she laughed. Was Jamie Ford also being bedded by Ray Steiner? First things first. Grace set up an appointment with her for the following day.

Jamie assured Grace there should be no problem finding out about Trudi what's-her-name. Continental had a contact firm in Albuquerque. Jamie promised to get in touch immediately. If all Grace wanted to discover was Trudi's financial condition, she should have her information inside of a week. 'Plus any gossip about her,' Grace added belatedly.

'The bill rises,' Jamie warned.

And indeed it did. Grace was only thankful that she didn't have to hire a private investigator to deal with an errant husband.

A week later the report came via the mail from Continental Assurities. It was triple-sealed, so Grace had to use her scissors to get it open. But she soon held the truth about Tommy's dumping of Trudi Heidi Halley, aka Trudi Surefoot.

What upset Grace most, she supposed, was Trudi's loss of her child. Tommy Patterson, the great destroyer, had done it again, only this time the child was alive. In one way or another, Tommy managed to rip motherhood away from all of them, except Odelle. But Odelle was strong. Odelle knew what she wanted: marriage, a family. When Tommy deserted Grace, she knew only that she had to keep going before the furies caught up with her. But Trudi, did she know anything at all? The report said she was known about town for spending her salary on various pharmaceuticals and exotic plants. The world was moving on, but Trudi Surefoot still occupied the stoned age.

What was Grace to do about this? Could she give a hot tip to one of the scandal mongers and let them take over? No. Tommy was too clever. There were so many excuses he could make for the way he had treated Trudi. Look at how little censure he had faced when the story of how he treated Grace and Odelle came out. The scandal sheets loved his flaunting of convention. After all, bigamy was a minor affair for a man who openly stated his belief that all laws constrained the human soul.

Grace held on to her Trudi Surefoot report. She did nothing for the next several weeks because Odelle was out of touch. Oh, she did go into New York and talk to Craig about NANNY'S BOY. He read a few sections and agreed with her that it was a bit too twisted even for her readers, especially the section where Nanny spanks the P.M. when

165

she didn't like his decision concerning British activity in the Persian Gulf. 'Stick with young romance,' Craig told her.

Grace wanted to reply that she had been faking young romance lately. Matter of fact, she could barely remember young romance. The trust, the hope, the foolish disregard of reality, where had they gone?

She took a trip up to Boston to be with Ray for the weekend, her thank you for his tip on Continental Assurities. 'Did it help?' he wondered. She was surprised he even remembered.

'I found something out about my ex-husband.'

'He of the slapped face?'

'You saw the story.'

'Stories,' Ray corrected her. 'God, there's a guy who's raking in the bucks. If only I were smart enough to state the obvious in words of one syllable, I too could write a book about today's society.'

'You're much more complicated than a single syllable,' she flattered him. 'Anyway, Adam Stead's too good to give up. He's so – umm – so real,' she tried.

'You mean when he held on to the helicopter runner as it tried to lose him over New York City? Or was it the time he took six shots in his chest from the gun of master villain Richard Denton, but still managed to hogtie the bastard and call the police, only to end up in hospital having to choose between his male and female lover?'

'I liked that touch. Especially when the male lover said, "Shall we make it a threesome?"'

Ray laughed. 'That's your books, honey. Adam Stead's never involved in sex unless it degrades someone. I play to the male mind.'

Grace chuckled into his shoulder. 'We're both such whores.'

'Speaking of whores.'

'Yes?'

'If you want my advice, stay away from your ex-husband. You don't need the aggravation.'

'Even if he's done a wrong I think I can right?'

'I thought he didn't believe in right and wrong, only power.'

Power. Women had so little of it. What did women excel in except the power to annoy, also known as the power to nag? Women, even women who worked outside the home, were relegated to life's details – car pools, menus, household budgets – while men had time to appreciate the broader sweep of their existence. Men insulated themselves from everyday worries by having their women handle them. Maybe Ray was right, Grace should just forget the private investigator's report. Life trundled on. Women were either stepped on or stepped over. And what could she do about it but watch men's feet?

166

In mid-August, while everyone else was on holiday and Grace was trying to come up with an idea to replace NANNY'S BOY, which she had grown quite fond of in their short time together, Odelle called. 'I'm back!' she exclaimed.

'Nice trip?'

'The children and Sy are still alive. And I think that in itself is a testimony to my patience and my diligent attention to creating an atmosphere of harmony. In other words, it was an extremely stressful experience, and I don't want to see any of the family again for at least a year.'

'Isn't Julia going off to college?'

'Smith. I don't think it's really her type of school, but I'm hoping by the time she finds out how to get off campus and meet men, she'll have wised up enough about them to pick and choose. Unlike myself. I went to Cornell and met Tom Patterson. And the rest is history. By the way, did you move on the Trudi Surefoot thing?'

'I got it all. He left her with a twenty-dollar bill. She had to give her child into her brother's keeping. Now she waits tables and sells pottery and buys drugs with the proceeds. I suppose we should be thankful that she works in a restaurant. That way she must get something to eat.'

'Naturally, we'll take action.'

'Why, Odelle? I've been thinking. Maybe we should just forget it.'

'Forget it? When the opportunity lies in front of us to right a wrong with a certain panache, you would turn your back? Grace, this is not the you we all know and love. What did Georgiana do to the Earl who ravished her, stealing her virginity, thus making her an outcast in Northumberland?'

'She had him ambushed in East Africa, castrated and cannibalized.' Grace fondly remembered LADY OF THE PIRATES. 'But that was fiction.'

'Well, of course, I agree that castrating Tommy would probably get us arrested, and as for eating him – well, he's probably pretty old, so I imagine he'd be tough, but with a good dose of tenderizer . . .'

'Odelle!'

'Oh, all right, Grace! We'll stick to an American form of torture. We'll hire a lawyer.'

# Chapter 28

# Legal Aid

By the time Odelle arrived in New City, New York, Grace was finally deeply involved in another plot line. In other words, she was less than pleased at the interruption. She was unloading herself at her typewriter at record speed, chronicling the adventures of Edwina, lusty daughter of a Viking lord.

Grace didn't really enjoy doing historicals like this in one respect: they involved research, at least a little. On the other hand, historicals freed her to impose any moral code she wished upon her heroines. After all, no one was going to invite Edwina to afternoon tea. Unfortunately, Edwina had gotten a little bit out of hand in the morality department of late.

As Odelle descended, Edwina, who had just taken part in the vicious sacking of the Saxon coast, floundered about in a Viking ship which had been set fire to by a well-placed Saxon arrow. She was about to go into the drink to be rescued by Rolf, illegitimate son of Ethelred the Readiless. Love would naturally ensue after three hundred more pages of complications. And here was Odelle, expecting Grace to take off for New Mexico into someone else's romantic fiction. 'I will not take no for an answer,' Odelle warned.

Grace was definitely annoyed. What did time matter to Odelle? Julia was ensconced at Smith; Sy was out of the country for a month; and Luke was with his babysitter. All Odelle would be missing was a few days of voluntary work. Grace would be taken out of Edwina's life at a most critical point, like how diaphanous would be her Viking garb as she floated in the drink, and who knew if she would ever get back to her own people?

So naturally Grace was huffy on the flight to New Mexico and the drive into Taos. But her sympathy was roused somewhat by eating lunch at the Cantina Sante Maria. She observed Trudi surreptitiously, noting the woman got half the orders wrong as she stumbled through her day of drugs and sorrow.

Odelle and Grace reserved rooms at the Adobe Inn and argued about when was the best time to tackle Trudi. Finally, they decided to do it while the woman of the three lives was at her pottery stand. Trudi worked at the Cantina from six in the morning until two in the afternoon. Then she became Trudi Surefoot, potter. So at four, after they had enjoyed a short rest from their journey, Grace and Odelle walked over to the old section of Taos and approached Trudi's stand in the marketplace. Grace kept urging Odelle along as her interest was several times redirected towards some Indian jewellery. Grace wasn't about to look at Indian jewellery, not while the Vikings were uppermost in her mind.

Trudi was glad to have customers standing in front of her, examining her works. Grace and Odelle smiled at her and nudged one another, neither wanting to be the one to start. Finally, Odelle took charge, as she usually did. 'Pardon me for being inquisitive,' Odelle said, 'but are you by any chance Trudi Surefoot?'

Grace moaned at the clichéd approach, but Trudi seemed pleased. 'Why, yes, I am. Do I know you?'

'We have a mutual acquaintance,' Odelle said.

'Tommy Patterson,' Grace got to the point. Odelle would take eons!

'Tommy?' Trudi replied. And they were both surprised because she said the name with love and adoration.

'You were married to him, weren't you?' Odelle asked.

'I still am,' Trudi replied.

'You still are? Does he support you then?'

'Well – uh – no.'

'Does he call or visit you?' Grace wondered.

'Well – no.'

'So what exactly does this marriage consist of?' Odelle wondered.

'Gee, these are awfully personal questions,' Trudi caught on.

'Trudi, both of us are former wives of Tommy Patterson.'

'Golly.'

'He married me when he was still married to Odelle,' Grace cut in grimly.

'Gee.'

'We're worried about your legal and financial status,' Odelle stated, warming to her subject.

As it turned out, they were the only ones who were. Trudi had given neither a thought. After about ten minutes of talk, Grace suspected Trudi was not only on drugs but had been none too bright to begin with. Just Tommy's type of woman, she thought ruefully.

It took Odelle and Grace two days of incessant persuasion to convince Trudi to let them hire a lawyer for her. The lawyer would press Tommy not only for a legal divorce, which Trudi really didn't want, since she was under the illusion that he was coming back for her, but also for Trudi's share of the profits from WOMAN OF THE THREE LIVES.

Tommy Patterson hit the ceiling when he was served both with divorce papers from that drudge in Taos and a suit demanding payment of funds from royalties received upon WOMAN OF THE THREE LIVES. Jesus! What was Trudi up to?

He turned the matter over to his attorneys and tried to dismiss it from his mind. After all, he had suffered several suits in the course of his long career as pater familias to a growing mass of followers. Some reporters wrote that he was head of a cult, a guru, but he was no false messiah. At least as far as he knew. No, he was head of a feeling, the feeling of GOOD; and to feel GOOD, some women had to be screwed. So they sued him for breach of promise, a weakness of his – he had a habit of promising things when he was about to come. But as long as he was married to Trudi, he couldn't be held to any promise of marriage.

Still, what had set Trudi off now after so many years? He decided to call her. She had always been such a reasonable, complaisant creature, he was sure he could talk some sense into her. And he was right! She was delighted to hear from him. She even asked him when he was coming "home".

'Trudi, I'm calling about these suits of yours,' he explained.

'What suits?'

'Law suits.' Maybe there was some *weisenheimer* behind the suits, aiming to get Tommy's money, not for Trudi but for himself. 'Whatever made you sue me for a divorce and for all this money? You know the money's not yours. You never earned it. You sure didn't write the book.'

'Oh, Tommy. My lawyer says that you appropriated my life story and then led me around on all those television tours. It's sort of like you ghost-wrote my story. So he feels I'm entitled to at least half of everything you made on that book.'

'Half! You moron! Do you think you really had those three lives?'

'I know I did!'

'It was the power of suggestion, Trudi. My suggestion.'

'You're wrong. You just brought out what was inside me. You can't take my lives away from me, Tommy, so just stop acting so horrid!'

She was screaming at him. Little Miss Shit-For-Brains was screaming at Tommy Patterson! 'All right, look, let's not worry about that right now,' he tried to calm her. 'What about this divorce thing? What makes you think you need a divorce?'

'Well, Grace told me that you married her while you were already married to Odelle.'

'Grace? Grace Mandling!' He should have known!

'She is so sweet. And Odelle too,' Trudi crooned. 'I don't know what I would have done without their support. They've given me money and everything, like for the lawyers and things. They say, when all this is over, I should be rich. Then I'll be able to get Free back. Isn't that wonderful!'

Tommy hung up on her. He could not stand for one extra second to listen to her mad drooling. Grace and Odelle, they were behind all this. There must be some law against persecution. He would find it and he would pin them to the wall with it.

His lawyers came back to him and told him there was nothing illegal in his ex-wives giving his present wife advice. Well, goddamn it, there should be! He would call those bitches and let them have it. Odelle . . . what the hell was her number? Where did she live even? He had read something about her in all those articles that had come out after Grace had slapped him. Odelle had remarried and was living in some Midwestern city, served her right. Either Chicago or St Louis. Remarried. Probably to that brute he had met in Ann Arbor, the one who hung around while the lawyer served him with divorce papers. Better not call Odelle, who knew what connections her husband might have. But Grace . . . now there was a different story. Grace was all alone.

Her number was listed. That's the sort of idiot Grace was. He would never let his number be listed. There were all sorts of nuts in the world, wanting to get even, like a lot of those who took his seminars and afterwards claimed it was a rip off.

Tommy arranged his call to Grace very carefully. He went to sleep that night at twelve, after winding down from his ten to eleven stint on *Dr Feel Better*, where he took calls from all over the Los Angeles area, he himself having a well-fenced home in Beverly Hills. He was asleep for two hours before his alarm woke him. Two in California, five in the morning in New York. Man at his weakest then. Woman too, he assumed.

Yes, when Grace Mandling answered the phone, Tommy knew she had been in a deep, deep sleep. 'I don't appreciate your childish little vendetta,' he grimly told her without any introductory pleasantries.

'Excuse me?' Grace's first thought flashed to Rolf's half brother, legal heir to the throne of the Saxons who had tried to seduce Edwina and had been rebuffed. But then she shook her mind clear. Where would Rolf's half brother have learned to use the telephone?

'What did you and Odelle think you were accomplishing by going to Trudi?'

Grace laughed slowly, seductively. 'Why Tommy. This is Tommy, isn't it? Tommy the great?'

'Cunt!'

'Gee, Tommy, aren't you the one who goes around the country espousing the philosophy of ME? And now all of a sudden you don't want Trudi to get hers? Grab it while you can, Tommy. You're getting older, even if the world doesn't seem to be getting any wiser. And don't call this number again. I'd hate to charge you with harassment.'

'The statute of limitations hasn't run out. The whole world saw you slap me. I could have you up on charges of assault.'

'Please do, Tommy. It would make such a great story, which I'm sure all your supporters would relish.'

And then the bitch hung up. The bitch hung up on him! There if anywhere was the essence of ME.

Tommy Patterson lay in bed, bereft of sleep. But then it occurred to him that he was approaching things the wrong way. His fight wasn't with Grace or even with Odelle. The suits came from Trudi. It was her he would have to face.

He'd have to fit that pothead into his schedule somehow. New Mexico wasn't far. He would be able to do it in a day and still be back for his soon-to-be-syndicated radio call-in show. He told his lawyers exactly what he wanted them to draw up. They warned that it might not stand up in court, but conceded it was worth a try. Legal papers in hand, he flew to New Mexico.

The trouble with most people is they just don't grow. He could see the minute he entered Taos that Trudi had not grown at all. She had expanded neither her consciousness nor her horizons since the last time he saw her. And when he met her face to face, he knew that his intuitive assessment had been right on the mark.

When she spotted him, her face lit up, her eyes widened, her lips broke into a smile. 'Tommy!' she screamed and ran into his arms. He was loved. As usual.

He convinced her to leave her job at the cantina and come away with him for the day, despite the fact that the owner threatened to fire her. 'Listen, Pedro,' he told the obvious immigrant, 'You wouldn't have hired her in the first place unless you were desperate.' Her hand in his, Tommy led her from the cantina, back to the apartment they had once shared, only to discover that Trudi no longer lived there but was a boarder in one of the older, more rundown houses. Jeez, he hoped he could stand a day there.

He made love to her. He was sure this would look good in court. If she really wanted to divorce him, why did she spread her legs to

172

eagerly for his entry? Of course, she smelled a little bit like jalepano, but he tried not to let that bother him. Then, after he was through with his part of the love-making and she almost came, he got down to business.

Hours later he had got nowhere. It disturbed him that all the sweet talk in the world could not convince her to drop her divorce suit against him. 'But why?' he wondered.

'I just was very affected by Grace's story,' Trudi said, 'especially the fact that she lost her baby. I lost mine too, you know.'

'Free? Free's dead? Dear little Free,' Tommy mourned. 'We are on this earth such a short time.'

'What are you talking about?' Trudi wondered. 'Free's with my brother and his wife in Cartersville, Texas. I'm hoping some day, with the money you owe me for my share in the book, to get Free back with me. That's why I can't give up on any of this, Tommy. I hope you understand.'

'I understand,' he conceded. 'You want money. We all do. I came here prepared to give you a settlement. And I think it's going to thrill you.'

Trudi smiled expectantly. He knew he had her where he wanted her.

'How does one thousand dollars each month for the next twelve months sound?' he suggested enthusiastically.

Trudi sat up. Her breasts, still perky, bounced up with her. 'Oh, Tommy!'

'I knew you'd be pleased.'

'Twelve thousand dollars! Oh, but that's so much. Can you afford it?'

'Not really,' he admitted. 'But I want to be fair with you. And if you say I haven't been, well then, I haven't been; and we've got to do something about it.'

In no time at all, even though she did have qualms about calling her lawyers first, he had her signing a document, relinquishing all claims, all rights to WOMAN OF THE THREE LIVES. He flew back to L.A. a happy man. By courier he had his agreement with Trudi delivered to his lawyer. It was all settled. Now he could move on to a further refinement of ME.

His lawyer called back just as Tommy was preparing to go to the studio and help the bozos of the world overcome their mental and moral trepidations. 'There's a bit of a problem,' the lawyer said.

'Yeah? What is it?'

'Trudi Surefoot signed over her power of attorney to her lawyers. Nothing she agreed to is worth a damn.'

173

# Chapter 29

# Trudi Surefoot's Fourth Life

Tommy Patterson made it to *People* magazine again. Grace took some satisfaction from that. She should. She had instigated the article. She was surprised they actually did the story. Usually, they stuck to such fluffy, good-news, feel-good pieces. But even *People's* editors had to concede that this was a story not to be missed. The propagator of ME had definitely lived down to his own philosophy.

Actually, the story was focused on Trudi Surefoot, "noted woman of the three lives", as *People* called her. A reporter and cameraman followed Trudi through her day as a waitress and artist, showing the poverty to which she had been reduced. Accompanying the article was a photo of her crying bitterly when talking about the loss of her daughter. Fortunately, they mentioned nothing of her extensive drug use. There was only so much reality the readers of *People* could take.

Tommy didn't help himself much. He was quoted in the article as saying, 'I can't speak about this. It's in the hands of my lawyers.' When asked why Trudi got nothing from the wildly successful WOMAN OF THE THREE LIVES, Tommy snapped, "Who wrote the damned book!"

Ah, Tommy dear, your MENESS is showing, Grace thought deliciously.

For Tommy Patterson the *People* article was disastrous. He was making a swing through the Midwest, Kansas, Nebraska, Illinois, Ohio. In Kansas and Nebraska hardly anyone knew who he was. The takings were meagre. Perhaps he should have promoted himself as more of a Dale Carnegie figure, as people definitely would have to think positive to live in those desolate states.

In Illinois and Ohio Tommy hit the big cities. Everywhere he went, there were some of those dippy women's groups, spurred on by the *People* magazine article, out picketing. Cunts!

He had called the police in Chicago. He was scheduled to appear there for an entire week. By the time he arrived, most of his seminars

174

had been sold out for months. But to get to the auditorium where his seminars were held, his flock of followers needed to pass through the barricade of drooping breasts, created by strident feminists. He simply couldn't understand it. What was Trudi Surefoot to them?

Had he but known, Odelle Hampton was one of the organizers of the protest, along with others in her Volunteers Against Masculine Oppression group, known throughout the women's movement as VAMO. She had already moved from her work at Planned Parenthood to the more tragic enterprise of saving women from the men they loved. She joined VAMO in reaction to the outrage her new work instilled in her. However, she couldn't allow herself to be visible in the protest movement against her ex-husband. Had she been arrested, Sy would have been furious. However, Odelle was gratified by VAMO's picket line and the ladylike way they scurried along once the police arrived, only to reform when the police left. Several protestors even made it into Tommy's seminars in one guise or another, only to ask him embarrassing questions in the middle of his Meditation on ME sessions.

Tommy thought he could ride the whole *People* magazine out. After all, Americans had notoriously short memories. If they could elect Richard Nixon, they could forget about Trudi Surefoot. By the time he reached Columbus, Ohio, though, he knew he'd have to take some action. He thought of Columbus as being prosaic. He had forgotten it was also a college town. More militant feminists! You give these girls an education and what do they do with it!

He gave in. He figured if he couldn't survive in Columbus, he wouldn't survive anywhere. He called his lawyers and ordered them to settle. 'Under what conditions?' one asked for instructions. 'Under any conditions!' he shot back. 'I'm losing a fortune out here!'

Trudi received half of everything Tommy had made on WOMAN OF THE THREE LIVES. She would continue to receive half of the royalties and any other monies accruing from the sale of the book. And now there was talk of a movie deal, or perhaps a mini-series on television, six hours' worth, two hours for each life.

And what of Trudi? Her lawyers were overjoyed at the settlement, and she supposed she should be too. It meant she could give up her job at the Cantina Sante Maria and sleep late in the morning. That was good. She had the feeling she really was never meant to be a waitress anyway. Getting up in those early hours, especially after a full night of cannabis or whatever, had lowered her creativity level. Now the lawyers assured her she could pursue her art full-time.

She called both Odelle Hampton and Grace Mandling to thank them for their efforts on her behalf. Even though their help meant she

175

would now be divorced from Tommy, it was probably a good thing to try to get on with her life. Tommy, well, she still loved him, but she had to face the fact that maybe they had moved beyond each other. Not that she wouldn't take him back if he really wanted her again. But only time would tell, she warned herself bravely.

Grace Mandling made an interesting suggestion, which Trudi took up with her lawyers. Grace suggested that Trudi put all her new-found wealth into a trust fund and live off the interest or the interest and part of the principal, depending upon what sort of lifestyle Trudi wanted to adopt. And Trudi found that suggestion good. She didn't really understand money. She knew it was used to buy things, a new-fangled way to barter, which she sometimes did when she lent her kiln to one of her friends and received raw materials in return. But she'd never had real money before, like excess money. She'd only barely had enough. Therefore, she did let her lawyers set up a fund at some bank in Taos.

In the beginning, the details were unclear with this new trust fund of hers because, despite the bank manager's insistence, Trudi couldn't calculate how much money she would need. She knew the first thing she had to do was rent a two-bedroomed apartment and then buy a ticket to Cartersville, Texas. Now was the time to bring Free home.

Cartersville was much as it had been three years ago when she left Free with her brother and his wife, Buster and Libby Halley. Trudi felt guilty because she hadn't really been back to Texas as often as she planned. It just seemed so hard to collect enough money and find the time. She called though. She spoke to Free on the phone. She also sent her daughter drawings. She missed Free terribly. Being a mother was a part of her life. Maybe she wasn't the best mother in the world. Okay, she would concede she should get off drugs. But her child was her child. She had given one up for adoption. She still wondered about that. She didn't want to wonder what Free was doing all her life.

Buster and Libby called Free "Carrie". And when Trudi arrived on their doorstep – they had bought a house since the last time she had seen them – she saw a little girl playing in their yard who looked like a Carrie. Free's hair was cut. It used to be long and trailing, now it was short and curly. And Free was dressed in the cutest little playclothes, just like you'd seen in magazines or on television.

'Free!' Trudi called to her daughter, even before she rang the doorbell.

The little girl in the yard stopped what she was doing, looked up at the strange woman with the moon face and long swinging hair, and was puzzled.

'Free, it's me; it's your mommy.' Trudi bent down, expecting the little girl to run into her arms. Instead the girl looked more puzzled and possibly scared. Trudi was confused. What should she do next?

Libby solved her problem by opening the door. 'Trudi!' she exclaimed. Libby didn't look too pleased to see her.

'Hi, Libby. I've come to get my daughter.'

Buster came home from work early. Trudi guessed Libby had called him. No sooner had Buster arrived than Trudi's mother and father came over from East Diablo. Trudi was happy that everyone was so anxious to get together with her. If only Free had been more responsive, her day would have been complete.

Libby made a family meal of macaroni and tuna fish, with some good, fresh salad. It was a welcome change from the Mexican food or hamburgers Trudi usually ate. They all sat pleasantly together, eating and having a good talk. Everyone had read the story about her in *People* magazine. They were suitably impressed when she described all the photo-taking and interviewing that took place.

Then she told them about the money she was receiving as a settlement from Tommy. 'Alimony?' her mother asked.

'Oh, no. I wouldn't take alimony from him,' Trudi said. 'This is all from the book we did together. So the first thing I did with that money was to rent a two-bedroomed apartment so Free can come home with me.'

And there it was, that deadly silence again. Everyone looked away from her except Free, who stared right at her, as if Trudi were talking about someone else.

Libby let Trudi help put Free to bed. Oh, what a lovely room her daughter slept in. It was all pink and white, with teddy bears and dolls and a little playhouse, blocks and Legos. Libby and Buster had given Free everything. Trudi was so pleased about that.

When they got downstairs again, Mom had already made them coffee. Everyone sat around the living room looking sombre. Trudi was afraid. Maybe one of them was sick and she hadn't been told, like maybe her Mom or Dad had cancer. It was so long since she had really been together with them.

'So how does Carrie look to you?' her mother asked.

'She's just so beautiful,' Trudi said, 'Libby, you've made a beautiful little girl out of her.'

'You haven't visited your daughter in over eight months,' her father said censoriously.

'Oh, I know,' Trudi answered. 'I'm so sorry about that. It just seemed that every time I got enough money or time together, both just slipped away from me. But she's been in my heart every day.'

'Libby can't have children,' Buster said sorrowfully.

'Carrie's become our child,' Libby said. 'We love her like our own.'

Trudi studied each member of her family. And then she understood what they were saying. Her own family wanted to take Free from her. 'But she's not your child,' Trudi said carefully to Libby. 'She's my child. I left her with you until I could take care of her again. Now I can.'

'We bought this house for her sake,' Buster said.

'She's in kindergarten now,' Libby added. 'The teacher says she's real bright.'

'There are kindergartens in Taos, too,' Trudi said.

'We won't let her go,' Buster told his sister. 'Not without a fight. Maybe we don't got your high-powered lawyers, but we're going to take this to court anyway.'

Trudi turned to each member of her family. Her brother and Libby stared purposefully back at her. Her mother sat with eyes downcast, playing with her hands. And her father stared at her like the Last Judgment.

She didn't stay with any of them that night. She stayed in a motel over in Jonesboro along the interstate. She tried to think, but her mind wasn't clear. All she knew was that she was dying.

She returned to Taos and consulted with the lawyers who had handled her suits against Tommy. She wanted her child back.

She hated lawyers. They gave her a checklist of the positive and negative. On the affirmative, she was the child's natural mother. Courts favoured natural mothers. She had explicitly stated that Free was being left at her brother's only until she was able to take care of her daughter again. Now she could amply demonstrate before the court that she had the financial means to support her daughter.

Negative, the child had lived with Buster and Libby for over three years. During that time, Trudi had visited Free only five times. 'But don't all my phone calls and letters count?' she protested.

Buster and Libby provided Free with a stable environment. The little girl was happy, healthy, well adjusted in her new home. What would become of her if she were wrenched away from that and the "parents" she had known over the last few years?

Also on the negative side was Trudi's lifestyle. 'You mean because I'm an artist?' she objected.

No, it wasn't the arts. It was the drugs, the sleeping around, the instability.

'But I can change,' she promised.

'Even if you became like a nun now, it might not do any good,' they told her. 'And all of your past failings will come out in court because

178

your brother and his wife will make sure the judge knows about them.'

The only good thing the lawyers did for her was arrange for visitation with her daughter. She'd called Buster earlier, demanding to see Free, and he had refused. So now she needed a court order to see her own daughter!

Trudi returned to Cartersville with a heavy heart. She couldn't understand why this was happening to her. What had she done to find her life so screwed up? She couldn't even get Free alone. She had to visit the child under court supervision at Buster and Libby's house! They were afraid she would kidnap the child. How could she kidnap her own daughter?

The saddest part of that visit was that Free no longer knew her. Oh, she knew a person named Trudi because Libby always told her Trudi was asking for her when the phone calls came from Taos. But Libby was "Mommy" to Free, and Trudi was simply "Trudi". How clever Libby was on that one. The bitch!

So here Trudi sat in the living room or played in the yard with a child who looked upon her as a stranger, a voice on the phone. She kept asking Free, 'Do you remember . . .' but Free remembered nothing.

'How would you like to come and live with me?' she finally asked.

The little girl shrugged and smiled. One of her front teeth was missing. Trudi vaguely remembered the pain of losing teeth and her pleasure at a visit from the Tooth Fairy. 'If I lived with you, would Mommy and Daddy come too?' Free asked.

Trudi had known many dark days in her short life, but that day with Free was the most deathlike.

When she returned to Taos, she was sick at heart. She loved her daughter. She wanted her back. She hated her brother, his wife, her whole family. What pleasure it must have given them all to turn against her.

She could fight for her daughter.

She could destroy her daughter's life.

She looked around her two-bedroomed apartment, at the empty room which was for Free. Trudi was disgusted with herself. All her life she had trusted people. All her life she had been used. And now she would lose the only person of value she had left, her daughter.

Yet to win Free would be, maybe, a victory not worth having. Not if it destroyed Free's life.

Her lawyers told her the battle could go on for years, with suits and countersuits, various arcane custody arrangements that would wrench the girl from one place to another.

179

Buster and Libby had betrayed her, but Trudi couldn't deny that they loved her little Free.

She gave the child up for adoption. There was only one condition: she wanted to have no contact with her family ever again under any circumstances.

Libby tried to call her and thank her. Trudi said shortly into the phone, 'Don't ever try to contact me again or I'll change my mind and fight you tooth and nail.'

Now she was totally alone. No children, no husband, no family, no love in her heart, just a deadness that crept over her, bringing her so far down that not even the drugs helped. Through that haze, Odelle Hampton called to ask how Trudi was doing. It was sweet really, the call. Maybe that was the only sorority she would know any more, the sorority of Tommy's ex-wives. Trudi unburdened herself to Odelle, told her all about her family's betrayal and the loss of her child. Even the ever-optimistic Odelle didn't have anything upbeat to say, not for the longest time. Then she said, 'Free won't always be lost to you.'

'Oh yeah?' Trudi replied dolefully.

'Didn't you say Cartersville was small-town Texas? Not to mention East Diablo. So Free'll hear through family and friends that she was adopted, and she'll probably find out she was adopted from Buster's sister. She'll come looking for you, Trudi, and then you can tell her the truth. You daughter will come home again.'

But until that day, what was left to Trudi? She sat in her beautiful, new, two-bedroomed apartment and tried to figure it out.

180

# Chapter 30

# Sign or Be Damned

Grace Mandling woke with a smile on her face. Despite the alarm's insistent beeping, the memory of her dream stayed with her: Galen's body, Galen's eyes, Galen's love raining down on her. She was happy. She was in love. She had carved in her heart, "Grace is giddy over Galen."

But love was a mistake. She already had enough experience of making mistakes, first with Tommy, then with Darrell Templeton. She had trusted, she had loved. In return, she was deceived and burned.

Since Darrell's betrayal all those years ago, men were her friends, her lovers, her enemies, her business associates, but never her heart's desire. She would not let herself suffer love's weakness again. So, turning off her alarm – and how appropriately symbolic it was, waking her rudely from dreams of overwhelming love – she tried to convince herself that Galen was simply an infatuation. She was flattered by his continuing attention; she delighted in his touch; but she couldn't love him because love was so dangerous.

Yet, day by day, she was welcoming her state of jeopardy. Grace was beginning to believe she could have it all. Oh, insidious hope, as she might have put it in LOVE IS A WALTZ. Galen did love her. He wanted a child. They could be married; she could get pregnant again. After all, thirty-eight wasn't that old any more. There were all these tests they could do to assure a healthy birth. Why shouldn't Grace seek personal happiness instead of living in and brooding about the past? Why should she spend her time shielding herself from hurt instead of seeking the light of perfect romance once more?

Why? Because she wasn't an idiot!

Oh yes, she confronted herself, you are an idiot! And that's the problem. If you continue this freefall in love with Galen, some day you are going to wake up in your bed all alone. Men are like bees;

181

women like flowers. Men are great pollinators, but they keep all the honey to themselves.

But is there not a single man of redeeming value?

Don't, Grace, she warned herself. Once you start thinking that way, you'll be stuck to the tar baby of the weakness that is love.

She lay back in bed with a deep sigh. She felt better. These slugfests with herself always made her realize how basically sensible she was. Maybe she wasn't smart, but she was definitely sensible. And if she did marry Galen, what would the publicity be like? "Grace Mandling robs the cradle!" Yes, her marrying Galen was a plot line that would never sell with her fans. She was sure they would prefer to see her with someone strong, older, distinguished. And yet, maybe she could sell Galen as a tempestuous young artist, wild and ranging, who needed mature love to help him settle down to his greatest work, even if that work turned out to be an infant.

Impulsively she picked up her phone. She tried to reach Craig Epstein in New York, but he was at a meeting. She couldn't stand it. Lately, all editors ever did was go to meetings. Who the hell was reading the manuscripts! Oh yes. She forgot. Publishers farmed them out to English majors in Connecticut.

Craig finally got back to her a little past eleven. 'Sorry. Weekly staff meeting,' he informed her. 'What did I miss?'

'I've continued to ruminate on my sequel to LOVE IS A WALTZ . Lydia is middle-aged now.'

'Oh God, Grace. Does middle age really sell?'

'Her first husband, Cecil, Earl of Montcrief did not die in World War I, as I had at first envisioned. Instead, he's wounded and evacuated to the hospital where Lydia is nursing. She doesn't recognize him until she cuts away the bandages. He recovers under her loving care. But he wonders, after the war is over and so many of his friends are lost, what life is all about. He decides he must serve a nobler cause. Unfortunately, in serving that nobler cause, he dies of malaria,' Grace plunged on. 'He caught it in an African jungle while they were searching for a new species of moth. End of Part I.

'Part Two: Lydia, after a period of mourning to which all of London bears witness, remarries. Her husband is the suave but heartless Dabny Cockerell, heir to the Cockerell china fortune. For their first anniversary Dabny is having her portrait painted. Cockerell has hired the artist Richard Bonningham, also known as Bonnie Big Dick. He's younger than Lydia and wild as the Welsh hills from which he comes. Helplessly, needlessly, Lydia and Big Dick fall in love with each other, though she's a married woman and he years younger than she. They set off together for the South of France and from there to

182

more exotic spots so that Bonnie Big Dick can release the latent, Gaugin-like talent within him. Meanwhile, Dabny Cockerell is on their trail, an ever-increasing threat to their well-being. Until, that is, Big Dick returns to London with an enormous output of work and his new wife and child, Lydia and Little Dick. Despite the fact that Lydia had not been divorced in England, she and Bonnie Big Dick were married by the chief of the Zambezis and have drunk during their wedding night out of the skull of the Zambezi's chief enemy. Now nothing could separate them except death. And maybe British law. I see a trial scene at the end, a dramatic confrontation between the laws of love and nature and the laws of civilized society. Well? How does it sound?'

'Hmm,' Craig said meaningfully. 'Is Lydia going to be too much of a libertine, I mean, with – uh – Bonnie Big Dick?'

'Craig, darling, one has to have passion.'

'But will we actually see the – uh – '

'Big dick? You know that's not my style, Craig. A lifted hemline, an unbuttoned pair of trousers, custom-made by tailors because of Bonnie Big Dick's, um, rather impressive appendage, perhaps two tousle-headed lovers in the morning. Nothing explicit. Though I expect the Zambezi will have something to say about phallic pro-tuberances, not to put too fine a point on it. One is just so much more open to nature in the jungle.'

'Well, it's different, Grace. I rather like your simple, little-did-I-know women better. But, hey, why not give this a try? And while we're on the subject of giving things a try, what's been happening with all of Tommy Patterson's papers? Have you had a chance to delve into them yet?'

'Craig, does one like to clean the toilet?'

Grace extricated herself from further conversation with Craig Epstein on the subject of Tommy Patterson. She had no time for that now. She was too excited by her new plotline. She would work through her relationship with Galen in this book. Now what should she call it? She always liked to have a title to define the first page. PILLAR OF LOVE? Well, it would do for a start. The blue screen of the computer floated emptily before her, waiting for the loving touch of her fingers. And then the phone rang.

Damn it!

She picked up the phone in a huff, only to discover that her agent Edna Waitz was attempting to unload gloom and doom upon her. 'Bad news,' Edna said.

Bad news? Grace tried to think. She hadn't even written anything that could have been rejected. Had her latest HELL HATH NO FURY dropped off the best seller list so soon? Was Craig Epstein leaving her stranded at Adams & Westlake, while he went off to a better job elsewhere? Had her publishers been taken over by a German conglomerate? What exactly qualified as bad news to Edna Waitz?

'Grace?'

'Yes, I'm here. I'm simply involved in my sequel to LOVE IS A WALTZ.'

'Forget that. Doubleday has just signed Tippi Moonstone to do a biography of Tommy Patterson.'

Tippi Moonstone. Where had Grace heard that name? Oh yes, of course. Tippi Moonstone. The woman had a long and distinguished career as a gossip journalist. First, she had written that rather lethal piece in *Rolling Stone* about the Bowel Movements when punk was so popular. Then she did that full-length study for *Cosmopolitan* on Washington, D.C., as the capital of sado-masochistic sex practices, especially as it involved United States Senators. From there she had moved on to a best-selling campaign biography of a certain well-known, philandering politician whom she had probably met in her study of sado-masochism in Washington. Hmm. Grace wondered. Had the release of those photos in the *New York Post* of Tippi in bed with her senator subject been part of her publisher's publicity campaign or was it just serendipitous?

Tippi's latest subject was even more money-making. Her study of self-love practices among Catholic clergy and religious orders certainly made Grace pick up a copy when it came out in paperback. Whoever knew when one could use such diligent research? 'All things considered, Edna,' Grace told her agent, 'I think Tippi is the perfect choice to write a biography of Tommy Patterson.'

'You don't get it, do you?' Edna said.

'No.'

'If Tippi writes that biography, what happens to you?'

'I write my sequel to LOVE IS A WALTZ.'

'Do you think Tippi's not going to ask for access to Tommy's treasure trove of literary jottings, which is now in your possession?'

'Well, she can ask all she wants. His papers, as you say, are in my possession. I am his literary executor.'

'And if she goes to court to get them? Which she very well may do. After all, it would keep her forthcoming biography in the forefront of public awareness. You know what a sensationalist she is.'

'Oh, I wouldn't go that far, Edna. Some people look at life from a political point of view, others a religious, others economic. Okay, so Tippi looks at life from a sexual point of view. Hey, it sells.'

'Yes. And let us just consider who was part of Tommy's life. Let me see. There's your friend Odelle Hampton. And that girl you two

184

helped, Trudi Surefoot. Kitten Fairleigh might relish the publicity as long as Tippi doesn't make her out to be a murderer. And then, I wonder, what will Tippi Moonstone make of you?'

'Yikes!' Grace shouted. She knew exactly what Edna meant. Tippi would not only go into the old story of Tommy the bigamist and the still-born birth of their child, she would also swim against the stream up to dear old University of Iowa, maybe to discover that Grace left there with Darrell Ahmed Jemal Mohammed Templeton. What would Tippi make of RAGE IN BLACK AND WHITE, whose leading female character is named Grace?

Grace saw her martyrdom stretching out before her. What if Tippi Moonstone found Trudi in that drying-out clinic? Oh Jesus. Trudi never could keep her mouth shut. And if she told Tippi how Grace had helped her squeeze the bucks out of Tommy, would Tippi paint Grace as a vindictive woman instead of this sweet champion of romance, an image Grace had nursed since her first book? Hell, yes.

Something had to be done about this. Grace did not intend to see herself ripped into little pieces and plopped between the pages of a prurient best seller. 'How can we stop her?' she asked Edna.

'We can't.'

'We can't! Then why the hell did you call me and bring all this worry down on me?'

'We can't stop Tippi Moonstone. But we can take defensive action. We can stall Tippi in her search for the dope on Tommy and his women.'

'Okay, how?'

'You also sign a contract for a biography of Tommy Patterson. Your legal case for refusing Tippi access to Tommy's papers is all the stronger, plus you can put the story of Tommy Patterson forward in your own way.'

'There's just one thing wrong with that, Edna. I don't want to write a biography of Tommy Patterson.'

'You don't have to write it, just sign the contract. Let Craig beg for it. We'll give him to understand that your sequel to LOVE IS A WALTZ comes first. And then, well, who knows? Though, Grace, you have to realize that if you're in the business to make money, besides raising the literary tone of the nation, a work on Tommy, no matter what shape it takes, will bring you in a pretty penny.'

'It wouldn't be pretty,' Grace said dejectedly. 'Okay, how soon do I have to fake this commitment to Craig?'

'Can you come in this afternoon?'

'This afternoon?'

185

'Darling, they have been panting for this opportunity ever since Tommy's will was made public. Let's let them drink at the well of your generosity. For a price.'

'It had better be a good price. A damned good one. I don't sell my soul for less!'

When Grace put down the phone, she knew her system was sliding quickly towards a state of shock. First of all, she hated putting on tights midweek. She worked in her tracksuit or an old bathrobe, then she wore jeans to the shops. Now she would have to look romantically elegant. Second – oh, Jesus, did she really have to deal in depth with Tommy Patterson's life? She had married him oh so long ago, and she was still being screwed.

Protection. That was her aim now. For herself, for others. She put in a call to Chicago. She would have to warn Odelle about Tippi Moonstone. The only present-day reading Odelle did was Grace Mandling. Odelle claimed that Grace's books were enough for her to get an idea of what was happening in the literary community. Aside from that, Odelle was slowly going through the University of Chicago's list of great books. 'They're my sleeping pill,' she told Grace once. So Tippi Moonstone would mean nothing to Odelle. She had to be warned!

Odelle's phone rang four times, and Grace got annoyed. Why was Odelle never home? Then the click. 'This is Odelle Hampton, executive director of Sisters of the Storm. Right now I am working for the betterment of battered women and children. If you are battered or in danger, please call 772-HOME and we will direct you to our nearest shelter. If you are a batterer, please get help because, when we find you, we will press charges. You days in Chicago are numbered. If you are a contributor to Sisters of the Storm, our women and children's shelter, please leave your name and number and I will definitely get back to you with delight. If you are calling to advertise your product, please don't bother me. Find child care for your child and get out into the real world where you don't have to annoy people at all times of the day and night with your phone calls. If you are a robber, forget it. I am hooked up to a security system, and there is a neighbourhood crime watch. When we find robbers, we castrate them. With the kitchen scissors. If you are a member of my family, leave a message but don't expect me to run your errands for you. If you are a friend, well, you wouldn't be calling me during the day. Here comes the beep.'

'Odelle, this is Grace. Can I help you edit that message down a bit? Just say, "This is 892-372. Please leave your message at the sound of the beep." If you do so, people won't become hysterical waiting for

186

that fucking beep. Okay! Listen now. If a woman named Tippi Moonstone calls you, pretend you're mute. She's writing an un-authorized biography of that schmuck we both married. She very much digs for the dirt. Call me back immediately upon your arrival home and give me Trudi's number. I have got to see her and warn her because you know what a blabbermouth she tends to be. Too much of the old peyote in the brain. And for God's sake, Odelle, change that fucking message before I call you again!'

She sat back, aggravated. Why was nothing in life perfect? Where was that eternal sunrise she felt as a child? Gone, gone with her youth. Damn it.

Speaking about youth, as long as she had to go into the city, she might as well make the best of it. She put in a call to Galen's office. 'May I please speak to Mr Richards?' she wondered in her low, seductive voice.

'Who? Oh, Galen. Hey, Galen, it's for you.'

No class anywhere any more!

'Yeah?' Galen came on the phone, sounding very masculine, hip – and young!

'It's "Hello, may I help you?"'

'Grace?'

'Who else would correct your telephone etiquette?'

'Hi, babe!'

He was hopeless. So she gave up. 'I have to come into the city. Do you want to have lunch?'

'Oh, Jesus, Grace, that's fantastic! Hey, there's this great new hamburger place. You can almost see the cows being slaughtered in the blood than runs from the – '

'Galen, dear, I hate to be pushy, but do you think I could choose the restaurant?'

'Hey, no problem.'

'All right. I'll make reservations. I should get in about one. Can you take a late lunch?'

'I'll take the whole day to be with you.'

Grace sighed as she put down the phone. Okay, so he was a little rough around the edges. But he had what it took: complete devotion to her. She hoped.

## Chapter 31

# Chow Down on West 47th

Grace made it into Port Authority at ten to one. The only good thing about coming into New York at midday was that one didn't have a forty-five minute wait at the Lincoln Tunnel.

Port Authority was humming with its usual mass of homeless and perverts, but Grace swept on by and was out of the door before she could be pushed, jostled, solicited or mugged.

New York, as usual, was beautiful but dirty. The sun shone; the dirt swept up from the sidewalk. Since Galen worked at 56th and Sixth, Grace saw no need for a taxi. She hugged her coat to her and stepped smartly up Eighth Avenue, ignoring various comments thrown her way in Spanish.

Grace had been to Galen's office but once before, last Christmas at the cocktail hour, which had extended from around one to around four-thirty when they all fumbled home. She had made Galen promise not to tell anyone she was *the* Grace Mandling, though she suspected she would be recognized in any case. That didn't happen. Was it because everyone was too drunk? Or did she really appeal only, as one critic claimed, to frustrated *hausfraus* and pimply-faced, young, female commuters?

Galen was waiting for her in the reception area of his firm, so she merely stuck her foot in the elevator to hold it and called him over. As the door closed on them, he gave her a kiss and nuzzled her ear. 'It's so good to see you,' he told her. 'You look marvellous, as usual.' He stood back. 'Elegant.'

She smiled. 'You look fantastic too.' And he did, of course, in his jeans and leather jacket, covering his grey wool sweater. His hair was slightly wild and his face was flushed – with the pleasure of seeing her, she hoped.

She had made a reservation at Bonita's on West 47th between Eighth and Ninth Avenue. It was a pasta type of day for her. She

188

needed the comfort. Grace only hoped they had some red meat to satisfy her macho lover.

Bonita's had just recently become popular among the theatre crowd. Unlike some along restaurant row, Bonita's took reservations. Grace had no intention of queueing to eat. Yet she couldn't go to the more magnificent and expensive eating palaces in New York because she knew Galen wouldn't appreciate them. Also, he never wore a tie. Bonita's was perfect.

"Was perfect" because, when she entered, she discovered her favourite Italian chef had fled to establish his own restaurant on Tenth Street, and Bonita had hired a Haitian to replace him. They now served Carib. What was happening to the restaurants of New York? Hadn't she just been here four months ago?

Galen looked at the blackboard specials while they were waiting for the maître d' and said, 'God, I love this food. Spice is what it's all about.'

Grace wondered if she could just have a banana maybe. But she smiled politely at the maître d' as he led them towards the mirrored booths. Great. She would be able to sit and watch herself looking eleven years older than Galen.

'Grace?'

Ah, her public. Grace turned with a polite smile on her face. Then her jaw dropped open. 'Kitten!' she exclaimed.

'Oh, wow,' she heard Galen say behind her.

'Won't you join us?' Kitten asked. 'We've just ordered.'

'Well, I – ' Grace was going to refuse, but Galen slid into the seat next to Kitten's friend. Grace was left with no choice but to nod at the maître d' and slide in next to Kitten who delicately moved her small rump over, but not quite enough for Grace to feel comfortable, unless she liked sitting with half a hip hanging over the edge of the banquette. 'This is quite a surprise,' Grace said. She'd be nothing if not fatuous.

'Have you met David?' Kitten wondered. 'David Turner, Grace Mandling, one of the women Tommy divorced.'

Grace looked into the perfect blue eyes of David Turner and wondered what type of contact lenses he wore.

'God, I love you in *He Who Must Die*,' Galen said to David, holding out his hand. 'I'm Galen Richards, by the way.' He nodded first at David and then at Kitten, who purred her greeting in return.

'Whatever are you doing in New York?' Grace asked.

'David's been offered a starring role in the revival of *She Stoops to Conquer*,' Kitten said.

'I don't think you have to call it a revival,' Grace corrected, 'not when it's a classic like that.'

'It's not really a revival anyway,' David agreed. 'They're turning it into a musical.'

'Oh my,' Grace said. 'I didn't realize you sang.'

'I don't. I'm taking lessons. This is the opportunity I've been searching for for quite some time. It'll be good to get back to my roots in the live theatre.'

'Oh, were you on the boards before?' Grace wondered. He was so young – handsome, but young. With all his fame resting in movies, she couldn't imagine him having time for much stage work.

'On the boards?' he queried. 'Oh! You mean, on stage. Well no, I haven't been on stage yet, but all actors feel that their roots are, as you so magnificently put it, on the boards. Besides, I've always looked forward to doing a play by Oscar Wilde.'

Grace pondered telling David the real author of *She Stoops to Conquer*, but what the hell? Let him make the mistake before some newspaper reporter, who probably wouldn't know the difference either.

'Okay, he was a fag,' David continued. 'But if you're an actor, you learn to deal with these things.'

Grace fortunately did not have to bear the full brunt of the conversation with this moron. Galen took up the cudgels. He at least was delighted to be sitting with the delectable Kitten Fairleigh and her charming escort, whom some had called a Paul Newman without talent. Not that Grace planned to repeat that remark to him.

It was not until the tail end of lunch, when Grace had eaten her fill of black beans and rice, about two forkfuls, that Kitten alluded once more to their mutual connection, Tommy Patterson.

'How is the murder investigation going?' Grace wondered. 'I haven't heard from or about Detective Morris for the longest time.'

'Oh, he's a devilishly hard worker,' Kitten assured her. 'He's made several very interesting discoveries. This is confidential of course. Not for public knowledge.'

'Then how did you get it?'

'Did you never see *L.A. Rape Squad*?' David asked Grace. 'Kitten played a decoy who actually gets raped. Then she finds the rapist and accidentally shoots him to death. She rode in a lot of squad cars, researching her role. She made a lot of friends.'

'I bet,' Grace concurred. 'So you have an inside informant?'

'Several,' Kitten bragged. 'Detective Morris has found out some very intriguing facts about Odelle and Trudi.'

'They've lived very intriguing lives,' Grace said noncommittally.

'For instance, did you know Odelle visited Tommy three days before he went over that cliff?'

'Really?' Galen said.

Grace tried to kill him with a look, but he was paying no attention to her this lunch. His eyes were on Kitten. She would have to kill him later. 'And what did Odelle say to that?'

'I don't know if Detective Morris has sprung it on her yet,' Kitten said. 'Though I myself called and gave her fair warning.'

Grace was surprised. 'That was decent of you.'

'We're all in the same boat where Tommy is concerned, aren't we?'

'Tommy was concerned,' Grace corrected her. 'And Trudi?'

'Trudi was exhibiting at the Colosseum the week Tommy died. She was there for the opening of Native American Artists of the Southwest. Whether she stayed the entire week is unknown. It seems she's not traceable at the moment.'

Thank God, Grace thought. Damn! Now she'd have to call Odelle again. What if her phone was tapped? How could she put this in code? But first, she'd have to sign that damned book contract. Today was a day she would gladly wipe off the slate of her mind as soon as it was over.

The only good thing about lunch with Kitten Farleigh and David Turner was that David picked up the bill. Galen objected weakly, while Grace kept her VISA safely in her purse. 'We'll meet again,' Kitten promised vaguely in the doorway, as they were about to leave. She learned forward to press cheeks. Grace warmed slightly. Kitten probably hadn't always had an easy time of it, despite the fact that she was a raving beauty and men fell all over themselves to do whatever she asked. So Grace put her angst aside long enough to say, 'I should warn you about something.'

'Umm?'

'Tippi Moonstone has signed to do a bio of Tommy.'

'Oh, shit.'

'My sentiments exactly.'

The couples parted, Galen walking backward until Kitten's rump was out of sight. 'Hot damn! Wait till I get back to the office and tell people I had lunch with Kitten Farleigh.'

'And David Turner,' Grace added.

'Who? Oh, yeah. Gee, Grace, have you ever seen such a beautiful woman? I mean, up on the screen they look so large. It's hard to believe they'll be just as gorgeous in person. Hey, I've worked with models. I know how disastrous they can be without the trimmings. But Kitten, that's a live woman. Like, words just kept coming to my mind during lunch. You know – ripe, voluptuous, lip-licking, giving, warm, wet. Oh Jeez, I could go on and on. A real movie star. Oh, hell. I'm no good at words. What would you call her, Grace?'

191

She gave him an ice-cold smile. 'It's not what I'd call her that you should be worried about – darling.'

Slightly hurt and puzzled, Galen watched her walk away from him. He wondered, had he said anything to upset her?

# *Chapter 32*

# Adams & Westlake, Inc.

Adams & Westlake, Inc., Grace Mandling's publisher, kept itself in a windowed skyscraper, overlooking the East River, just south of the UN. The windows-on-the-world effect was deceptive for upon entering the building you were watched carefully. Who knew? You might be a writer, and those people were dangerously irrational. There was a guard at the door and two guards by the bank of three elevators. The only place that didn't have a guard and probably needed it was the company bookstore, where Grace was sure shoplifting was highly prevalent. She hated shoplifting anywhere, but here it especially hurt her. These were her books thieves were taking through the turnstiles. Unless their tastes led them in more esoteric directions, which she found hard to believe.

Grace walked over to the bookstore's display window and examined it closely. Centred in the window was WALKING TOWARDS WISDOM: THOUGHTS WHILE HIKING ALONG THE APPALACHIAN TRAIL. To the left was BOMBSHELL: AN INSIDER'S GUIDE TO THE NEW ADMINISTRATION. To the right TICKLED PINK, touted as a family saga of beauticians in Memphis, Tennessee. Only in the far right corner was there a display of her many titles with the firm of Adams & Westlake. True, her latest book HELL HATH NO FURY had come out six months ago, but was that any reason to be shunted aside? And they wanted her to sign a contract! Edna would have to put some clause in there about extensive publicity.

Sniffing and in a huff, Grace returned to the reception area and went up to the man at the desk. 'I'm Grace Mandling,' she told him. 'I have an appointment to see Craig Epstein.'

His face turned from bored to interested. 'Ms Mandling,' he said, and stood. She shook hands with him while he told her that his girlfriend loved her books. Why was it that no man ever admitted to reading them? Grace couldn't even be sure about Craig. She was royally escorted to the elevator, past the two hounds from hell, and sent shooting up to the eleventh floor.

Once on the eleventh floor, Grace knew her way to Craig's office without any problems. Even if she hadn't, she would have been able to locate it from the sounds of swilling liquor and raucous laughter. Selling her soul obviously didn't bother anyone but herself.

She stood in the doorway to the office, unnoticed, and saw the champagne bottle resting in its ice bucket. She hated champagne. Everyone knew that. Couldn't they just have provided some Dos Equis and nachos?

'Uh-hum!' She cleared her throat meaningfully.

They turned. It took them a second to focus on who it was. Then Craig came over and it was all hugs and kisses, enough to communicate any disease that might be going around.

Grace wasn't going to make this easy for them. Despite Edna's assurances that the contract was exactly what Grace wanted, she went over it carefully, as did a member of Adams & Westlake's own legal staff. The lawyer was just as nervous about this contract as Grace was. He liked to have months to study anything that was going to be signed by anyone.

The sum Adams & Westlake was willing to pay for a biography of Tommy Patterson was mind-boggling. She could retire on the advance, if only she didn't have to write the book. She picked up the pen, then stared straight at dear Craig. 'What if the book I write is not the book you want?' Grace asked him coolly.

Craig raised his shoulders. 'What does that mean?'

'What if I write the truth – the real truth – about Tommy?'

Craig started salivating. Grace sighed and signed the contract. But she was in no mood to celebrate. She stayed long enough to have her picture taken for the news bulletin Publicity was planning to issue to the local television stations for their Five o'clock News "culture" segment – that was, if they could fit culture in between all the crime, AIDS and arson stories. Then she bowed out of the party, claiming a pressing appointment. And indeed she did have. She planned to rush to Port Authority and get the first express bus out of the city.

The elevator provided a moment of serenity. When she reached the ground floor, she stepped out into the real world again. Walking briskly across the lobby, she was halted by a man at the reception desk who called to her, 'Oh, Ms Mandling!'

She turned. He was not alone at the desk any more. Two guards were there, watching over a man in a shabby overcoat who was gesticulating wildly. The reception desk attendant stepped aside and held up a pile of books. 'I know it's an imposition, but could you please autograph these for me?'

Grace smiled. A paying customer. She hoped!

The dear man had five books. One he wanted for his mother, one for his aunt, one for his sister and two for his girlfriend. She could see that he was disappointed in her crablike scrawl. Everyone wanted her signature to be an extravagant display of penmanship. However, she had never been able to write legibly.

While she was trying to get the dedications straight, she vaguely tuned in to what was happening with the man and the two guards at the other end of the lengthy reception desk, with its banks of phones and security cameras. 'If you have an appointment,' the guard said, 'just tell us who it's with. We'll check it out. We can't let you into the elevator without an appointment. Hey, it's our job, man.'

'Do you know what I have in my hand?' the man replied angrily.

Jesus, Grace hoped it wasn't a gun!

'I have a best seller in my hand. I have a book that I have poured my life's blood into for the last five years.'

'Yeah? Well, you can send it in and someone will read it,' the guard tried to explain.

'I don't want just someone to read it. I want to explain it first, explain what I am trying to do. You are keeping me from my destiny. Don't you understand that!'

'Look, brother, there's nothing I can do for you. Can't you hear what I'm saying?'

Well, Grace certainly could. She finished the final dedication, closed the book and smiled her appreciation. Then before she left, she made the mistake of looking across at the man arguing with the guards. Silly her. It was always dangerous to make eye contact with the insane, which in New York counted for about 40 percent of the population. The man for the first time seemed to notice her. Perhaps he was annoyed that someone had dared pay attention to his humiliation. In any case, he glanced angrily over at her. And she froze.

Quickly, she turned on her heel and pushed through Adams & Westlake's revolving doors. She wished she had her sneakers on so she fled faster, surer. 'Hey, brother!' she heard someone, probably one of the guards, call behind her. She picked up her pace. She had to escape.

A hand grabbed her sleeve, slowing her down. She pulled away and kept on walking. The hand came from underneath and hooked her upper arm. 'Grace,' the voice said near her ear.'

'Let go,' she said, without looking. 'Or I will call the police.'

'Grace, please,' he begged.

She stopped and squared off with Darrell Templeton while pedestrians stepped gingerly around them.

195

Darrell Templeton, or Ahmed Jemal Mohammed, whatever he was calling himself now, looked none too good. She could see that the clothes he wore had, when new, been expensive. At this point, they merely looked shabby. His face was more grey than the pale tan it had been when they were lovers, and his hair was every which way, as if it had been tied in dreadknots that had come loose. Despite the worn leather briefcase he carried in his left hand, he looked like a bum.

Whether he had sunk below the poverty line or not, Grace had no idea. For the first few years after publication of his RAGE IN BLACK AND WHITE, she had followed his career. She had had no choice. He was flamboyant enough to draw the attention of the media. He spent most of his time emoting about racism in America, claiming he had no home but was still a slave, socially, psychologically and economically, in the United States. For violently exposing America's faults, he was acclaimed as a new and gifted voice among the younger generation of black writers. Of course, all violent voices then were understood as being new and gifted. Today they would simply be labelled "strident".

But Darrell Templeton in his prime had shone. He was invited to the cocktail parties of the rich and glamorous, symposia of the bright and stately. He entered a stratum of American society where Grace, despite her renown and commercial success, still wouldn't be welcomed. She knew he had received several grants to continue his writing, had been invited to return to Iowa to conduct a seminar on politics and the novel, had spent a summer at Laurel Pines, an artists' retreat, finishing his new novel. But after RAGE IN BLACK AND WHITE, she had never read a thing Darrell wrote. It wasn't that she chose to ignore his work, fearing she would again find herself the object of his broad contempt. It was that, as far as she knew, despite all the grants and acclaim, after his first book he failed to have a second published, though there were jottings published in all the right magazines, touting the second coming of Ahmed Jemal Mohammed.

There are some writers who write and there are some writers who talk. It's very easy for a writer with controversial material to make a living talking. But Darrell's subject was black rage, which could only be successful as long as there was white guilt. White guilt died with the coming of the Reagan presidency and, more importantly, the Yuppies. People were too busy dressing for success, celebrating the golden calf of greed, sticking it to each other in the boardroom, climbing to the top of the greasy executive pole, making money, while dragging business into a state of ineptitude and inefficiency unparalleled in American history. Spare moments were spent perusing biographies of successful executives, learning new management

196

techniques, worrying about a lack of sex drive, taking seminars on success from people like Tommy Patterson. There was no more time to fret about the less-than-successful, those who couldn't or wouldn't keep up. Darrell's rage was out of fashion, therefore out of mind. And unlike Tommy, Darrell lacked the ability to change what he was selling when the fashions moved on.

Did Grace feel sorry for him, standing there before her now, looking so dishevelled? Not really. She felt more sorry for herself that she would have to undergo the ordeal of speaking to him. Her rage towards him had turned to ashes; her hurt had faded, replaced by bemusement at her own stupidity. But anger at being used was still strong. Women needed that anger to survive.

'Grace, you got to help me,' Darrell told her.

'Why?' she questioned coolly. She turned from him and began to walk on. He kept pace with her.

'I got to get someone to see this novel,' he told her. 'It's the best thing I've written since RAGE IN BLACK AND WHITE.'

'That bad?'

'It's all about a black Jesus, the Second Coming. I've found God, Grace.'

'Really? Where has she been keeping herself lately?'

'Look, you can help me. There are no coincidences in life, only God's plan for us. He threw us together today because he knew you would help me. He knew how much we meant to each other. All you have to do is call your editor, tell him to take a look at my book. That's all it needs, a look. It'll speak for itself.'

'If it's that good, Darrell, someone will pick it out of the slush pile and buy it. Anyway, what happened to your publisher? Why don't you take it to them?'

'They were bought out by some English firm. You know the English. Still the old colonial mentality. Will they buy a black Jesus? Please, Grace. As a favour to one who loved you. Or if you won't call your editor, how about giving me the name of your agent?'

'And your agent?'

'I can't get him on the phone.'

Grace was making steady progress on the sidewalks of Manhattan, crossing Madison now, heading towards Fifth, then on the home stretch towards Eighth. It was after four in the afternoon and the streets were filling with the beginnings of the rush hour. Traffic cops were at several intersections to guard against grid lock. Grace was beginning to feel safe. She felt now was the time to let Darrell know exactly what she would do for him. She stopped and turned to face him. 'I wouldn't introduce you to my agent, my editor, my friends,

197

not even my enemies, Darrell,' she told him. 'Like so many men, you think you can kick women in the teeth, then smile and say you love them and all will be well again. Well, not this woman. Some of us kick back. But I do want to thank you for one thing, Darrell. If you hadn't treated me in such a despicable fashion all those years ago, the million or so I now have in the bank wouldn't have been possible. You live on rage, I live on love. I guess love travels better. So long, loser.'

'Bitch,' he hissed. Then 'Bitch!' he screamed. 'Cunt! Cocksucker! Slit! Fucker! Fucking bitch!'

Grace crossed Fifth under the watchful eyes of a traffic cop who was moving slowly across the lane towards the mad black man screaming obscenities at any woman passing him by. The cop didn't really want to engage this fellow. Who knew what the nut would do or what diseases he was carrying? But, hey, being a cop was a job with good benefits, so he took out his nightstick and made the approach.

Grace moved swiftly on, the sound of the shouting fading as she travelled with the pedestrian traffic, streaming towards home.

Home was warm and cosy, home was safe, home was a hot shower, which she took as soon as she managed to remove her dress and throw her underwear in the hamper. She washed her hair, her skin, she washed under her nails, down her body to her toes. She let the water run over her until she was sure the soot of the city was swept down the drain. Then she stopped the water and stepped out, towelling dry.

The phone rang while she was halfway through drying her hair. The answering machine was on, but she rushed to pick up the receiver anyway. It could be Galen, letting her know he was flying to Hollywood to follow his dream, Kitten Fairleigh. But, no, it was Craig. She should have let the machine take it. He again thanked her profusely for coming to her senses and deciding to write a book about Tommy. Then he added, 'By the way, some fellow just called and said he was a friend of yours, that you suggested he call me. He has a book you thought I should look at?'

'Oh, really? Who was that?' she faked. 'I hope I didn't scatter your name around loosely at some cocktail party.'

'So do I,' Craig agreed. 'This guy's name is Ahmed Jemal Mohammed.'

'Oh God!'

'You know him then?'

'He's someone I knew a long time ago from the Iowa Writers Workshop. An awful man. I really hate this guy, Craig. It would be terribly upsetting to me if you had anything to do with him. Not that I want to be a temperamental author or anything, but – '

'Enough said,' he assured her.

198

'How did he get your name anyway?'

'It happens all the time, Grace. They know the author's name, they put a call in for the author's editor, then claim to be a friend. I always check.'

'Thank God you did. I would have been so pissed had he benefited by that limited and painful acquaintance years ago.'

Dear Craig. He was so understanding. Of course, if he actually did read Darrell's work and decide to publish it, he would have seen the last of her at Adams & Westlake.

Grace finished drying her hair, then dressed in jeans and a sweatshirt. Wanting her skin finally to breathe, she had planned not to put any make up on. Then she though better of the idea. After all, Galen had spent lunch in the glow of Kitten Fairleigh's make-up artistry. Grace had better put some effort into her own looks. At least she wouldn't have to make dinner. Galen could have something frozen, or make himself a sandwich. One good meal a day was enough.

Going downstairs, Grace checked her machine. There wasn't a single message on it. Damn. Didn't anybody have the sense to call her with something interesting to say? Like Odelle? She had to get in touch with Odelle. She checked the time. It was still early in Chicago, and Odelle was probably being a martyr at her shelter, but Grace had to try. The sooner she got in touch with her, the better.

Luke was home. His mother was not. So Grace engaged in him a conversation about what colleges he had applied to and where he really wanted to go. He really wanted to go live in a foreign country for a few years before he went to college, but his parents wouldn't let him. They warned him he would simply have to settle for junior year abroad. Parents were so unreasonable, Grace thought. If he were her child – hell, what would she do?

'Hey!' Luke said, as Grace contemplating how easy it was to give advice when the pain wouldn't be yours, 'I think she just pulled up.'

Grace heard the phone dropping, then Odelle's voice in the background, saying, 'Get the groceries in and put them away.' Then she heard Luke say something that resembled, 'Oh shit,' but she was sure Luke had better manners than that. Then, 'Hello?'

'Odelle. *C'est moi.* Why won't you let Luke travel? I'm sure Sy could find him something safe.'

'Jesus! I have to go through this with him every day and now you!' Odeile exploded.

'Okay, I rescind my advice. Besides, we have more important things to talk about. Is your phone bugged?'

'Bugged?'

'Are your phone calls being taped?' Grace put it more simply.

'I know what bugged means, Grace. I do watch television. But so far, I am not approaching paranoia.'

'I had lunch with Kitten Farleigh today.'

'Oh?'

'She told me that Detective Morris has discovered you saw Tommy three days before he died. I hope you were not – involved in any way in Tommy's – uh – demise. Not that I would object personally, but on legal grounds, committing murder is a bit iffy, sort of considered a major character flaw.'

'I didn't murder Tommy. If Detective Morris deigns to get in touch with me, instead of snooping around, looking for answers without my input, he will discover that I went to Tommy because I needed money for the shelter. I thought that not only could Tommy easily afford to donate some, but that his talking on the subject of battered women and children would give the problem the prominence it deserves.'

Something didn't ring quite true there, but Grace would analyze Odelle's words later. 'Trudi was there too, you know,' Grace added.

'What!'

'Trudi may have been in Los Angeles when Tommy did his head first over the hill. That has yet to be clarified. Morris can't find Trudi. It seems she's disappeared from the face of the earth. Which is why I asked if your phone was bugged because it sounds to me as if Trudi's disappearance might be fortuitous. For the time being. However, if one could psychically contact her, there are a few things one might ask her and inform her about.'

'Such as?' Odelle wondered. 'Just assuming that I might have this psychic ability.'

'Find out if she was in L.A. when someone deep-a-hundred-twenty-fived or so our ex-husband.'

'And?'

'Let her know that Tippi Moonstone has signed to do a bio of Tommy and will be snooping around in no time.'

'What? Grace, this is impossible! I've read all of Tippi Moonstone's books. She's going to rip us to pieces and let us bleed all over the pages. I don't care about me so much, but what about Julia?'

'With the murder unsolved, dear, what about all of us? You can count on Tippi trying to solve the mystery via her book. And she'll find out about you and Trudi being in the area.'

'Grace, we have to do something!'

'I have. I've signed my life away this afternoon. I've agreed to write a biography of Tommy myself. This way I can keep a firm hand on his papers until I decide what to do with them, like burn them, most likely. Also, I'll be able to write the story from our points of view. I already warned my editor that the real story of Tommy Patterson was not what he might opt for. No warm fuzzies. Anyway, get out the word to everyone not to talk to Tippi, including our friend of the flowers.'

No sooner had Grace hung up the phone rang again, probably Odelle with some thoughts to consider. But no. It was her agent, Edna. 'Dear,' Edna said, 'Tippi's book is scheduled to come out in exactly eighteen months. Craig just called to tell me. Adams & Westlake wants your book to debut before then. I thought I'd let you know.'

'Well, they'll just have to wait, Edna. I am working on my sequel to LOVE IS A WALTZ, and I can't stop now.'

'Oh? So Tippi shall have the first word?'

Dear Edna. She knew how to get Grace where it hurt.

Galen was still glowing from lunch when he got home. She broke the spell for him by having him carry into the family room, as they called it, despite the fact that they didn't have a family, all the boxes of Tommy's papers that had been shipped out to her. 'I thought you didn't want to see any of this,' Galen commented as he hoisted Box No. 9.

'I don't. But I have no choice.'

By the time they finished the moving job, the family room looked more like an obstacle course. Both were tired and hungry, so they ordered Chinese and had a couple of beers to go with it. That relaxed Galen enough to let the crazy smile come back on to his face. 'She was something, wasn't she?' he said.

Grace didn't bother to ask who was something. Unfortunately, she already knew. 'Galen, dear, I do have feelings,' she reminded him.

'Yeah. So?'

'So could you please stop talking about Kitten Fairleigh.'

'Why?' he replied. 'She's not real.'

'She's very real.'

'Yeah. But she's not really real. Like, she's not touchable.'

'I have the feeling she's very touchable,' Grace said grimly.

Galen smiled wickedly at her. 'I like it when you're insecure.'

She looked at him from under her eyelashes. 'I like it when I'm not.' But she let him pull her to him. She could taste the kung pao chicken on his breath. 'It's going to feel so good not to have anything between us but love,' he reminded her of her promise to forego birth control.

She flinched inwardly, but as usual Galen didn't notice. She wondered what caused her to flinch. Fear of getting pregnant? Or, more likely, Galen's clumsy imagery. Never before had she imagined a condom stopping the flow of love between two people. 'How do you feel about your child taking a few years off before he goes to college?' she asked him.

'Is it a boy or girl?' he wondered.

'Does it matter?'

'Hell, sex is destiny. Didn't anyone ever tell you that, Grace?' he whispered, as he lay on top of her.

## Chapter 33

# Kitten Fairleigh Speaks

'What do you say when someone tells you you're the sexiest woman alive?' the reporter asked Kitten Fairleigh. They sat together high above street level in her suite at the Pierre. The man was wearing a brown suit, yellow shirt, yellow tie with pink flowers. He had dressed for the occasion, though denigrating the necessity for interviewing a movie star to his friends. Secretly, his hands sweated and his heart beat faster, knowing he would soon be in Kitten Fairleigh's presence. Dreams do come true.

Kitten herself was dressed in a light pink satin pants suit. The material shimmered and slid sexily when she crossed and uncrossed her legs, when she lifted her hands to push back her hair, so blonde, so pure, so exciting. She smiled crookedly and repeated his question as though she were giving it some thought. She tried not to let the boredom show. After all, she had only been asked this question a million times or so. 'What do I say when someone tells me I'm the sexiest woman alive?' Her voice was husky, vibrant. 'Usually I say thank you,' Kitten replied. God, she hoped he would try to come up with questions that evinced a little more intelligence. Or would this interview be spent playing "The Body", instead of "Actress with a Soul"?

She warned herself to be careful. This reporter was from the *New York Times*. It would do her a world of good to be written about in the *Times*. Usually, she was relegated to the tabloids. Now that was slowly changing. A few daring souls had ventured to compare her to Marilyn Monroe, and maybe this reporter was digging to see if there was anything to it.

Meanwhile, he was salivating. It was a talent she had cultivated, setting men drooling over her. Now it was so automatic, she no longer had to put any energy or imagination into it. She'd noticed her effect over lunch on that young friend of Grace Mandling's. How terribly

203

easy it was. Would she ever lose it, her not so elusive attractiveness to men? She didn't like to think about it. But maybe. Maybe she would some day when she got old. The years would pile up on her, pushing her under. That's why interviews like this were so important in the game plan for her career. In California, where she lived and worked, she could be the ultimate bimbo and still be respected. California thrived on bodies without minds. But here in New York bimbos were perhaps a trifle bit less appreciated. She'd have to show some flashes of intelligence, but not too many. She didn't want to disconcert her many fans. Indicating to a small extent that she had a brain would be rather like deciding how much thigh to flash.

'You've had a very interesting life,' the reporter informed her. 'Born Gretchen Marie Corelli in Baltimore, you became Kitten Fairleigh. How did that come about?'

'The name change?' Kitten headed for the fastest exit from her past. 'Kitten Fairleigh was the name of the character I first played upon the stage. She held enormous appeal for me. She was witty and beautiful, and she got all the guys. At the time, I was very much an introvert.'

'That was at the University of Southern California.'

'That's right. I enrolled there to specialize in computers. But I got bitten by the acting bug.' Ouch! Even she winced at that cliché.

'And very quickly you made the leap from university stage to Hollywood scene.'

'Not exactly by choice,' Kitten said. 'You see, when I played the character Kitten Fairleigh in a student review called *Girls! Girls! Girls!*, I wore a skimpy outfit and a blonde wig. The image was so successful for me that when I switched from computers to theatre arts, I dyed my hair blonde. After that, no one took me seriously as a student or an actress.'

'So instead of learning your craft – '

'I think I'm pretty good at my craft,' Kitten cut him off, recrossing her legs and letting the satin shimmer. She enjoyed watching his eyes move dramatically downward.

But he recovered quickly. 'What was it that really started your career rolling?'

'I appeared in a commercial for a chain of gas station/convenience stores. I wore a khaki shirt with the name of the chain over my left breast and a pair of short shorts. At the end of the commercial, the camera came in for a closeup, and I said, "Come in and let me really pump your gas." Customers found it stimulating.'

'I bet,' the reporter said, a little globule of drool beginning to gather at his mouth's right corner. His pad dropped farther down on his lap. 'How did you get the part in the commercial?'

204

'You mean, was there any casting couch?'

'Oh, no, no, no. Certainly not. I was just wondering what that first audition was like?'

Kitten recrossed her legs, stretched and rested her head on her hand, letting her honey blonde hair sweep loosely around her neck. 'Well, that wasn't my first audition. I had auditioned many times before that, but had never been chosen. However, I knew the director of this commercial. He was a friend of my mother's. And he gave me a chance. Naturally, I will be forever in his debt.'

'Now, your mother . . .' The reporter saw something he could be serious about. 'Didn't she desert your family when you were a young girl?'

Kitten's expression cooled. 'My, my. You have been doing your research.'

'I think our readers would like to know. I mean, there's such a dichotomy, isn't there? You a sex symbol, your mother a raging feminist.'

Kitten laughed tightly. 'I'm having trouble getting your point on this.'

'Well, as I understand it, and please correct me if I've got it wrong, your mother was married, had two children, then decided that being a wife and mother might have been what she was programmed to do, but it wasn't really what she wanted to do. So she picked up and left. How old were you at the time?'

'Nine,' Kitten said, remembering all too well the day her mother left them. Not even a word of farewell, Mom told them she was going to the grocer's to get some milk. It turned out to be the longest trip to the shops any Corelli had ever made. No one ever wildly imagined what had happened to Catherine Corelli. Gretchen had been heart-sick with worry. She sat there with her six-year-old brother Danny while their father, Mark Corelli, one of Baltimore's finest young dentists, as his parents called him, telephoned police, hospitals, friends, everywhere, searching for his errant wife. It was only days later that she called from some place in Tennessee to let them know she would not be returning with the milk or anything else.

Dear mother, Kitten thought. In freeing herself, she had enslaved her daughter. Kitten, or Gretchen as she was then known, at nine years old became the main character in the house, even though her father hired a woman to come in from three to six each day. Kitten was the one who got up, threw in a load of laundry before she woke Danny up and made him breakfast. Then she made sure they both hopped on the school bus for the day's lessons. Their after-school activities had to stop because there was no one to chauffeur them. All

205

the kids knew their mother had fled, so they were constantly subjected to those humiliating taunts. The teachers also knew, which made it worse. They were treated like orphans. And their father had no time for them. He worked all day and on Saturdays besides. They had to depend on aunts and uncles and grandparents, when they were alive, for their nurturing. Then two years after their mother deserted them, Sharon, their stepmother, entered the picture. Not exactly wicked, Kitten would have to concede at this late date, but certainly not exactly loving either, especially not after she and Mark Corelli had two children of their own.

Kitten became reconnected with her mother seven years after Catherine Corelli fled. She finally sent letters to both Kitten and Danny, explaining why she had to leave them. Kitten didn't really understand what her mother was trying to say. Her mother talked about expanding her horizons, freeing herself, being her own person, being human not female. It was too confusing to fathom for a teenager who realized, as her body filled out, how very female she was.

But what was exciting and understandable was that the letters her mother sent came from California. California! Another world.

Kitten wasn't involved in the legal wrangle that followed when Catherine decided she wanted some visitation rights. She could have heard about if she had wanted to, there was certainly enough screaming going on in the family. But she closed her ears to it. All she knew is that the Christmas after she received the first letter from her mother, both she and Danny were bundled up and sent out to Los Angeles for a visit with Mommy, who at that time was living with Sam Goldsmith, director of commercials, which is how several years later Kitten got the part as the gas pump girl.

'What does your mother – who, I believe, is president of her NOW chapter – think of you?' the reporter asked.

Kitten looked at him strangely. Shouldn't the question have been put the other way around? What did she think of her mother? What did she think of a woman who had two children and abandoned them? Left her children bereft of love and protection in what really was a cold, cruel world? But anger was not the emotion Kitten wished to project. So she said, 'I don't think I quite understand the question.' The sour thoughts circulating in her brain she would keep to herself.

'Well, here's a woman who some might call a bra-burner, or as I did before, a raging feminist, definitely a feminist, in any case, and here you are, symbolizing all that feminists despise.'

Kitten laughed, pretending to be mystified. 'You obviously know more about feminists than I do. What exactly do they despise?'

'Sex,' the reporter answered automatically.

'I didn't know feminists despised sex,' Kitten said with a puzzled expression on her face. 'I thought feminism was a movement working for equality between the sexes. In status. In wages. I think I've achieved that for myself. At this point in my career, I can pick and choose my roles. I may not earn the biggest salary in Hollywood, but I'm certainly able to maintain myself and a certain style of living. Anyway you want to look at me or my career, I have established my independence. I have achieved all that any feminist would aspire to.'

'But haven't you done that by selling out?'

'Selling out?' Kitten was afraid her voice rose slightly.

'Kitten Fairleigh is a sex symbol. You've achieved what you have by becoming a male masturbatory fantasy.'

'Well, whose problem is that?' She leaned forward, perhaps proving his point as his gaze fell from her liquid eyes down the front of her satin, v-necked top. 'America's a marketplace for buyers and sellers. I sell what I have. If people don't buy it, then I'll change my merchandising. Do you consider what I do, acting, any more disreputable than what you do? You write for a living. You write what people want to read. You're writing about me because people want to read about me. And with these questions you're trying to get some good copy. I don't knock you for that, don't knock me for what I do.'

'Touché,' he said. 'You image doesn't do you credit.'

Either that or he wasn't as bright as he thought he was, Kitten thought maliciously.

'So you consider yourself a feminist?'

'I consider myself a woman. And I'm damn proud of it.'

'But not a feminist?'

'What is a feminist? Would I trample over another woman to get to her man? No. Would I refuse to work with a woman director or producer, should one have the sense to ask me? No. Do I support women's rights to be valued as human beings and not as sex objects? Yes. Equal pay for equal work? Yes. A segregated society, women separated from men? No. I like men. I like them as lovers and companions. I like having women friends, but I also like having men friends. So while I would say, yes, I'm a feminist, I'm not an angry one. I don't think men are trying to do me in. Of course, all work, especially in Hollywood, is guerilla warfare.'

'Your latest work,' the reporter began, giving up on the feminist tack, 'perhaps we can move on to that? Here, I believe, you've really branched out into a more art-oriented film. Even though you're a big star, a movie star, *Vanilla Loves Chocolate* was not a big success.'

'No, it wasn't. But you're right, I wanted to branch out. And I also wanted the chance to work with Robert Guterri. Making a film in

Italy was certainly a different experience. One definitely appreciates American efficiency all the more.'

'*Vanilla Loves Chocolate* was based on that best seller of many years ago, RAGE IN BLACK AND WHITE. Did you feel you offended any of your fans by portraying, first of all, such a cold-hearted bitch, secondly, such a cold-hearted white bitch, taking advantage of a black man? And did you feel the material was dated?'

Kitten lifted her green-blue eyes up to the ceiling and thought. 'I didn't see the material as a black/white confrontation. That, I believe, was a surface issue. I would say *Vanilla Loves Chocolate* dealt more with the issues of oppressed and oppressor, enfranchised and disenfranchised – also the issue we were just talking about, man versus woman. I think the see-saw of relationships between Grace Goldstein and her black lover was what fascinated me when I was reading the script.'

'Some critics say you played the part of a cold-hearted bitch to perfection.'

Kitten smiled graciously. Some say she played the part to perfection in real life also, but why give him a quote he'd be bound to use?

'How did you feel about the protest of Ahmed Jemal Mohammed, the author of RAGE IN BLACK AND WHITE, who threatened to set himself on fire in the centre of Rome because his work had been misappropriated?'

'As I understand it, the book was bought for the movies when it came out. I saw his signature on a contract. Because I asked about it. Certainly when someone threatens self-immolation, one takes notice.'

'Are you planning to do any more art films?'

'If another interesting part comes along, I will. Right now, as you know, I'm scheduled to start shooting *Fantasies* next month. I'm very excited about it. It deals with a man's midlife crisis. He has this fantasy, this dream woman he believes he's been searching for all his life. And now, suddenly, whenever he thinks about her, she appears. It makes for many embarrassing situations. In the boardroom and in the bedroom. It should be a bright, fast-paced comedy. Until that starts, I'm here in New York with David Turner, while he goes into rehearsal for *She Stoops to Conquer*.'

'David Turner,' the reporter repeated. 'Could we talk for a minute about the men in your life?'

Since Kitten understood that the interview would at some point get around to the men in her life, she simply smiled and waited.

'Tommy Patterson,' the reporter said. 'Sum him up in one word.'

Several words came unbidden to Kitten's lips, but she held them back. 'I can't,' she confessed falsely. 'He was much too complicated for a single word.'

'Your relationship. Was it love? Infatuation? It's said that, while Tommy Patterson had the whole of America enthralled, you managed to enslave him.'

Enslave him? She didn't know if that was exactly the case. They met on the *Billy Natterman show*. "Nattering Natterman" he was called in the trade. His television talk show captured Los Angeles air waves at ten o'clock every morning with a series of celebrity guests out to plug a new movie, a book, or simply themselves. It was easy listening for housewives, except there were no housewives any more. Kitten didn't know what the demographics of the show were, but obviously someone watched it. It had been on the air for five years now.

Kitten appeared on the *Billy Natterman Show* to plug her new movie *April Ice*. She was the first guest because Billy liked to get an attractive woman on fast to catch everyone's attention. She wasn't really up to the show. Not only did she think *April Ice* was going to be a bomb, but she had also just slid out of a love affair with her co-star in that movie, Dirk Semiroff. Despite the exotic last name, Dirk was a British actor trying to make it in Hollywood for the sake of the money. His problem was that he had trouble hiding his contempt for everything Southern California represented. This included, as it turned out, Kitten Fairleigh, as he had let her know just the week before.

So there she was, sitting with Billy Natterman, depressed and dejected. But she rallied with a reminder to herself that she was an actress with an image to project. So she said as many kind and meaningless words as she could about Dirk Semiroff and *April Ice*. She also talked about her charity turn as one of the honorary sponsors of "Have A Heart", a fundraising effort to build a gym for senior citizens.

Then, after one of those five-minute commercial breaks during which Billy Natterman tried to paw her when he assisted her in moving one seat over, Tommy Patterson was introduced. Kitten had never met Tommy before. She had seen him, of course. He was a difficult man to escape. Tommy was everywhere, even on billboards, with his feel-good philosophy. Nothing's wrong if it makes you feel good. That was a bit hard to take. Kitten still harboured a big dose of resentment against her mother, who, to feel good, had deserted her children. However, it was now the age of greed and getting while the getting was good. And Tommy seemed a person for this age.

But it wasn't to advocate his feeling-good-is-good message that he was appearing on Natterman's show that day. It was to push his latest book, WHAT IS A COMMITMENT AND HOW TO MAKE ONE IN 10 EASY STEPS. 'People have everything they need except love,' Tommy said. And it struck Kitten how absolutely true that was, especially in her own life, especially after being dumped by Dirk Semiroff. She sat up and paid attention.

Before meeting Tommy Patterson, Kitten had never considered herself a stupid woman. By a series of hard choices and smart moves, she had propelled herself into the movies and on to the pages of fan magazines and tabloids throughout the country. Her brain led her, not her heart. Perhaps because her working life was so lop-sidedly in favour of the rational, she made the biggest mistake of her life that day on the *Billy Natterman Show* by falling irrationally in love with Tommy Patterson.

It was the simple truths that got to her. Tommy's words seemed to conjure up her most elemental thoughts and feelings. But then he was so popular, it should have alerted her to the fact that he was saying what everyone was thinking and feeling. In other words, in order to say everything, he said nothing – at least nothing of value. His messages were variations on age-old themes: Live life to the fullest. Eat, drink and be merry, for tomorrow you die. Look on the bright side. Keep your sunny side up. He offered to an anxious public all the childish bromides that life had subsequently disproved. Tommy led people to believe that they could return to the cocoon of innocence from which the later years had so rudely ripped them.

Kitten Fairleigh wanted that cocoon. She had never really had much of a childhood to begin with and now she wanted remnants of it back. She wanted someone to love, cosset and comfort her. And in return she wanted to be able to love someone completely, give her heart away and not have it broken.

Being with Tommy was in the beginning like sliding naked into a warm Jaccuzzi. Everything was so comfortable, so right. It was also so brief. One couldn't stay in a Jaccuzzi too long; and when one got out, the cold wind was all the more biting.

At what point did she discover that Tommy Patterson was a phoney? She supposed when, before every interview they faced as a couple, he readjusted her blouse so it showed more cleavage. He was reaffirming his masculinity by making sure everyone knew how sexy she was. He was saying to the world, 'I own this very desirable woman.' And he did try to own her. He tried to manipulate her every emotion. At first, because she was so insecure and so in need of love, he succeeded.

He left her career alone. He was smart enough to realize he knew nothing about Hollywood deal-making, though he wasn't above giving her agent hints about how much she should be making and what sort of percentage of the gross she should be getting. It was her psyche he tried to destroy by making her totally dependent on him. He kept her emotionally off balance, giving and refusing love without reason. Instead of perpetually sitting in a comfortable, warm Jaccuzzi, she soon found herself watching for and wondering over every little sign. How was Tommy feeling that day, what was he thinking, what did he want of her, what would make him happy? Did he love her or couldn't he care less?

Sexually, her life became a nightmare. She knew men. She had slept with enough of them. She wasn't bragging, it just happened. Usually, all they would have to do was get her alone and they would rise to the occasion. When she removed her blouse and those tits that loomed so large up on the screen loomed just as large in person, men generally broke out in a preparatory sweat. She enjoyed that. She liked to be appreciated. She liked to know she had a body men would die for. But Tommy – sex with him was like dropping quarters into a candy machine. It was over so fast, you never really got what you wanted, even when you pulled the right handle.

Then there were the many times when he was impotent. The only way he could become erect was for her sexually to humiliate herself. Sometimes she had to undress way across the room, then crawl on her hands and knees over to him and beg him to let her suck him off. Other times, he would have various vegetables prepared and encourage her to masturbate with them. Or she would have to sit in front of him and tell he had the biggest cock she had ever seen and all she wanted out of life was for him to fuck her.

What did she get out of this? When he was finally up and semi-hard, he would go into her, release himself as if he were taking a long needed pee, and then back out so quickly she scarcely lubricated. Afterwards, he would whisper to her, 'The whole world thinks of you as a sex goddess. Only I know how really frigid you are.'

But that wasn't true! She wasn't frigid. She hadn't been with Dirk. She hadn't been with other men. Seeing them turned on turned her on. She could come just on their worship. But Tommy made it clear he didn't worship her. There was to be only one lord and master, and that was Tommy Patterson.

A year passed between her honeymoon and her first affair. During that time Tommy parlayed WHAT IS A COMMITMENT AND HOW TO MAKE ON IN 10 EASY STEPS from a best seller and a local radio call-in show to a national radio call-in show, where he did "relationship

211

counselling" on the air. She found it ironic that people would call in to discuss their most intimate problems on a nationwide hookup. She was tempted sometimes to call in herself. Would he recognize her voice or her problem? Or would he simply say, 'Lose the schmuck. He's not good enough for you.'

One year. One year of complete fidelity to the master of manipulation. How had she ever lasted so long? Even now, she remembered exactly how she had stumbled into infidelity. It was a night shoot. She was in her trailer, waiting for her call. Tommy was on the radio. She was still trying to figure him out at that point. He was giving advice to a woman who found some of her husband's sexual habits disgusting to her. Tommy was suggesting that she go along with them anyway because a man's sexual appetites had to be appeased. In other words, even on radio Tommy Patterson was a real pig.

Steven Kane, the director of her last effort, knocked on her trailer door, and she invited him in. He had come personally to apologize because the male star, who shall remain nameless, was having another nosebleed. 'Why doesn't he stop using that stuff?' Kitten wondered.

'He can't,' Steven replied. They looked at each other, as man and woman have since time immemorial. And then, as if he had scripted it himself, Steven came to her and pulled her into his arms. His lips were on hers, his hands upon her breasts, and she was begging him to make love to her. It was awkward in the trailer, very awkward because she was sure she screamed as he drove into her over and over again. It was a scream of passion and of relief. He ripped her blouse away from her skin, and she felt exultant. His wet lips were on her nipples, sucking at her, demanding, demanding, while he grew harder again inside of her. She died in his arms, she needed him so. Here finally was a man who wanted her and who could appreciate her without demanding anything of her, except later, before the cameras, a heartfelt performance.

That was one of her better films when she thought back on it. She played a young woman who discovered that the man she thought she loved was actually a contract killer, hired by her brother to do away with her, so that the brother could inherit the family fortune. Finally entitled *Love Her Till She's Dead*, it was her first attempt at slapstick comedy. The critics called her performance "warm, knowing and witty." She had Steven to thank for that. He was the one who took the time to help her polish her craft. Well, okay, he polished elsewhere also. Still, it was fun!

It was a one-movie stand with Steven Kane, but she would always be grateful to him for reawakening her common sense. There was

212

nothing wrong with her, personally or sexually. It was her relationship with Tommy that was so destructive. And she wanted to put an end to it. She wanted a divorce.

'I will never allow you to humiliate me,' was his reply. In other words, no one with her sex appeal was going to be allowed to reject the all-knowing master of good feeling, Tommy Patterson. He came across with threats of what he would do to her if she filed for divorce; stories he would tell about her so-called sex appeal. 'There's nothing you could say,' she assured him.

'You'd be surprised by my vivid imagination,' he warned.

'Say what you want,' she retorted. 'If I have to, I'll sleep with every reporter alive to prove you wrong. Women included!' But Kitten was scared. She had obviously married a nut. She spoke to her lawyer. In strictest confidence. 'People are used to messy divorces,' he told her. 'Don't worry about it.'

But she did worry. Tommy's lies could ruin her career. So she stayed married to him for appearance's sake – his appearance. They shared "Mi Hacienda", but not a bedroom, not a life. And then she found David Turner.

It was true, as the fan magazines said, she did have a habit of falling in love with her co-stars. But she didn't sleep with all of them. However, David Turner came along at exactly the right moment. When she saw him, saw his body, his eyes, she knew it would be a long-lasting – at least as long as they were shooting the movie – satisfying affair. Their movie, an action/adventure flick, was shot on location in Yugoslavia. He played a gun runner, she a nun doubting her vocation. They combined to work the scam of the century on a world-wide gang of terrorists-for-hire. At least the writers assured them it would look like the scam of the century once they filmed it. Even though she was a nun, love scenes with David abounded. At first there were gentle, then alluring looks. Finally, there came the intensely erotic seduction in which she casts off her habit while he unzips his trousers. They had practised that scene in private many times before. 'The chemistry's great!' the director assured them after viewing the dailies.

The chemistry was great, and the papers didn't have any trouble picking up on it. Her affair with David Turner became an open secret. 'I find my relationship with David very – satisfying,' was the way she put it when asked by *Entertainment Tonight*.

'And your marriage to Tommy Patterson?' the reporter wondered. 'On the rocks?'

'Tommy has a very open view of marriage,' Kitten lied. Tommy had been hysterical – ranting, raving, telling her she was making him look like a fool. But her lawyer told her the longer she kept up the affair with David, the better. She and Tommy had signed a prenuptial agreement. He could get nothing from her, offer her nothing except the divorce she wanted. Any accusation he tossed around now, except that of adultery, would be looked upon as sour grapes.

Neither she nor her lawyer expected Tommy to be murdered. Certainly, her alibi was enough of a blow to her reputation. While Tommy was being pushed over a cliff, she was in bed with David Turner, trying Position No. 36.

Not only had Tommy had the bad grace to be murdered, two days before he was murdered he cut her out of his will, leaving only bitter words; and the day before his murder, he ordered his lawyer to draw up a divorce decree, which the public soon knew about. In other words, Tommy's murder and the events surrounding it made her look a real villain.

To save herself, she had to play the worst part in her life, the distraught widow. She gave interviews in which she vaguely spoke about love, some difficulties she and Tommy had been trying to work through, sorrow, despair. And all she could do was pray that it worked, that not too many of her fans had been terribly offended.

She had enslaved Tommy Patterson, the reporter from the *Times* had suggested. But she had enslaved nobody. It was Tommy who held the whip, both literally and figuratively. 'Tommy's gone,' Kitten almost whispered to the reporter. 'I think we should let his life speak for itself.'

'Your marriage wasn't trouble free?'

'No marriage is.'

'You didn't murder him, I take it?'

Kitten smiled. 'No. I didn't murder him.'

The reporter laughed nervously. 'I just thought I'd ask. It would have made quite an exclusive had you confessed.'

Kitten took in a deep breath, increasing the air in her diaphragm, pushing her chest forward toward the reporter. 'I can't believe Tommy was murdered,' she said, 'despite what the police say. I still think it was an accident. After all, he was a man everybody loved.' She shrugged. 'So who would kill him?'

# *Chapter 34*

# The Visit

'How much progress has she made?' Odelle asked her friend Madelaine Stevenson.

Madelaine looked over the flat front lawn of River Range Clinic and sighed. 'I wish I could tell you that Trudi Surefoot has made a commitment to change. But she hasn't. She's fighting us all the way. I have a feeling it's just a waste of our time and her money. We can keep her off drugs here, but as soon as she leaves, she'll go right back on them.'

'Has she spoken about leaving?'

'No, not yet. I don't think she realizes she can leave. But we can't carry her indefinitely, Odelle. Our program generally runs six weeks. Trudi's been here much longer. We have a waiting list. Parents call me every day, begging a place for their child. Businesses want to put their top executives here. We care about Trudi, and sure, I feel like a failure for not being able to help her. But sometimes I have to harden my heart. We can't help someone who doesn't want to be helped.'

'I'll speak to her.'

'Do,' Madelaine urged. 'Remember, this is another favour I'm doing for you. Our patients aren't supposed to have visitors. But you said this was a matter of life and death.'

When Odelle left Madelaine's office, she was directed towards one of the smaller dormitories. Everywhere in the grounds of River Range she saw people exercising, walking, jogging, playing soccer, heading towards the crafts building. Only Trudi remained in the dorm, sitting in her room, looking sad and grim, living still the unexamined life.

Trudi's eyes brightened when she saw her friend. 'Odelle!' she enthused. 'God, that guy got away with your money! I was so upset. What a pig, huh? Gee, I'm so glad you came. You've got to help me get out of here.'

215

Annoyed and angered, Odelle sat down on Trudi's bed and said, 'It was I who helped you get in here. Remember? You came to me and begged my help. You said now that you were in charge of Tommy's Fund for the Betterment of Humanity, you were going to get off drugs so you could handle things responsibly?'

'That was before,' Trudi said.

'Before what?'

'Before I found out how hard giving up drugs was going to be.'

Odelle looked at Trudi in her washed out exercise clothes, her pale little face and sad eyes. She shook her head. She simply did not understand addiction. Ever since she had been told to give up caffeine, she didn't even have a cup of coffee in the morning. Yet here was Trudi. Because of her drugs, she had lost everything in life that was important to her: her chance for love, her children, control over herself and her surroundings. Still she yearned for what would eventually kill her. Why? 'Why?' she asked. 'Why do you need drugs so, Trudi?'

'Because life is so boring without them,' Trudi replied. 'My mind just sits here and goes nowhere.'

Odelle was shocked. Boring? Life? She only wished it would be a little more boring, a little quieter, more sedate. But no, life was always like a thunderstorm hovering menacingly just over the horizon. Sooner or later everyone was going to get drenched. She took Trudi by the arm and pulled her over to the window. 'Look,' she ordered her.

Trudi looked. 'What?' she wondered.

'See that tree over there, that oak? I bet it's been alive for over a hundred years. The grass, listen to it. You can hear it growing. Every week it has to be mowed. Look up in the sky at that cloud. Where do you think it's been before it circled over us? See over there, that group of people playing soccer? Consider how their bodies are working without them even thinking about it, their hearts pumping, their internal thermostats making them sweat, their brains connecting foot to ball. And all that's boring?'

Trudi look askance at her friend. 'Have you taken to writing greetings cards?'

Odelle was shocked. Trudi had never employed sarcasm before. Maybe she did need drugs. 'Okay.' Odelle pushed Trudi back towards her bed. 'You don't want to change. You've made that obvious to the staff here at the clinic, those who have been trying to help you. Now you've made it obvious to me. So leave. I want you to pack up today and get out of here. There are hundreds of people waiting to take your place. Go back to New Mexico and live your life in your perpetual fog, Trudi.'

216

'You don't have to get mad, Odelle. It's my life, not yours.'

'True. But I thought finally you were going to make something of it. I thought maybe you could start over. How old are you anyway? Thirty? Thirty-one, thirty-two? You can still get married and have children, Trudi. You can still have love. But that's obviously not your choice. So I'm giving up. However, before you go back on drugs, there are things we must discuss and get straight.'

'Fine.' Angrily, like a stubborn child, Trudi folded her arms across her chest and waited.

'What were you doing in Los Angeles that week Tommy was murdered?'

'What?'

'Don't play dumb, Trudi. Kitten Fairleigh told Grace that Detective Morris – remember him at "Mi Hacienda" after Tommy's funeral? – found out that you were participating in an exhibition of Native American crafts in Los Angeles the week Tommy was killed.' Odelle watched while Trudi thought. If eyes were mirrors to the soul, Trudi's was a little bit nebulous. 'Do you remember nothing?' Odelle asked in frustration.

'I remember being in Taos,' Trudi said.

'Yes, well, this is L.A. we're talking about,' Odelle reminded her.

Trudi thought. 'Umm. They were gathering art works for a craft show that was to caravan through the Southwest and up the Coast. It was the – uh – Native American Artists of the Southwest, that group. I submitted my work because, honestly, my pottery is really very good. It sells. And they told me I couldn't exhibit because I wasn't a Native American. Well, goddamn it, I was too! I mean, how native can you get? I had lived three lives in America, one as Rising Surefoot, Indian princess. And, hell, what is East Diablo, West Texas, if not the heart of the Southwest? So finally they let me in. And then I forget what happened exactly. We went touring with the exhibition to demonstrate our craft firsthand. I remember being in a big, ugly city. Could that have been Los Angeles?'

'Sounds like it.'

'Tommy was there!' Trudi's eyes lit up.

'You saw Tommy?'

'I think so.'

'What do you mean you think so!' Odelle shouted.

Trudi looked confused, almost hurt. 'I'm trying to remember, Odelle. Like, his aura came to me. We've always had very strong, interconnecting auras.'

'Lord help me control myself,' Odelle prayed quietly. 'Did you see Tommy or not?'

217

'It's like he came and went several times. He faded in and out of my consciousness.'

'You mean, when you weren't so heavily doped, you could see him; when you were, you couldn't?'

'It's not like that, Odelle. It's a good, healthy feeling.'

'It sounds great. You can't even remember whether you saw your ex-husband or whether it was simply his aura, whatever that's supposed to mean. Do you at least remember whether you murdered him?'

'How could I have murdered Tommy? I loved him.'

'Did you push him off the cliff accidentally?'

'I have a vision of him falling. I see the pain in his eyes and his surprise. Yes, there was his wonderment that the world would soon have to do without him.'

Odelle stood up. 'Oh, Jesus!' She jammed her fist against her thigh. 'You murdered him!'

'I don't think so.'

'But you don't know.'

'Our spirits intermingled at the moment of his death. I guess that's why I felt so bad about it.'

'Temporary insanity, drug-deranged, unable to distinguish real from unreal. Is that the kind of defence a lawyer could work up? And you need a lawyer, Trudi. You need one desperately.'

'Do you think so?' Trudi wondered with those innocent eyes of hers.

'I mean, I can see why you would murder him. We all at one point or another in our lives have been angry enough at Tommy to murder him. But actually to do it – '

'No, I didn't murder Tommy!' Trudi said with more force. 'I think.'

Odelle sat down on the bed and grabbed Trudi's hands. 'Listen to me. After I leave, take a good look at yourself in the mirror and ask yourself what you have become. Trudi, it's time to stop being a zombie. I'll consult Grace about your latest revelations. Meanwhile, there's something further we have to discuss. There is a woman by the name of Tippi Moonstone. She's a writer. She's writing the biography of Tommy Patterson.'

'Oh! Isn't that nice?'

'No, it's not nice, Trudi, because Tippi Moonstone is the sort of writer who reveals all. All our dark, ignoble secrets. And we all have plenty that we have to hide. Under no circumstances are you to talk to Tippi Moonstone. Grace, meanwhile, has also signed a contract to write a book about Tommy. She will protect us.' Odelle stood. 'It's time for me to leave. I have to confess that I am almost at the point of washing my hands of you, Trudi. And I don't do that to very many people. I only wish I did. I would probably be a much happier woman.

'But that's not your problem. Your problem is yourself. Look in the mirror. Try to find the woman you could be if you gave yourself the chance.'

Trudi sat on the bed for the longest time after Odelle left. She didn't really feel like getting up and looking in the mirror. She didn't really feel like doing anything. There was an emptiness in her she believed only drugs could fill. She had tried to fill it with love, with motherhood, but she had failed at both. Drugs were something she could definitely depend on.

She didn't know how long she sat there. The gong sort of woke her from her self-induced trance. That meant lunch time. She wasn't very hungry, and she hated to eat with the rest of the druggies. They always looked so reproachful. But she supposed she should get something to eat.

Trudi got up and stood in front of the mirror to pat down her hair. Odelle's advice came back to her. What did she see in the mirror? She saw a woman getting older. Her skin was sallow, her eyes sinking. She had nothing to show for her thirty-odd years except two previous lives and two lost children. If she did push Tommy off that cliff, she should have gone over it with him. Because she had nothing left to offer anyone.

What had Tommy been thinking of, putting her in charge of the Fund for the Betterment of Humanity? And how had she gained the energy all those weeks ago to think that she could change? She was who she was. She was nothing. An empty vessel.

She left her room to fill at least the stomach part of that empty vessel.

'Hey,' someone caught up to her, as she crossed the yawning lawns of River Range. 'I haven't seen you for days. Have you given up on nature?'

Trudi looked over at her companion and ran her fingers through her hair, only too well aware that she really hadn't combed it thoroughly for days. 'Oh, hi, Don. How are you?' she said to the River Range nature enthusiast who led hikes each day, the ones she had so enjoyed when she first came here.

'I'm great!' he replied. 'I suppose the big question is, how are you?'

Trudi sort of grimaced and smiled at the same time. 'Not so good,' she admitted. 'I guess I'll be leaving here a failure. As usual.'

'You don't have to leave here a failure,' he said to her, his eyes deep and warm.

219

'I know, I know. Everyone can change. That's what they tell you. But I can't, Don. I just can't. I have no – no inner strength. You know what I mean?'

'Hey! Anyone who has the strength to lead three lives has the strength to give up drugs.'

She laughed. 'Sometimes I wonder if I really did have three lives.'

'Never stop believing in yourself, Trudi. You are strong and beautiful. You may doubt that now, but I don't. And there's someone else who doesn't doubt that either.'

'Oh yeah. Who's that?'

Don pursed his lips. 'I can't say. It's not allowed.'

She didn't understand what he was talking about, but that didn't worry Trudi. She usually didn't understand what people were talking about anyway.

Trudi filed into the dining room with the other residents of River Range and went slowly through the cafeteria line. She didn't know why, if they were trying to wean people away from addictions, they had so many chocolate desserts. Perhaps because somehow they knew Trudi didn't fancy chocolate.

After collecting enough food on her tray to satisfy her meagre nutritional needs, Trudi ignored her assigned seat and found herself at one of the round tables for eight. Three people were already sitting there, and they looked at her coldly. It bothered her to be a pariah. But she knew why people resented her. She wasn't participating, she wasn't contributing. Everyone else was working to conquer the common enemy of addiction. Seeing her just hanging around was like seeing a ghost of their old selves. Trudi felt ashamed. And yet she was defiant. She chose to be a druggie. She chose death in life.

She ate as quickly as she could. They didn't want to sit with her, and she didn't want to be in the cafeteria any longer than was necessary. No one talked to her the whole time she was at the table. She got up, stacked her tray, and left even before Madelaine made the announcements for the afternoon's activities.

As she walked back to her dorm, Trudi looked up at the sky. The sun was obscured by clouds. Did Trudi wonder where the clouds had been? With drugs she could ride upon them. Odelle had said some trees were over a hundred years old. Trudi had lived longer than that. The grass grew. Trudi knew that. With her sacred mushrooms, Trudi had talked to individual blades of grass to ask them what it was like, if it hurt when people walked on them or cows grazed. On drugs there was nothing Trudi couldn't do. Except remember if she had killed her ex-husband.

The dorm was quiet when she returned to it. Everyone else was eating or enjoying a social hour in the library. She was alone. All alone. She opened the door to her room. Now she was annoyed. Someone had been in here while she was in the dining hall. Was nothing sacred?

A book had been left on her bed. It was bound in an awful shit-brown. It had a bookmark sticking out from it. She picked it up and it fell open to where the bookmark was placed. Two passages were underlined: "I am the light of the world: he that follows me shall not walk in darkness, but shall have the light of life." And, "You shall know the truth, and the truth shall make you free."

Trudi caressed the pages of the New Testament with a smile on her face. She knew these words. She had heard them since her birth when her soul stirred. But her soul had since died and she was in darkness. The pages of John's Gospel flipped through her fingers. "I am come a light into the world, that whosoever believes in me should not abide in darkness."

And yet wasn't darkness all that she knew? Darkness, emptiness, where no hand could reach her, where no one could save her. "Let not your heart be troubled: you believe in God, believe also in me. In my Father's house are many mansions: if it were not so I would have told you. I go to prepare a place for you. And if I go and prepare a place for you, I will come again, and receive you unto myself; that where I am, there you may be also. And whither I go, you know, and the way you know. I am the way, the truth and the life."

And for the first time since she was oh-so-young, when Cousin Earl had his way with her and Trudi knew she was lost, she knelt down upon her knees, clasped her hands and prayed, 'Lord, forgive me.'

She didn't ask for a sign because Trudi was always self-effacing. But the clouds that had obscured the sun moments before were swept away, and the sun shone down on Trudi and on the Bible she held in her hands.

221

# Chapter 35

# Delving into the Big Muddy

'Anal retentive,' Grace spoke aloud into her empty house. She didn't want to get to work that morning. It annoyed her that she had to set aside the adventures of Lydia and Bonnie Big Dick in order to deal with her ex-husband's garbage. But there it was. And here. And over in the corner. Everywhere! Her house was overflowing with the sewers of Tommy Patterson's mind! Boxes and boxes and more boxes. When did he have time to collect all this stuff!

He travels fastest who travels alone, Tommy. Or had he enjoyed visions of donating his papers to some vast university complex, desperate for name recognition? More likely, Tommy had intended to establish his own memorial library.

Galen had left a razor on the kitchen table. Was he making what she considered at this point a rather sensible suggestion? No. He had put a little note under it. "To open boxes." This was so annoying of him. He knew she didn't want to do this damn book. And here he was, helping the project along.

If only Galen would stop asking if she thought she'd have to interview Kitten Fairleigh! That was this book's big draw for him. She supposed at some point she would have to interview everyone. Even herself. It would be necessary to reopen the wounds of her youthful innocence – innocence, hell! Naivety! – and let the blood flow once more. Long ago and far away, bleeding by leeches brought restored health. There were still leeches in the world today. They walked on two feet and assumed the shape of men.

Grace sat back and forced herself to calm down. If she kept getting carried away by anger, she would soon be tempted to turn to tranquillizers. This would be a breach of her mother's code of medicine whereby aspirin solved all problems. She smiled. What would her mother make of someone like Trudi? When she read the book – and her mother read *all* her books – Grace would find out.

And thinking of Trudi, what was happening with her? Odelle was supposed to find out and get back to Grace, but she hadn't. Angered and upset once more, Grace supposed this silence must mean she would have to do everything herself: write the book and save their skins at the same time. Why could she depend on no one!

The phone rang. Grace looked suspiciously at the clock. It was only ten to nine. Who had the gall to call her at this hour? Maybe Odelle! She picked up the phone, prepared to hear the latest. But it was Galen. 'Hi,' he said brightly. 'How's it going?'

'How's it going?' Grace wondered angrily. 'Is that anything like "how's it hanging"?'

There was a puzzled pause at the other end of the line. 'I guess I shouldn't have called you so early,' Galen assessed. 'But I just wanted to know if you found the razor and everything. Like, I usually get really excited at the beginning of a project and – '

'Galen, shut up, will you? It's too early in the morning to talk. I've found the razor. Thanks. It was thoughtful of you. You've probably saved me from running right down to Chez Jackie's and having a manicure. Now was there anything else?'

'Yeah. How are you feeling?' he almost whispered.

'Feeling?'

'I mean, like are you nauseous yet or anything?'

'Did you have sex ed in high school? You don't get nauseous until the second or third month. So far I haven't even missed my period!'

'One of the women here is going to one of those infertility clinics. Do you think we should seek help?'

'You should, Galen. Definitely!' She flung down the phone. Men were such idiots! How long did he think it had been since they stopped using precautions? People didn't become pregnant instantly. Galen should know that by now. All he did at night was read those books about pregnancy and prenatal care. What was the publishing industry coming to? Who would be stupid enough to buy these books which focused on starting your baby off right in the womb, what foods to eat, what music to listen to, what books to read to your foetus? Only Galen would plunk down $17.50 for a book like that. She hoped. The rest of the world had to have more sense. After all, being pregnant was supposed to be fun, exciting, natural – not hard, intellectual work.

Grace sank down on one of the boxes. How excited she had been the first time she was pregnant. That was with you, Tommy, she communicated silently to the boxes lying about her. God, all those miserable years ago, and only now was she starting over. How you wrecked my life, you bastard. She held the razor in her hand and looked at it. Was she ready to take the first slice into the past?

No. She'd call Odelle. Maybe her friend wasn't at work yet. After all, in Chicago it was an hour earlier. Avoidance, Grace chastised herself. But she didn't care. It was her life. Or it had been before Tommy moved into it, at least his very mortal remains, his writings. And she was hoping that they were only mortal, not immortal. God save us from that.

Odelle, Odelle, Odelle. Grace flipped through her little black book, then dialled her friend's number. Better to get everyone's status straight before she began working. The phone was ringing. Good. Three times. That meant the answering machine wasn't on. 'Hello. There have been so many complaints over the last message on my answering machine, that I have decided to change it. Obviously, there are objections to explicit instructions in this very free-wheeling world we live in. Why, I don't know. People just don't seem to believe in taking orders any more. Not even from telephone answering machines. It's sad, isn't it, when we're constantly vying for position like this? So let me just say, and this is not an order but a suggestion, that you leave your name and number at the sound of the beep, and I'll get back to you whenever it's convenient. After all, I have a life too.'

'Odelle, it's Grace. May I say that this message also sucks. You were supposed to – '

'Grace?'

'Odelle?' Grace said, when she had turned off the machine and its screeching stopped.

'Grace, I meant to get back to you last night but it got so late. I didn't want to disturb you, especially after speaking to Galen the other evening.'

'You spoke to Galen?'

'Yes. You were out dropping something off at the library or something. He told me that you two are trying to have a baby.'

'He what!'

'Grace, I think that's absolutely wonderful. You need a child in your life. Why should I be the only one to suffer? Only joking, of course. But Galen seems so excited about it. I have to meet him some day. Do you realize this is the longest affair you've had since – oh, well, I suppose it's best not to mention Darrell.'

'You know, Odelle, I'm beginning to prefer your answering machine. Did you find out anything from Trudi?'

'She's in sorry shape, Grace. The cure is not taking. And she admitted she was in L.A. the week Tommy died. She thinks she saw Tommy. She's not clear on that. I take it she was heavily sedated, shall we call it, the entire time. But she says she felt his aura. Which might mean she and Tommy fucked for old time's sake.'

'Hmm.' Grace considered that, pacing in and around the boxes scattered in the hallway, dragging the phone with her. 'And you? Let me get it straight for posterity. What's your story again about your visit to Tommy the week he died? I was thinking about that. For instance, he changed his will after he saw you.'

'My conversation with Tommy isn't relevant, Grace. If it were, I would have told you about it. Surely you can believe that.'

'In other words, you're throwing yourself on the mercy of Tippi Moonstone?'

'Grace, I have complete faith in you. I must run now. Sy's home. I'll give him your love.'

Grace put the phone down, twisted her face into a frown and sat down on one of the boxes. It occurred to her that she was the only ex-wife of Tommy Patterson who lacked the opportunity to murder him. Kitten was in town, albeit shacked up with the charming if mentally vacuous David Turner. Trudi was displaying her art while inhabiting drug heaven. Odelle saw Tommy a few days before his murder then flew back to Chicago – she said. Any one of them in a moment of rage might have pushed Tommy over that cliff. Tommy had that effect on women.

She looked around at the closed boxes. 'Who killed you, Tommy?' she asked the brown, sagging cardboard. She took up the razor. It glinted in her hand. She made the first slice in her disembowelling operation.

## Chapter 36

# Hallelujah!

It was two weeks now since Trudi rediscovered Jesus Christ as her saviour.

Rediscovered, because there had been that tent meeting over in Plattsville where Reverend Jerry and Sister Ginny Mae came to preach the gospel and call upon all sinners to be redeemed. Lord, if anyone had been a sinner, she had been one, even though at the time she was only twelve. She had gone forward when they made their call and been washed clean in the blood of the lamb. The only trouble was she hadn't stayed clean. She had strayed. Lord a'mighty, she had strayed. All we like sheep, yeah, Lord, have gone astray. But the Lord is a mighty shepherd and he has rounded up his flock once more. She had come home to him and was now rocking her soul in the bosom of Abraham. Praise the Lord!

She carried the Bible with her constantly. Its very presence in her hands gave her inner peace. When she was young, she had received prizes for reading the Bible, for attendance in Sunday School. Those days of innocence had gone down the drain with drugs and sex and abandonment of the ways of the Cross. Now the words of her youth called her home. The Bible sang to her a song of love, of forgiveness, of strength. She didn't need drugs. She didn't need sex. All she needed was Jesus Christ as her saviour. From the dull grey of her dark ages, life took on differing hues. The sky was blue, the grass was green, the trees were budding, flowers perfumed the air about her. She was once again alive. And she was grateful. As Jesus raised Lazarus, so he raised Trudi Surefoot from the dead.

Of course, Jesus had not done it alone. He had his disciple to whom Trudi would be forever indebted. And that disciple was Don Harrington. It was Don, Trudi later discovered, who placed the Bible on her bed. It was he who knew that the path to salvation lay in the straight and narrow. It was through Don that Trudi found the love of Jesus Christ rekindled. How could she ever thank him?

Still, despite her gratitude to him, she knew that the River Range program would not work for her. Group therapy, individual therapy, what did she need of them? She didn't need Freud when she had God. She didn't even need Skinner.

Exercising, yes. Exercise renewed her by getting in touch with her physical being now that her spirit breathed new life into it. And hiking, yes. She needed those moments with Don to renew her acquaintance with Nature. Order or disorder, she didn't know. God the great gardener worked his wonders along the path of her life as she reached out to touch all living things.

But God had a mission for her that could not be fulfilled by staying cooped up in River Range. God was calling her to set her hand upon Tommy Patterson's Fund for the Betterment of Humanity. Too long had that money lain around, uselessly collecting interest. There were people out there who needed her help. There were people out there crying in the same wilderness she had inhabited just a few short weeks ago. And this is exactly what she told Madelaine Stevenson in her exit interview.

Madelaine doubted her cure. 'I know you're excited now by your newfound belief, but – '

'There are no ifs, ands or buts when one accepts Jesus Christ as one's saviour, Madelaine,' Trudi chastised.

'Trudi, I'm happy that you've found a way out. Just don't expect miracles.'

Trudi smiled condescendingly. 'Madelaine, Jesus's love and sacrifice for us is the eternal miracle.'

'Trudi, please, just open your mind and listen to me for a minute. You have what we call an addictive personality. You expect what you're addicted to to solve all problems. Drugs couldn't do that, as you now realize. Maybe religion can. But what we all need, each of us within ourselves, is an inner core of strength that can see us through, no matter how depressed and deserted and alone we feel.'

'Madelaine, I have Jesus by my side. I will never be alone again.' The poor lamb just didn't understand the rightness of Trudi's cause. Trudi mourned for the head of the River Range Clinic.

Exit interview completed, her bags packed, a taxi called, Trudi had only one person left to see. And Don Harrington seemed to know it. He was waiting for her at her dormitory door. 'I'm so happy for you,' he told her. 'You've found the way.'

'I wouldn't have found it without you, Don.' She shrugged her shoulders. 'Why don't you tell everybody about this secret we share, this great joy in the love of Jesus Christ, our Lord and Saviour?'

'Because Jesus isn't the way for everyone.' Don said.

227

'Oh, but you're so wrong! The Bible explicitly states that we may not come unto the Father except through – '

Don held up his hand. 'Trudi, for you it was an answer, and I'm grateful. But for others there are different answers: love of family, rededication to life, art, music. Whatever saves, that's what we must pursue.'

Trudi placed her hand on his arm. 'You are truly a good person, Don. Though what you just said doesn't make you that good a Christian. None the less, I won't forget you.'

Trudi picked up her satchel, which she had woven herself, much like Rising Surefoot had woven her first Indian blanket where the buffalo roamed, and started down the long trek towards renewed entry into the world of challenges. But then she stopped and turned to find Don still watching her. 'You're wasting yourself here,' she told him over a distance of some twenty feet. 'Have you ever heard of the Tommy Patterson Fund for the Betterment of Humanity?'

'No,' Don admitted.

'Well, I'm in charge of it. I have tons of money to give away to make people happy. I don't have any staff yet. Would you be interested?'

Don didn't have a chance to answer. Trudi turned once again and started walking, casting one more look over her shoulder to say, 'I'll be in touch.'


Odelle was at work in the shelter when one of her counsellors called her to the phone, saying there was an emergency at home. Odelle knew immediately what had happened. Luke had been in an accident. Damn! She knew she shouldn't have let him drive to school and back. All those teenagers did when they got into a car was show off. It was like boys in a shower room, assessing whose penis was biggest. She grabbed the phone and shouted into it, 'Luke, what is it!'

'Mom,' Luke was whispering, 'there's this religious fanatic in the living room, and I can't get rid of her.'

'What! You're not to let anyone into the house. How many times have I told you? Does she look dangerous, deranged? Can you call the police?'

'I – hey, she said she was a friend of yours, and I recognized the name from hearing you talk to Dad and Aunt Grace, so I thought that's who it was.'

'What name?'

'Trudi Surefoot.'

'Trudi? It can't be Trudi. She's at the River Range Clinic. It's probably some other druggie who got released and then somehow got my address from Trudi and is pretending to be her. Look, you're right next to the cellar. Go down into it and – '

'Mom, the door to the cellar locks from the outside. Besides, I don't want her chasing me down into that cellar with an axe!'

Jesus! What was she to do?

'Mom, I'm going to make a dash up to my room. If the worst comes to the worst, I can jump out of the window.'

Right. Two storeys down. He'd break his leg and probably his head too. 'Okay. You do that. I'm hanging up and calling the police.'

Odelle dialled the Glencoe police station and told them there was an intruder in her home who was threatening her son. She gave her address and informed them she was on her way home. Then she had one of her assistants put in a call to Sy. She could not face this alone!

Damn! Everything took too long: red lights, stop signs, other cars. By the time she reached home, she was hysterical. Odelle was sure someone had murdered her son.

Thank God! Two police cars stood in front of her house, blue lights flashing. She prayed they had made it in time. She rushed into the house and into the arms of this big, beefy, brawny man in blue. 'I'm the mother,' she shouted at him and tried to push him out of the way.

'Mom!' she heard Luke call. Thank God! He was alive!

A car screeched to a halt outside, followed by wailing sirens. But she had no time to worry about who it was. She pushed past the officer into the arms of her precious baby. She'd thought April 15, the day he learned whether he was accepted or rejected by the college of his choice, was going to be her major day of anguish. But nothing could beat this. 'Luke, Luke! Are you all right? she asked him. She hugged him tight, squeezing the life in him.

They heard screams from outside the house, a male voice calling, 'My son!' It was Sy. He had brought along his own police escort, and this one had his gun drawn. How many traffic laws had Sy broken in getting here from Chicago at such a speed?

'Do you have her?' Odelle asked the officer. 'Has she – is it – safe?'

Auditory impulses assaulted Odelle from all directions. In one of them, showering her from the living room, she thought she heard a rough voice saying, 'Look, lady, I don't care right now if Jesus loves me. I want to see some identification and I want to see it this instant!'

Sy burst into the hallway. He saw Odelle and Luke standing closely together and came up to embrace them. 'Thank God!' he said, perspiring with relief. He took his son's face in his hands and kissed him, embarrassing the hell out of Luke. 'You two go outside,' Sy ordered. 'I'll take care of this.'

They didn't argue with him, though Odelle thought it was some-what silly, seeing as there were at least five cops in her house, one

229

with his gun drawn. By the time they went outside, several of their neighbours had gathered, especially the teenagers home from school. They called to Luke to find out what was happening. 'A Jesus freak, and I mean freak,' he said before Odelle hushed him.

'Oh Lord, they're going to murder all of us,' Odelle heard one woman say, a woman she knew did nothing but interfere in other people's business.

Neighbours called to Odelle and she waved them off. 'I don't know anything yet,' she told them. 'Please, why don't you go inside?' And leave us alone, she wanted to add. It was too miserable, waiting, wondering what was going on in her home. What pollution had settled in her living room.

One of the neighbour's kids brought Luke out a coat. He needed it. They were left standing in the cold for fifteen minutes with no news whatsoever. Finally, Sy stormed out of the house and raged up to her. His mouth was moving but he wasn't saying anything. 'Sy? Sy!' she tried to make contact. All she needed now was for Sy to have a heart attack. She just wasn't that proficient in CPR.

He turned away from her and folded his arms across his chest. She knew better than to talk to him when he stood like that. They waited.

Half an hour later, when some of the neighbours had finally given up and gone inside to watch *People's Court*, the police brought out a woman, trussed up in handcuffs. It was Trudi Surefoot!

'The Lord be with you and with your spirit!' she called to the Hamptons, just before the police pushed her head down and shoved her into the back of the squad car.

The cop who had followed Sy up from Chicago walked by to say there would be no charges, but from now on he should ask for a police escort. The Glencoe police came over to let the Hamptons know that their house was now secure. 'She says she knows you,' one of the officers said.

'Yes, she does,' Odelle admitted, very confused. What was happening to Trudi?

'She's wanted for questioning in California on a possible murder charge.'

'Jesus!' Luke said.

'I think I've heard just about enough about Jesus for the time being,' the officer told Luke Hampton. 'We might be back to question you.'

'Any time, Officer,' Odelle said. 'And thank you so very much.'

'That's what we're paid for, ma'am,' the officer replied.

Slowly, the police cars made their way through the crowd, which had regathered, augmented by men and women returning from work.

230

After the police left, the neighbours waited around for an explanation, but none was forthcoming. Sy grabbed Odelle by the arm and led her firmly inside their house. Luke meekly followed.

'I cannot believe this,' Sy said, as he closed the door on the crowd. 'I warned you all those years ago in Taos to leave this alone. But did you listen to me? No. Your first husband has cast a shadow over my life from the day I met you. And now, even though he's dead, he's still doing it. I'm not forgiving you for this day, Odelle.'

He turned for her and started climbing the long staircase to the upper floor. 'Where are you going, Sy? Where?' she called tearfully.

'I'm going up to take a shit,' he enunciated clearly.

'What's Dad talking about?' Luke asked.

'I think sometimes when people become overly excited, they – '

'I know that Mom. I mean what's all this stuff about your first husband? Who was that woman?'

Odelle placed a hand on Luke's shoulder. 'Dear, have you ever read a book called WOMAN OF THE THREE LIVES?'

'No.'

'Good. Don't.'

## Chapter 37

# Beloved Martyrdom

As she watched pictures of Trudi, handcuffed and accompanied by several police officers, being marched into the courthouse in Los Angeles, Grace Mandling realized that she had never before seen Trudi in an undrugged state. Usually, Trudi wore a moony, moody expression on her face. Now her eyes were bright, her face was fresh, and her spirits definitely looked uplifted. In other words, Trudi no longer looked drugged; she looked mad. Crazed. Loony. Yes, loony. Someone who has been affected by the full moon.

Trudi certainly had been affected by something. Without benefit of counsel, or, more appropriately in her case, clergy, Trudi Surefoot confessed to the murder of Tommy Patterson. As the papers put it, she said, 'I take the burden of Tommy's death upon my shoulders.'

What an idiot!

How did Trudi get into such a fix?

Odelle blamed herself, as well she might, Grace thought viciously. If only Odelle had vouched for Trudi in the first place, or rushed down to the police station to explain after Trudi was arrested. If only Odelle had found a lawyer to represent Trudi before their little Indian princess voluntarily agreed to extradition. But Odelle did nothing! Her explanation: 'Sy was so mad already, I just didn't want to upset him.' God, what a mouse!

So Trudi was put on a plane with only a Bible, a police officer and her fractured mind for company, and flown into the arms of a waiting Detective Sam Morris.

If the Hamptons thought this was the end of the matter for them, they had another think coming. Detective Morris intimated, during his television interview, that charges would be pressed against a certain someone in the Chicago area who for months had helped Trudi Surefoot elude the L.A. police. Odelle might have to take refuge in her own shelter.

232

Grace, as usual, was the last to find out what was happening. She never turned on the radio or television until evening. That was soon enough to be slugged in the stomach with the day's events. But this story broke in the early morning, New York time. And she found out from Galen. He called her from work with his usual morning check on her period – did she get it or not? Then he casually dropped the bomb on her. He heard from coworkers, Tommy Patterson's killer had been caught.

That item was shocking enough in itself. But when Grace discovered it was Trudi Surefoot who supposedly did the dirty deed, she was flabbergasted. Trudi Surefoot? Murder was simply not in the woman's heart. And Trudi was still fond of Tommy, despite everything she had been through because of him. No, Grace would never believe that Trudi had murdered her – their – ex-husband.

Trudi needed help. When Grace found that none would be forthcoming from Chicago, she put in a call to Tamar Litowsky, the lawyer who handled Tommy's will. The woman was not in; she didn't get in until 10.30, L.A. time, which made it 1.30 in New City, New York. By then Grace was angry and hungry, since she couldn't eat until she got this thing settled.

Tamar acted as all lawyers will, disregarding the human element – in this case, a nut being charged with murder. All Grace got from Tamar was some legal verbiage. Decoded, the message was that Tamar could do nothing, not even recommend a good lawyer for Trudi. Tamar's main concern was Tommy's estate. She had been his lawyer. And if Trudi did kill Tommy and was convicted of same, she would inherit nothing from the estate. Trudi could not benefit from the death of someone she had murdered. There were laws against that sort of thing. In conclusion, Tamar must protect the interests of the estate over the interests of an ex-wife who was charged with murder. 'But by not being any help at all, aren't you assuming she's guilty?' Grace pointed out, to absolutely no avail.

Stymied, and not knowing any criminal lawyers herself, thank God, Grace called the only other person she knew in Los Angeles who might be of help: Kitten Fairleigh. Or rather she called "Mi Hacienda's" private line, whose number she found in Tommy's magnificently revealing address book, which she had come across in one of the many cartons she had opened.

The phone was answered by someone whose comprehension of the English language was thrown in doubt by her refusal to understand either Grace's or Kitten's name. Grace wondered once again why she had taken French in college. It had been a futile pursuit to capture a dying language. No one spoke French any more except the French, whereas Spanish was becoming the second language of the United States. And she knew it not! In desperation, she resorted to a rather abbreviated form of dialogue without her usual polite flourishes: 'Get Keeten on phone or I come keel you! Call immigration pronto!'

That seemed to have made an impression. The woman said something like '*madre mia*' and rushed hurriedly off, dropping the phone in the process. About a minute later, a tired, husky voice said, 'Yes.'

'Kitten, wake up.'

'Who is this?' the voice dreamily asked.

'Grace Mandling.'

'Grace Mandling? How did you get this number?' The voice became a little brisker.

It took Grace about fifteen minutes to explain not only how she got the number but exactly why she was calling. Naturally, Kitten had heard about the arrest. She was even sick of being pestered by reporters who wanted her response to Trudi's "confession". That was why Rosalita had strict orders not to let anyone get through to her. But now, like a town gossip, Kitten wanted to hear all the details the reporters didn't have, up to and including Trudi's conversion and her run-in with the Glencoe police at Odelle's house. She agreed with Grace that if Odelle had just stepped in a bit sooner or been a bit swifter mentally, Trudi wouldn't be in this mess. She concluded, 'I never liked Odelle. I think maybe it's because she's going through menopause and not doing it very gracefully.'

Grace was surprised. As far as she knew, Odelle was too young to go through menopause, but she was not interested in checking Kitten's medical diagnosis at this moment. 'I called for your help,' she explained. 'Tamar Litowsky refuses either to represent Trudi or recommend someone who will represent her. You must know someone, or you must be able to give me names of a few lawyers who might –'

'Hold on, Grace,' Kitten said, and Grace could immediately hear worry in her voice. 'Do you think we should really get involved in this? How is it going to reflect on our careers? I've already been damaged enough by being in bed with David when Tommy was murdered. If you want to see hate mail, I've got plenty of it. I don't think hiring a lawyer for Tommy's murderer is going to do me any good. Or you!'

There were many things Grace could say, such as, 'If we don't hang together, we'll all hang separately.' Now was not a time for petty, personal concerns. Instead, she simply informed Kitten, 'It's Trudi's basic constitutional right to get the best representation possible.'

234

'What about her constitutional right to remain silent? Had she employed that, she might not need a lawyer. If she murdered Tommy – '

'Trudi doesn't know if she murdered Tommy. Weren't you listening to anything I said, Kitten? Trudi was in a drugged state the entire time she was in L.A.'

'Hmm.' Grace could almost hear the movie star thinking. Then she spoke again. 'You know,' Kitten said, 'one of my public affairs announcements has to do with drunk driving. Some people say that being an alcoholic is a disease. But you still have to take responsibility for getting drunk and for what you do while you're drunk. Tommy and I had our differences, but if Trudi – '

'If, again. Shouldn't she get a chance to have someone defend her against that "if"?'

'Maybe,' Kitten conceded. 'But I can't become involved. I'm sorry, Grace. I've got my career to think of.'

'Thanks, Kitten. Thanks a lot. I'll remember your generosity.'

Grace was about to hang up the phone when she heard Kitten say, 'Look, this is a case that's going to get a lot of publicity. There are going to be prominent criminal lawyers waiting in line, willing to take it. What I can do is contact a friend of mine; he's a reporter, but he does a straight city beat. I can let him know, confidentially, that you're interested in hiring someone to take Trudi's case. How would that be?'

It was the best Grace was going to get. So she put down the phone and began her wait. While doing so, she turned on the television to CNN and began to open a few more of Tommy's boxes.

Aside from fan letters, a goodly portion of the boxes was filled with manuscripts of Tommy's published writings, first, second and third drafts of the pearls of wisdom he let fall on an unsuspecting public. That was before computers. After computers, there were print-outs and cases with discs inside. These she would have to check out later. In one box yesterday she had found several appointment books Tommy had kept. He was very meticulous. Perhaps he had so many appointments he had to write them down. She didn't know. She used the loose scrap of paper method. True, she missed appointments that way, but she also left no tell-tale trail of her life. Or her opinions. Tommy's appointment books had notations on those he was meeting. Written after the names were such words as "cunt" and "fag". Such a charmer, her ex-husband. But even though he left evidence of whom he had seen and when, there was no indication of what the meetings were about.

She let the material slide down her lap on to the floor. Her house was becoming a fire hazard. About the time Galen was to return

235

home, the phone rang. It was Kitten Fairleigh. 'I have a name for you. Leon Cohen, should he call you. As I predicted, there's a rush on to defend Trudi, especially now that they know someone's going to pay for her defence. My reporter friend tells me Cohen's not the most flamboyant; he won't turn the trial into a circus. He's quiet, circumspect – for Southern California – and he'll get her off.'

'Thanks, Kitten. I owe you.'

'You'll pay,' Kitten promised.

Grace took calls from three lawyers before Leon Cohen called late that night around eleven, when Galen had just sunk into bed and was wondering where she was. Grace had hedged with the other three, knowing she might have to accept one of them if Cohen didn't come through. But when he called, he explained that he had been on a case, and that, if she wished, he would consult Trudi's public defender tomorrow and see what he could do about getting her bail.

'Yes. And how much of a cheque do you need as a retainer?' Grace wondered.

When he told her, Grace was glad that both she and Galen were working. She would need every penny she could get her hands on.

Depressed by thoughts of depleting her fortune, Grace was in no mood for sex. She tried to explain as gently as possible to Galen, 'Keep your hands off me! Not tonight!'

'Look, my darling, we've got to keep trying.'

'Galen, do you know anything at all about the rhythm method?'

'Oh yeah,' he said disgustedly. 'There was this Catholic girl I dated once who assured me it was the only form of birth control she was allowed to practise. Therefore, if I wanted to sleep with her, I'd have to take my chances.'

'Hmm.' Grace was interested. 'And?'

'And? Do you think I'm crazy? I found someone else who used at least three different barrier methods, I used a condom, and we were energetically happy. For a while.' He placed his arm over her waist.

'That's the trouble, isn't it?' Grace said. 'We can only be happy for a while, not forever.'

'Happy in spurts. The rest of the time content. I'm content with you, Grace.'

'I know you are.'

'And you?'

'I'm tired. Anyway, my dear young man, what I was going to tell you about the rhythm method was that theoretically one can only get pregnant a few days a month and I'm way past that. Matter of fact –'

'Umm?'

'My period is nearly four days overdue.'

236

'Umm.' He moved closer and smiled into her shoulder.

'Of course, it doesn't mean anything,' she warned him. 'I've been under a lot of stress lately. Delving into Tommy's life certainly hasn't been pleasant.'

He touched her shoulders. He could always tell how tense she was by her shoulder muscles. 'You need a massage,' he informed her. 'Turn around.'

She followed orders. She lay beside him in bed and enjoyed the sensation of his fingers pressing into her neck, shoulders and back. It made her realize once more how much she needed Galen. It was unfair to need – to want someone so much, especially when life was so uncertain.

Life. She fell asleep thinking about life, the creation thereof. Was she pregnant?

The next morning Galen woke her up by kissing her stomach. He usually kissed either higher or lower. But now he kissed her stomach because he thought there might a child in there. His child. When she was alone, she felt her stomach herself. It didn't feel any different. Maybe she should go out and get one of those pregnancy test kits. But no. She had received a D in college chemistry. She wasn't about to let her future rest on her own laboratory techniques. She would wait. Time would tell – a nine-month chunk of it.

When she finally got up, she lazily washed and put on her tracksuit. She planned to spend the day opening boxes and examining contents. She was beginning to feel like a pathologist. For background, she decided to break her own rule and turn on the television to one of the many talk shows that proliferated in the morning. It occurred to her, and not for the first time, that this was why Tommy had been so popular. He was presentable; what he had to say was very palatable; and people who watched these talk shows seemed to be looking for a quick fix that would solve all the problems in their lives by noon. Tommy specialized in the quick fix.

'Stay tuned for *Hollywood Today*,' the announcer informed her. Hmm, and just as she was becoming involved in the previous show's intriguing question of why women have fewer orgasms than men, not that the men cared.

'*Hollywood Today*, an exclusive interview with Tippi Moonstone coming up,' the next promo came on.

Tippi Moonstone again! Now there was a one-woman publicity machine. She was hyping her book about Tommy so totally, no one would even know Grace was publishing one of her own. She'd have to speak to Craig Epstein about Adams & Westlake's advertising budget for her book.

237

Several commercials for long-playing records of country stars Grace had never heard of before and never hoped to hear of again flashed and faded on the screen. Then the spotlights of *Hollywood Today* swung into action, 'With your host, Gene Jackson!'

Gene spewed out a few hot headlines about arguments on movie sets, breakups and coming togethers, pregnancies and deaths – sadly noted. Then he swung his chair around to come face to face with Tippi Moonstone, looking terribly young and terribly glamorous. Grace caught sight of herself in the mirror. Jesus. No wonder she didn't get the publicity. In the gloom of her living room she could see age growing upon her like waxy buildup.

'And now, Tippi,' Gene Jackson was saying, 'tell us the latest on this new twist in the Tommy Patterson story. His ex-wife Trudi Surefoot was charged with murder. What do you know about it?'

'I have an exclusive for you, Gene.'

Gene Jackson sat there, eyes gleaming, tongue hanging partially out of his mouth, waiting expectantly. Thank God the camera didn't swoop lower. He probably also had a hard-on.

'Leon Cohen is defending Trudi Surefoot.'

'That was on the news this morning,' Gene pointed out. So much for Tippi's exclusive.

'But do you know who's paying for Trudi Surefoot's defence? Who hired Leon Cohen!' Tippi demanded.

Gene panted in anticipation.

'None other than Grace Mandling.'

'Now, she's the romance writer.'

'Tommy's second wife.'

'And she's also writing a life of Tommy Patterson.' Thank God someone had got word to him.

'One can only ask how objective it will be from a woman who would pay for the defence of her ex-husband's murderer.'

Get in the knife while you can, Tippi, darling, Grace thought mercilessly. And see if you get your hands on any of Tommy's papers whatsoever! She went over to the television and flicked it off. Who needed more aggravation?

Obviously, people thought she did. Edna Waitz called, ostensibly to ask how the book was coming. 'Now listen, dear,' she said, finally coming to the point, 'I understand that you hired a defence lawyer for Trudi?'

'I'm making sure she receives her full measure of the law's protection,' Grace pointed out.

'And I'm sure Trudi's grateful. Of course, it's a financial burden for you, but one I might be able to take off your shoulders.'

238

Grace waited. Over the years she had learned to be leery of offers of help. Nothing came without strings.

'You know that Dell is rushing to reissue WOMAN OF THE THREE LIVES? Certainly, that will put money in Trudi's coffers. Also, here's something to consider: what wouldn't some publishers give to get exclusive rights of Trudi's story, as told to – need I fill in the name?'

'Oy!' Grace uttered. She could only get Edna off the phone by promising to think about it. What happened to the Son of Sam law? Trudi couldn't profit from writing about a murder she committed. Unless Leon Cohen got her off. Hmm.

A point Craig Epstein brought up when he called. 'I just wanted to find out how everything was going,' he lied. 'By the way, it was a master stroke of publicity, hiring that lawyer for Trudi. However, I hope it doesn't generate too much hostility toward you. We're promoting you as an ex-wife, not as a vindictive ex-wife. Also, how would you feel about hyping the book by doing a magazine article on the inside of a murderess's mind? What makes Trudi Surefoot tick? Something like that.'

After Grace assured Craig that no one knew what made Trudi tick, and she certainly wasn't going to waste her time trying to find out, she finally got back to work. However that didn't last long, as she found she had no stomach for it. Instead, she went upstairs and lay abed, immobilized by her surprising lack of drive.

Somehow, that day got away from her. When Galen came home and suggested they go out for some gyros, she realized so far she had accomplished nothing. She only wished she could adopt Galen's laissez-faire attitude towards life. 'You're heaven for me, Galen,' she assured him. He smiled back lovingly. He was so much like a warm puppy. She thrived on his devotion.

They had Greek wine, Greek salads and gyros. Who could ask for anything more? Galen didn't nag her with questions about Tommy or Trudi. Instead he regaled her with stories from work, about his coworkers and their clients. He made her laugh. And isn't that all one really needs from a man?

When they got home, Galen undressed her and put her to bed. She loved to be undressed by him, just let her body become a dead weight and have him tumble her this way and that until they were both naked and entangled within each other. Heaven was having a man by you whom you loved.

When the phone rang later that evening, long after their languorous love-making, they were watching the news. AIDS, rape, robbery, murder, traffic jams – they lay in each other's arms and let the world sweep through the sewers under them. Galen picked up the

239

phone. She waved to him, indicating she was not available. But Galen, with a serious expression, handed the phone to her. Shit!

'Leon Cohen here,' the voice said, crisp and very much to the point.

'Yes, Leon,' Grace replied at her most melodious, helped on by the wine and Galen's lingering art of love.

'I've had a long talk with Trudi. I'm not going for bail.'

'Why not?'

'She's more of a danger to herself than to society. My assessment is that she's definitely out of touch with reality. She spent half our time together trying to convert me to Christianity. Tomorrow I'm going before the judge to have her transferred to a private clinic, where they can examine her and run tests on her, both mental and physical. I have a feeling that part of her brain might have been wiped out by years of drugs. We'll do a CAT scan.'

'But what does her defence look like?' Grace asked.

'Whether she killed Tommy or not, she doesn't know; and the prosecutor has only circumstantial evidence. I think we can get her off on mental or medical grounds. However, that would always leave a shadow over her life. It would be better if we could clear her.'

Grace wondered. Trudi had lived with a shadow over her life in any case. And how could they clear her?

'You, I understand, have all of Tommy Patterson's papers,' Leon continued. 'Have you found anything in them, diaries, what-not, that could exonerate Trudi or at least point the finger in another direction?'

'Not yet,' Grace admitted. 'But I haven't opened all the boxes.'

'What about if I send someone out there to help you?'

'Look, right now I don't think that's a good idea. There are too many people who want to get their hands on Tommy's papers, and I'm in charge. We have time, right? There is no such thing as a speedy trial in the United States of America. So I will make it a point to work through the boxes as fast as possible. If I find I need help, I'll contact you,' Grace promised.

'Okay,' Leon agreed. 'In the meantime, let's try to cool the publicity. If Trudi is ever allowed to open her mouth, we'll have enough of a circus to deal with. Until then, I don't want passions inflamed or opinions being formed.'

Grace wanted to tell Leon that the publicity machine was hard to stop once it started rolling. And with all of them involved, Kitten and her, Odelle and Trudi, and now Tippi Moonstone, the story would continue to snowball. But instead of piling any more grief on his plate, she said, 'I'll call you the minute I find anything.' If she found anything.

240

# Chapter 38

# A Piece of the Puzzle

Five days after the news broke that Grace Mandling was paying for Trudi Surefoot's defence attorney, the mail started to roll in. It was not a pretty sight. Grace had always assumed that Tommy's fans were terribly middle class – in other words, bereft of moorings in an alienating society. Who else would listen to that jerk? However, from the letters she was getting, she would have to assume that, instead of common, ordinary, rootless folk, Tommy attracted the lunatic fringe. The death threats weren't so bad. It was the letter writers who threatened to torture her before they killed her that really got Grace worried.

Now her problem was should she call the police? That decision was fortunately taken out of her hands by Galen. He picked up several of the letters, thinking they were from her fans. When he read them, he became first enraged and then weakened by the thought that something could happen to her and the hoped-for-baby-to-be. He called in the New City police, who called in the FBI. As Galen put it so poignantly to the officers, 'How could anyone write this filth to an expectant mother?'

She made one mistake before she got pregnant with Galen's child. She forgot to have Galen's IQ tested. Oh well, she would have to hope the child took after her. No, that wasn't entirely true. She wanted it to have Galen's sweet, inoffensive personality. Maybe some of his artistic flair also. Not that she knew she was pregnant for sure, but already she had moved her tampons to a less prominent space in the bathroom cabinet.

Craig Epstein, her beloved editor at Adams & Westlake, was naturally upset about all the mail. He bemoaned the time it took for his assistant to forward it to Grace. His assessment of the hate-mail situation was gloomy. He conceded the fact that these people now knew her name and obviously who her publishers were, but he doubted they would shell out the money to buy any of her books. 'We might be facing a boycott,' he worriedly told her over the phone.

'Craig, do you honestly think that Tommy and I had any readers who overlapped?'

'Demographics – '

She had to cut him off. Ever since Adams & Westlake had gone to computers, all Craig could talk about was his pie charts. Meanwhile, she was trying to impress upon him that she really didn't want any more hate mail from potential murderers. But Craig said, 'Dearest, the mail's addressed to you; I must forward it to you.'

Galen, her white knight in blue jeans, took care of the problem. He got in touch with the FBI and warned them that forwarding mail from New York to New City, an hour by bus, a week by postal service, left Grace vulnerable, timewise. The authorities should intervene while the mail was still hot.

Galen's suggestion made so much sense to everyone except Craig. 'We're setting a precedent here that I don't like,' he complained. 'This is state interference with the mails, and I feel I must protest!' So much for his concern about her welfare.

'Darling,' she replied, 'the state interferes with our mail every day by non-delivery in a timely fashion.'

So Grace got used to patrol cars circling around her quiet New City neighbourhood. And she also got used to a certain notoriety, especially after the story of the threats made against her appeared in banner headlines on the front page of the *Daily News*. "Death Stalks Love Queen: Grace and Tommy, Together at Last?" Underneath the headlines was a picture of her with her breasts flopping out of her blouse. She could only suspect a composite by a clever photographer, as even her bathing suits of late covered everything, including as much as possible of her thighs. How had the *News* got hold of this story when she wanted it kept as quiet as possible?

It was Galen in action again. And he was quite pleased with his handiwork. An "undisclosed source" had given the *Daily News* snippets of the death and mutilation threats made against her. 'Why?' she asked him, when he bragged about it to her. 'How?'

'One of my friend's a courtroom artist who freelances. She knew someone from the *News'* crime beat.'

'Jerry Harry? He of the byline?'

'Yeah. I met him in a bar for lunch. He was an old guy, already drunk. I guess being a reporter takes a lot out of you. Anyway, I gave him all the details of what's been happening. And he investigated the rest. Look at how prominently he plays up the FBI. That's good. That's real good.'

242

'Why is it real good, Galen? And why for God's sake did you go to the *News* rather than at least a more respectable *New York Times*?'

'Do you think a *Times* reader would write that sort of threatening letter?' Galen asked her. 'Go to the source, Grace.'

Galen was right about one thing. The death threats did diminish after these nuts learned the FBI was on their trail. Papers all over the country picked up on the *News* story, and a few investigative reporters even followed up by finding some of the letter writers. One who had threatened to cut Grace's breasts off and shove them up her – well, elsewhere, turned out to be a seventy-nine-year-old great-grandmother. "Tommy Patterson was the Second Coming," the *Gravel City Gazette* quoted her as saying, "I went to Des Moines to see him once and he smiled at me."

Such was the irrational nature of Tommy's following. However, all the hoopla gave Grace the chance to reaffirm on radio call-in shows all over the country her belief in the Bill of Rights, including the right to a lawyer. Of course, she didn't know if that was in the Bill of Rights or the Constitution itself, but no one listening to her did either. So they were all happy in their ignorance. Further, these interviews, aside from giving her a chance to wave the flag in the face of intolerance, also allowed her to push her books and her upcoming biography of Tommy Patterson. Take that, Tippi Moonstone. All Tippi could get was a continuous five-part booking on *Entertainment Tonight*. Thanks to all the free publicity, Craig Epstein was finally happy.

Grace was happy too. Usually, while working on a book, she didn't like to speak to anyone. Plotting took all her concentration. But Tommy's writings were so swollen with excessive, nonsensical verbiage that she found herself taking telephone breaks every hour or so. She called people she hadn't spoken to in years. Her phone bill would be enormous, but she would put it down on her tax form as research.

Meanwhile, out in Hollywood, Trudi was being tested and re-tested. Leon Cohen kept calling to find out what was normal for Trudi. Did anybody know? Also, had Grace found anything? Grace assured him she was definitely looking.

What she had actually done was overlook. She had come across a box with a manuscript and some discs nestled inside. The title page read PARENTING: THE HOWS AND WHYS OF BRINGING UP YOUR CHILD. She supposed the thought of Tommy writing about being a parent was what threw her. What had he done for Julia, his first born? Where had he been when Grace lost their baby? And what about Trudi with Free? Wasn't Trudi's loss even greater than Grace's own? So it took Grace a while to get up the stomach to go back to that box. She lifted

243

the manuscript out of the box to place it on a small, bare patch of rug, and the title page slipped from the contents. On the contents page, she saw ELONGATION: A THEORY OF LONGEVITY, by Tommy Patterson.

What did elongation have to do with parenting?

The phone rang before Grace had a chance to find out. When she came back, her attention was distracted from the manuscript and swept back into the box from which it came. There, formerly concealed by the manuscript, was a disc holder and a black leather bound notebook that Grace had come to recognize as one of the number of Tommy's appointment books.

To her, the black leather notebooks looked more like ledgers. But maybe that was how Tommy accounted for his life. She turned this one over. 1988 was embossed in fake gold on the front cover. Eureka? She didn't quite know.

Grace sank down with her back against the sofa. She flipped through the pages of the month before Tommy died. Like the rest of the appointment books, this had one or two word notations. Sometimes there were no words, just jotted initials. Take for example the many notations of KFDTF. Did these refer to Kitten Fairleigh and David Turner? Did the F mean fucked? TL with a line drawn from four in the afternoon all the way down the page. Did Tommy do business and conclude with pleasure? Was TL Tamar Litowsky?

Initials, initials, and more initials that she had no way of recognizing. Maybe Kitten could help. Or even Tamar, should she be willing. Or maybe Grace should just turn this over to Leon Cohen and let him do the searching. She shuddered when she thought of what her bill would be. Like, for example, what would a private investigator make of NUT. NUT was scattered all through that month and picked up its pace during the month Tommy was murdered.

But on the other hand, also picking up its pace in the month Tommy died was KFDTF. And then after one KFDTF was "see lawyer".

Grace let the diary rest on her knees. She cleared her mind and tried to think. Odelle had said something at Tommy's graveside. Something about divorce papers and Kitten had seemed surprised. How had Odelle known?

Her hands shaking because she didn't want to discover anything, not really, Grace flipped to the last week's entries in Tommy's appointment book. "KFDTF surprise". Okay. What was the surprise?

TS. TS. TS, on the day he was murdered. Trudi Surefoot. Oh Jesus! Grace was going to burn this book. But hold it! After the

244

second TS Tommy had written, "Out of mind". Tommy's own assessment was that Trudi was insane! His own words could be used against him.

Three days before his murder, OH. Odelle. She had been to see Tommy but everyone knew that. Why had she seen him? Tommy had written "threat". Threat? What did Odelle have to threaten him with after all these years? Did Odelle know anything more about Tommy than Grace knew herself? Did it have to do with Julia? Odelle would have to come up with an explanation.

The day after Odelle had seen Tommy there was TL underlined twice. Tamar Litowsky. Tamar had said Tommy came in to draw up a new will. Maybe Leon should look into what the old will was like? Did Tommy know the day he came in to draw up the will that he would be dead within thirty-six hours?

The next day, the day of his death, TL. To sign the will? And of course the already mentioned TS. But no KFDTF. Did that mean that Tommy didn't know Kitten was out that night with David Turner? This would be strange, because he seemed to know every other time. Or was Kitten at home with Tommy the night he was murdered, despite what David Turner claimed?

Grace shook her head. She flipped backward in the diary to the week before Tommy's death. Here was NUT again. Several NUTs. One "NUT trouble?" Who was NUT?

Grace closed the diary. Regretfully, she knew what she had to do. She put in a call to the coast to Leon Cohen's law office. 'He's in court. May I take a message?' his secretary inquired. It didn't surprise Grace to find Leon out. He was always out. Maybe when he was in he was out, not wanting anyone to think he had nothing to do. Important people were never in. Right?

'Please tell Mr Cohen to call Grace Mandling. It's urgent.'

Dejectedly, Grace put down the phone. She left the diary on the phone table and looked around her. The boxes were still waiting. Where should she begin?

She was still intrigued by the box she had just attacked and what she had found in it, not only the 1988 appointment book but the manuscript. Was it for Tommy's last book? On parenting? And what is elongation? Hmm. Whilst waiting for Leon to call back, she might as well delve into Tommy's latest assault upon the human mind. ELONGATION: A THEORY OF LONGEVITY. A lot of good that did you, Tommy, she told the print-out.

Grace pushed past the table of contents and started reading. As she did so, her eyes began to widen. She could actually comprehend what Tommy was saying. Usually, he couched everything he wrote in such

245

a stream of psycho-babble that she never understood what point he was trying to get across. She supposed that his obfuscation was the point. Each reader could pick from Tommy's message what he or she chose. But this, this was a guide to what foods to eat to live longer. "Longer" was the operative word. Eat only long things, like bananas, green or yellow beans, squash, pea pods, not just the peas, chilli peppers, spaghetti. Grace flipped through the pages, becoming more mystified. Had Tommy become a vegetarian?

And look at all these tables of nutrients. Did Tommy even know what a nutrient was?

A history of longevity settled itself into the middle of the book, seeming a bit out of place. But an editor could fix that. Now this history was more like Tommy. It included not only biographies of the long-lived, but details of their eating, drinking and sexual habits through the ages, with an emphasis on oral sex. Definitely Tommy's idea of a good time.

But after the murky doings of history, there followed a month of elongation diets. No. Not Tommy at all. Had he collaborated with someone? Grace flipped back to the first page of the manuscript. No. His name stood alone. But he must have had a researcher. Or two, or three.

Grace put the manuscript down. Intrigued, she picked up the box of discs. She went over and turned on her machine. Then she placed one of the discs in her B drive and tried to bring it up. Unless it were written in Greek, Tommy had not used the same word processing system she had. What was she to do?

Rockland Community College lay in Suffern, New York. It served the needs of those high school graduates not ready to go on to a four-year college or not willing. Not only did it educate, it also provided vocational training. In other words, it had a computer lab. It was the nearest college Grace could think of. So she turned on her answering machine, got into her car, and drove to Suffern.

The computer lab was a veritable bee hive of activity. The man in charge of it was young, had red hair and his name was Carl. She explained her problem to him and showed him the discs. She didn't know what computer had been used or what word processing system. Could he help her?

'Gee, I'd love to,' Carl said. 'But, as you can see, all the terminals are taken. Besides, straightening out your problem could mean hours. It could be stored in ASCII, it could be stored in EBCDIC.' He shrugged.

'Hours?' Grace said, assessing the solution. 'How does a $200-an-hour consulting fee sound to you?'

'I – '

'You're allowed to consult, aren't you?'

'Well, I – '

'I'll write you a cheque for two hours to start. I'll wait here until you go to your bank and cash it. I'm desperate.'

Carl assured her it wouldn't be necessary for her to wait until he cashed the check. But that didn't stop him from going out to cash it anyway. She wasn't bothered. She waited patiently. She was sure she was on to something. Tommy had no background in nutrition. He was not a health nut. So how come ELONGATION: A THEORY OF LONGEVITY?

Carl came back and got to work. It took him less than an hour to find out what machine Tommy had used and what system. 'I owe you some money,' he said.

'Keep it,' she waved him off. 'I have to use this machine.' She sat down at the desk and got to work.

After three hours of going into and out of every disc, what did she know? Nothing. Not much more than she knew when she saw the printed copy of the manuscript. Word processing leaves no dead phrases behind. Spell-checking leaves no telltale spelling errors. And there was no header in the text to indicate who had written what. Still, she fervently believed Tommy had not written all of ELONGATION. But who had?

## Chapter 39

# Grace Mandling, Girl Detective

Grace made copies of the discs holding Tommy's perhaps last opus. She quickly checked her watch. If she rushed, she could make it to her bank and toss the discs inside her safe deposit box.

On her way home from the bank, it occurred to her that if anyone would know what Tommy was up to and with whom he was working, it would be his agent. After all, it wouldn't be like Tommy to write an entire manuscript without getting some money up front. If his ideas didn't sell, he dropped them.

And yet, if he had sold the manuscript, why hadn't there been some publicity from his publishers? Wait a second. There had been. They claimed LOOK BACK FOR LOVE was his last book. Had he fled to another publisher?

When she got home, she found her answering machine flashing at her like there had been a nuclear emergency in her absence. But the messages would have to wait. First she put in a call to Edna Waitz, her agent. Grace vaguely remembered Tommy's agent calling her after Tommy's death, but she could not remember her name. Edna couldn't either. Grace's call simply served to arouse her curiosity. 'Why would you want to get in touch with Tommy's agent?'

'Tommy left another book. A completed manuscript,' Grace confessed.

'And you're calling his agent!' Edna screamed. 'You're his literary executor. You call the shots on whatever's left.'

'Not if he's already sold it,' Grace pointed out.

Grace was put on hold while Edna called over to William Morris. 'Carmen McCall,' Edna came back on line to say. 'Don't let her talk you into anything. We can make a fortune on that book.'

Disgruntled, Grace put down the phone. Whenever anyone talked about making money out of Tommy's writings, she always felt she was feasting off the dead. And with Tommy there was a very bitter aftertaste.

Carmen McCall. Now Grace remembered. When she reached Carmen through two layers of subordinates, she introduced herself. 'This is Grace Mandling. I'm Tommy Patterson's lit – '

'I know who you are,' Carmen cut her short. 'Tommy told me all about you. He used to have nightmares about you. Did you know that?'

'Guilt-induced?' Grace wondered.

'I don't think so. They all had something to do with castration.'

'Hmm. Uh – Carmen, I've been going through Tommy's papers – '

'I'm sure. I heard you're writing his biography.'

'And I've been wondering,' Grace continued, seemingly oblivious to Carmen's interruptions, 'did Tommy leave you with another book?'

'LOOK BACK FOR LOVE is coming out next month. It's already being shipped.'

'I know. But I understand that was in production when Tommy was – '

'Murdered,' Carmen cut in again.

'Thanks. I was floundering for the right word.'

'I've noticed you have that trouble in your books also.'

It seemed obvious from the direction of the conversation that Carmen was not one of Grace's many fans, that she was one of Tommy's many lovers, and that she still felt deeply defensive about her man, despite his corporeal non-existence. Well, New York is a hard place to meet someone, so maybe it was just as well Carmen was clinging to the dead. Safety first.

Grace ploughed on. 'What was Tommy working on after LOOK BACK FOR LOVE?'

'I don't – '

Grace retaliated. 'Did he show you a manuscript? Did he tell you what he was researching? Did he sign another book contract?'

'No, no and no. Why? Do you have something?'

'He never discussed any book after LOOK BACK FOR LOVE?' Grace tried to make sure.

'Look, if you have something, maybe we can discuss it. Money is money, and I'm sure my connections with the sort of editors who handle works like Tommy's are better than Edna Waitz's.'

'Gee, I don't know, Carmen. Edna represents Thelma Di-Giovanni, and her book is No. 3 on the *New York Times* non-fiction best seller list.'

'Oh, you mean – '

'Yes, GARLIC: CLOVES OF SPLENDOUR. Was Tommy, by the way, interested in garlic or other nutritional aspects of food?'

'Tommy? He saw red meat and he'd growl.'

'Yes. I seem to remember that. So he hadn't become a health nut in the last months of his life?'

'No. Well, he did say once, very lightly, that he was going to start filling up on carbohydrates to strengthen himself for the ordeal of his upcoming book tour. He hated those book tours. He told me that everyone tried to suck the love out of him.'

Which probably meant he was getting a blow job in each city, but why let dear Carmen in on Tommy's private metaphors. 'Well, thanks for the information, Carmen,' Grace said. 'I really appreciate it.'

'Yeah, sure. Just remember, no one can sell Tommy better than I can.'

Grace put down the phone, almost lost in thought. She tried to transmogrify herself into Tommy Patterson. It was a disgusting effort but someone had to do it, if only to save Trudi. There Tommy was, on a tour, promoting his books, his tapes, his videos, his philosophy, whatever. Tommy never stopped promoting. And someone approached him. That happened all the time. Even though she only did interview shows and book signings, someone was always coming up with the idea of a lifetime and wanted Grace's opinion on it. Grace always backed off. One, she had enough ideas of her own. Two, she didn't want to be used by anyone paranoid enough to assume she would steal an idea. But Tommy?

So maybe someone – some NUT – had approached Tommy with this great idea about increasing one's lifespan. And Tommy thought, 'Jesus Christ, here's an idea whose time has come. All my life I've been tracking the baby boomers, trying to keep one step ahead of their neuroses. I've gone from selfishness to angst to reminiscence. So what comes next for the aging swell of our population blunder? Fear. Fear of death. They see it all around them. Their parents are dying. Their own skins are wrinkling, their bodies are sagging. Age has crept upon them unawares. They are no longer babies. They are no longer booming. They have discovered that life has limits.

'But limits are off limit to this surging generation. There always has to be a way out, an escape, even from death. ELONGATION: A THEORY OF LONGEVITY.'

Oh, it fit so nicely, Grace thought. Someone had approached Tommy with a path towards immortality and he was going to take it, or at least take credit for it.

Except, how could he do that while he was still eating meat? He would need a religious conversion, much like Trudi's but not so wacko. Yes, Grace could see Tommy acting it out now. At first he

250

would refuse red meat, then chicken and fish and eggs. Slowly, ever so slowly, but not too slowly, he would work his way around to the vegetarian diet in ELONGATION. And then he would deliver the manuscript into Carmen's hot little hands.

Except it hadn't happened that way. Because someone had murdered Tommy first. But perhaps things had worked out for the best. It would have been awful had he already given up the food he loved only to be killed before he could profit from his sacrifice.

Of course, this was only conjecture, and conjecture wouldn't help free Trudi. Grace had to find the person embodying the initials of prime suspicion – NUT.

Brimming with determination, she was about to pick up the phone to call the airlines when it rang, startling her. It was Leon, asking if she had got his message. She confessed to not listening to her messages yet. He seemed put out until she told him about the appointment book. 'Good news and bad,' she confessed. 'Tommy did see Trudi the day he died. On the other hand, he does state that she was not in control of her mental faculties. However, did she really kill him?'

'I'll send someone for that appointment book. We can't afford for anything to happen to it now.'

'I'm coming out to L.A.,' Grace informed him.

'The book – '

'I'll duplicate it.'

This she rushed out to do. It was tedious, but life isn't all metaphysically super sleuthing. And while she stood and mechanically copied the pages of Tommy's last notations, she let her mind wander ahead to what had to be happier times. Category fiction. So far she was considered just a romance writer. But there were other categories, and now she knew which one was beginning to appeal to her: murder mysteries.

Okay, so she would never be another Agatha Christie. Locked rooms made her claustrophobic. However, she could see herself as, yes, Christi Agamemnon: Assignment Murder! Christi lived in – humm – Milwaukee? Does anybody live in Milwaukee? Would anybody want to read of Milwaukee? No, something more romantic. Hawaii? Alaska? Yes, Alaska!

'Miss!'

'Hmm?' Grace turned to face an agitated middle-aged man.

'You copied that page a couple of minutes ago.'

'Oh! Sorry,' Grace said. She'd better get to work. Christi Agamemnon, yes, she liked it.

After finishing with the appointment book and giving a false apology to the long line behind her, Grace rushed to the counter, bought a jiffy bag and placed the duplicate of the book inside. She addressed this to – well, she was going to send it to Edna, but Edna wouldn't get the charge out of this that Craig would. So she addressed the duplicate to Craig Epstein and on the bottom, wrote, 'To be opened on the event of my death!' He would love it!

By the time Galen arrived home, Grace had finally called the airline and bought a ticket for the earliest plane out of Newark for Chicago. Then she booked a later flight from Chicago to Los Angeles. She also called Odelle and got Sy instead. She explained she would be out there tomorrow morning, Odelle should not go to work. 'And why?' Sy asked, none too pleased.

'I'm about to solve the murder of Tommy Patterson,' she informed him dramatically.

His response was simply, 'Holy shit,' in that annoyed voice Sy sometimes got when life became too much for him. He really should retire. Grace would have to tell him that if she saw him.

She was doing the washing when Galen stepped through the door. He was surprised because the laundry was his purview, and he only did it when they were both almost out of underwear or there was a special pair of jeans he wanted to wear. But he had already read in one of his many books that expectant mothers had these surges of energy, so he tried to take her activity in his stride. Now if only he could get her to fold the clothes after she washed them. But, hell, he supposed it was just as easy to wear them right out of the basket.

'Hi,' she called when she heard him. 'How are you?'

'How's the little mother?' he called back.

She snarled, showing her all too sharp incisors. 'Galen, I'm leaving you for a few days.'

'What! Have you checked with the doctor?'

She came into the kitchen. 'Galen, stop this incessant nonsense about my alleged pregnancy. Women have been having babies since Eve. So try a little benign neglect. Okay?'

He sighed. 'Why won't you let me pamper you?'

'In nine months you can Pamper the baby.'

Galen rested his elbows on the table and placed his head on his hands, while he emoted sadness. 'Where are you going?'

'Chicago first, then out to L.A. I've got a murderer to catch.'

Galen was shocked. He stood up straight. 'You know who did it?'

'I have my suspicions. But I'd rather not say right now, until I verify them.'

'Well – who are you going to see out there?'

'At this point, aside from Trudi's lawyer, Odelle in Chicago and Kitten in L.A.'

'Kitten?' Galen's eyes lit up. As he was standing behind the counter, Grace couldn't see if his pants bulged. But was that drool at the corner of his mouth? 'Galen, just remember, I am the mother of your child. I am still your beloved, I assume?'

'Oh yeah, sure.' He came around the counter and hugged her. 'You are, Grace.'

'Then why do I get the feeling you're constantly fantasizing about Kitten Fairleigh?'

'Isn't every healthy, red-blooded American male fantasizing about Kitten Fairleigh?' Galen backed off to ask innocently.

Grace's eyes narrowed, but Galen was too far away for her to practise her karate kick to his crotch.

# Chapter 40

# Hurtling Westward

Depression always descended when Grace flew into Ohare Airport just west of Chicago. She supposed it was the symmetry that bothered her, the land cut up into blocks, houses lined up on those blocks one after another, the same model repeated over and over again. It was so ugly. What could she say? She had grown up in the Midwest and lived there a large part of her life. But it was, along with the pronunciation of the a's, flat. She had become used to the beautiful, richly rewarding hills of the Northeast.

It was funny, she thought, as she swung her overnight bag, clearing a path for herself on her way to the taxi stand. Odelle had been born in Connecticut and here she was living in the Midwest. They had exchanged geographies.

The taxi hurtled along the flat, evenly paced streets. One thing the suburbs didn't have and that was traffic, probably because everyone was moving out of Illinois, down South, out West, away from the cold and the flatness.

Grace paid off the taxi in front of Odelle's house. She was looking forward to seeing her friend and having one of those chats over coffee. But it wasn't Odelle who met Grace at the door. It was Sy Hampton. For the first time, Grace noticed that he was indeed getting old. She had always thought of Sy as being strong and virile. She supposed that was because he was definitely muscular. Even though he owned his own company, he worked in the field, not in some office. But now he was slacking off. And he looked worried.

He kissed her cheek as they stood on that familiar porch together. Then he welcomed her inside. 'Home from work?' Grace wondered. 'I hope you're not sick?'

'I'm taking a day off,' he confessed.

'Sy doesn't trust me any more,' Odelle called from the living room. Grace came over and gave her friend a big hug. Although she had

254

spoken to Odelle often, this was the first time she had seen her since Tommy's funeral.

While Odelle left the room to bring coffee and Danish, Grace made herself comfortable on the sofa, noting it was new, as was the rug. 'Luke's learned to wipe his feet when he comes into the house, he's almost on his way to college, so we decided to go the whole hog and get the furniture we want to last us the rest of our life,' Sy explained.

'You're forgetting grandchildren,' Grace reminded him.

Odelle smiled as she came back in and set the tray down on the coffee table. 'Grandchildren,' she said wistfully. Grace hoped Odelle was thinking more of Julia than of Luke. 'Or what about a godchild?' Odelle suggested slyly.

Grace tried to look as blank as possible, but Sy said, 'Congratulations! Your friend Galen called about half an hour ago to tell us the news. He wants to make sure you're rested before you fly on to the coast.'

'I will kill him!' Grace shouted.

'Why?' Odelle wondered. 'He sounds like such a nice boy – I mean, man. He was very excited.'

'If it were possible, Galen would be the first pregnant man. Matter of fact, I think he *is* pregnant. At least with expectation. He won't let time take care of itself. He has to hurry it along.'

'It's nice that he's so concerned about you,' Odelle said. 'I remember when I was pregnant with Luke – where were you, Sy?'

'Christ!' he said. 'Let's not have a list of my crimes now. Grace has obviously come here with a purpose. What is it, Grace?'

'Sy, as much as I love you, this is really between Odelle and myself,' Grace said sternly.

Odelle sat primly, knees together, hands folded on her lap. She looked at Sy: Sy looked at her. Grace's eyes flicked between the two of them. 'Sy felt rather – umm – put out by Trudi's invasion and capture by the police, right here in our living room. He made me promise that anything that had to do with Tommy or his wives would be shared. Therefore, Grace, whatever you have to say can be said to both of us.'

Grace pondered that. She wondered how much Sy knew? Did he know that Odelle had seen Tommy three days before his death, after which Tommy changed his will? How much of this matter had husband and wife shared? If only she could get Odelle into the kitchen or somewhere to find out. But, well, 'You asked for it,' she told them both.

Grace launched into her history of finding the appointment book containing Tommy's notations of his last days. 'Trudi was there,' she told them, 'but so was everyone else.' She looked meaningfully at Odelle. 'There was also another weird thing I found in the box with his last appointment book. A manuscript.' She explained the nature of the manuscript, and Odelle heartily agreed with her that Tommy's favourite food was steak, either that or barbecued ribs.

'Matter of fact,' Odelle said, 'he took me to a rib place when – ' Then she fell silent.

'When you met in him L.A. three days before his murder,' Grace concluded for her.

Sy looked at her. Oh God, Grace thought. She hadn't told her husband.

'I've explained my visit with Tommy to the police,' Odelle defended herself before the verbal blows could come. 'When they called me about Trudi, I felt the whole story of my involvement should come out.'

'You visited Patterson!' Sy exclaimed. 'Why?'

Odelle stood and gave herself distance from both of them. She sighed. 'The shelter needs money. It needs money desperately. Every year with all these budget deficits, the government's funding of the shelter had decreased. Before I saw Tommy, I had approached everyone I knew who has money, organizations who could have held benefits for the shelter, even the Junior League. But charities go in and out of fashion. Battered women and children are out. There are new diseases to conquer, new political causes. But just because we turn our faces in another direction doesn't mean there aren't still husbands and boyfriends out there kicking the living daylights out of their so-called loved ones. I have to live with this every day, knowing there are so many more people who need my help and there is nothing I can do but watch them fall by the wayside. I've exhausted my own small inheritance from my parents, money I meant to leave to my children; I've donated to the Shelter all that Sy allows for charity from his salary. But the shelter is like quicksand. Who, I thought, who has more money than he would ever need? Who took more than he ever gave? My answer: Tommy Patterson.'

Odelle returned to the couch and sat down, as if the effort of what she had just said had been too much. 'I like to think I don't hold a grudge. Tommy deserted me; he left me on my own with a young child to take care of. But I made out all right. There's no reason to hate. Things straightened themselves out. I found Sy or he found me.' Odelle smiled at her husband. 'Now, everyone gets a divorce. Back then it was humiliating. I will never forget the humiliation of having a man I loved, with whom I had what I thought was a mutual commitment, walk out on me. He hurt me, but as I say, I survived. Nicely.

256

'Sy adopted Julia and Julia grew. I always felt there was no need to tell her about her real father. You know that old expression, "If you can't say anything nice about someone, don't say anything at all." I saw Tommy manipulating millions the way he manipulated me. And you, Grace. Furthermore, he was getting away with it. So why bring such an inheritance upon Julia?

'Of course, she found out. I kept it from her as long as possible. When she got her driver's licence, I faked it, told the officials I couldn't find her birth certificate, and they accepted her social security card and school records. Julia didn't question it. But then, remember Sy, when she and her friend went to Europe that summer? You can't plead with anyone for a passport. So Julia found out that Tommy Patterson was her real father.'

'I remember,' he said painfully.

Odelle smiled. 'Yes, you had that nice fatherly chat with Julia that lasted, oh, all of one minute.'

'Well, hell, I've always considered her my kid. What more did she need to know?'

Odelle reached out and squeezed her husband's hand. 'Julia, sappy as all girls are, romanticized her real father. At least that's what I think happened. I know once when I visited her in college, I saw a collection of Tommy's books on her book shelf. And then, finally, she had a chance to meet him. He was speaking in Boston about positivation or something dumb like that, and Julia went with a few of her friends from college to hear him. Afterwards, she hung around and watched while Tommy signed books and cassettes, that sort of thing. And then when the crowd had thinned, she approached him. "Hi," she said, "I'm Julia." When there was no reaction, "Your daughter."

'Tommy could have said, "Well, hi, long time no see," or something else innocuous and that would have been it. That's all she wanted, some acknowledgement. But he just looked past her as if she weren't even there. And she wasn't. For him.

'Julia told me how humiliated she had been. That was much later. Years later. All her friends in whom she had confided thought she was a liar. One even called the mental health clinic and tried to get her into therapy. She laughs about it now. But you could tell it cut deeply.'

'Tommy's idea of getting close is to destroy,' Grace remembered.

'So that's why I went to him. To get money.'

'How could you humiliate yourself so?' Grace asked angrily. 'To beg Tommy for money? God, why didn't you come to me?'

'Darling, you had already given $10,000. I don't know what your finances are like. I didn't want to be a leech. And I didn't say I begged

257

Tommy for money. I didn't ask Tommy for money. If you had to use a word for how I got the money from Tommy, I think it would be "extorted".'

'Extorted?' Sy repeated.

'Yes. Tommy has a private number, as we all know, to protect him from his fans. So I had to plan my route of attack very carefully. I wrote to him care of his publishers a month ahead of time. I told him that I had something mutually beneficial to discuss, gave him the address of the hotel where I would be staying. I wrote that if he didn't show up, I'd have to go public with it on my own. And it might be damaging if I did.

'At the appointed hour, Tommy showed. Perhaps he had in the back of his mind the publicity job we did on him about Trudi Surefoot. Anyway, he came to the hotel and then took me to a rib place for lunch.

'I explained, over a plate of ribs and coleslaw, how my shelter was having trouble raising funds, how it desperately needed an influx of money. Real money. I suggested strongly that this would be a good charity for Tommy to invest in. He laughed, sort of like it wasn't any of his concern. He reminded me that I had written I had something mutually beneficial to discuss. So I told him support of my shelter was mutually beneficial. Then he asked, how so?

'I wondered if he had any idea of the sort of people my shelter saved. He didn't, but he suggested first the homeless, then drug addicts. Neither, I told him. It's for battered women and children. He sort of dismissed that with a wave of his hand. And then I said to him, "You remember what that was like, don't you, Tommy? How you used to slap me around and – '

"Immediately, he objected. "I never laid a hand on you!" he protested. "Of course you didn't," I agreed. "But who's going to know that except you and me?"'

Sy looked shocked. Grace smiled. 'Wonderful,' she told her friend. 'I love it!'

'But that's – unethical,' Sy pointed out.

'Did ethics ever stop Tommy Patterson!' Grace had to ask him.

'Anyway,' Odelle continued, 'after that, Tommy got very hot under the collar. And I didn't think it was the tabasco sauce on his ribs. He said he'd see his lawyers and sue me for everything I had. I told him I had nothing. I had given it all to the shelter. Besides, I reminded him, once the accusations were out of my mouth, nothing would recall them from people's minds.

'Then he started to bargain. A thousand, five, ten. Nothing satisfied me. I wasn't going to be paid off so easily. I told him I wanted a constant source of income so I didn't have to be grovelling around all the time. He backed off again. And then I reminded him about VAMO – Volunteers Against Masculine Oppression – the organization that had done such a job on him when we were trying to get him to be fair with Trudi's settlement. I warned him that they would picket his every lecture, his every book signing, his every seminar. "And think of how much money you'll lose that way," I said.

'Finally, after much bickering, which I won't bore you with, we came to what I considered a satisfactory arrangement. The book: LOOK BACK FOR LOVE. He would assign the copyright to my shelter. I didn't know until the will was read that he also left me $10,000. That I've divided between Luke and Julia. But I can assure you that all the monies from the book will go to Sisters of the Storm. His publisher says I'll get a cheque twice a year for a very long time, but now I'm wondering how can I live on a cheque that only comes twice a year?'

'You'll learn,' Grace said. She sighed. 'Anyway, it's a relief to know finally what really happened. I didn't want to get Trudi back into the frying pan and you into the fire.'

'No,' Odelle said. 'I didn't murder Tommy. I really was back here in Glencoe the day he died. But what about Trudi?'

Grace then explained what she had found in the appointment book. Trudi did see Tommy that last day. The question was did she murder him? There were other initials Grace wanted to look up while she was in L.A., including the curious NUT. And of course Kitten Fairleigh might be able to supply important information.

'You're going to see Kitten Fairleigh?' Sy wondered.

'Another man with his tongue hanging out,' Grace said dispiritedly. 'What does everyone find so attractive in Kitten Fairleigh?' From the look on Sy's face, Grace would rather he didn't tell her.

Grace rose. 'Well, the airport calls. Again.'

'Keep in touch,' Odelle urged her. She looked down at the tray of undrunk coffee and uneaten Danish. 'I should have served you milk,' she said thoughtfully. 'I think I read coffee is dangerous for expectant mothers.'

'Everything is dangerous for expectant mothers,' Grace said. 'Galen's given me a list. I don't think there's anything I can eat or drink for the next nine months. One wonders how our mothers and grandmothers did it without all the benefits of this medical advice.'

'Pregnant,' Odelle said wistfully.

'Are you marrying this Galen?' Sy asked sternly.

Grace thoughtfully put her finger to her lips. 'I suppose I'll have to. After all, if it's a boy I don't want him to be called a bastard right off. Though I suppose that appellation comes in time to all men. *N'est ce*

259

*pas?'* She smiled sweetly at them both, kissed them goodbye, and was once again on her way.

# Chapter 41

# Kitten Country

Grace Mandling disliked L.A. And that wasn't merely because of its congested airport and crowded freeways. Hell, any city could boast those. Frankly, she had suffered through several bad experiences in the Los Angeles area. When MAY I HELP YOU? her first novel, set in the heart and soul of Chicago, was being made into a mini-series, she was hired as an advisor to the scriptwriters. The rationale behind her hiring was the producer told her endearingly, that she alone could help them capture her original flavour. If that were the case – and she was smart enough to wonder about this only after the fact – why was the location of the department store changed to L.A.? 'Easier to shoot,' the producer explained graciously to her. 'And let's face it, who understands Chicago?'

Needless to say, her job as an advisor was a mere boondoggle dear Edna had arranged. But Grace stuck around anyway in hopes of soaking up not only the sun but the atmosphere. Who knew when she would have to set a novel in California? Fortunately, that day had so far not yet come.

Grace would freely admit she didn't understand Southern California, but she could see why it and Tommy Patterson had a love affair going. There was a constant running, almost diarrheic, conversation about feelings, relationships, emotions, i.e., "Where his head is at", in this case with no sexual connotation.

However, here Grace was, back again on the West Coast, this time set upon freeing her crypto-martyr Trudi Surefoot. Or at least she would give Leon Cohen the ammunition to do so. She wondered how Trudi was holding up in a mental institution. Did she know the difference between that and real life? Or, alternatively, were all the nuts out on the street?

NUT. NUT was the reason Grace was postponing letting Leon Cohen know she had arrived in L.A. As soon as she did, she realized he would send someone over and relieve her of Tommy's vital last appointment book. Before that happened, Grace wanted to get in touch with Kitten Fairleigh and see if Kitten could come up with a name to match the initials – NUT.

Kitten, naturally, was not in. Grace was again faced with communicating in fractured Spanish with Kitten's maid. She left a message that she needed to see 'Keeten pronto.' It was '*muy urgento*'. Faced with the prospect of waiting at the hotel for Kitten's call, while avoiding Leon's, Grace had a choice of taking a short nap or going out by the pool for sun and a swim. From her fifth-storey window, she looked down at the pool. All the bodies beneath her glimmered young and perfect. That decided it for her. She needed her rest anyway.

The phone woke her like an alarm. She was surprised to note that she had slept for more than two hours. Maybe being pregnant, even in the early stages, did exhaust one. She couldn't remember. Her first pregnancy had been so long ago.

It was Kitten Fairleigh returning her call. 'We must meet,' Grace told the movie star. 'I can't say anything over the phone.'

'I'll send my car for you,' Kitten conspired agreeably. 'I've just had my workout so that'll give me time to shower and dress.'

Grace could get used to having a car chauffeur her around, instead of foraging through traffic herself, especially here, where traffic clogged the arteries like cholesterol. But soon they were off the freeway and out into the countryside she vaguely remembered from the drive after Tommy's funeral. They rose along the cliffs, as the sea majestically roiled against the rocks below.

Rosalita, Kitten's housekeeper was waiting for Grace. She said something in Spanish as a greeting, then led Grace into the living room. This room Grace definitely remembered. It faced straight out towards the Pacific, which today was blue and as calm as its name. Trudi was truly nuts. Any lawyer in the world could have proved that fact by bringing a jury here. Who in her right mind would give up a house like this?

'Impressive, isn't it?' Kitten had come silently into the room. Grace moved away from the picture window and stared at one of America's foremost movie stars who had certainly dressed the part today. She had on a slinky white jumpsuit, accessorized with gold, all complementing her hair.

'It's beautiful,' Grace said, not knowing if she meant the ocean view of the image of womanhood Kitten presented. Now why couldn't she have been born looking like that?

'Sometimes I stand at the window, as you were doing, and I'm afraid. When the earthquake comes, as it inevitably will, all this beauty will be destroyed and me along with it. On the other hand,' Kitten said, walking slowly towards the window, 'when I've had a really bad day on the set or in my personal life, I come here, look out at the endless ocean and realize how insignificant man is.'

'Most men definitely,' Grace agreed.

Kitten gave that musical little laugh that drove men wild when she did it on the screen. 'Not that cute little Galen of yours, though, I'm willing to bet.'

'Oh, did you like Galen?' Grace asked. 'It would definitely be mutual admiration then.'

'I could tell. I hope you didn't mind. It's very hard for me to turn of my sex appeal.'

'It's very hard for me to turn mine on,' Grace said into the undertow.

'I know,' Kitten caught her comment anyway. 'That's because you think too much. Sex is all a matter of feeling. You're tight. I've noticed that every time I've met you. You're wary, juggling the possibilities of a situation. You need to – urm – just let life happen. Life really is like an orgasm, building, exploding, descending. And we can have orgasms over and over again. I try to portray that in my work.'

Before Grace could compliment Kitten on her success, Rosalita reappeared, rolling along a tea tray, which carried a bottle of chilled white wine and a selection of hors d'oeuvres. It was only then that Grace realized she was famished. She hadn't eaten since that awful airline snack on the plane out. 'Pardon me while I make a pig of myself,' she said to Kitten.

'Please do,' Kitten urged. 'It's all delicious, but very low calorie. Wine is my only splurge.'

'You can't have to watch your weight.'

'All the time. Such a bore.'

They sat down together on the couch. Kitten poured the wine and handed Grace a glass. 'To what shall we drink?' she asked. 'Success?'

'We have that. What about emancipation?'

Kitten shrugged. They clinked glasses and drank, savouring the cool chill of one of God's first gifts to humankind. Silently, they spread low calorie cheese dip on low calorie wafers. When the first pangs of hunger had abated, Kitten asked, 'Now, what was so *urgento*?' She smiled.

Grace took a napkin – linen – and wiped her hands. Then she reached into her purse and pulled out Tommy's appointment book. With a touch of drama she hoped Kitten appreciated, Grace handed it to the movie star. Kitten took the appointment book and literally curled up with it.

263

Despite Grace's firm belief, being brunette and only normal look-ing, that all beautiful blondes had to be dumb, if only as a comfort to the rest of womanhood, she could see from the concentration on Kitten's face that this blonde wasn't dumb at all.

Several pages into the book, Kitten looked up and said, 'He must have had me followed. He had a lot of sexual hangups, but I suppose you knew that.'

'I was young and innocent when I met him.'

Kitten shrugged. 'And maybe he wasn't impotent then.'

'Tommy was impotent!' "Wait till I tell Odelle," Grace was thinking.

Kitten looked puzzled. 'Could it be that I overwhelmed him?' She returned to the appointment book. 'Obviously, he was jealous.'

'What do you think KFDTF means?'

'It's me and David. F? Fucked?'

'That was my assumption.'

'And that's just what it is, an assumption, because some of these evenings we didn't. We were just helping each other with our lines. But naturally, Tommy would see David as a threat. David was so much younger and more aware than Tommy. He presents such a virile image. You know, like I'm sex, David's a stud, an image he's trying to dispel with this venture on to Broadway.'

'I see he's managed.'

Kitten smiled. 'You mean the reviews, where some critics sug-gested he came off not so much as a fop but a fag. Poor David, he howled in pain.'

'So did one of the critics David caught up with. I suppose he'll get probation on the assault charge.'

'I'm planning to appear in court alongside him for moral support. Also, I'm hoping the judge is a fan.'

'And what if the judge is a woman?'

'Hmm,' Kitten considered. She took the easy way out and went back to the appointment book. 'I assume OH is Odelle Hampton and that TS is Trudi Surefoot.' She looked up. 'This book is not going to help Trudi any.'

'What about the other initials?' Grace said.

Together, they worked for the best part of two hours, figuring out whom the letters stood for. When they were done, there were few unknowns. One of those unknowns was NUT. Kitten could see that Grace was obsessed with NUT. 'Why?' she wondered. 'Is NUT important? The initials don't appear the last week of Tommy's life.'

'And yet before that last week, NUT appears several times a week, sometimes every day. Why?'

264

Kitten shrugged.

'Was Tommy having an affair with anyone?'

'I don't know. Gauging from his inability with me, he might have been afraid to try. But I honestly don't know. Even just after we were married, Tommy informed me we were to have a very open marriage. Later, after I found out too much about him, I took him at his word. But if he was seeing someone, I didn't suspect. Nor, finally, did I care.'

'He was working on a new book. Did you know what it was about?'

'No.'

'Nutrition?'

'Tommy!' Kitten peeled off that laugh again.

'He was going to divorce you. Maybe he was going to divorce you for someone else.'

Kitten leaned forward. Grace couldn't help but think of Galen. How he would have loved the sight of her boobs trying to make an escape from the white jumpsuit. 'When I married Tommy, everyone knew who he was, while I was just becoming known. Tommy gave me a boost up in name recognition. But before we married, we both signed prenuptial agreements. So I had nothing to gain or lose by the divorce. Certainly, it was a difficult moment when news of our impending divorce came out on the day of Tommy's funeral. It made me look like a suspect. But, believe me, there was little passion involved in our marriage. Analyzing it now, it was based on reasons of status, on both sides. I wanted Tommy because he was somewhere between God and Gucci loafers. Tommy wanted me at his side to make him look more of a man.'

'What bothers me, Kitten, is that Tommy did not write down KFDTF that last night of his life. And yet you claim he knew you were with David Turner, going out to a première of a new movie. Then afterwards it was back to David's place for an evening of – romance? If Tommy knew ahead of time that you would be with David, why didn't he write it in his book?'

Kitten's mouth dropped open in a half idiotic smile. 'You're trying to pin the murder on me?' she said in astonishment.

'No, I'm not!' Grace objected. 'I'm trying to eliminate suspects.'

'What would be the point in my killing Tommy? The divorce? I can give you the name of my lawyer. I wanted a divorce from Tommy long before he filed against me. Honestly Grace, I thought you came here as a friend.'

'I did!' Grace protested.

'And why would I smash in my own front door? That's how the killer got in.'

'The killer could have had a key. Or the killer could have been invited in by Tommy. Then some argument might have ensued. In a fit of rage, or even acting in a premeditated fashion, the killer could have tossed or pushed Tommy over the cliff, retreated in panic, and only then might the person have decided to cover his or her tracks. So the murderer or murderess smashes the front door to make it look like attempted robbery.'

Kitten stood up. The white jumpsuit slinked over her perfect form. 'Brilliant. Is this a plot for your next book? Because if it is, let me give you a little twist you're going to have to work in. The police found glass splinters all over the house and on the patio that leads to the cliff where Tommy took his swan dive. Which means, Ms Mandling, that the person who broke the front door was coming in, not going out.'

Grace poured herself another glass of wine, oblivious to the fact that Kitten still stood and obviously wanted her out of the house. She thought carefully, not as Grace Mandling but as Christi Agamemnon, Alaskan super sleuth. What would Christi do?

Grace stood up with a suddenness that startled Kitten. 'Where were the fragments?'

'What?' Kitten said, confused.

'You said the police found glass fragments all over the house. Where exactly was all over? In the kitchen?'

'No.'

'Bathroom?'

'No.' Kitten was faltering.

'Where then? Trace the fragments for me.'

Mystified, perhaps intimidated, Kitten led Grace to the front door, whose glass had been replaced with teak. From there she walked Grace back into the living room and then hesitantly towards a side room and out to the patio. 'I don't know how many fragments were along the dirt path,' Kitten said. 'You'd have to check with Detective Morris about that.'

'Fine.' It was then that Grace realized she had never been outside the house before, except by the front door. Here on the patio a pleasant afternoon breeze was blowing, sweeping from the ocean up towards the hills. This was the place where her former husband must have realized his life was in danger.

Grace looked around her, trying to get a sense of the scene. The patio was blocked off from the hill in front of it by a three-foot high brick wall. Behind the patio, leading away from it, lay a dirt trail. Grace walked towards it. As she did, he noted that not only could one see from the patio into the living room, but one could also see the other room where glass fragments had been found. 'What is that room?' she asked Kitten.

266

'Tommy's office. Where he wrote.'

'Ah ha!' Grace said.

'Ah ha what?' Kitten wondered.

But Grace as yet couldn't formulate exactly what she meant. Had Tommy been working when the murderer broke in on him? 'Was the computer on?'

'The computer?'

Grace sighed in exasperation. 'The night Tommy was murdered. Was the computer on?'

Kitten lifted her shoulders and let them drop. 'How the hell should I know!'

'What I'm trying to find out is did the murderer find Tommy at his desk?'

'God! Well – wait a second. I don't think so,' Kitten said excitedly. 'I think Tommy was out here. He liked to come out here at night and watch the stars. He was, in his own way, a romantic. I think there was something good in him,' Kitten noted sadly, almost wistfully.

'We're not analyzing Tommy's character now,' Grace reminded her. 'We're analyzing his movements.'

'Right.' Kitten pulled herself together. 'What I just remembered was that the police found a glass out here on the patio. It held Tommy's favourite drink and had his fingerprints on it.'

'So, he was out here. Looking at the stars. He hears the front door being bashed in. What does he do?'

'Who knows?'

'How true. However, if I had heard the front door being smashed, I would have hidden immediately. What Tommy did, what his male hormones led him to do, only Tommy knows. And the murderer. But one thing we do know is that Tommy goes up this path.' And at that, Grace started up the path also, the one that slowly wended its way along nature's gardening to the top of the cliff. 'And then he stops,' she said at the edge.

'It was dark,' Kitten reminded her. 'Even with the patio lights, it's dark up here.'

'So he might not have known when he took that last fatal step. It might have been an accident, not murder,' Grace said excitedly. 'Then Trudi – hey, they might have been up here together, looking at the stars, and Tommy got so overwhelmed he took one step too many and – '

'But why would Trudi break in? And Tommy was standing with his back to the cliff as if he was facing someone. That's what his footprints showed.'

Grace sighed. Kitten was obviously going to be no help in constructing a favourable scenario. At the edge now, Grace looked down, way down. She grimaced. It was an ugly way to go. Tommy must have bounced off several outcroppings of rock that lay beneath this edge. 'I hope it was quick,' she said to empty space. She turned back to Kitten. 'As much as I hated Tommy, I don't think he deserved to be murdered.'

'Neither do I,' Kitten quickly agreed.

'I've just realized that now, standing here like this, feeling his pain at the moment he must have realized he was going to die.' Grace strode quickly down the path towards the safety of the patio. Kitten trotted at her heels. 'Further,' Grace said, flinging her words behind her, 'I don't think you killed him.'

'Gee, thanks.'

'I would have seen guilt written on your face at the cliff side.' She stopped on the patio and turned to face Kitten.

Kitten was smiling. 'But I'm an actress. Remember?'

Grace overlooked her remark. 'I don't think Trudi could have done it either. Unless it was an accident. Unless she reached up to hug Tommy or something and threw him off balance. But still, it doesn't make sense for Trudi to have done it, does it? Why break the door?'

Kitten shrugged. 'I think it was just some thief.'

Grace shook her head. 'No. If it were anyone else but Tommy Patterson, I would agree with you. But to come out here, to this wilderness, just to rob someone? No. There are easier targets. Someone came out here specifically to confront Tommy. And that confrontation turned to murder.'

Grace went back inside the living room and picked up her purse. She smiled at Kitten and said, 'I've taken up enough of your time. Thanks for seeing me, Kitten. And for the food and wine. I hope we meet again.' She held out her hand.

Kitten took it. 'Some day you'll write a script for me that will have meaning. When I form my own production company, I'll be in touch.'

They shook on it.

# Chapter 42
# Mentally Yours

So that was it. Her efforts to find Tommy's killer by herself had come to naught. The next morning Grace turned in the appointment book to Leon Cohen and told him all she knew, her conversations with both Odelle and Kitten. 'I believe them,' she judged.

Leon glanced quickly through the appointment book, then took more time studying the listing of names with initials Kitten and Grace had compiled the night before. A few initials neither of them could figure out. Leon was worried. 'We have to find out who everyone in this book is. But it's going to cost to check on these,' he warned her.

Naturally, she thought.

There was really nothing left for her to do in Los Angeles. She had called Galen six o'clock L.A. time to find him miserably in bed with morning sickness. She knew that younger men were being urged to let the feminine side of them creep out, to be warm and sensitive, but Galen was taking it a bit too far. She could not stand nine months of this! She told him this in no uncertain terms. He was to straighten himself out by the time she returned. God, was she to be a mother to two babies!

Her only remaining wish, she told Leon, was to visit Trudi. 'She needs a friend. Now more than ever.'

'I don't think there'll be a problem,' he told her kindly. Well, those are always famous last words. Leon's assistant not only had to get in touch with the mental hospital, he had to get in touch with the prosecutors. In other words, Grace would be spending another night in L.A.

But by nine o'clock the next morning, red tape surmounted, she presented herself at the pristine glass doors of the Phoenix Institute for the Correction of Slight Imbalances. It didn't sound like a nut house. But since Trudi was confined there, that's exactly what the Phoenix Institute had to be.

The woman who greeted her was dressed very California, which meant she looked like a slut but probably wasn't. Grace was politely informed that she was expected, and then she was escorted to the waiting room. The room was plushly done in beige and rose. Grace did not occupy it alone. There was another person who sat with his head in his hands. He looked up only once and that was to tell Grace to 'Stop staring at me!'

Naturally, she had not been staring at him, but he was now certainly the centre of her attention. As a matter of fact, she was wondering whether it might be the better part of valour to get up and walk out of here before this madman strangled her.

One of the staff came in. Grace rose. But the woman said, 'Reverend Baker, you may attend to your flock.'

Jesus.

Grace sat back down, gratefully alone. She leaned forward to the reading table and noted that xeroxed copies of the menu and the day's activities had been run off. How thoughtful. Grace picked up one of each and looked them over. The menu seemed well balanced and interesting, hopscotching from one ethnic favourite to another. She would admit though that tacos with a side of spaghetti might be a little bit unnerving if she were schizoid. The activity sheet was also impressive: tennis lessons, swimming therapy, arts and crafts. She was sure Trudi must be involved in those. As Grace remembered, clay was Trudi's life. There were even movies shown in the great theatre, while at the same time "acting out" took place in the little theatre, and aerobics in the gym. The movie tonight would be, hmm, *The Gods Must Be Crazy*. How comforting that must be to most of the patients here.

'Ms Mandling?'

Grace looked up. A woman in a white jump suit, much less sexy than the one Kitten had worn last night, stood in the doorway. 'Yes?' Grace said.

'I'm Kathy Wilmot, staff director for Trudi's cottage. Would you like to come with me now?'

Grace quickly folded the menu and activity sheets and put them in her purse. She stood and followed Kathy Wilmot down a long corridor and then out into the grounds of the Phoenix Institute. 'We have quite a way to go,' Kathy explained, 'as Trudi is in our restricted area.'

'Oh?'

Kathy noted the worry in Grace's voice. She gave her a reassuring smile. 'It could be called our criminal wing, but we don't use terms

270

like that here at the Phoenix. It's more for those whose maladjust-
ments, or as we like to put it, whose slight imbalances, may pose a
threat to society.'

'Trudi doesn't belong in any criminal wing,' Grace objected. 'She is
not a criminal.'

'That's what they all say.' And then Kathy laughed. 'Oh, I didn't
mean it to come out like that. We don't have serious, hardcore
criminals at the Phoenix, obviously. What we have are people whom
the district attorney's office doesn't consider dangerous. For instance, a lot of people charged with white collar crimes come here,
hoping our doctors will find that they acted under the influence of
some psychotic disorder. Or there are those who claim to have
committed their alleged crime while they were drunk or on drugs. Or
those on probation who come here to prove they are well intentioned
in their efforts to reform. That sort of thing. Trudi's lawyer, Mr
Cohen, did a good job getting her in here. Actually we have several of
his clients here now, including a seventy-three-year-old dowager
charged with running a group of teenage break-in artists. She re-
cruited them through her grandson, or so we understand.'

Grace nodded as she walked briskly alongside Kathy. The Phoenix
Institute from the inside was very impressive. The lawns were well
manicured, with tennis courts and baseball diamonds and a swimming pool. It looked like a health resort. But ahead Grace could see a
fence with a gate. The gate was guarded. That must be where they
had stashed Trudi. 'How's Trudi doing?' she asked Kathy.

Kathy mulled that over. Finally, she came up with, 'I'm not her
doctor. You'd have to speak with him.'

Grace grabbed on to Kathy's unease instantly. 'You mean she's not
getting on well. She's depressed. She's – '

'She's unpopular, if you really want to know, Ms Mandling. Matter
of fact, the best thing you could do for Trudi Surefoot while you're
here, if you really are that good a friend, is tell her to lay off.'

'Lay off? I don't understand. Trudi is always so dizzy, she never
bothers anyone. So lay off what?'

'Trudi may have been dizzy when she was high on drugs. But she's
not on drugs anymore, Ms Mandling. Now she's high on Jesus Christ,
no one is safe from her. I have several times had her come up to me
when I was very busy with my administrative duties; she grabs my
hand with the pen still in it, and asks me, "Have you taken Jesus
Christ our Lord as your saviour?" I ask you, Ms Mandling, is that any
of Trudi Surefoot's business? And I'm not the only one she ap-
proaches. Staff and patients alike, none of us is safe from her
proselytizing. She holds Bible readings in the common room while

271

others are trying to play cards. At crafts workshops, she makes crucifixes for everyone, with various mangled bodies of Christ glued on. Believe me, it is not a pretty sight, especially for one patient who is here because he drunkenly ran his car into a crowd of pedestrians, killing two. I had never felt especially sorry for him before, but when Trudi handed him one of her gruesome crucifixes, he went absolutely off the wall. He's been in restraint ever since. In other words, Ms Mandling, do us a favour and tell her to shut up!'

With growing unease, Grace began to wonder what she had got herself into. What had happened to the Trudi she knew and cared about? She had time to ponder that as Kathy was gaining access to the privileged grounds for the criminally insane. It looked much like the rest of the institute but with a fence around it, barbed wire at the top. The cottages here were adobe, giving the impression of a vacation village. Kathy informed Grace that Trudi was in the one labelled "Idaho". 'We give our cottages state names. It seems safest. Each cottage has four single rooms with locks on the door, if necessary. But since these people know, if they escape from the Phoenix Institute and are caught, they go to the state mental hospital, the locks are basically unnecessary.

'Here we are now. And one other thing you might mention to Trudi – the staff doesn't have time to make all the dietary concessions she is asking for. We serve well-balanced, nutritional meals. That should be enough.'

They entered "Idaho" while Grace puzzled over Trudi's dietary needs. Wine and wafers? Kathy knocked on the second door to the left. 'Trudi,' she called. 'There's someone here to see you.'

'To see me?' Grace could hear the excited voice from inside. Did Trudi think it was the Messiah?

The door opened and Trudi Surefoot stood there. Grace almost didn't recognize her. She looked – older. Her face was thinner. Her hair had been cut short, a sophisticated bob that the old hung-over hippie would never have worn. Trudi was a different woman. Drug-free. Reborn. 'Grace!' she shouted. She grabbed her friend and hugged her tight, then pulled her into the room.

Kathy followed them in. 'I'll leave you now,' she said. Then she showed Grace the red button near the air vent. 'This is an intercom. If you need anything, just push it and we'll be here immediately.' She smiled and left them, closing the door after her.

Trudi waited like an animal for the outer door of "Idaho" to close. 'It's not really an intercom,' she whispered to Grace. 'It's the panic button. That's if I should suddenly decide to attack you.' She laughed heartily.

'You look – so – ' Grace shook her head, wondering how to put it.

'Beatific,' Trudi completed. 'Like the angels. I've been reborn, Grace. I've found the way, the truth and the light. But I suppose Odelle's told you all that.'

Grace frowned slightly. 'Odelle is really sorry about what happened at her house. When her son called and said some nut had invaded the homestead, she had no idea it was you.'

Trudi waved the explanation aside. 'Oh, that doesn't matter, Grace. Anyone could have made that mistake. People aren't used to religious intensity any more. If humankind could only realize that finding Jesus is better than a multiple orgasm, what a happy world this would be.'

The frown did not leave Grace's face. 'You've had multiple orgasms? Because, like, I'm older than you and I've never – '

'Oh, there's nothing to it, Grace. You just have to relax and let them come.' She sat up straighter. 'Of course, I haven't had any lately. So full of the love of God has my life been that I haven't had time to think about men or masturbatory pleasures. Anyway, it's so good to see you.' Trudi reached out and took Grace's hand. 'You must tell me everything that's been happening!'

'Well, I've been working hard, Trudi, to get you freed.'

Trudi withdrew her hand. 'You mustn't do that, Grace.'

'Why not?' And then the truth began to dawn on her. 'Did you – you did kill Tommy?'

'Didn't we all kill Tommy? Like we all killed our beloved Jesus.'

'Trudi, Tommy was not Jesus. Nowhere near it.'

'And yet – and yet, Grace,' Trudi said, shaking her finger in Grace's face, 'if we had all been better people, Tommy would not have had to die. If we had all been kind and thoughtful and helpful to each other, he would still be here, walking among us. Didn't He come into this world to show us a reflection of ourselves? And even in His death are we still not being revealed? No, Grace, I consider it an honour to accept my martyrdom. I only hope I can bear it with as much grace as Jesus our saviour bore his.'

'I don't think anyone's planning to crucify you, Trudi. Look, all I want to know is did you kill Tommy – hold it! – in person? Did you go to Tommy's house that night and push him over the cliff?'

Trudi's brow creased. 'Not that I can remember,' she said.

'That's what I thought,' Grace replied with relief. Then she informed Trudi, despite the fact that the woman didn't seem to care at all, of all the steps she had taken to assure Trudi's freedom. Martyrdom was fine, she pointed out to the ex-druggie, but didn't Jesus ask his disciples to go out and preach the gospel? 'How many people can

273

you reach in prison?' Grace wondered. 'Compare that to just one street heavily laden with condominiums.'

Trudi gave that some serious thought.

'Also,' Grace continued, 'if you are convicted of Tommy's murder, what will happen to the Tommy Patterson Fund for the Betterment of Humanity? You can't be in charge if you're in jail. And think of how many sick and dying, widows and orphans, you can help with the money Tommy left.'

Trudi took that into consideration.

Grace saw she was making some serious headway here, so she decided to move on to even more difficult matters. She explained to Trudi how in this world we all had to try to get along with each other, not bother each other as much as possible. Therefore, until Trudi was free, she should lay off her efforts to convert everyone, especially here at the Phoenix Institute.

'You don't understand,' Trudi said. 'I'm just worried about their souls.'

'When the time comes for them to see the light, Trudi, they will. Isn't that what happened to you? Jesus was there all the time; and when you were ready to receive him, he came into your heart.'

Trudi laid her hand on top of Grace's head. 'Bless you, Grace. And how perfectly your name fits you. Once again, I have seen God's grace, His plan for me through you. I have spread the word, and now the word must carry its own weight. By the way, have I told you about Don Harrington?' No, she hadn't. So she proceeded to enlighten Grace about this wonderful man at the River Range Clinic who had laid a Bible on top of her coverlet. 'I just feel that Don and I can change the world together,' she enthused.

'When you get out,' Grace cautioned her.

'Right. How soon will that be, do you think?'

'Soon. I hope very soon,' Grace said, though with Trudi's initials in the appointment book on the last day of Tommy's life, she knew she was giving her friend false hope. 'Now, another thing: What is this about you and the food they serve here? I saw one of the menus, and it looked perfectly healthy to me. Is the food ill-prepared?'

'Oh!' Trudi said, all enthused again. 'I'm just so afraid I won't have time to spread the message of Jesus Christ to all those who need it. It's just hit me since I've been off drugs that I'm not young any more. There's no much lost time I have to make up for. I know that my soul is immortal, but just how long do I still have to inhabit my body for the greater glory of Christ our Lord?'

'That's a question we all ask ourselves at one time or another, Trudi,' Grace said as kindly as possible.

274

'But what do we do about it!' Trudi ranted. 'Our body is our temple. God wouldn't want us to defile it. Yet, we do. With so much new scientific evidence coming to light, we go about eating the same old junky things.'

Grace frowned. To what extremes was Trudi willing to go for her temple? 'You've become a vegetarian?'

'Oh, Grace, I've always been a vegetarian. You know that! But what kind of vegetarian? That's what concerns me now. Because just a while ago I was watching this cable channel on TV, and this woman came on, and she just made so much sense. She talked about how long vegetables are better than short ones. Like string beans are better than radishes. You know what I mean? She called it, umm – her theory of elonga – aiiii!'

'Trudi!' Grace shouted, digging her fingers into Trudi's arm.

'Ouch!' Trudi protested.

'Her theory of what!'

'Elongated fruits and vegetables,' Trudi said, sucking the pinholes Grace's nails had made. 'Honestly, Grace!'

'What program was it! Which channel were you watching!'

'I don't remember. There are just so many thousands of channels on cable. I never knew there were so many things to watch until I came here. I wish you could have heard her, Grace. She sounded so sensible.'

'Trudi, think!' Grace begged. 'What channel? Please!'

'Umm.' Trudi thought. 'I think – yes, it might have been – or – no – well, it could have been the Lifetime cable channel.'

'When?'

'Oh, gee, how long have I been here? Hmm. I can't remember exactly when I saw the program. But it couldn't have been too long ago.'

'Do you remember the name of the speaker?'

'No. I'm not interested in names. I'm interested in theory. Anyway, she was just this little brown-haired thing, and I was thinking she sure didn't look too elongated herself. You don't have to worry though. If you're really interested in her diet, you might be able to buy a book about it. She said something about having it privately published for her clients and then it was picked up by, what was it, the Brown Rice Press?'

Grace stood up and pushed the red button on the wall. 'I'm ready to go now!' she screamed into it. Less than a minute later two guards rushed to her rescue. All the while Trudi was protesting, 'But, Grace, we hardly had time to say anything to each other!'

With one of the guards agreeing to escort her to the gate, Grace yelled over her shoulder to Trudi, 'Pack your bag. You're getting out of here!'

275

# Chapter 43

# NUT

Her name was Natalie Ursula Trent, and her story was much as Grace had suspected. She had met Tommy at one of his "Good Love Good Life" singles seminars and had gone up to speak to him later about her theory of how to have an even better, longer life.

'Tommy seemed excited,' she said in a tearfully taped confession at the police station. 'He said I had something here and that we should really work on it together. He told me that with his contacts and name recognition and my theory, we could write a book that would sell in the millions.

'So we divided up the work. We each wrote our separate sections. Then we got together over the manuscript for the final push towards submitting it. That's when it happened, when I realized what a fool I had been. I was over at his house once while we were working, and I saw a print-out of what we had done so far. Included was the title page. It had only his name on it. I asked for an explanation. Tommy said I would be mentioned in the acknowledgements and get a consultation fee, but, really, the heart of the book was his critique of diets through the ages. Well, that was bullshit, wasn't it?

'Anyway, I argued with him. Tommy Patterson was stealing my life's work. He knew it too, but he didn't care. He had used me and drained me dry. Now he was getting ready to toss me aside. I just couldn't let him get away with it. The more I thought about it, the madder I got. I called him and told him I was consulting an attorney. He just laughed at me, said he was sued all the time by people like me who claimed his work as their own. It never stood up in court, he told me.

'And it just galled me because I knew, with our legal system, he was going to get away with it.

'Then I decided to do something about it. I would go to his house and steal his discs and the printouts. How could he claim then that

276

what I had was his? Everyone – all my friends – knew about my diet. With the repossession of my work, I would have him cold.

'I had read in the newspaper that Kitten Fairleigh was attending a movie première that night. And you always saw pictures in the paper of Tommy and Kitten together, didn't you? How was I to know she was attending the première with another man?

'I went to "Mi Hacienda" with a crowbar, intent on breaking in to take back what was mine. There were no lights on in the house. I took the crowbar and smashed in the glass front door. "Mi Hacienda" is so far from any other house, I knew no one would be around to hear. But there was someone around. It was Tommy. He had been outside. On the patio. I didn't know though. I didn't see or hear him even after I broke in. So maybe he was out on the patio, afraid to come in because – well, because he thought whoever had broken in was a thief. But I wasn't! I just wanted to retrieve my property.

'I searched through his office, trying to find the printouts and discs of my work. Even though I thought at the time there was no one in the house, I was scared. I had never done anything like this before. I wanted to get out of the house as soon as possible. I kept hearing noises, you know, like someone was around. And there was. He must have seen me through the office window. I don't know. All I know is that suddenly the lights went on in his office and there he was. I was terrified.

'There was a lot of screaming then, shouting, threats made on both sides. He promised to ruin me. Then he tried to call the police. But I pulled the phone from him. I picked up the crowbar. At first I didn't even know it was in my hand. But then he said to me, "Put that down!" I didn't. I just held it in my hand and started walking towards him. I didn't mean to do anything except take what was mine. You've got to believe me!

'Anyway, as I came towards him, he backed away, out of his office, through the living room and out of the sliding door to the patio. I followed. I don't know why I followed. I was just so infuriated that he was getting away with my book and now he was going to have me arrested for breaking into his house, when he was the thief!

'I don't remember clearly what happened. I wish I did. All I know is that he kept backing up, first out of the house, then on to the patio, then up the dirt trail. And then – over the cliff. I didn't lay a hand on him. I swear to God I did not lay a hand on him. Or a crowbar. He just backed away and I followed. Until he was at the edge of the cliff, where he took one step too many.

'There was this look of surprise on his face. I was surprised too. I watched while he tried to grab on to the air as if it were a tree branch.

277

One foot was swinging free. His other foot had got caught on some rocks, and I rushed towards him to pull him back from the edge. But by the time I reached for him, he was falling. Falling. Until I couldn't even see him. I didn't even hear him land.

'Did I murder him? I don't think so. Do you?'

Well, naturally the police did think Natalie Ursula Trent had murdered Tommy Patterson. But Leon Cohen felt the circumstances made a conviction mighty doubtful. He was willing to take the case, and this time Grace found a way to finance it at no cost to herself.

Through Leon, she approached NUT, as she could only think of poor Natalie Ursula Trent – after all, anyone who trusted Tommy had to be a little bit insane – and promised to arrange for the complete manuscript of ELONGATION: A THEORY OF LONGEVITY to be published, 'With Tommy and you jointly sharing authorship.'

Natalie at first was adamantly opposed, until Grace pointed out to her that a good defence cost a lot of money. 'Besides, you had a theory which you wanted to see promulgated. Believe me, interest in ELONGATION: A THEORY OF LONGEVITY is never going to be hotter than it is now.'

'But why should Tommy get money from my ideas?' Natalie continued to protest.

'Tommy is dead, dear. Remember? You're being charged with his murder? His estate gets it. More specifically, I get it,' Grace pointed out. 'I will donate the profits to your defence fund.' And by putting this in writing and getting Natalie's approval, ELONGATION was ready to face the world of publishing. The book was snapped up, after hearty bidding, by one of the country's most prominent publishers, which unfortunately wasn't her publisher Adams & Westlake. Craig was, needless to say, totally pissed. 'Darling,' Grace told him, after listening to his diatribe for more minutes than she cared to remember, 'you know old Gracie wouldn't make any arrangement that would make you unhappy.'

'You already have!' he shouted at her.

'Oh really? I guess that means you don't want to sign up my book NUT-PATTERSON: A REAL CLIFFHANGER, to be further subtitled, "The Inside Story of Tommy Patterson's Last Moments". Natalie and I have come to an arrangement. I have exclusive rights to her story. But, of course, if you're not interested – '

Dear Craig. Not only was he interested, he parlayed his relationship with her into his own imprint at another publishing house! Meanwhile, Edna Waitz brought a villa in the South of France. Poor Grace was left to build castles in the air with her pen, figuratively speaking.

So, everyone was a winner. By the time NUT's trial rolled around, her ELONGATION: A THEORY OF LONGEVITY had been rushed to press and was number one on the nonfiction best seller lists around the country, helped along by free publicity from every tabloid to be found in the grocery store and plenty of play in *People* and on *Entertainment Tonight*.

NUT wasn't found innocent of Tommy's murder, but she was found not guilty of second degree manslaughter, which is what the prosecutor's charge had come down to. Natalie sat at the defence table, looking so thin and fragile that the poor jury couldn't conceive of this woman holding up a crowbar to threaten anyone. They concluded Tommy's death was an accident. More specifically, couldn't it be called death by misadventure?

Of course, it helped that Leon Cohen was able to pick as a jury twelve good men and true, who claimed never to have read not only Tommy's books but any book. Ignorance is sometimes bliss.

Meanwhile, in a step unprecedented in publishing history, ELONGATION and Grace's reportage of the NUT murder trial, although issued by different publishers, would be boxed together for the upcoming Christmas season, Grace's book finally being entitled PASSION'S TORTUOUS TANGLES. 'Less confusing for your public,' Craig informed her.

NUT was less free to enjoy her success than Leon had hoped. True, she wasn't convicted of manslaughter, but she was convicted of breaking and entering. She would have to pay for the door she bashed in and serve one month in the county jail and two years on probation, which definitely hampered her author's tour. But all in all, as she told the judge tearfully, 'I've learned from my experience.'

As Grace would conclude in her reportage, 'Everyone learned from experience when it came to Tommy Patterson.'

# Chapter 44

# Love, At Long Last

NUT's trial ended just in time for Grace to speed home with her notes and have her baby. She faced a slight problem when she almost couldn't get on a plane because they kept telling her she was too far along. She would assume they meant her pregnancy, not her age.

Galen, her stalwart little soldier, fainted in the delivery room, but at least he didn't have labour pains. She had those all by herself. He insisted they do Lamaze because having natural childbirth was the only way to go. She humoured him up until the time he fainted, then she asked for a caudal.

She had a boy. Galen, after they revived him, was so excited that he fainted again. Was he perhaps too much of the new man? Well, it was too late now to worry about that. They were stuck with each other, married in Las Vegas one weekend during the NUT trial. Husband and wife, mother and father, Galen and Grace. They named the child Joseph Andrew after their fathers.

J.A. was three months old and Grace was diligently breastfeeding when she got the call from Trudi: 'Come west to my wedding.'

Grace learned later that Trudi had originally intended to have her wedding take place at "Mi Hacienda", so that the spirit of Tommy could hover above them, but fortunately with all the publicity from the NUT case, Kitten Fairleigh found she could no longer live at peace on her quiet hillside. So she sold "Mi Hacienda", at a loss for the tax deduction, to a religious order of bread-baking nuns.

Trudi was devastated but found a country club overlooking the Pacific Ocean that would serve her just as well.

Her intended was Don Harrington, whom Grace had never met until the night before the wedding. But she had to admit, she approved. True, he might have made a Jesus Freak out of Trudi, but he seemed sombre and solid enough for the both of them. 'We're going to have tons of children,' Trudi promised Grace. 'And this time I'll get to keep them.'

Don himself was deeply involved in good works, via the Tommy Patterson Fund for the Betterment of Humanity, helping the homeless, the medically indigent, the working poor, all the people Tommy himself could never relate to. Trudi occasionally stepped in and wanted to give money to one or another of the false messiahs who predominated in Southern California, but Don stayed her hand, much as God had stayed Abraham's.

Odelle had come out for the wedding, not only because she wouldn't miss it but because Luke had decided to go to Stanford and she wanted to see what Sy was giving up half his life savings for. And Kitten was at the wedding, looking lovely as ever, as Galen told her over and over again until even she began to become uncomfortable. Kitten had formed her own production company and made Grace promise she would come up with something suitable for Kitten's first feature. Grace was tempted to write a screenplay from her book VIKING PRINCESS. Kitten would made a perfect Edwina.

So they were all together again, much as they had been for Tommy's funeral. But this time the occasion was a happy one. Grace was married with a child. Odelle's home for battered women and children, Sisters of the Storm, was well financed, and she was looking forward to a productive middle age. Kitten had formed her company; further, had just received rave reviews for her portrayal of a woman obsessed with Oriental men. And Trudi was off drugs and finally getting the stability she needed.

Tommy Patterson? He was a voice fading in the wind. Tippi Moonstone had come out with her glorified biography of him, which was termed a paste-job by the critics. Her titillating book of gossip hit newsprint then died. The world awaited a definitive biography of Tommy Patterson, which Grace was diligently working on, page by page, memory by memory. It would not be a pretty sight.

But as Grace stood there, next to Galen, who was ogling Kitten, holding J.A., their bond and joy, watching Trudi and Don pledge eternal love to each other, she mellowed. Finally, after long years of pain and rage, each of them had survived and surmounted their encounter with Tommy Patterson. And they were happy? As Trudi might put it, all things work together for good. Eventually.